TRINITY
FIELDS

BY THE SAME AUTHOR

Come Sunday
A Bestiary
The Almanac Branch

TRINITY
FIELDS

Bradford Morrow

VIKING

VIKING
Published by the Penguin Group
Penguin Books USA Inc., 375 Hudson Street, New York, New York 10014, U.S.A.
Penguin Books Ltd, 27 Wrights Lane, London W8 5TZ, England
Penguin Books Australia Ltd, Ringwood, Victoria, Australia
Penguin Books Canada Ltd, 10 Alcorn Avenue,
Toronto, Ontario, Canada M4V 3B2
Penguin Books (N.Z.) Ltd, 182–190 Wairau Road,
Auckland 10, New Zealand

Penguin Books Ltd, Registered Offices: Harmondsworth, Middlesex, England

First published in 1995 by Viking Penguin,
a division of Penguin Books USA Inc.

1   3   5   7   9   10   8   6   4   2

PUBLISHER'S NOTE
This is a work of fiction. Names, characters, places, and incidents
either are the product of the author's imagination or are used
fictitiously, and any resemblance to actual persons, living or dead,
events, or locales is entirely coincidental.

Grateful acknowledgment is made for permission to reprint excerpts from the following copy-
righted works: "Thank God for You" by Sawyer Brown. © 1993 Mark A. Miller, Travelin'
Zoo Music, Mac McAnally, Beginner Music. "Howl" from Collected Poems 1947–1980 by
Allen Ginsberg. Copyright © 1956 by Allen Ginsberg. Reprinted by permission of Harper-
Collins Publishers, Inc. "Mr. Housman's Message" from Personae by Ezra Pound. Copyright
1926 by Ezra Pound. Reprinted by permission of New Directions Publishing Corporation.

LIBRARY OF CONGRESS CATALOGING IN PUBLICATION DATA
Morrow, Bradford.
Trinity fields: a novel / Bradford Morrow.
p.   cm.
ISBN 0-670-85728-9
PS3563.08754T75   1995
813'.54—dc20   94-20125

This book is printed on acid-free paper.

Printed in the United States of America
Set in Fairfield
Designed by Brian Mulligan

For my
mother and father

Heraclitus said that war is the parent of all things; this could more properly be said of love; but his paradox seems to be confirmed in the case of friendship.

—George Santayana

TRINITY
FIELDS

PART I

THE HILL

Los Alamos to New York
and Long Tieng,
1944 – 1969

We came careening across the desert toward Chimayó, dry warm wind over our faces hysterical with laughter, crazy with our sudden freedom, while over our heads an enormous sky wheeled, studded with stars, and the Milky Way shed its ghostly glow over the buttes and piñon trees and junipers. We were fifteen and we were in some kind of trouble. We were tickling the dragon's tail hot and heavy. And though our eyes were tearing from the wind that scratched them, the tears dried on our temples as fast as they flowed, and our tongues felt thick from the scotch whiskey we'd taken from Fuller Lodge back on the mesa. It was me and Kip and this kid we picked up hitching in the middle of the night out along the stretch by San Ildefonso pueblo, not Indian, a Hispanic named Fernando Martinez who was probably younger than we and who kept standing up in the back seat as we accelerated across the landscape. The bottle went around from hand to hand. Words were shouted but flew away behind us into arroyos and sagebrush. We were the most unholy trinity on the face of the earth, or else the most holy.

Grim and giddy, we'd have been a sight to see if anybody had been there to see us, but the highway between Pojoaque and

Chimayó was empty. We stopped once to walk into the desert a few hundred feet and throw ourselves down on our backs and look up at the stout stars and wobbly moon and howl and curse and dance, and just be cool, bad outlaws, while back on the road the radio blasted "Tutti Frutti" and this Martinez began to carry on because Kip asked him what he was doing at the pueblo if he lived over here on the high road to Taos, and the kid started bragging that he'd just popped his first cherry. I said, —No you didn't, and he said, —Did so, and Kip said, —You lie like a dog, man, and he said, —You lie like a rug, man. But it didn't really matter because when he asked us what we were doing out here in the night in a stolen car, good boys like us, crewcut and white as soaptree yucca petals, here in our T-shirts and bluejeans cuffed over brown shoes, when we told him what we were doing, he didn't believe us any more than we believed him. We told him we were from up on the Hill and we were making a pilgrimage to the valley of the little church where the dirt is sacred, because we were sick and our parents were sick and every last one of our neighbors was sick. All of us were guilty, tainted black to the pit of our souls by what had happened at our home. This is what we said. We, they, all of us needed to be cured, and the only way to be absolved of the infamy of so many murders was to go, pay homage, and partake of the magic purifying soil at Chimayó. Fernando Martinez coughed loud, spat hard, and rolled around in the arroyo laughing like somebody who didn't have the sense God gave an apple, and said, —You guys are nuts, and we said, —Are not, and he said, —You're out of your minds, and we started running like jackrabbits to the car, and Martinez was at our heels shouting, —Hey, wait for me! and though we didn't, he managed to leap into the back seat on the fly in time to stay with us all the way down into the village, and we didn't mind because nothing mattered, we were in such trouble by now, nothing mattered at all except getting to the church in order to be blessed with the miraculous dirt that would sanctify our great escape and confirm our newfound manhood.

The plaza of El Potrero was dead. After we pitched to a halt, a willowy cloud of dust came washing over us, and what descended in its wake was a glorious silence, sweet and haunted. We sat, staring up at it, awed almost to sobriety. A dog barked in the near distance, short choppy echoing yelps, then everything was silent again.

El Santuario de Chimayó, humble in the moonlight, an enchanted godhouse whose curved lines and organic shapes made it seem like a thing built by fairy-book creatures, so phantasmagoric were its adobe towers and rounded mud walls. It was more sublime, more modest than anything we had ever witnessed. At that moment, without having to confirm in words what we were thinking, we knew, both of us, that we had not guessed wrong. Chimayó was just where Kip and I had to come, we night riders in the tradition of Las Gorras Blancas who journeyed across New Mexico from dusk to dawn a century ago cutting the cursed barbed wire, fighting the bosses who were bent on fencing us in even then—our people, our land, our lives—we kids, we midnight penitentes burdened less by our own sins (ours were still ahead of us) than those of our community. And this was why we were here. Because we had finally gotten it through our adolescent heads, finally comprehended our exile and why our fathers were both revered and hated—revered because they were heroes who brought the war to an end, hated because in order to end the war they created something that in turn promised to destroy the very people it was meant to protect.

Deep in the heart of our ambivalence it took moonlight to shine in upon certain truths, for, back on the hill of poplars where we lived—poplars are *los álamos*—there were things so buried in the dark, the sun didn't know how to make them manifest. Good old pock-faced buttery yellow daddy moon, we drank to him, lifting our bottle high to where he nested in the cottonwood trees and big box elders. All was aglow and appeared to pulse. I can remember feeling scared and happy. I believed in what we were about.

For whatever kind of night this Martinez had already managed to have, he was not ready to give it up just yet as history. No doubt the chance to watch what these two strange children come down from the Pajarito Plateau were going to do was more compelling to him than going home. We didn't pack him off. We had come in our way to like him by then. He was a saintly outlaw was Martinez, we'd decided, and probably yes it was true he was not a virgin anymore. Even if he were, we had to admire if not covet the way he wandered around in the night, unprotected and unsupervised. We'd never met anyone quite like him, having ourselves been overprotected and overseen from as far back as either of us could remember—literally corralled at birth by barricades, censored and surveilled, isolated and cloistered, sworn to silence, and guarded by military police in hutments and on horseback. Though it had been seven long years, nearly half our lives, since the roadblock gates had been lifted, and one no longer needed a pass to get in and out of our town, the sense of constraint, of being different and apart, remained. Even the few dangerous games we had managed to invent and play up on the Hill, games we worked at hard in the hope of seizing vital freedoms, paled before Martinez's ranging independence. Look at him down here on the desert floor running free as the breeze. Listen to him brag and laugh. Watch his head jerk, his fingers point, his knees snap. See his clothes flap casually around his arms and legs—even his old baggy denims gone white with age and cotton shirt thinned to silk seemed untamed. He was absolutely fluent with his freedom, wore it with the same unself-conscious grace a ponderosa wears its bristled boughs.

So, yes. We'd begun to admire this Fernando for where his hasty feet could carry him. Also, being our parents' children and therefore not entirely unpragmatic, we kept on with him because it had become clear he knew the way far better than we.

Now Martinez leapt from where he had been perched on the dusty cream canvas boot behind the back seat. In the moonlight I could make out the merest trace of a moustache and dark down in his chin cleft. He was an old young boy, I thought. We followed him down the mild slope of the plaza under the zaguan, the arched entrance into the courtyard of the church. A creek trickled and gurgled out below and ahead of us somewhere, water that would twine, like all running water in this stretch of scratchland, down into the Rio Grande and find its way to the Gulf of Mexico. The birds were all asleep, the dog had gone back to sleep. Everyone was slumbering but us three. Martinez had the bottle and knew the way, so we were as much in his wake as the lunar-gray highway dust had been in ours back on the desert.

—How do we get in?

—See, I was baptized here, I know this place good, Martinez assured us, his voice a low mewl, ignoring my question. He was more talkative now that he'd become one of the impromptu gang, the leader in fact for the moment. We didn't speak, but studied him as he tried the carved wooden doors that led into the sanctuary. —Damn, he said. The doors were shut tight and it was too dark to jimmy the old lock. After a few elastic moments of silence Martinez reappeared, ran his forearm over his mouth, and led us around to the west side of the church. The stars burned cold and bright above the steeples and through the tree limbs, but seemed different here than back on the Pojoaque flats, more razorlike and frozen and sharp. The sky between them was purple toward the horizon, bluish black at the center overhead, and dirty white like aspen bark around the body of the full moon. On the far side of the river, over at the margin of several hectares of pasture rose Tsi Mayoh, the hill from which the valley takes its name. It was a long, curvilinear granite hump that resembled some dozing, ancient beast. Scrub bushes crowded its backlit profile like crooked teeth. The moon kissed its horizon and I thought if I were the moon, I would, too.

Martinez was carrying on.

—Yeah yeah, I was saved here when I was little, you know. See, I was born too small, size of a grasshopper, my bed was a shoe box, and I kept getting bloody noses and headaches and when I'm in third grade they're afraid I'm gonna die, and the doctor in Taos say I got a brain tumor and he wants to operate and my mother decides to bring me to Chimayó, so we go inside the church here, we pray, and after we pray we go in the little room and I kneel down, I bend over, and they sprinkle the dirt right there on the back of my head. Sprinkle dirt just like you sprinkle holy water. I still remember the smell of that cool dirt. It smells like . . . *real earth*. You'll see. God he lets things happen bad and good, but for me it was good.

Along the length of the plaza side of the santuario runs a room that, I later discovered, used to be a vestment chamber where the priest would don his robes for Mass, but was converted to a sacristy where pilgrims pause to give thanks, having visited the posito and partaken of the sacred dirt. It is in this room the faithful leave behind their crutches, after experiencing the miracle of the soil. Martinez pointed to a dormer window that protruded from the roof of the sacristy. —Up there, he said. The edge of the roof was just high enough that Kip and I had to boost Martinez on our shoulders to hoist him up. Once there, he whispered,

—Come on, and extended his hand down to us. Kip climbed on my shoulders and Martinez pulled him onto the roof.

—Now what? I said.

—Jump, said Martinez.

I tossed the bottle up to them and jumped high as I could, my arms outstretched over my head. I touched their fingers, but fell back to the ground. Jumped again, again fell. The third time one hand caught mine, then another, and I swung freely in the night until the two of them hauled me aloft. We sat on the corrugated tin to catch our breath, then Martinez crawled to the dormer. Panes of glass were missing, and when he reached in to unlock the window frame he disturbed some roosting pigeons that launched themselves over his shoulder, making a raucous exodus of wings clacking and bleats like terrified babies. As Martinez slid backwards on the tin we all let out our own cries of terror. But then, at nightmare speed—too slow, too swift—we saw Martinez open the window and disappear into the crawl space.

—Yeah okay, he said from within, as if he were talking to somebody inside, his voice echoing off walls we couldn't see. Kip shimmied into the blackness after him, and I after Kip.

Now it was fully pitch-dark. —Come on, we could hear Martinez ten or twenty feet ahead of where we lay on our sides, breathing hard from fear. We heard him crawl on all fours forward, and we heard him pause before he jumped. When he landed he gave a grunt as if the wind were knocked out of him. Footsteps down in the nave. We scraped along, edged forward, bumping into one another, feeling our way deeper and deeper into the church. Suddenly the square opening ahead became illuminated—a faint white flickered in vague space. We crept to the end of the shaft and looked down into the void. Fernando Martinez stood below, a ghost shedding light upon ghost altar, ghost santos, ghost pews. He'd lit a candle and held it over his head. He wore a broad smile on his face. —Told you I know this place good, he said. I looked at Kip and Kip looked at me, and we dropped down feet first into the sanctuary, two drunk virgins, larcenous and saturated not just in hot, smooth swig but the innocence of angry idealism, hardly believing where we were. —Now we go to the well of earth, Martinez said.

Years later I discovered that there is a word for the act we performed on behalf of all the guilty souls back home on the Hill. Geophagy, it is.

Having hit our heads on the lintel of the doorway near the altar, we found ourselves in a claustrophobic chamber, a cell whose air was humid and ceiling low, with one small window. Here it was, the posito, a primitive circular hole carved a forearm's length wide and about as deep in the ground. We knelt. First we washed our hands with the dirt, then our faces, and finally we began to eat. From the tips of our fingers, from the bowls of our palms, we ate from the bottom of this hole handfuls of damp, crumbly loam known as the tierra bendita, choking, hacking and spitting, holding it down though it wanted to come up. Fernando Martinez sat against the wall and regarded us, amused and sodden and calm. He forbore to join our earthen feast. The candle flickered and made our shadows jump, giant and grotesque on the walls, while he finished off the whiskey and soon enough drifted into a dreamy stupor.

December 1944. Here is Los Alamos, New Mexico, an invented town, an extemporaneous city made for men at war, a secret district that couldn't be found on any map, a community that did not exist two years before Kip and I were born, between Christmas and New Year's, into a world of opposing ideas, of rage and determination, of fire and death, a community that was still in its rural infancy when we came crying into the slantlight —Kip morning, me evening—that poured through the windows of the delivery room.

Los Alamos. Sometimes in the night to frighten myself I will whisper those words into my pillow. Los Alamos. *So low, so almost, so lost all souls. Los álamos,* poplars, cottonwoods, the quaking aspen—*álamo temblón.* I'll whisper these words and I, too, will begin to tremble.

And yet it would be an easy falsehood to claim that I didn't love the place. However spartan, it was in many ways a veritable paradise back in those earliest days, as most who lived there would agree. We sometimes called it Shangri-la, though the military preferred the less expressive designation of Project Y. But by whatever name it went, Los Alamos was rather utopian—a successful experiment in socialism, perhaps the most successful socialist community ever to be founded in this country, paradoxical as that might have seemed back in the fifties, when our principal purpose was to develop a hydrogen bomb to deter the spread of Communism, to bring socialism down so that the free-world markets might thrive and the concept of state ownership be passed into extinction.

Our parents were so young and so brilliant, and in our brand-new home there was no undertaker, no cemetery, there were no elderly people walking the streets, no widows gazing out windows. None of our citizens owned real property, nor were we subject to municipal tax. Unemployment was unknown to us. Loneliness was rare among us. Racism and casteing did not much occur to us—though it must be said there was certain social status attached to living in one of the houses of older vintage, because those were the only structures on the Hill furnished with bathtubs, but this rare honor went more often to the scientists than the military men. Still, we were a pretty integrated group. None of us was rich, none of us was poor, and because our town was unknown, drifters and grifters were never seen to walk our unpaved streets. In the war years our secret citadel was free of crime—no one had time to contemplate theft, and besides, none of us back then had anything worth stealing except ideas. Our skies were blue daubed silver and white and the purest black, and nowhere was the taint of smog that beleaguered other cities. Disease was more or less absent from our lives. That is, our doctor might set a broken arm, the result of a construction accident or a fall down a scree-strewn hiking trail, and later, as the bomb neared completion, might treat an early victim of radiation exposure, but the hospital was used above all as a place for delivering babies.

We were known as the Hill people. We lived in an embryo of hiddenness and generally kept to ourselves up there in the Jemez mountains during the last years of the war. To hold the outside world at bay, our community was cordoned off by fences that ran up and down the long lengths of the finger mesas. Men on horses rode the perimeters, studying the cliffs for unusual movements, poring over the canyons down where the Anasazi used to make their homes. No one left or entered without showing a pass to the guard at the gate. None of our movements was unmonitored. All our needs were, as much as possible, attended to within the precincts of the town itself. They preferred that we did not leave the mesa; laboratory members weren't allowed to travel more than a hundred miles away without permission, and no one—friends, relatives, it did not matter who—was allowed to visit us. Our telephone conversations were eavesdropped, letters were posted unsealed and read by censors before going out into the world. Codes took the place of English. Our names were converted to numbers on driver's licenses and our common address was a post office box down in Santa Fe. All the adults who worked on the Manhattan Project, as the entire undertaking was called, were required to sign the Espionage Act, and all were fingerprinted and photographed. Neither expense nor time was spared to assure our sequestration. In history there have been many secret societies—the Iroquois had theirs of medicine men, I think of the medieval guilds and cathedral masons, in Persia there was Mithraism and in Greece Orphism—but never was there one more secret than ours. We were asked only to make the bomb, devise it and construct it as quickly as possible. We had our hardships, the winters were tough and the summers were dusty and hot, but our lives were rich. We were shepherded by our patrons, parented by them in some ways, were given a quiet place where we could think, experiment, learn, build. In a way, we were all children—from the geniuses who walked among us down to the kids who ice-skated on Ashley Pond. We were, in the end, protected from everyone but ourselves.

This was our home. Magpies, bobbing-tailed phoebes who loved nothing better than to pronounce their name *"fee-bee fee-bee"* over and over while raucous, cranky scrub jays cried back *"pi-ñon-es,"* chattery finches, vast turkey vultures that lazily floated above the land stippled by arroyos flushed with runoff water, plump robin redbreasts drilling for worms in the dewy orchard grass—in spring it seemed every bird in the world was here. Elk, deer, bear walked our vegas; brookies, rainbows, browns swam our streams and ponds. When we looked out toward the east we could see long violet vistas that as if by sorcery changed to blue to amethyst to opal to the pink of a child's cheek within a matter of minutes. The Sangre de Cristo range, its peaks mantled by clouds or snow, defined the farthest edge of our view, beyond the sere badlands of sandstone and granite, beyond the lowland pueblos, beyond the long, serpentine red roads that led to villages where Indians conversed in the patois their ancestors had used for hundreds of years, still discussing the same problems—how to get a decent crop of corn or beans to grow out of ground dry as a liar's tongue, how to restore the Pajarito Plateau to what it was before the mestizos came into being, before the Spanish came to subordinate the Indians, before the Anglos came to subordinate the Hispanos. Although those from San Ildefonso and others of the pueblos in the valley became our friends, in the beginning we Hill people shared little more than one thing with the Indians, and for that matter with all of us who made our home here—like them, we were at war, and we were brothers and sisters with a common purpose. We were allies, the good guys. And knowing ourselves to be on the side of righteousness, we knew we must not lose.

He, William Calder—known as Kip from as far back as I can remember—and I, who was his best friend, were so tight that if born in the same skin, we would hardly have been closer. We were brought into the world within not quite a full day of each other, eleven hours apart to be exact, in December 1944. How we came to share the name of William—though my middle name is Brice, and Brice I have always gone by—is that our grandfathers bore that name, and before them in both families there were Williams, uncles and cousins, populating the ancestral tree. The two Williams. It was thought of as an amusing coincidence and was the subject of various jokes at the time. —Well, they're certainly a *willful* pair. That sort of thing. Kip—whose nickname derived from his mother calling him her little Giddy Kipper—and I were born, were named and nurtured at the simple clapboard hospital, that long low hut with its wooden floors and enameled walls, and our mothers took us home to the Sundt houses on the same block where we grew up, near each other, as the winter snows came and went and spring forced the flowers into bloom.

I remember life on the Hill, so many shards of detail. Like everyone, I remember Fuller Lodge and the purity of the air around it, so often washed by walking rains. The grandest structure in town was the lodge, where the youngsters used to room back in the twenties and thirties when Los Alamos was a summer camp for boys from wealthy families in New York and Boston and St. Louis. Its architecture of ponderosa logs and white oakum, its long porch and high windows put one in mind of both a cathedral and a cabin. I remember the happy gatherings that took place there, and the fun we had tying together the red ristras of chilies and hanging them so they could sway in the wind along the grand portal. How delicious smelling were the baskets of fresh garlic when the farmer brought them up from the valley. How much fun the Easter egg hunt every year on the lawn. I remember the mechanical Santa Claus, arm waving back and forth, seated in his plywood sleigh and the reindeer that lunged and lurched on their trestle, and how very fine it was to build big snowmen with coals for eyes and a carrot nose out on the yard below Fuller Lodge and how we made hard round snowballs and smothered them with raspberry syrup and ate them out under the morning sky too cold to flurry.

I know—and knew—my mother was quietly unhappy about living the way she lived, and in this she probably wasn't alone. Most of the wives on the Hill were kept in the dark about precisely what it was their husbands did at the lab. This was the sine qua non, the sole pact made between the government and each of the men hired to participate in the program, the Project. To an outsider my mother's life might have looked idyllic, and any hint of grievance toward it fussy, trivial, ludicrous, spoiled. She lived in beautiful surroundings, her life was wholesome and protected in many ways that other people's wartime lives weren't. She was loved by her husband and blessed with two healthy children, neither of whom had as yet learned that the birthright of adolescence is revolt. She taught in the school, all grades from elementary up to high school, and was adored by most of her pupils who studied English and tried their best to learn Latin under her guidance. The kids that didn't revere her at least respected or feared her.

For a schoolteacher's son—a lot in life only a step above being the pastor's daughter—I didn't fare badly. I was only teased a little when I couldn't conjugate a verb or diagram a sentence, was reprimanded with the same gentle care she showed any other student when I was guilty of not paying attention. By the same token, when my work was good and showed improvement, I was rewarded with the very praise that my classmates might receive, no more and no less. Her impartiality stood me in good stead. Evenhanded toward us all, as well as a real scholar—disciplined, original, largely self-taught—she was admired by her peers, even beloved. Students of hers from years ago write my mother letters, and keep her abreast of their own children's progress.

Still, I just knew she wasn't with it, was never quite content. She worked hard, relished work. She was a meticulous, but not maniacal, housekeeper. She was better than a good cook. She knew that she was more fortunate than most, especially during those days when she was a young mother living with husband and children in an America where thousands of mothers and wives didn't have that luxury, their boys and husbands off in the European theater in some muddy trench, the Pacific theater taking salvos in heavy ocean. My mother was aware of this much. There was a lot of sanity to her. She read to her children every night when they were young, raised us on *Treasure Island*, on *Ivanhoe*, on *The Alhambra*, on the King James Bible. She spoke to us, when we were babies, in the language of adults. She took us to pick watercress at the edges of Pajarito Springs and taught us how to tell cress from monkeyflower, which is terrible to eat. She knew things, and what she didn't know she tried to learn. She delighted in the names of plants here, like pipsissewa and kinnikinnik. When the birds passed overhead in spring she told us that they were sandhill cranes migrating from their winter home in Bosque del Apache to their nesting grounds in Idaho. She played piano, and sang, and we all tried to sing along. She had the charming if eccentric habit of smoking a small clay pipe in public and try as he may my father was never able to talk her out of it. She was cool before cool was cool. I can remember going to the famous parties in the great room at the lodge, and we kids would gunnysack-race across the lawn and dunk for apples, pin the tail on the donkey, clasp hands and go round and around in a circle and fall down together when London Bridge was falling down, limbo the limbo (Kip was limbo champion) and scrape knees and elbows, and eat canned peaches and sugary homemade fudge, and the adults would drink and dance, and if she'd had just enough tipple, my mother could dance crazier, more reckless, more full of life than any of them. To this day her mediating sadness—a misery she has always kept to herself as if it were some precious treasure—is an enigma to me, though sometimes I do remember her feeling especially tired and having to go to bed and how the water in the glass at her bedside table smelled different from the water the rest of us drank, and how once when she was dozing I took a sip and it scorched my tongue. I spit it back into the glass, as quietly as I could, and left the room filled with the special guilt of a child who knows he has done something wrong but doesn't have the vaguest notion what it is, or why he knows it is wrong. I must have assumed at the time the clear burning liquid was medicine. Now I may know better, but mother as enigma remains just that. In later years, when I could have risked asking her about it I didn't, perhaps out of embarrassment or a fear of knowing the truth. And so I'll never have an answer because now I'll never ask. She is still alive but not, as they say, all there. Years and declining health render certain questions pointless.

My father I seldom saw, though I have a memory of him riding me on the backs of a pair of wide wooden skis, and the bite of the snow on Sawyer's Hill being so cold it felt hot. For some reason, there resides in my head a song sung by him, in the voice of a twanging radio cowboy, about how he was so tall that when he laid himself down to sleep he rested his head in Colorado and his feet in Montana. But my poor father wasn't so tall as all that. We weren't allowed to speak about the blessed Project at dinner, or any other time. —What you don't know won't hurt you, was how he put it, trying but failing at levity. Stealth from dawn to dusk, stealth was all and everything to these men. Their tasks were compartmentalized to insure security, so that even the exchange of information between scientists working side by side in the Techs, as labs were called, was often limited, and ideas had to be fed through the intricate cat's cradle of what my father called speakaround. Very little in Los Alamos didn't travel by nonlinear means. Just as electrons circle the proton and neutron heart of an atom in constant ellipses, now near, now not near, now far, now not far, on and on with every passing second, so did we, each of us, in our ways circle one another, elliptically, near and far. Relativity was, here, among physicists, more than theory. It was a given, a way of life. Silence was golden—which may be part of the reason I revolted against it, and now still equate silence with cowardice. Mum was the word, but whatever the word might have meant was so mum, you didn't dare say, —Mum's the word. All in all, Dad is less clear a figure to me than Mom. They are both in different ways gone now, my father dead and my mother having mislaid her memory, to use the delicate phrase of her physician, and to get her off her one dear subject of religion is all but impossible.

Still, the hows and whys of their absences are less important than the absences themselves. I regret that now, when I could finally talk with my father about his part in the making of the bomb, now that I could muster some historical curiosity unobscured by the deep and often blind anger I displayed toward him during my days of antiwar activism, he is gone. During his last years he would have welcomed the chance of a discussion with me, and the reconciliation of sorts we'd begun at the beginning of this last decade might well have been accomplished. But I guess that wasn't to come to pass, any more than has my talk with my mother about her problems and her hopes.

I remember my Kip, too, of course. I confess to remembering nothing and no one better than Kip, my parents and sister Bonnie Jean included. Indeed, almost myself included.

When summer came to the Hill, Kip and I took our shoes off and never put them on again until we had to go back to school in September. We were young and our waking hours were given to games. All the windows in the Sundt houses where we lived were wide open, and front doors—never locked in any season—stood ajar to catch the morning breeze. Because the Sundts looked alike, in June my mother put out two potted geraniums on the porch, so I'd never get lost in the evening when I walked home. Some of the men who came by in winter to stoke up our furnaces showed up in summer to paint the two-story apartment houses a flat regulation green and the roofs dull brick brown (the Sundts were meant to resemble boulders scattered around the meadow if viewed from a high altitude by enemy reconnaissance, and were set at angles rather than in uniform rows to enhance this mirage, though I always thought these spies would have to be morons to mistake houses for rocks). As the smell of fresh paint drifted through the air it became linked for us with summer and liberty. We trailed off into the canyons, and pitched tents under the conifers. We burned pinecone pyramids, we wrapped ourselves in our soogan bedrolls and looked up into the night sky for shooting stars. We heard scary footfalls in the dark, we had stare-downs, we danced like Indians we'd watched on the reservations. In the potreros we explored cliff dwellings and whenever we came upon a rattlesnake taking its siesta we would kill it with a stick and hang it in a nearby tree. Anything that hinted of danger was what attracted our interest above all.

We treasured one game in particular, though my love for it came gradually. Peppers was what we called it.

Says Kip one day, —Hey boy, wait till you see what I got.

—Yeah, what? I ask.

He doesn't answer, but jerks his head to the right over his shoulder, turns on his heel, and begins to walk fast down the dirt street toward the old sawmill at Central and Diamond. Pollen floats in the sunlight, grainy yellow sheen. The afternoon is windless and warm.

There are some kids down at the mill. They're climbing up the steep pile of sawdust, playing king of the mountain. One of them has a bloody nose that looks like a bloody mouth, all red. Another, the son of an engineer, a sweaty crazy kid, is upside down on the rope swing, way out over a pile of scrap lumber studded with rusty nails. —Drop! drop! some of our friends are screaming, daring him to plummet headfirst into the dangerous rubble. Kip walks right past him and his audience, still ahead of me by a few paces. —Kip, Kip, Kip can't be king, this other boy taunts, and his sister joins in, —Kip can't be king, Kip can't be king, but Kip can't hear them, or pretends not to and keeps moving. I look over at them. They shrug and I shrug back. We are, what, nine or ten years old.

—Where we headed? I ask, once we're out of earshot.

—You'll see, and before long we come to a half-finished Tech building. Kip stops, looks around behind to see if anyone has followed us, and now around back slithers belly down into the crawl space, knees wide apart, shoelaces trailing behind him, both untied, looking like dirty mop strings chasing his tennies over the tan dry ground. I get down on my hands and knees and peer into the darkness but can only hear him grunting. In a minute he's back, with a beat-up saddle blanket wrapped around something long and narrow. —Come on, he says, and we're off again, this time down into the woods. The manner in which he's cradling the mysterious bundle under his arm makes me a little afraid, I have to admit. Something secret, something very precious he's got.

We walk side by side into a clearing and he says, —Sit down.

I'm getting tired of this and say, —No, just show me what you got there.

He makes me promise not to tell a soul, and I promise.

Kip unfurls the blanket. What he's got is a shotgun.

—Where'd you find that?

—It's a four-ten, he tells me.

—But where'd you get it?

—Isn't it the best?

I agreed it was pretty fine, but asked again, —Where'd you get it?

—It doesn't matter.

—You stole it?

—I didn't steal it.

It was probably the first time Kip had ever lied to me, and I took it to be a special moment in our friendship. Something new and strange got born between us, passed in a twinkling, difficult to define just what. It was as if his lie caused everything to feel suddenly more important—the dumb wind in the high boughs of the ponderosa became smart, the hiss of the needles was significant, everything was changed, matured, honed. The wedge this deceit drove between us only served to make me love Kip more. I wanted to please him so he wouldn't have to lie again. In a way, it was the lie that midwifed our game of peppers.

What's next is I want to know what we're going to do with the gun.

—We're going to shoot it, of course, boy, he says.

—You got ammo, boy? I say.

—'Course I got ammo.

And sure enough he's got a box of shells.

—What're we going to shoot?

This is getting exciting, because it's really going to happen, I say to myself. But what's going to happen?

He doesn't give it to me right off. He waits. He lifts the butt of the shotgun to his shoulder, draws the barrel to a nice, steady horizontal, aiming straight into my eye, and says, —We're going to play peppers.

—So what's peppers? blinking, despite myself.

I almost say, So what's peppers, boy? but that's harder to do with a shotgun pointed at you, even if it's in the hands of your best friend, and unloaded, which it is.

—Peppers is one of us goes way over there . . . and he is pointing to the far edge of this canyon we are standing in, one of our favorites because none of the other kids seems to know about it, and it's always been a place where we could come and loaf around in private. —One of us goes way over there, and then the other one shoots and the one who's over there gets peppered.

—Forget it.

—No, look, I know how to do this, Kip says.

At his insistence, the first shot is to be taken by me at him: a display of trust. I watch him stride away across the field, long arms swinging alongside his narrow hips, his slightness belying the obstinance which at times like this can saturate his character. He is determined and casual at the same time. There is an ease, a carelessness to Kip I've always envied, occasionally attempted to affect. It must have seemed sophisticated from the first time I recognized it in him, but it's something I have never achieved.

To get our bearings, first he has me shoot from a distance too great to reach my target. He moves forward twenty paces, while I load again—Kip has shown me how—and then look up at him.

—You're too close now, move back, I shout.

—Go ahead and shoot, he answers, his voice reedy in the thin, still air.

—Move back.

He takes some steps backward, not many, and I shoot.

Nothing; a little dust kicks up off to his left and shy of where he stands.

—What'd I tell you? You're wasting shells, he shouts out, his hands cupped around his mouth. —Shells-*ells-ells* echoes neatly down the steep canyon walls. I look up. The sun is retiring over the trees. A redtail hawk is ovaling back behind me toward the east. I reload. Kip has walked up much closer now, and all this begins to make me nervous. I'm thinking, How come we got to play this game? It isn't very fun anyway. And what happens if I kill him?

—Come on, boy! Kip is calling, and I aim dead at his dancing figure. I can't do it, begin to lower the barrel. He is hollering, —Pull that trigger, babyman, come on, pull! Up goes the barrel again, and I hold my breath, see Kip jumping up and down, eyes closed so the bird-shot doesn't blind him, and we both know that unless my aim's off this time he'll get a pelting. I squeeze the trigger, recoil, smell the metallic smoke, hear the shotgun crack. It's like it is not me doing any of this, like I am watching someone else accomplish it all.

Kip is on the ground. He's screaming—kind of a high-pitched squeal I'd never heard him make before—and he is writhing. I am running to him. I've dropped the shotgun in the dirt. I'm afraid I've started to cry from fear, and my breath is heavy, my chest heaving by the time I reach him. His screams sound like laughs. His face is strangely smiling, but he's not smiling. It's a grimace. I guess I expected blood, and yet there isn't any blood. His face is purple-pocked, and his shirt is torn. I try to put my arm around him, but he shoves me off. He doesn't say anything to me. If he were to speak, I know it would be to scold me for crying like I am. His chest and cheek the most repulsive sight, a negative constellation of buckshot bruises.

The peppers game.

Kip has won.

He sits silent as a monk, then when he finally stands, his first words are, —Where's the gun, little fella? It's your turn now.

*B*orn in a place set apart from the cultures surrounding it, we naturally developed a deep detachment, a separateness that all of us carried forward from youth into adulthood. Growing up as we did in the afterglow of genius, in a place whose triumph it was to create the finest death machine ever conceived by human beings, we expected that our games, games like peppers, games that involved defying injury on the monkey swing, games like the one we loved where we roller-skated as fast as we could down the sidewalk that approached Central School and crashed into the wall and fell down laughing so hard our sides ached, were all games that in their childish ways attempted to match the perils we surely sensed our parents—mostly our fathers—were courting day and night in their labs.

Kip and I had been too young, of course, to have registered what was happening on the Hill before the first bomb was detonated downstate at Alamogordo, and the dream of Trinity became in one bright instant on a predawn morning, after a long night of cold rain and driving winds, an actuality.

That was July 16th, 1945, 5:29:45 Mountain War Time. Dawn in which black became white, the white of absolute death, and then white became black, blacker than the black of Otowi glaziery, as the desert gave birth to a fiery tapbell, a flowering kale of light whose unprecedented pressure of a hundred billion atmospheres caved the earth in beneath the tower even while it disintegrated everything in its immediate path, caused a blind girl a hundred miles away for a moment to see its flash, and in a matter of instants changed forever the world back home at Los Alamos, not to mention the world beyond.

Like atomic particles, emotions have half-lives. Emotional climates linger, like radioactive clouds, in rooms where human beings have lived, fought and loved, eaten and shat, worked and slept. We'd grown up, Kip and I, inside an atmosphere changed and charged. We sensed—no, we *knew*—we were different from anybody who didn't live on the Hill. Trinity only confirmed this difference. We had been delivered into the midst of a birth far more significant, profoundly more potent than our own. The principles and tenets of Nature herself were being tested. Mere unfledged babes, we were set forth in the shadow of something far greater than ourselves. And we knew it.

Who would have thought a community could become so prepossessed by the invention of a device that would supply neutrons to start a chain reaction of nuclear fission? It is no exaggeration to say that never in the history of modern man—possibly never in mankind's history, period—has a collective of individuals lived together in such isolation, defined and motivated by such clear purpose, freed of distraction, fully focused on solving a single problem. It will never happen again.

My earliest impression about what it meant to split an atom was that the atom—which I mixed up with Adam, from my Sunday school lessons—preferred to remain whole, would never want to be broken in two, in the same way that Eve would probably not want to be halved like some circus performer laid out in a coffin-shaped box and—head sticking out one end, feet the other—sawn down the middle by some metaphysical magician in top hat and ratty tails. For me, then, the horrific, miserable explosion that resulted from smashing this helpless atom was a manifestation of its unhappiness. Poor Adam the atom! Your pain seemed understandable to me. Poor bantam building block, what had you ever done since the beginning of time and space to deserve such shabby treatment? After all, you were already the littlest thing in the universe—how cruel it seemed for people to want to make you tinier again by half. After all, when I asked my father what your name meant and he told me, That which cannot be cut, didn't I shout it was wicked to harm you? Were I an atom and they busted me like they busted you, I felt I would respond with a similar burning rage. I, too, would burst into tears of fire.

Every schoolboy knows they call it a mushroom cloud, but every schoolboy who has ever considered the contents of his undershorts is also aware it looks like a penis, a phallus with thick stem and knolled head that swells and rises into the arched, indignant clouds above. One of our wickedest games of childhood was to *pants* some kid—pounce on him and pull down his pants—and then, once he was revealed for all the world to see, we could cry out, —Look here, look here, the boy's got the bomb in his britches! This game gave us the greatest pleasure until one time the boy who had been pantsed responded, with what dignified calm he could summon, —That means if I piss on you, you're gonna wither up and then you're gonna start to glow and bleed green gunk all over the place and then you're gonna die! And what did he do but lift his precious little member into his hands and direct it toward us, saying, —Oh, I think I got to pee, I think I got to pee bad now, I just can't *hold* it anymore, and had us running in a scattered fury, still laughing, but not so confident we shouldn't get some distance between him and ourselves.

Hurt and disgust live near one another, maybe they're married. Both have, over the years, been occasional companions of mine. I wonder if they haven't been constant friends to Kip. Many of us kids from up on the Hill share an understandable ambivalence about our home, where we came from, from whom we descended. They, our parents, were, then, the good guys, or at least that was how we saw them before we knew about them from more complicated angles, which forced us to recognize that they were also the bad guys. It was the moral conundrum that defined our home. Sure, they were duped and deluded. Sure, they were naive. You build a bomb for a government, you can't expect the government not to use it. There was a war going on. Hitler was a monster, a brute with a black blot above the lip and pale palm thrust into the sky as if he were about to punish the earth itself with a hard slap. Hirohito was a demon surrounded by a band of suicidal fiends who loved nothing better than to raze and maim and send sleeping sailors to watery graves. Mussolini was a bully and scoundrel, pig-eyed and bullet-headed. All three of them were burned in effigy down at the Santa Fe Fiesta each August during the war. Men set torches to the huge devilgod whose name was, by tradition, Zozobra—a creature of gloom and moral pollution, an icon of papier-mâché and chicken wire hung from a pole on a hill so to be seen by the thousands of fiestagoers—but who in those years was nicknamed Hirohitlmus. To the sounds of ritual drums, the flames consumed Zozobra's gown and climbed through its loins and up its chest to its shoulders and then its head, sparks flying high into the night to join the stars, and soon enough, just as Christ died for man's sins, this paper statue bristled, flared, crumpled, and finally died for mankind's sadnesses.

Yet ritualistic bonfires were not enough. Zozobra was made of paper and wood and wire, but Naziism and its kin were forged of stronger stuff. The war blanketed the earth. The war bosses were going to take our lands away from us. This was what was faced, this is what we were told. Look at Poland, look at Pearl Harbor. Our boys were dying, they were killing and being killed. They were dying in foxholes, dying on the sands of beaches, dying in air, in fire, in water, elements passing back into the elements. They were being gored and flensed and gassed. They were being tortured, blitzed, mutilated. They were suffering across the continents. It was incumbent upon us now to make a torch that would burn the living Hirohitlmus beyond resurrection. Of a flame so hot it could sear those hearts of steel. And this was why our parents came to the Hill. The Germans had been experimenting with fission, had already split an atom of uranium. It was imperative to develop our bomb first and to deploy it before anyone so much as suspected we were in the nuclear business to begin with. Even if the Germans would ultimately surrender before the bomb was ready, and even if the Japanese were considered to be conquerable without the use of the bomb, it was as if what had been set in motion had assumed an inertia and life of its own—so that once it was proven and ready, the bomb simply had to be dropped, both of them had to be used, the plutonium and the uranium, as if new laws of momentum had been awakened together with all the other revelations that those on the Hill had witnessed. And to think, all of it had been accomplished in a bubble, behind a mask. No wonder the world was so surprised.

Before our fireball atomized shy lizards and blooming yuccas, sagebrush and coyotes of the flats at Alamogordo in the Jornada del Muerto, before word got out that there was a connection between what had happened down at Billy the Kid's old stomping grounds and what had been going on in the secluded tranquility of Los Alamos, nobody understood what we were doing up on our magic mountain. But in Santa Fe the rumors about us had always been as plentiful as they were arcane. Some said we were building electric spaceships. Some said the Hill was a hideaway for pregnant WACs. Some believed we were engaged in making windshield wipers for submarines, or even constructing submarines themselves, rivergoing subs that, when finished, would travel down the Rio Grande into the gulf and on to the seven seas. Others, less inventive, thought we were manufacturing poison gas, yet others that we were distilling scotch, or that our enclave was really a posh internment camp for dangerous, dissident Republicans.

Stories about us Hill people kept the valley people busy. I imagine them sitting in the shade under the rough-hewn portals of the Palace of the Governors on the square in Oldtown, and discussing the curious spaceship people who hid high in their covert desert perch, studying comets and the movement of planets. It seems of a childlike charm, the notion of us Los Alamos hillies riveting tin like Mars-bound elves and fashioning silver nose cones and rocket wings, or as if we were a lost tribe of industrial zealots, innocent and harmless, tipsy with ideas if not our own bathtub brine.

It was the Trinity morning that gave us our public face, at last. We were the makers of death by light. It was as if we'd usurped for ourselves what had always been God's right—to bring on the apocalypse. We didn't need Him anymore, but could institute doomsday all on our very own. And we were proud about it. You don't pinch the sickle right out of Death's hands and establish yourself as a reaper of skill and consequence without feeling some tremor of vanity. Domus felix, it's a happy house where Master grasps the greatness of his power. Our secret was known across the face of the earth. We were horrified, and yes, we were proud.

When I think of it now, I still can't help feeling a wave of cynicism that has matured into a numb sadness over the years come urgent, thick, and finally smothering over me. I can be walking down a street in New York, making my way toward home, say, carrying a bag of groceries, and something, the cry of a baby or the weight in my arms, anything, will remind me of the paradoxical world into which I was born and at whose creative epicenter I was reared, and it makes me gasp for air. Hill people, valley people, what does it matter if gullibility remains unaffected by our environments? What a quaint appellation was Hill people for these bittersweet geniuses who were our parents, these brilliant naifs come to save the world, uninnocent innocents—as I came to see them—betrayed not just by the Truman administration but by their own love of a scientific challenge, a warm lust to push the envelope of theoretical and applied physics to the limit, as if to test its own tensile strengths, and all under the cloak of patriotism. Hill people, what a charming designation in which to frame our industrious little community. The Project and its Gadget, such dainty nicknames for what we did and built up in that windswept aerie during the war, the very war our somber, real work brought to its garish end.

As Kip once put it, —You can paste feathers on a snake, but that still don't make it a bird.

So what am I doing here now? New Mexico has always been a difficult place for me to return to, however evocative were the views of the front range, the vistas out toward the Continental Divide seen this morning from oval windows of the little Beech-craft turboprop, destined for Santa Fe on the commuter flight down from Denver.

What am I doing here? A fair question.

The towering clouds convene, palatial over the mountains, and the back ranges of Colorado are mantled in late winter snow, the snow brighter than the cumuli, and we are skirting along just above the thick white, from time to time catching the thermals, which pitch the plane upward heavily and knock us into a crab-walk sideways before hefting us down again. In the foothills and into the higher valleys snow collects in drifts under the conifers, the green of the pines almost black. Tracery down in the iced fields resembles ebony capillaries in the white meat of the snow —trails made by deer, or deltas of cold water rushing down de-clivities beneath the slushy crust—and the massive, convoluted zinc ranges interrupt long flat stretches of a soft powdery pale brown. These valleys well below timberline are dusty already, even though it is early spring. Winding across them are trees that must be hugging rivers hidden in purple shadows. The blue mountains like a photograph of primordial ocean. The ridges are waves, the clouds spume, the houses small schools of square fish. And all of it, the turbulence of this ocean and the movement of the creatures in it, is as if locked in a continuous instant.

So beautiful, it makes me ache. How lucky you were, I think. To have grown up in a place of beauty so unbroken that it invited you to take it for granted. Lucky and unlucky. Once left, home becomes an impossible place. It wants you back, it wants you out. It pushes as hard as it pulls, like some mad gravity that resists the very mass physics demands it attract.

It is true I have missed this part of the world, more than I would want to admit. But what I have missed is the world itself, and not those in it, or those who were in it. That's harsh, though. And then I'm thinking, Are you still the same unforgiving boy who abandoned so much, or so you flattered yourself, for an *idea*? Or, if not an idea—because I can hear Kip's voice, even now as it challenges me—if not an idea, then what? —*It was you, Brice, you and Jessica both. You gave me no choice,* I hear you say, old Kip. *You were both mine and then you weren't mine anymore, so what did you expect me to do?* She wasn't yours any more than I was, I respond without hesitation, even though I know we both were in your thrall, each of us in a different way. And I think, as my eyes come back into focus on the world outside the window, What would life have been like had I chosen to stay in New Mexico, live my years out in Los Alamos, or in Santa Fe, and let Kip go off to follow his fate alone? That is, let him follow it even more by himself than he did. I draw a blank. For one, I honestly cannot imagine for myself a life—here, there, anywhere—without Jessica and Ariel at its center.

Reddish black lakes the color of the water when rains have been heavy and rivers are dense with runoff, and another lake, man-made, whose color is celadon with a green-lace border where the shallows come up to the shore. It has the shape of a ginkgo leaf. Seems dead, a dead lake. I see narrow roads contoured into the sides of steep slopes. Not much sign of life on them this morning, but think what persistence it took to carry dynamite in on muleback to make the initial blasts, get the cliff-hung channels mined out, think of all the hard work to level out the strait passes. Men, always busy.

"You're not really going, are you?" Jessica had said. "I mean, it's obviously a hoax."

"Hoax? why would it be a hoax?"

"I don't know. What else would it be?"

That was the day before yesterday. The budding ailanthus and Norway maple out the windows of the apartment had shivered in the weak April breeze. The sky over Manhattan was that mid-season white, a ubiquitous, brutal light that blinds even as it fails to cast a shadow. It was a bleak day when I received the letter, an overcast that would neither snow, rain, nor shine. It was in-determinate, the weather, not cold enough to warrant wearing my overcoat, not warm enough for a jacket. I'd walked home from work. The letters on a small table by the door, as always. With no return address and written in a hand I had not immediately recognized, the envelope drew no attention to itself. It lay among the daily stack until after dinner. Some bills. Law review. Read a brochure for an ornithological excursion in Costa Rica, knowing I'd never go but daydreaming my way through the description of the rainforests, rare birds and their habitats. My consciousness still maundering over some photograph of colorful plumage, I had read half the letter before registering what it proposed. —Kip? I said.

Jessica's response puzzled and relieved me. She seemed more distant from him than I might have anticipated, and less inter-ested in finding out what had finally happened to Ariel's father, her estranged fiancé, than my paranoia ever allowed me to expect. After all this time Kip remained, however unrealistic my fears, a threat to my contentment and the stability of this life I had worked long and hard to establish. As the years had passed and Jessica and I settled into our marriage, as we raised Ariel—whom we'd named after the splendid sprite in Shakespeare's *The Tempest*, and an aunt of mine whom I had never met but whose wit and strength were legendary in our family, a woman who was listed in the Who's Who of American pioneers—as present after successive present rubbed away at the past, that fear lessened. But it was a treacherous fear, with an energy all its own. It had the habit of visiting me at unexpected moments, and would haunt me whether I was downhearted or happy, exhausted or full of spirit. I was never protected from the sudden realization that there was one person in the world who could take everything I love away from me. This fear became a regrettable visitor on certain anniversaries, my birthday, for instance, or I should say *ours*. Jessica might refer to something about the "bad old days" back at school and Kip would come up—a passing, innocent but inevitable reference—as the mutual friend who'd introduced us. However unjust, however childish of me, all too often I would catch myself studying her during those moments, shamelessly scrutinizing for some lapse, some chink in her fluid facade, some awful hint of a lingering attachment, or love. Because Jessica and I had never been able to confirm his whereabouts after Operation Homecoming in the middle seventies—whether he was truly dead after those violent confusing times when he found himself the maddest of the mad boys in Vietnam and ultimately in Long Tieng, Laos—it would have been love wasted on her part, for all we (that is, *she*) knew. And Jessica was not given to wasting love or anything else. She was romantic, true, but she was also a practical woman. Kip was never finally listed as killed or missing in action. Nor was he listed as a prisoner of war, although in plain fact that was precisely what he'd become and, in a way, we with him, all prisoners to that war.

He was a vacuum, an omission, a rebuff. He was simply a grand absence, unanswerable and unanswering. Jessica might love still what she had once loved about him, but she had been hurt, and now there was nothing to love—this was how I interpreted her view of him. He had gone, he had returned, he had gone again, and never returned. —You are my husband, you're the one I love, she would say to me, and she said it just often enough that I came to trust it as the truth, at least most of the time.

And when I didn't? Well, then I watched, fool in the extreme though I might have been, and sometimes saw what wasn't there. Jess and I seldom fought. When we did, chances are it was because I believed in ghosts, and she didn't. The result was forever the same. My apology always carried the sworn coda that I'd never bring it up again. I'd let bygones be bygones, deny the past, with its barbs and biases, any chance of ruining the present.

—I'll never mention it again, I would promise.

—You've got to let it go, she'd reiterate.

—I will, I would say once more.

The wonder is, the words from my mouth weren't hers and vice versa. "You've got to let it go" is the language we use when we're hoping to console a friend who's been spurned by a lover. Not the words the one who was left behind should have to say to make the friend feel better.

Still, nostalgia idealizes. And while my intentions to let it go may have been genuine, I indulged myself from time to time in visions of Kip, and conjured nightmare scenes of his triumphant return. He had become a secret agent of some sort, conspiring to save the world, such as it was, while the rest of us slept, and like some Ulysses who, having quenched his desires with the occasional Circes of Bangkok, would know the time had come to return home and had but to eject this pretender from his doorstep to liberate his Penelope, and live happily ever after.

It may sound far-fetched, immature. But these gilt daydreams and mangled myths were real enough to me, and I tended them like a gardener does her choicest rose, a storyteller his favorite fairy tale. At the same time, I knew they were stupid fantasias but believed that I was helpless in the face of them. It was an addiction, I thought. It varied from year to year, but never failed to abide deep down, no matter how I might reason with myself about its injudiciousness and deep absurdity.

"Who would bother with a hoax?"

"Look, he got himself involved with some strange characters over there."

"Wishful thinking, Jess."

"You can't just up and go out there because you got some letter in the mail telling you to."

"It's his handwriting."

She paused before saying, "I think what you do is you put the letter away and forget about it."

"I don't really see what choice I've got."

"You always do what Kip tells you to do?"

"That's cruel," I said, with a half-smile. "But you admit it might be him."

"I don't get you, Brice."

"What's there to get?"

Jessica slid out from where she was seated across from me in the kitchen and took a small silver box down from the top shelf of one of the cupboards. Inside the box were some cigarettes she kept for occasions such as this. She lit the cigarette on the ring of flame at one of the gas burners on the stove, and said, "Of course you've got a choice. You simply ignore it."

I asked her, wasn't she at least curious?

"Hasn't the time come and gone when either of us can afford to be curious about Kip?"

Cigarette smoke ribboned upward, my eye followed its wavering. The next morning I made hasty arrangements, told my partners at the office that I had to go away for a couple of days. During the night before I left, Jessica whispered to me, "I'm scared."

Neither of us had slept.

"Stop being scared. There's nothing to be scared about."

"You know what there is to be scared about."

"Let's don't talk about it anymore, Jess."

"But we haven't talked about it at all."

She was right. My diffidence had cooled my interest in looking too much harder at the possible reasons my oldest friend had like a Lazarus come forth from the quiet, and wanted now to speak.

"Well, maybe this is a blessing in disguise. Maybe the time has come."

"He can't have Ariel. Isn't that what they all do, runaway fathers? See the light and try to worm their way back into other people's lives?"

Her adamancy came as a surprise. "Ariel's all her own now. He can't have her any more than you and I can have her at this point."

"He can turn us into liars in her eyes."

"Nothing can change how Ariel feels about you, Jess. You know that."

"What about how she feels about you?"

We slept. And when I said goodbye, her fear was replaced by a different kind of seriousness. "You're going to come home, aren't you?"

All my fellow passengers in the turboprop are asleep. The

young girl in the seat opposite mine closes and opens her hand as she dreams. Dark-haired and dark-skinned, a pale blue dress and ivory sweater. Her small mouth, pink as the corolla of a locust flower, is open, and the light catches her lower lip and tongue. Wonder what her dream is. The updrafts over the mountains buffet us, and I watch as her doll—horrid scrunched witchlike face and a long shock of purple hair, a troll I guess—comes loose from her embrace and tumbles into the aisle. I reach down to retrieve it and, having glanced around to assure myself that no one would see, lift the doll, scented with the odor of childhood, to my face. Ariel, I think. Her rag dolls and teddy bears smelled just the same when she was this girl's age, maybe four or five, back when it became clear her "uncle" Kip had permanently disappeared. I lay the doll back on the sleeping girl's lap, and marvel how she could feel maternal affection toward an ugly lump of molded gum.

Once we are over New Mexico there is less snow, and the same rumpled pale brown desert is studded with green-black points, piñons I would think, and there is a miles-long mesa off to our right, due west, and a fire in the lower mountains—I can see the white cottony smoke. Burning their fields in preparation for planting crops? Seems too early in the season to be a forest fire. Rectangles of manifold green appear now, as do tumbledown structures, farms here and there, islandlike hamlets. The edges of town are coming into view, and as the plane descends toward this animated map, everyone wakes up, except that now I am beginning to feel sleepy myself. My feet are frozen, my legs tingle. My mouth is parched.

So, yes, what am I doing here, I who left so long ago vowing, as only an idealist gifted with the nature of a true mule could, that I'd never return except for weddings and funerals? Why allow myself to be provoked? What do I possibly hope to accomplish? And why have I been so quick to dismiss the idea that the letter isn't a prank, a fabrication?

One obvious answer would be this. What would be the point of making up such a thing, of writing such a letter and mailing it? What would anybody gain from such a prank? The only problem with a rhetorical answer such as this is, of course, it's just another question.

While it is fair to say I've lived a life, and in doing so have made friends and enemies, just like anyone else, I think there are more of the former than the latter. I'm more sinned against than sinning but need no blasted heath on which to howl it out to whomever in the world would care to hear me. I have been burned and have felt adversity brush my life, but in ways no different than the next man. By the same token I have been the sharer of good times, many good times. These last have been unexpectedly quiet years, comparatively apolitical and socially disengaged, given how my adulthood and earliest years of practice began. It may be that I willed my life to be ordinary after a certain passage of time, but there's no crime in that. I was tired of catastrophe, sick of the strife, and once I decided I couldn't carry on trying to fill someone else's shoes, fight someone else's fights, those of my father or Kip or anyone else, began to devote much of my strength to sizing things down, to making my life *human,* if you will. My withdrawal from the antiwar and antinuclear movements, from all the various honorable causes, from the world of activism and philanthropy in the form of unbilled labor, from the days of countercultural this and that, was an act of positive reductionism—or so I informed my disgusted but very understanding colleagues.

—I can see where you're coming from, Brice, they would say.

—I'm not really turning away from you guys. I'll be here if you need me, I would say.

—We'll be here if you need us, too.

I'm okay, you're okay. Whatever might have been the merits of my rationale, I knew it was time I try to save my own life, and to let the world go its way, since that was what it was going to do with or without me contributing my voice to another chorus of protesters, my body to another march, my name to yet one more arrest warrant. To this day I believe it truly was less disillusionment and more an embrace of sober realism that moved me to change. I'd just turned thirty. The war was over—our undeclared war, the debacle of our generation. My practice as a lawyer would of necessity move away from defending what we used to call our dear old Antis—anti-Nuke, anti-War, anti-Establishment—and toward work with other clients. There would always be good and decent people who took stands against the flow of conformity, but the courts moved on with history, and so perforce did I. Thirty seemed as good a year as any to take a measure of where my life was headed. Kip had gone to Vietnam and Laos, had tried to come home and failed, had left me forever, it seemed. Jessica and I had settled down. My father wasn't going to change his mind about his contributions to military science but he was then starting to slow down into the last decade of his life; my mother was daft and content; my sister had married, was raising a kid, and hoped that another boy would follow. Ariel was growing up fast. Five years old, hard to fathom. It was time I grew up as well.

There was a Chinese saying my mother sometimes used, an inside joke we shared, that went, "May you live in interesting times." It was an inside joke because on the surface it sounded like a blessing but what the saying meant was, "May you be cursed."

We had lived in interesting times. And now I believed the curse must be lifted.

*I*t is a commonplace that we all depend once in a while upon the kindness of strangers. Strangers have a curious way of coming through for other strangers. But having to depend on the kindness of friends is a more unpredictable business. After all, there is something to lose with friends, whereas between strangers the freedom to say no allows one to say yes, even acts as a strong incentive to say yes. It is kind of my old friends to take me in on such short notice.

I feel both unnerved and grateful when Alyse picks me up at the airport. And more so, when she tells me that I will stay in her studio on Mountain Road, just across the river from their adobe. "Martha won't be in your way there."

It is more that I don't want to be in anyone's way. "How old is Martha now?"

Martha is four. Alyse and Michael were late bloomers, together since forever but held off starting a family until the last possible moment.

"She won't remember me."

I had met Martha once, when she was still a baby, in New York one Christmas when her parents had come east to introduce her to her grandparents, Michael's mother and father. She was memorable for her clear, round face and dark eyes. There was strength in her brow and grip. "But I remember her."

"With Martha you never know. I wouldn't be so sure she won't have all sorts of questions for you about Jessica and Ariel and what do you think of the new president. Nothing surprises me anymore. How does it feel to be back?"

"I don't think I want to feel anything about being here, if you

want to know the truth. I'm not completely sure I *should* be
here."

"You told me not to ask, so I'm not asking."

"Good. Don't. You wouldn't believe me if I told you."

"Try me."

Instead, I look out the window and express real amazement,
and not a little dismay at how quickly things have grown and developed. If you come back to where you grew up as seldom as I do,
you are bound for shocks of various kinds. People your memory
holds in time, changeless and smiling, have moved away or are dead;
places you cherished—a shallow crossing in a river, an old tree
whose cherries you loved to pick and then eat sitting in its generous
shade—are silted or sawed down. It all goes merrily or unhappily
along whether you stick around to watch or not. Commonplaces,
but they come at me in full force as we encounter the outskirts of
town where once there was nothing but piñon and tumbleweed.

"It's changed a lot since you were here last."

"Seems a shame," I say.

"We got too famous for our own good. All these Los Angeles
people commuting in for the weekends, New Yorkers too, artists
and dealers, and not just art dealers but people who made a lot
in drugs, got away with it and now are legitimate, into crystals,
organics, whatever all, a lot of money now. We're being califor-
nicated is how they put it. Are you tired?"

"No," I say. But I am. Or, maybe less tired than enervated.
And unnerved.

The studio is secluded. An adobe cottage cantilevered over a
steep ridge and surrounded by forsythia in full bloom, lilac and
apples, cottonwoods and aspen, and bushes whose names I don't
know or cannot remember, all beginning to bud. I'm left here to
wash up. Dinner will be later over at the big house, as they call
it. The studio is a smallish house built between the First and

Second Wars, I would guess, though maybe earlier. Whitewashed walls, three modest rooms—sitting room, bedroom, the studio itself—a smell of winter must in the air. I open a window that looks out over the valley. The river bursting with runoff is loud and steady, and I think, White noise, and suddenly come to the recognition that this is the first in a long time, years perhaps, that I have been alone, without Jessica somewhere nearby, without Ariel an at least distant presence.

Red tile floors, uneven and cool underfoot, rough-hewn lintels and doors, the traditional vigas—round heavy beams of timber —running lengthwise across the ceilings, and set in at alternate angles between beam and beam the latillas, like herringbone lath: it is all so familiar. I lie down on the horsehair bed and stare up at this geometric wooden ceiling, marveling at how easily I'd remembered Southwestern architectural terms I learned with my mother so long ago. Off the kitchen is a veranda in need of some carpentry. The vines have succeeded in pulling in several directions the arbor roof that runs along the terrace end over the patio. A pair of purple finches bound about in the tangle of grapevines that meander like coarse hair through the comb of the bower's rafters. Spring, time to multiply, hatching time. Dusty out here, and warm for April.

Let me try to lie down, see if I can't get myself centered—in that gentle sixties idiom, a potter's term that means to get your clay perfectly balanced and formed at the center of the turning wheel, and felicitous in this context given how my thoughts are wanting to spin off and prevent me from forming some sort of design or intent. A shortness of breath, is it the altitude?—I have lived at sea level for so many years now, and I can feel the seven thousand feet, the thinness of the air here—or is it nervousness? The birds are making a din. The will to reproduce, the will to squabble, the chorus makes me feel suddenly tired. I arrange a blanket over my feet like some old gentleman, lay my forearm over my brow, and despite my usual inability to nap during the day, drift off into a deep and dreamless sleep, but not before I have scolded myself for letting a flock of randy birds make me feel old. Let them chirp.

When I wake up the light in the windows is half gone. I panic for an instant, look at my watch. Five, not a problem. Calm yourself, I think. Alyse told me to come to the big house between six-thirty and seven, and pointed out a footpath down to the narrow river—more a glorified irrigation ditch than a real river, at least up here toward the head of the canyon—across a plank bridge, and up through a rocky corral to their house. On the far side, she'd told me, the landmarks that would guide me to their house were a Depression-era windmill that moaned whenever the wind made it work, and a walled inconspicuous zendo, a stupa, the oldest such Buddhist retreat in the country. Those who erected it thought this valley to be worthy. The birds are still chattering and I'm reminded of a line attributed to Lucy Audubon, the wife of John James: "I have a rival in every bird." I've never understood why I always get such a kick out of that quip of hers—it shouldn't make me laugh, but never fails.

As I begin to unpack my few things I realize that there's not much point—I'll want to be on the road as soon as tomorrow, go up to the Hill or else Chimayó itself—and then I notice something else, how awkward I feel in my shined black shoes. They look suddenly ridiculous to me, all wrong for the desert. Off they come, as does my gray suit, which is nothing special but seems strangely fraudulent here. Idem, my tie, conservative enough with its narrow bands of maroon and white, but here superfluous. I pull it off and stick it into my bag. Idem, the white shirt. Idem, the thin black socks. Baptismal dishabille, like a good purging of pretensions and disguise, not that they don't wear suits here, just that I never did. I replace my urban costume with jeans and a sweatshirt and feel more at peace. That accomplished, I search through the cabinets to see if there isn't some scotch—could use a drink—but find nothing. The refrigerator light doesn't come on when I open the door, but I can see it is empty save for a plastic bottle half full of water—flat and fluorinated—an earthenware jar of crusty browning mustard, and an unopened box of baking soda. There is a chill in the room now. Time to pull the windows closed, the evening air rising out of the canyon is cold. The birds have quieted down and, of course, what is my response but to miss them.

Do I reread the letter now or tomorrow? I've already read it half a dozen times, but I sense that reading it here on the high desert is going to be different—very different, perhaps—than from the distance of home and city.

I have gotten used to its look. Cockled white paper in a plain white envelope. Paper heavier and too large for the envelope, folded several times to fit. The letter is written in pencil, as is the address on the outside. Pulling it out of my pocket again I am seized by the prospect that all my sudden attention to it is an act of wretched credulity.

Being alone, I am able to read it aloud, granted in a kind of whisper, and with the greeting "Dear Brice," I begin to hear the letter as if it were spoken in his voice, a younger voice than that he must have now, but still distinctly Kip's. "How does a specter go about making his confession? And where could I possibly start in my apology to you, not to mention the explanation I owe others, you know who they are, who she is. I can't make what I need to make clear to you in a letter, but I didn't think it would be fair for me to suddenly show up, the ghost of a lost soldier come alive in his flesh. I couldn't bring myself to phone. So I got your address, you were as easy to find as I thought you'd be. It takes a kind of strength to go away and another kind of strength to stay. I was right to think you would still be in New York.

"I won't go on here like I'm some sort of friend of yours anymore, I know I haven't been. It hurts to write that out in so many words, but how could it be otherwise. If I'm wrong about this, I'd welcome your friendship but I count on nothing. What is imperative to me is that you believe I have a good reason for writing and that I'm not being cruel.

"Well, maybe it is cruel, a kind of cruelty you'd never have thought me stupid enough to have brought down on myself.

"I don't know much about your life, but there are people in everyone's lives who would be capable, I'd think, of practical jokes. Whether for fun, or to get you back for something you'd done to them. There must be such people in your life. Who knows? I want to save you time and trouble trying to authenticate this, Brice. There are secrets we have shared that you still must have kept secret. They're nothing to be proud of but we shouldn't be ashamed, either. If you have told no one else about Mary Bendel and the infamous visits, for instance, you'll have your proof that this is no fake. We saw a blue pony once in the sky. You'll remember that. I still have some charming scars from the peppers game, as you must. After our car accident I called you a traitor. I did because you were.

"I think these few details from the days we knew one another should be sufficient to legitimate my request. Or that is, make legit that it is me making the request and not somebody else.

"Time is no luxury for me. I need to meet you. I will assume that you will know where. It is the place where we became adults together. It would be understandable that you might not want to open things up after all these years, but for me there isn't much choice in the matter, not if I'm to complete something I started a long time ago. I need to entrust you with a story and there is someone I hope you will pass it along to. I need you to be my friend just one time more.

"Don't be a traitor twice, Brice. Even the walls of Jericho fell, and believe me or not but my purpose here is to make sure some walls don't. I will meet you there in a week, you know where and I think you know when, pilgrim. Please come, please listen.

"As ever, Kip."

As ever, Kip, indeed, as forever and always—you're too much as ever Kip. Shock, fear, relief, unhappiness, confusion, a sense of betrayal, a rending I could almost hear across the tenuous fabric of my contentment; then—and all this occurs within the briefest time—these sensations are drowned under a single wave of hope that the letter *is* a hoax, precisely because it goes so far out of its way to proclaim itself the truth. Why does it try so hard? I think, and for another instant I say to myself, Brice, you're a fool, you're here on a fool's errand, and even if it is Kip who's written this, Jessica was right, it may be a grave mistake to give his airs any credence. "Don't be a traitor twice"? I mean, *come on.* The audacity of it takes my breath away, the nerve of the man. I stuff the letter back in its envelope and find myself studying the stamp, an image of a wood duck, stern, even fierce, with his green and brown feathers and piercing red eye. The postmark, Los Alamos. Where else? Put the letter back in my pocket and pace the narrow kitchen. A story to entrust and someone to pass it along to, more mystery than I like—is this a story I'm going to want to hear? As I pace I notice a framed photograph hanging over the glass-front cabinet. In the image are a couple of gold prospectors, old-timers with big ears and shabby hats, one of them caught in the act of blowing away dirt and scratching gently in his pan to see if there is gold, while the other looks down over the shoulder of his crouching friend. It is an old black-and-white glossy but has the feel of some daguerreotype, and in white ink someone has written in the corner of the still *Russell Lee, Pinos Altos, May 1940.* Smile at the convergences. They emanate youth.

They want for there to be gold in the wide-brimmed beat-up pan. In their way they seem to be gentlemen. The days of the gold rush long past and yet look at them, they haven't given up one whit of hope that their future will turn up in the bottom of a pan.

No, it's not a hoax, the letter. It is Kip. And I think, Yes, I have to be here. Yes, I have to know what story he wants me to know.

The sky has evolved into a mute deep blue, huge and high. The evening star is faint but visible. I make my way down the hill toward the river. It sounds like a thousand chattering children. I slip a couple of times during the descent and set rocks running. Soon I cross the river on a rickety plank and begin to climb toward the silhouette of the windmill above me, knowing better than to think that it's a giant in need of a proper lancing.

—Part of your salvation is you were never meant to play Sancho Panza to his Don Quixote, Jessica said once, a long time ago.

—And what part am I supposed to play? I asked.

—You're both Don Quixote, as far as I can see.

—I'll take that as a compliment.

—Do with it as you like.

Both Quixote. Maybe so, maybe not, but there was a time when we knew we would never die. We might get sick. We might get hurt. But we knew we would get well and our wounds would heal. If we were sad, a new day would bring us happiness. If we had lost hope, the desert dawn would restore our faith. We knew that those who betrayed us, if we were betrayed, would suffer, just as we would suffer if we were the authors of some treacherous act. Sure, there would be suffering, but it would come to an end. We knew it, we just knew it. Sickness would end, pain would end, the blues would come to an end, guilt and betrayal would be forgotten, we would forgive, we would be forgiven.

And we knew we would never pass away. We knew, being kids,

that daddy death would look and look but he'd never find the likes of Kip and me.

It really was quite a friendship, wasn't it, I think. With everything ahead of us and little by way of qualms.

I am up the hill. There is the zendo and there is the house.

What am I going to say when they ask what's brought me back to New Mexico? I managed to avoid answering that question all afternoon. Secrets inevitably create the need for more secrets, and before you know it the secrets become lies, no more stable than a house of cards in a playful breeze. But as I walk toward their home I realize I should have a story in place to explain my presence. It will have to do with Holy Week and Chimayó. That's becoming big now, and maybe I've decided to come out and see it one last time before the tourism and its shams and flimflam artists take over? Have one last look at it while there is still some semblance of what it was like in the quiet old days of our youth when the Lourdes of America was unknown to any but a few dozen locals, some anthropologists, the true faithful. In fact, I *am* looking forward to seeing my sacred site anew. Maybe this once, the world will display itself as immutable. That would be a precious relief, might be enough to get me to light a votive candle and say a prayer, or contemplate some saint or another in one of the antique bultos. So my secret can be hidden behind the sleight of a venial fib after all.

The light is on over the door. Moths circle it. The door is unlocked. I open it and say, "I'm here."

Chiming, echoed tones, like timbres that start as tastes in the mouth then work their way somehow into the ear. The chiming came from keys. It wasn't a dream but somehow I must have wanted it to be a dream, or wanted it to remain inside the fitful dream I was already having rather than graduate into something far less interior and circumscribed. The keys—brass tongues licking brass rings—clanged against one another, far away from where we lay in a heap.

I came to first. The sun was aloft.

We stank.

If my mother were there to behold us in our dirty glory she'd have said, —You boys stink to high heaven. My mother would do that, mix her schoolmarm side—which expressed itself in complete sentences, as well made as if with mortise and tenon— with her down-home side. She was forever calling Kip "antsy"— which at the time I misconstrued as "auntsie" because my aunt Ariel was reputed to be consumed by restlessness, as consumed as Kip I imagined, and I had not as yet learned about ants in one's pants, or had not in any event connected those ants to the state of being antsy.

Beam of light on my fingers, white with dried mud. Furrows at the joints of my fingers a matter of curiosity, something I'd not observed before, made me fathom that a baby's hands have the quality of antiquity to them, the creases and puckers in the flesh reminiscent of the timeworn. Silly aching child staring at his mitts. My throat was sore.

—Stink to high heaven, that was one of her favorite phrases and another concept I'm afraid I couldn't understand, or else just misunderstood, since wasn't heaven supposed to smell good?

Kip groaned; Fernando Martinez, who was still sitting against the dirt wall, was breathing through his mouth, making a rasping, scraping snore; and as I searched with my hands for my head I heard myself give out a moan that came up slowly from the depths of my first hangover. The keys were still far away, at least relative to where we'd slept in the bowels of the santuario, but I recognized, without having to think, what those keys meant.

—Kip, I whispered into his ear, which was right next to my mouth, as he'd fallen asleep with his head on my chest, —Kip? and I gave him whatever kind of shove I could manage, —Kip, wake up, man. His head was so heavy on me. I pushed myself up to my elbows, breathed quietly as I could, —Kip? once more, and moaned again from pain that flared in my temples.

I found I barely had the strength to hold myself up. A door, the great carved front door of the church, closed hard far down at the end of the main chamber and made a faraway clattering, like some great wooden wave crashing on a frail, jerry-built wooden shore, and both Kip and Martinez came wide awake. In the sallow ray that gave through the small window, the only source of light in this little cell, I could see Martinez blink, mechanically at first, three four five times, then stall with an open-eyed look of pure fear.

Wakeful, dreamily maybe, but conscious in an acid-blinded sort of way, I found my focus rise from my fingers, my head, my Kip, to Fernando Martinez's glare. The minutiae one takes in at a moment such as that! How I zeroed in on not just the red-flushed rims of his eyes but the damp lashes that unfolded, curling up and down and away from them—and then as quickly as the moment came it passed and the pace of things stepped up. Whatever middling state in which I'd lolled between the lofty and futile adventures of the night gone by and those to come was over in a flash. Turning point; and the world was about to tumble down around our ears.

The three of us began on hands and knees to crawl toward the doorway all at once. There was still the chance of making an escape if we could get out the side door of the sacristy and into the car before whoever was opening the church to worshippers caught us. Kip let out a yelp and the wildness of the yelp was that of a ferret caught in a bear trap, baleful and wretched, and he gave it full throat as he twisted back on himself to see he'd caught his foot and wrenched his ankle in the posito. If it weren't so pitiful, we'd have broken out laughing, but there was no time to laugh. Kip kept yowling and cursing now, and Martinez and I—responsive to our own fears—shrieked and our feet and arms churned. It was as if we were a single seething and sightless monster, like poor Caliban in Robert Oppenheimer's and my own favorite drama. Things went black and blank until a man's voice rose to challenge us in Spanish from down at the end of the nave, and when I heard—with ears that didn't seem to belong to me—just how distant that voice was, I knew if we ran hard we might evade, or at least postpone, being caught.

It was Fernando Martinez who showed a modicum of common sense. Kip and I would have been helpless, by ourselves, in the situation, and Martinez probably intuited it. Coming to, suddenly—or at least so it seemed to me—he clambered to his feet, hissed, —Shut up! then whispered what we were to do—I remember his face going very stiff—and we did what he said, no questions asked, no further ado. We bolted straight through the door by the altar that led into the nave, where we more or less faced, in the morning dark, our dilemma.

An old man. Like the church, he seemed out of a storybook, yet quite unlike the church, he was surely a spent thing. A spindle is what comes to mind as I think back, or a dying summer bee dusted by the first frost, a husk, a helpless wisp. He was, pathetically insofar as we could barely hear him over the music of his keys on the thick ring in his right hand, cursing at what we assumed was the top of his lungs, cursing us down and up, paying out a wheezy string of epithets in what might have been three languages, a little Tewa, some Spanish, some English. It was clear he was more terrified than we, and we knew, in the way boys like the commonest nasty predators can, we knew how to capitalize on terror. Martinez made his move first; and Kip and I followed suit. As we rushed toward this poor viejito whistling and windmilling our ungainly arms, I felt sorry for him, the caretaker, or custodian, or could he have been the priest? Seeing him there before me in what this shadowy light unveiled as a dismal suit, dark blue or a gray-blue, short at the cuffs and buttoned at the belly, the white of his shirt revealed in an inverted V above the waistband, there with his bola tie—turquoise lump set in dull silver was it? and no, I'd decided, he couldn't be the priest—half done up, there in his old body, and seeing him fix in slow shock on we who were bearing down on him, I realized he posed no threat whatever. So when Martinez, or maybe Kip—by accident, I assumed—brushed him with a flailing elbow as they ran by, not hard but enough to make him stagger, I caught the man in my arms and steadied him, felt just how tough he was, smelled the coffee, the old tobacco, and what must have been antiquity on his breath, and felt quiek sympathy toward him until he recovered his balance and thundered, —*Váyanse, hijos del demonio!* loud, louder than I could have imagined possible, and cried, —*Lárgansen, desgradiados,* get out of here, you disgraceful boys even as he sprang forward and swiped me across the face with his keys.

The look he must have seen on my face was some way equal to the unexpected swat he had given me. We each reeled backward a step, and locked eyes. We stood, a couple of generations removed from one another and descended down lines of thoroughly different blood and values, and gawked like two soldiers of opposing camps come unawares on one of the enemy, with arms drawn perhaps, but maybe not in the mood for any trouble after the day of heroics and warring, who try to back away, thinking, So these are the people we work so hard to do away with.

We stood, stared. I must have reached out to him, extended my hand, gave him a stolid smile.

Then that daydream soon was gone and Kip yelled, —Hurry up, come on, Brice, and I blinked and may actually have thought to give the old fellow an embrace before I regained my senses and dashed, my cheek on fire, toward the door at the end of the sanctuary.

The sun was so bright the light seemed stiff. We burst from the darkness into the hard white morning heat of the plaza, at a dead run. The reedy words of the old custodian receded as we piled, helter-skelter, Kip limping, into the car.

—Go, man, Martinez shouted, but Kip couldn't find the keys. Aside from a crumpled roll of dollar bills covered with a pale patina of the sacred dirt, his pockets were empty. He searched the floor of the car, and the seat. —*Picale, andale, ir'ya vacas!* cried Martinez.

Would that we had clung to the righteousness of our endeavor, is all I can think now, as I remember this scene from my youth; the vain panic, the demoralized and dishonorable flight from a helpless specter of a man. My cheek still has on it a patch of white, this tough welt, which I will always regard as an emblem of the series of bad if heartfelt decisions that were made on the morning following our idealistic—and after its own fashion successful—pilgrimage. While Kip and Martinez argued, and while the old fellow climbed the gentle hill from the zaguan to the top of the plaza, I lamented. Looked up at the hills that ascended above the irrigated flat fields of the valley, rose in parallel and curved mounds to converge, higher and higher, into the low mountain of Tsi Mayoh, and wanted—again, like a child—to bolt, flee my mates, leave behind my mess. I wondered how far away I could get on foot before they caught up. Remembered I had taken a piece of chicken from the refrigerator, a leftover from dinner the night before, wrapped it up in paper, and now I tapped my hands on my pants pockets.

Sometimes the mind can run in so many directions at once. I suppose I had thought ahead to the projected night before me, down in the valley, pictured myself under the heavy stars, hungry and far from the comforts of home. The chicken wing was gone. Must have lost it in the desert where some cayedog got himself a pretty easy morsel. I could picture my mother and sister sitting there at the table last night, talking of this and that, and remembered how I'd eaten second helpings and, bashful, asked for thirds against this secret prospect of famishment.

But then Martinez laughed and pointed, —The keys, man, there they are, let's go, and sure enough they were still in the ignition where Kip had left them. My mouth was as parched as the soil that covered my lips and cheeks.

—Go away, I shouted at the old caretaker, who was almost upon us, —go away, saying it as much for his sake as ours. Kip got the Plymouth started and slammed the column stick into gear just as he came hobbling to the side of the car, waving those church keys in the air, whooping and sputtering, the mongrel dogs—black, brown, white with spots, all nondescript but for their fat wet swinging tongues—running in close circles around him.

Our tires spun, kicked up pebbles. Our heads heaved forward, came to right. The moronic dogs stopped and, with the miraculous singularity of vision a pack can display, turned their attention from the viejito to us in the car, then one, then another of them bared fangs, and in an instant bounded straight in our direction. Kip, not having seen any of this, fumbled with the stick, hit the gas and suddenly backed up again, slammed into something, pumped the brake, pushed the shift stick to drive. The engine coughed and we lurched out forward as a painful howling rose from under the chrome bumper. I turned and saw that one of the mongrels, crackling with energy, powered itself in a furious scuffle with the earth, its hind end reddened and paralyzed, its head and forelegs churning as it pulled itself in a semicircle, and lunged across the powdery ground snapping in the direction of the car. The old man had sat himself down on the plaza. He watched the injured dog as it ran in arcs, fell, jumped up again, described a half-moon on the dust much the way we used to make snow angels on our backs after a fresh winter flurry, and collapsed once more. The other hounds were right alongside us. Martinez stood in the back seat. To him this was a marvelous circus, I guess. He threw the whiskey bottle at the closest dog, a black and muscular blur, and caught it square in the chops. Beyond the dogs, the bottle, the old man, I saw the santuario receding from view, glazed as it were by the scrim of dustlight. The stout twin spires seemed peaceful and eternal there in the delicate, protecting hands of the cottonwoods, and I knew with the same certainty one knows something in a particularly vivid dream that despite ourselves we had accomplished what we'd come to do, that while our simple-hearted wishes might be beyond the interests of fate to grant, our motives had not been construed as other than good and kind and compassionate. We could eat all the sacred dirt on earth, but still those who loved to make war would make war. My crooked halo whitened—could Kip, could Martinez see?—into the sincerest burning beam for that one small moment, then dimmed away.

Thinking back on it, I've come to adore El Santuario de Chimayó more and more over the years, despite my distance and the fact I'm not a religious man, don't attend church, don't *intend* to attend church in the future. Chimayó is more than a church, has to it a spiritual richness beyond what any religion offers. Sturdy and luminous, it is a holy yet secular place, secular as in saecular, *saecularis,* worldly and pagan, made of earth, of dust and water. Open to all, it shuns not the least among us. What else can a sinner say? Chimayó proposes, in its simplicity, that all churches should be made of hand-hewn timber and hand-plied mud, since wood and adobe sustain the spirit better than the finest marble or firmest granite. The Europeans can keep their pallid fortresses, with rose windows and spires to take your breath away, with golden doors to baptisteries and campaniles touching the lower stratosphere. The believers who, in the early part of the last century, fashioned Chimayó from the barest elements around them, knew that trees rise from wet earth, and that wood and mud are old biological friends. More than this seems an excess, and somehow faithless. If man is made of clay, why not his houses of worship? It remains as extraordinary to me today as it was then that not an hour's distance from this valley was the Hill where a fire was built that could burn not just wood but earth as well.

—Shut up, man, I turned toward Martinez. How could he find all this so funny? He hooted something in dialect at the old man, pumped a defiant middle finger into the morning breeze. I hadn't noticed, the night before, that he had his own brand. A scar ran from a point just below his eye down his smooth brown cheek to the edge of his jaw. It was thick as a worm and dull pink. He turned, offered me a smile—or rather, an inverted frown. His teeth were gap-spaced but there was a delicacy to him. Who was this guy? I turned around and sat back. And, of course, who were we?

Martinez laughed some more.

—*Cállete la boca,* Kip told him.

Martinez responded, —*Cállete 'l hocico* yourself, then pulled himself together, got serious all of a sudden, and said, —So what is next, my friends?

—What do you mean what's next? What's next is you're gone, is what's next.

—I think I'll stay along for a little while yet.

—You're crackers, boy.

—Kip?

—What.

—Maybe we better go back home now.

—No way, he said, and took a hard right turn, started driving faster, through what there was of this small village, past some broken-down wooden stalls and houses, toward fields with shade trees here and there and cattle with yokes of lashed sticks grazing in the mild calm of their simple world. I stayed quiet, was grateful that Fernando Martinez decided to be quiet. The determination in Kip's face made me ponder what we were going to do, where we were to go now.

We had no plan. What fragment of an agenda we did have in place the night before had been fulfilled, more or less. Kip and I each had a lode of tierra bendita in our bellies, as proposed, but beyond Chimayó, Kip and I had failed to scheme. There wasn't time to discuss it, and so having passed the Capilla del Santo Niño, surged beneath the trees that lined the narrow dirt lane, having sped down the main road, a road that would lead us not back toward Los Alamos, but rather toward Truchas and Taos, we found ourselves farther away from home and deeper into trouble. I glanced over at Kip again and saw him wince when he weighed down on the pedal with his hurt foot. I breathed in deep the pristine air off Tsi Mayoh, off the alluvial soil of El Potrero, off the Rio Quemado and Santa Cruz, and thought that I ought to have some say about what we were doing, but then figured, Leave it alone, after all what does it matter now that we're pure, now that we've eaten from the well of earth, there's nothing anybody can do to hurt us.

Still, fear has a way of tucking itself beneath a pretty quilt of optimism. We were all pumped up. The pain in my eyes and head and in my back from having slept on the ground disappeared some under the brilliance of the sky and clouds. We seemed to drift into tranquility once we reached the long plateau stretch on the high road to Taos. The dogs were far behind us now. I imagined that the old caretaker had bestirred himself, climbed to his feet, knocked the dust from his trousers, and walked back down to the santuario to finish his morning's business there, little the worse for wear from his encounter, and relieved to find out that we boys hadn't broken anything, and hadn't taken anything that God wouldn't be able quite easily to replace.

We encountered no one besides a farmer on a tractor going the opposite way, outside Cordova. Red-brown cattle munched orchard grass down in their pale green valley oases. The moon was setting. Smoke issued in whiskers from hornos and chimneys. Some silhouettes of swallows in the sky. A small herd of wild horses—one a tall lank roan with speckles the cast and shape of eggs over his back—stood beside the shoulder of the highway. Each faced a different direction, looking lost, which made me wonder, How can they be lost if they don't have a home? which in turn reminded me of Fernando Martinez who had curled himself up in the back seat into a fetal position and fallen asleep much like one of those dogs back there probably was doing right now, following his tail in a tight circle three times, lying down, maybe smacking his chops, the picture of contentment, and in a trice was dreaming.

As it was with Kip, Martinez seemed to be at home with himself. I stared at him. The wind whipped his hair in thatches. His shirt was untucked and missing buttons, and looked to be a third- or fourth-generation hand-me-down. Likewise his denims and fraying tennis shoes. His moustache, in the light of day, was in fact that of a boy, and when I turned around I allowed myself a moment to study Kip. If I could look like anyone in the world I would look like Kip, I thought. His contours were sharp and his movements astute. The darkness of his eyes belied such cunning light, his forehead was smoother than riverstone and browned by the sun, his cheeks and jaw and nose were so defined as to seem drawn in ink against the world around him. —What? he asked, sensing my eyes on him, and I said, —Nothing, and faced forward.

We were like a thrown rock. Never had I been on the road going as fast as this. What freedom and what fear, and as we carried on in silence I could feel those fears lift away just as our words and laughter had the night before, and tumble into nothingness behind. I was here with Kip, true brother. We'd done something special together and it was as if this car were our new home. Home is where you are most alive, most aware, most content, isn't it? I closed my eyes tight and watched the crystals of changing colors the sunlight played on my lids. The blood in my head sang.

By late morning we neared Ranchos de Taos. As the air got thinner and cooler among the rising peaks, the nausea we'd been feeling began to fade and with it faded our hysteria. Kip was driving slower now, one hand on the wheel and the other drumming his knee to the beat of the radio music. Borne forward in a haze of peaceful pleasure, we were above and beyond everyone and everything. The old Spanish saying *Noche alegre, mañanita triste*—a night of revelry, a morning of grief—didn't seem to apply to us anymore. We knew it couldn't last, but for an hour we didn't care. We wore the world like a crown.

We had stopped for fruit and candy bars in Las Trampas, one of the poor farm villages along the way. Kip decided to let me try to drive, but I wasn't good at it, had the car now on the center line, now on the shoulder, and without any protest from me, he took the wheel again. We counted the money we had taken—stolen, in fact—from hiding places back on the Hill. My contribution to our runaway money came from the cookie jar in our kitchen, a jovial Sambo whose gentle, foolish smile shamed me when I plunged my hand into his fat paunch in search not of pecan sandies but the plastic bag in which my mother stowed reserve cash. Kip had filched from his father's more ingenious but not invulnerable hiding place, which was simply a manila envelope taped to the underside of a table in their front room.

Most of my money was in single bills, with a few fives. I had folded it up and carried it in my breast pocket. When I thought about our thefts, I could feel the crown on my head begin to slip away. By the time I finished eating a hard green apple from the grocery, and tossed the core into the ditch along the side of the road, my euphoria had passed and my fears began to take its place.

I said, —We're pretty rotten, you know.

—What're you talking about?

—It's a pretty rotten thing to've done what we did taking our folks' money, don't you think?

—Hey, keep it down, Kip said, jerking his head toward the back seat. Then he said, quietly as he could, —Rotten? That's what you'd call *us,* rotten?

—Well.

—We're not the ones who're rotten, boy.

I didn't know what to say. Said, —I don't know.

—So, all right. We're rich and rotten.

I breathed in hard; I didn't want to be a stupid little kid anymore. I wanted to be strong. I said, —No more rotten than how the stuff got earned, I guess.

—All right, he said. —You said that right.

There were more and more signs of life, and with every person we encountered along the way, the dire nature of our quandary, the mess we were creating for ourselves, began to sharpen into greater focus, grow despite our unconscious best efforts to be oblivious to the thought of how worried our parents and friends must be, back up there on the Hill. We devoured our candy, squinted in the sun, and kept going. Onward was our only way, onward and upward. The flats at the foot of the Sangre de Cristos lay out ahead, and Colorado, secreted behind their snow-laden tops, beyond.

I knew my geography from school, I'd always loved maps, and it was nothing for me to close my eyes and conjure the land and life that lay ahead of us—north and north, through Colorado, maybe along the foothills up through Pueblo and Denver and on to Cheyenne, Wyoming, and north through Casper toward the Bighorn Mountains and Montana, where we'd hire ourselves out as ranch hands or vaqueros. Mow alfalfa and bundle it in bales, shear sheep, bust broncos. Then, after some adventures there, we'd get stir-crazy, and one morning before the dawn broke we'd be back in our car, headed north up into Canada, maybe high into Saskatchewan where we would become strong sawyers, build our own timber mill by some great river upon whose grassy shore we'd fish grayling or salmon for breakfast, hunt wild moose for our supper, and then we would go all the way up into the Northwest Territories, where we would wear sealskins and build ourselves a house of tundra peat, and let the rest of the world fare its wars below while we—heroes larger than life—sang songs, carved quaint scenes in reindeer horns, and smoked pipes by a fire crackling in the hearth.

Back and forth, back and forth. So my daydreams went. In the meantime, again more fellow travelers along the road, and by now more creeping remorse in my heart, and probably in Kip's as well. We were both quiet. I tried hard to keep my thoughts on the high times ahead rather than what might be happening back on the Hill. Time passed in odd blurts and shapes. More people saw us, a farmer on his tractor pulling his loaded spreader along the shoulder, headed probably from his tumble-down barn to a field, looked us over as we passed him slowly on a rough patch. I noticed Kip's eyes darting from the rearview mirror to the highway, felt us pick up speed again, and although he and I didn't say anything to each other, I sensed that Kip sensed that I sensed that we were being watched. We had every right to be paranoid.

Yes, a noble house of stone, with a crackling yellow fire in the corner hearth, and a big pot of black coffee on the cast-iron stove. And wives, strong wise wives, Eskimo girls with flat wide faces and knowing eyes, with bright woven clothing and reindeer moccasins.

A station wagon with side-by-side headlights and fins passed us, a woman and some children in the back, the eldest a girl with bangs and a coppery barrette not so much younger than we— they studied us too closely. There were others. One truck driver in particular who had come upon us when we were descending through the pine-forested mountains past Rio Pueblo, taking the switchback curves of Borrego Canyon much faster than we should have, bore down on our car and seemed to study the three of us from the height of his silver cab. Kip sped up, slowed down, but couldn't shake him.

—What are we doing, Kip? I heard myself say.

He didn't look at me, but had his eyes trained on the mirror as if in a trance, shifting them back to the meandering road from second to second, and said, —Not now.

The noble stone house and Eskimo wives faded, and I saw my

father's face as if it were right before me, saw his eyes, even saw that he'd cut himself shaving and could almost smell his styptic pencil, and I was afraid.

—Why not now? Let's pull over.

Kip yelled, —How'm I supposed to pull over? Look at this guy back here.

I didn't know. I didn't want to cry.

—You're in fifty-fifty here, Kip went on. —You tell me what we're supposed to do.

—I mean, maybe we ought to just go back to the Hill.

He slammed the butt of one hand against the steering wheel, shot me a look, muttered something like, —Okay, then set his jaw and began gradually to brake the car, gradually slowed us way down and, still driving, ignoring the horn blasts from the rig behind us, shouted, —Yeah, that's just great, that's a great idea.

I didn't know how to respond. Everything was happening at once, it seemed. Kip's move was working. As the car slowed more, the man in the truck behind us had apparently had enough and, blessedly, noisily, was passing us. Once the rig blew by, buffeting us as it offered one last deafening blast from its horn, the atmosphere completely changed. The truck—moments ago so massive, bearing down like guilt upon us—diminished before disappearing altogether around a sheer stone cliff. Kip, trembling a little, brought the car to the side of the road. We sat suddenly swamped by silence, intense and enveloping.

After a moment, Kip in a raspy whisper said, —You know, Brice, sometimes I really don't get you. I already told you we can't go back to the Hill. You know what's going to happen to us if we go back there?

—All I know is I'm not sure that what we're doing is the best idea.

He rolled his head back on his shoulders and looked straight up to the sky. —Okay, all right. You got a better idea?

He was still shuddering, but now I noticed that it wasn't so much from terror as anger.

I heard myself say, —Better idea than what? and as I said it, I thought, What a fool you can be at times, Brice.

—We been driving all morning and now you're going to ask what we're doing?

I said nothing because I knew it wasn't really a question he had asked, at least not a question he expected me to answer.

Soon enough he answered it himself.

—We just go on is all.

I couldn't look him in the eye. Again my mind drifted back to those horses—wild cayuses, by definition never lost—and I thought of being a cowboy twin with Kip in Montana, a homesteader with him in the North country, and about the original meaning of our pilgrimage. They, our parents and our people back on the Hill, were guiltier than we, this much we knew as truth. And so, given the nature of life on the Hill, why return? Kip, whose eyes I could feel were hard on me—Kip was right. I must have reddened, I sensed my ears burning bright. How could I have failed him like that? Yet, still, the tiniest flicker of dread kindled in me, too, a combined fear of losing Kip, knowing I would not have him forever for my very own as I'd had him when we were sequestered on the Hill, and inchoate perception of what the world might do to my friend, my heart's pal, especially in light of how unafraid of it he seemed to be. These must have been feelings. I doubt I'd have been able to put them into words.

Frightened eyes can be lucid eyes, and I remember feeling I was seeing Kip for the first time, as if through some clarifying lens. So it was I remember feeling, fair enough, but what was more likely was this. Not that my own eyes were sharper, instead that Kip's view of how he might approach his life minutely yet radically shifted. Last night was different from today. Last night we were both ecstatic. Our plan had worked. We'd been free, had freed ourselves. We'd toured across a landscape only dreamed at for months and years before. Yet this morning it was obvious that Kip was strengthened by being a runaway.

I stared at my hands and when finally I looked up I saw that he was smiling at me, a tight crescent smile, his lips brown in the flickering shadows thrown by the tall pines by the road. The ponderosas gave off a heavy scent of vanilla. I knew my lips were white. Suddenly, I would have given anything for a piece of angel food cake.

—We off now?

I said yes, and thought, Nice big piece with ice cream on top.

—Well, come on then, he laughed.

Sleepy, Jess says, "What's it like there?"

"You've been here, Jessica. More buildings, more roads, more people, more dogs, but still New Mexico."

"What's their place like, Lyse and Michael's?"

"It's all right. Where I'm staying tonight is new New Mexican. And their house is an old wandering adobe thing with heated floors, kind of old-new New Mexican."

"Heated floors?"

"Hot-water pipes, there's hot pipes just under the tiles so that the floor is warm in the winter."

Why are we talking architecture, I wonder, then Jessica—as if overhearing my thought—says, "Do you think you ought to come home now?"

"You know what surprises me?"

Jessica asks me what.

"What surprises me is that you still don't think I ought to be here. What would you think if I weren't here?"

"I don't know."

"See what I mean?"

"Maybe I'd think more of you if you hadn't gone is what I mean—no, I don't mean that. It doesn't matter, does it? I think you have to be where you are, and that's why you're there and I'm here, because this is where I should be."

"You're sure," I ask.

"Brice."

"Because if you think you should be here—"

"I don't. It's not my place. If I thought it were, I'd be there."

I say, "Have you talked with Ariel about the birthday party?"

"She'll be here Sunday."

"She doesn't mind that it's after the fact?"

"I don't think she cares about these things as much as her father does. Do you think she's too old for me to make that vile birthday cake she used to love?"

"Chocolate with peanut butter frosting—"

"—just disgusting."

"She may be too old but I'm not."

"You'll be here, no matter what?"

I could tell that Jessica had been crying before I called. When I hung up and turned out the light to try to get some sleep, I began seriously to contemplate apologizing to my impromptu hosts in the morning, and catching the bus to Albuquerque. I could be back in the city by tomorrow night. There'd be very little discussion about my change of heart. Bonnie Jean and Mother'd never know that I was here, so neither regrets nor explanations would have to be extended to them. Kip might wait for me all day Friday, but he'd get the picture by afternoon, and he'd have to accept my decision. Surely it would be unreasonable of him not to have considered that there was an excellent chance his long-ago friend Brice might determine to leave the past in the past. Resurrections have ever been dangerous business. Monsters resuscitate with the same alacrity as angels. How many times have I seen it happen in a courtroom, when I walk in, thinking my case is prepared and that my client has told me everything, only to have an entire defense go under because someone has remembered something, some small thing that capsizes all in its wake? I have seen it, and more than once. Kip, I think. More than half a lifetime ago, my friend. Are you angel or monster?

I can hear him, his taut, clear voice that I remember so well. His answer, Only one way for you to find out, Brice, and besides you know it's never as simple as sorting angels from monsters. You yourself were the one who always empathized with Caliban.

I did, it is true.

And his voice fades with the words, Well, what makes you think I'm not the same as Caliban, eh, Mr. Prospero?

*A*fter deciding to go forward, to match our emotional distance from Los Alamos in geographic measure, we'd continued down the pass below Picuris Peak half a dozen miles before realizing that Fernando Martinez was no longer asleep in the back seat. Indeed, he had vanished.

—What the—? and Kip turned us around. We drove back to the turnout where we had parked not a quarter hour before.

Nothing, no sign of our mercurial companion. We stood on the shoulder and peered down through the thick forest of old fir and knew he was there somewhere. We called his name. Wind tinkered its way in rising and dying waves, caused the shadows to play over the floor of brown needles below, heightened the eeriness of his disappearance. Clouds crept across the horizon above the serrate treeline.

—Martinez, we shouted.

It was as if he had been an hallucination.

—Should we look for him?

Kip shook his head. —You know what. I never wanted to bring him along in the first place.

—You were the one driving. You didn't have to stop.

—Who spotted him? Who said, Slow down, Kip, slow down, there's somebody standing there by the road?

—Don't try to blame this on me.

Kip stared ahead, chin forward, hands in his pockets, defiant. —I never liked that guy, he said again.

—What you want to do now? I asked in what must have been a revisit of my feeble voice, but uneasiness had settled in on Kip this time too, and he shrugged.

Again I wanted to broach the obvious with him, that this was not working, what we did last night was right and righteous but now we were coming undone, and wouldn't it be better to go back and take whatever is in store for us—after all, we did it, we suffered the remedy, we ate the dirt, nothing can hurt us—but instead we both stood there mute while the air walked through the sparkling pines, me left with my unanswered question and Kip with unmasked confusion until he said, finally, —Idiot.

The reference, I thought, might have been to me.

Then he finished, —Let's go, and once more we were headed down toward Taos. Kip peered into the dry canyon out to the east, peered out at the far peaks and frothing clouds, and without saying a word gave me to understand that he could read my silence, and that he had no intention of reversing course.

That we made it through Taos without being apprehended seems astonishing. Was this because a couple of boys said to be missing from up on the Hill didn't register with the authorities as being quite as significant in the great scheme of life as it was to me and Kip? Was it possible, Kip and I asked each other, they hadn't made a connection between our disappearance and that of the Wrights' Plymouth convertible? We'd left no note, had taken off in the middle of the night, silent and swift as elf owls that descend from their cactus-hole perches to dominate the darkness—or so we'd have metaphorically flattered ourselves. But was it possible that no one had deciphered our signature in the theft?—that of all the cars in town to take, we'd chosen one owned by the parents of our favorite childhood adversary, a boy who hated us as much as we did him, for no reason beyond our juvenile need to mark territory and dominate it in the time-honored fashion boys and wild animals have followed since ages immemorial, a kid Kip and I thought ourselves incredibly clever to have nicknamed "Wrong," the joke being, of course, that here was an instance where two Wrights made a wrong. It would not have been in the least foolish of them to have sent, by now, search parties into the canyons near home, down in Bayo where we used to ride ponies, or in Pueblo, or up higher into the Jemez toward the caldera, the opulent, grassy Valle Grande where one could walk for days without encountering another living soul. Insofar as we'd been rumored to have passed through Chimayó, a fact we found out later, isn't it true the caretaker back in the church might well have been half-blind and perceived to be a senile and unreliable witness? He had no corroborator—though, of course, Martinez was now a potential fink, if suspect and unreliable himself—and so our mysterious good luck at having not been caught was perhaps not so mysterious after all. We assumed that so long as we moved along shrewd and cautious and quiet we would be safe. By nightfall our second day we'd figured out how to raise the canvas top of the convertible over its steel ribs, and found some blankets in the trunk. We parked the car behind what seemed to be an abandoned bus station and slept as best we could, me in front, Kip in back.

In the morning, we indulged in 7UP and a tin of sardines for breakfast. It was when I reached into my pocket to pay for gas and a map that I discovered my money was missing.

—Damn, I said, as it came clear. —Damn damn damn.

Kip checked his pockets and his wad was there, and he paid, hissing between his gritted teeth, —I knew it. Did I know it, or what? I never liked that guy.

Once we pulled out of the station, left behind the peal of pneumatic bells and smell of oil, we both began cursing at the top of our lungs. What disaster, what stupidity. Born yesterday, wet behind the ears. Green as meadow grass and about as easy to walk all over. My fist came down on my knee.

—I told you so, said Kip.

—We gonna go back and find him?

—I didn't like him, I didn't like him one bit.

—You already said that.

And then I saw my wad of bills lying on the floor. Double fool, I thought, and held them up between my trembling fingers. Kip laughed so hard he had to pull over and idle for a moment.

—You're too much, boy, he said.

—I didn't think he'd done it.

—I'm not talking about him, I'm talking about you.

—Never mind, lay off. Everything's all right now. Like I say, I didn't think he'd done it.

—He might as well have.

We kept going, Kip chuckling every so often, me concentrating on the map.

Taos was left behind in a quiet fever of optimism. Gone were the high spirits of the first hours of our escape. Now our journey had matured; now we were going to find our way forward into the unknown. We would take our time, enjoy the views; or maybe it was that we wanted now to be captured, but could not admit it to ourselves. Hard to know, but the day was rich in its tardiness, and that was just what we wanted. Look at this, look at that—there were many lapses in our progress. Midafternoon drifted into dusk, the sunset of pale yellows in the cloudless sky, not so very memorable except that it, too, seemed to counsel calm. In an act of forgiveness, or trust, in an act of friendship maybe, Kip had handed me his money, saying, —Once lost twice found, you be banker.

Thus all was steadied between us again. I tallied our money, sorted it, found a sickly rubber band in the glove compartment to wrap around it. Seventy-eight dollars. Not bad at all. Into my pocket it went.

—Sorry, Kip, I said.

He ignored me. Maybe he hadn't heard.

—I'm sorry about losing that money.

—I don't know what you're talking about.

We settled back into the ride, indulging ourselves in self-congratulations only once, pulling over to the side of the highway up toward Eagle Nest, like we had back near the crossroads at Nambé pueblo, to try to dance and holler at the stars and moon. We did our best, but we weren't the same boys who'd driven hard across the desert to Chimayó. Gone was our giddiness, and now we'd begun to respond to an instinct that continued to lead us away from home, but without the comfort of knowing a destination. No, I don't believe we were afraid. We did dance, we did laugh, and we marveled at the mountains and stars. Maybe we were dazed by our own unexpected success. Deep down, I doubt either of us had thought we could carry our idea all the way to Chimayó, let alone Taos and Eagle Nest.

For all this, I still wasn't able to stifle my guilt about our parents, the looming, daunting actuality of what independence meant, or might mean, and the more simple, if as yet unadmitted, feeling of homesickness. These worked at me, gnawed at me.

—You still sure we shouldn't call, just to let them know we're okay? I tried.

—So then they'll know where we are?

—Not if we don't tell them.

—They could trace the call.

—That's just in the movies.

Kip said, —I'm not calling. You can do what you want.

Which left me without a choice. —Well, it's not like there's a phone around here anyhow.

It all means more in light of what is happening now, all these years later. I'm appalled by our selfishness and impressed by our temerity. We were, in our own way, deliciously irresponsible. When I think back, Kip's hardness interests me most; his hardness and also the strange prescience he unwittingly managed to exhibit during what happened next, what he caused to happen and how it prefigured something that would come to pass later in life. Uncanny, it still seems now, how our accident foreshadowed another—far more devastating—accident that lay ahead in his, and therefore our, future.

U.S. 64 up over the Sangre de Cristos. Wheeler Peak out to our left, over thirteen thousand feet. The snow on its summits glinted. On over Raton Pass through Trinidad—desolate ghost town, running dogs, the characteristic fingers of chimney smoke reaching up into the blue, birds like rags along the catenary power lines—and into Colorado. Route 25 through Pueblo and its stinking smelters loading the sky with burning black, and up past

Castle Rock, which looked like a punk fist of sandstone, through Denver at dusk, the city lights twinkling on either side of the highway and the great long stretches of foothills, front and back ranges, purple under black out to our left.

When Kip fell asleep at the wheel, our fifth night past state lines—overcast, the stars had abandoned us and with them fled our luck—all the way up near the Wyoming border, and flipped us clean over, his presence of mind, the resistance he showed the officers and ambulance attendants, was something to behold. Years of youthful animosity detonated in words.

—Don't touch me, man, he kept crying. His voice had moved down the register until it came forth as a kind of feral growl.

One of the men must have said something, moved to lift him out.

Kip's voice again, I can still hear it, —Leave me alone, man, get away from me.

And then, what I surely was hoping he wouldn't say. —Brice?

—Kip? I answered. I was standing clear of the wreckage, was in a daze, but could hear with wicked clarity.

—Brice, what're you doing?

There was nothing I could say. They were all over him. It was like he had fallen into derangement, and they'd come to put him away.

—Brice, you lousy—get these . . . get away from me—

It was humiliating. I simply froze. —They're trying to help, I managed.

—Brice, you traitor, you traitor.

How he did it, exploded at them with such vehemence, is more remarkable given he'd dislocated his shoulder and broken a leg in the flip. I had been tossed into a shallow irrigation ditch—the muddy water and weed-thick bank had cushioned my fall—and seemed to have come out of the smashup only scratched along the cheek and the palm of my hand. The car became altogether fascinating to me as I began to block out Kip's voice. I studied it where it lay at the end of parallel grooves in the soft shoulder, upside down beside the road, like some helpless insect, a glistening beetle. The men had Kip in a neck brace and he wasn't shouting anymore. Everything had gone from mayhem to a somber, peculiar hush. Movement, red lights illuminating faces, the stretcher, the vehicles, the trees nodding as if in approval at the edges of the scene. There was my friend at the center of it all, and there was my muddied, hurt hand, which I looked at with the same fascination I'd felt while observing the car, but also with horror as it quivered there in the night—red then black, red then black—as these men around me talked, asked me questions I couldn't hear over the extravagant racket in my head.

Kip, don't die resounded in my conscience, I might have said it aloud. More than ever it felt to me like he was something, and I was next to nothing. No, it was worse than that. I knew for sure in my callow, panicked soul that, compared to Kip, I was nothing, nothing at all. If he had been able to read my thoughts, he would have been disgusted.

*B*y dubious serendipity, we have fallen in love with the same woman more than once.

Charlea Hughes first, then Mary Bendel, and, finally, Jessica.

Our devotion toward Charlea, the fondness of young boys, was offered up from the base of her polished white, immaculate pedestal, which we erected without her knowledge and upon which we placed her so that we could stand in its and therefore her shadow, not daring to look up and see what was hidden under her skirt. Toward Mary Bendel, a married woman some years senior to our gawky not-quite teens, we felt the warmth of a more developed, unsavory passion, of bees intrigued by flowers for the first time. Mary Bendel awakened us mind and body without ever having meant so much as to disturb our thick pubescent sleep, and so was as innocent of our fervor as Charlea before her. Where Charlea might come to laugh at us, Mary Bendel, had she known, would have been enraged. And Jessica? Jessica was never much for pedestals. The thought of one would give her vertigo. Jess bore back toward us more ardor than we knew might exist in a woman toward a man, or men. Where Charlea was a girl, and Mary Bendel a young wife about thirty or so, Jessica, when we first met her, stood at the restive gateway between youth and womanhood, and was too young not to take risks, but old enough to know that risk is risk and can bring disaster as easily as it does any glimmer of joy.

They could not have been more different, at least physically. Charlea, agate-eyed with masses of wavy blue-black hair, olive skin, and full lips, her mother's Mediterranean characteristics coming through strong, a thick-limbed girl who stood resolute, content, smiling with her arms crossed on what she considered a stable earth, precocious, canny beyond her years. Mary we knew best by the smell of her clothing, her pillow, her rooms. Pale as eggshell, slender though not delicate, hair not so much flame red as the many-red embers in the hearth after the fire has blazed, reds of apricot and apple, her eyes the most bright blue, her lips a paler pink than the inside of a conch shell. A few fragmented details about her, this is all I can piece together because it was more the idea of Mary than Mary herself we loved, the mature sexuality of nonvirgin Mary. Jessica on the other hand we knew, and I know well. As well as one person can know another. My beautiful Jessica who refuses to cower before time's persistence. Jessica who was, I had always thought, the love of both our lives.

Each we loved in conspicuously different ways, but as sure as we knew them we did love them.

First, Charlea Hughes.

Part of the postwar wave—a changing of the guards, as it were, when many of the scientists who'd worked on the Project left for academic jobs around the country, and were replaced by others come to refine and advance what had already been accomplished, move forward into the age of thermonuclear capability, toy some more with apocalypse—her father had brought his family from Berkeley up to the Hill. Kip and I, who'd never seen the ocean, who'd never been west of dusty downtown Flagstaff, who knew little unto nothing about life, saw her and our heads spun. She was, to us, so sophisticated, a girl of the world. She was a superior being. A dark, desirable angel, she made us crazy with longing, vague, fuzzy longing, but longing nevertheless. We made a pact at once that since we couldn't both have Charlea neither of us would, and showed up one afternoon at Charlea's house, two lank and foolish boys in white button-down shirts and white trousers, virginal to a fault, to make our mutual confession of love and inform her of our decision that we were fated by a solemn brotherly bond never to do anything that would bring pain or shame on the other and that, therefore, although we both did truly love her, neither of us could express that affection by ever taking her out on a date lest we cause the other to feel jealous. Charlea burst not into tears but began to bite her lip and soon broke out into gales of laughter. Friendly but forthright laughter.

Her mother came into the room and said, —I believe you boys had better go on home now.

—But they haven't finished their iced tea yet, Mom.

—Still and all, I think it's time for the boys to get along, before their mother starts to worry.

After a pause of what I deemed to be an appropriate length, I

said, correcting her in as gentle and genial a manner possible,
—We have two mothers, Mrs. Hughes.

—Two mothers, she said and looked at Charlea.

—Two *different* mothers, I said.

—They're not real brothers, Mother, Charlea laughed.

Her mother straightened up, and said, —Either way, I still
think it is time for the boys to head back home now.

Oafs that we were, we'd actually begun to join in Charlea's
laughter, but now that we saw Mrs. Hughes was unhappy with
us our levity began to level off.

—Bye Kip, bye Brice, Charlea smiled without missing a beat.

—Bye Charlea, we said. Though we were not mature enough
at the time to understand it, this was surely one of the most
embarrassing moments in our young lives. How earnest, how pen-
sive, how sober—like stolid vaudevillians who'd got lost on their
way to the show—we must have looked wearing our selfish hon-
esty and adolescent pride on our sleeves, as we turned, no doubt
in tandem, to make our exit. Charlea was, on the other hand,
both self-possessed and not without a sense of humor. She was,
furthermore, forgiving. The next day in school, she acted as if
nothing had happened. No doubt she is now happily married and
raising a family of mature daughters and sons, or maybe running
a corporation with the same deft touch she showed that afternoon. Meantime, Kip and I proceeded, purblind soul brothers,
arm in arm through our youth, pretty much oblivious to the world
beyond our thick skins.

Mary Bendel; Mrs. Bendel.

You remember, Kip, as well as I, how we broke into her house
again and again. We were brash and brazen. Your mention of it
in your letter stirred sparks in the ash of memory. How could
either of us ever forget? We will always be linked in what must

be our most private secret, our presence there in someone else's privileged and intimate sanctum, giggling at first from nervousness, then giving ourselves over gradually to the deep, visceral pleasure of invading someone else's life in the most blatant way. But even if we'd been caught in the act, nothing we were doing, or more important, nothing we would have been perceived to have been doing, could possibly've been deemed serious enough to warrant our being arrested. It would have been glossed as harmless—as boys will be boys—and we undoubtedly would have played along with their presumptuous assessment in order to evade our punishment. After all, isn't it true we never damaged let alone destroyed or stole anything? We trespassed. Nothing more. No, I sense they wouldn't have done much had they caught us. But they would have made a mistake letting us off easy, they'd have been wrong not to punish us, and punish us good. And you know as well as I that they'd have been wrong not to do so, had they the wits or luck to trap us, because of the pleasure we derived from our trespasses, our visits as we liked to call them, flippant prudes that we were.

Kip, remember how it went? We were all of twelve, no older, and these were our first encounters with what could be described as the exquisite. Sure, we'd had many pleasurable experiences together before that (not to mention grim, unhappy ones), but they were all in one way or another purified by naivete.

The visits bespoke another nature. Part of their glamour lay precisely in their impurity. "Let the punishment fit the crime," isn't that the line you sang when you played the title role in our school production of *The Mikado,* warbling like some castrato before your voice cracked and your days as a caroling soprano came to an end? Well, if what you sang is true—and you certainly sang it as if you did believe it was, up there on stage in your imperial robes—it would be hard to think up an agony that would fit the plain, perverse joy we experienced those months of nights during which we made our visits.

Should I admit that I still get faint when I think about the process of it? How I loved not merely the execution of the plan, but the agreeing on what time we'd meet and where, loved the coming to a decision about whom we were going to "visit" after having thought about it, each of us alone, for hours on end? I do; it *is* shameful, but I would be lying were I to deny that it makes me giddy to remember saying goodnight to my parents, and how I went to bed with my jeans on, and my socks and shoes, how good I was at pretending to be adrift in sleep (the very slow, very shallow breathing, innocently deep and with the long pause before inhaling, I can still do this when the adult world forces me into a pretense of sleep) and how, after my mother'd checked in on me for the last time—bad habit of hers, she kept it up far too long into what I thought were my postyouth years—how I'd wait until everything was quiet before easing myself out of bed, and escaping through my window into the night. There was sex in the air. Every footfall was gravid, ripe with promise. My shoulders hunched up, my hands dug down into my pockets, each gesture made was grand as the movies.

First time we did it, we didn't know what exactly we were going to do once we'd broken into the house, but we did know what —that is, who—compelled us. The days of the peppers game were behind, the night of Chimayó several years ahead. Whose idea was it, yours or mine? It may have occurred without one or the other of us acting as the initiator, may have just come into being, as naturally as breathing, I don't remember. What I do remember is that the moonlight glazed the summer streets and yards with such brilliance, it looked like it had snowed. There was a mild breeze twisting up the canyons, switching back and forth across the mesa. We met behind a town barn. You were there before I, and I got there before I was supposed to. As in all small towns, in Los Alamos it was everyone's business to know everyone's business, and so we knew who was and wasn't invited to a wee-hours midsummer party. Your parents and mine, to be sure, but also the Bendels.

Our obsession with Mary Bendel was embryonic, so to speak, and yet it had taken a serious turn a couple of weeks before when we found ourselves crouching in the shadows behind some aromatic juniper, there in the late dusk, watching her in her kitchen, as she moved back and forth in the yellow-brown light, cleaning up the day's dishes. Her husband, we knew, often worked at night, though by no apparent schedule, just sporadic, and was said to be one of the more solid theoreticians at the lab. After Mary Bendel had finished with her dishes, she took off her apron and set out for her evening walk, and it was then, I think without any words said between us, just one step encouraging the next, we took it upon ourselves to sneak up to the Bendels' kitchen window and look in. We'd visited this kitchen half a dozen times in the past, for though they didn't have any children themselves (not yet, at least: —Mary Bendel's very young yet, my mother'd said once, —they're wise to bide their time), they sometimes invited us kids over. So you and I were peering in on a familiar scene, but our eyes were different eyes gazing in over the sill. The kitchen table was still damp from the sponge. The plates and glasses stood in the rack, glistening. The yellow light shone on the wall clock.

One of us must have said, —Let's go inside.

The other must have said, —What're you, touched?

We didn't go in that night, but we did sneak around to the back where we knew their bedroom must be, and peered into the windows and saw their bed, and the open closet in which Mary

Bendel's dresses—peach, mint, plum, black—hung alongside her husband's suits, and it was there that the meaning of our activities must have come into sharp, however inarticulate, focus.

—Let's move back over there, I might have said.

—Where?

—Back over there, pointing up the slight rise.

We moved away from the house maybe thirty feet to where there were some low crab apples, and waited.

What we had waited for and what we were given, finally, may not have been the same, but the glimpse of Mary Bendel coming back from her walk was mesmerizing to us. She entered by the side door, and we watched breathless as she moved from room to room in the Sundt house, turning a lamp off in the kitchen and on in the sitting room she had converted into a workroom for her many specimens of, and books on, butterflies—*her* obsession: she was an accomplished lepidopterist, and her workroom was furnished with big flat boxes with glass tops, like display cases for jewels, in which she'd pinned her specimens, each labeled in a neat hand, black ink on white tabs beneath the suspended colorful corpses. We crept closer, and watched her push her defiant hair away from her forehead with the back of her hand. She read, sitting at a table, and we crouched outside in the dark and watched her. It was exotic beyond anything you and I had ever done, Kip. And it must have been when she glanced up, from time to time, to stare out the window, stare right at us in the ink-black night, before going back to her reading, that inspired us to feel invisible.

Little creeps, how heartened we were by our bold behavior. We didn't know who Mary Bendel loved better, you or me, but we knew she loved us. It was like a queer game of hide-and-seek, where we who were hiding were really the seekers, and she who was the seeker had every reason to hide.

Two weeks later the visits came to pass. The Bendels were off at the midsummer party. That empty house solicited us, and we succumbed.

Though the time of absolute trust between Hill neighbors had passed with the end of the war, the gates had not yet been lifted; that was to come one day in February of 1957, a memorable day in that the Hill did not see it as an event to celebrate, but fear. We had to change our way of living, we knew the riffraff of the world was going to descend—that is, *ascend*—upon us. Before that day no one locked a door. You and I felt welcome, shrouded in the warm dark, confident on the quiet block. We might have paused, Kip, to think for a moment about what we were doing, but we didn't, and I believe that if we had, we'd quite easily have been able to cobble up some boyish justification that would have quelled our doubts. The night sky poured syrupy light over us, and we were daring. We might have showed some old-fashioned shame and entered by an open window in the back, but instead we looked around and, seeing no one, walked up the several wooden steps at the side of the house and entered by the kitchen door.

Is this how the insanely criminal feel? Welcomed because their desires are so comprehensive as to seem like needs? Confident that needs, like laws, must be upheld? Justified because so clearly embraced by circumstances they had only the subtlest hand in bringing into being? I mean to say, it *did* feel as if the house solicited us, that Mary Bendel's recent presence in it provoked our presence, too.

Whatever the answers to such questions might be, we moved through the Bendels' house slowly, deliberately. We felt strangely proprietary but not so much so that our hearts weren't heaving, in quick pumping bursts like those of a rabbit's heart when you hold him in your arms and pet him and place your palm on his breast. The moon lit the rooms enough so we didn't stumble into furniture, and soon we found ourselves in their bedroom, *her* bedroom, where we discovered the drawers in the chest that held her clothes, the soft cottons and dangerous bits of lace. That first time we hadn't thought to bring a flashlight, but I remember you so carefully lifting something of hers to your face and breathing in and how I said, —Bring it over here, boy, and you carried it to the window where we looked at it, a chemise, *Mary's* chemise, satin with narrow lace trim, a perplexity of fragile straps and fluid margins, looked at it rapt, smelled its trifle of perfume merged with a recognizable human scent, its Maryness. We must have been in the house for half an hour, maybe longer, touching and smelling and, yes, even kissing her woolen dresses in the closet, her sweaters arranged in piles on the shelf above, careful as we could be not to disturb how they were hung or folded, our heads in a swim—but a drowner's swim, slow-motion and learning to love the warmth of the water in our lungs. To anybody but us the scene we'd created for ourselves here would have been either ludicrous or disgusting; but Kip, for us it was a real passage. And after we'd done it once, there was no way for us not to do it again.

And so we did. And it didn't stop with touching and smelling and kissing Mary's things, it went a ways beyond just that. And it didn't stop with Mary, either. There were others. We learned a lot about many houses, and the wives and daughters who lived in them, how they lived, what some of their secrets were. But as the visits got more elaborate they became less struck by mystery. The clothes, these inanimate reminiscences of their wearers, became the point of the exercise—to touch, smell, and sometimes actually wear them for the dizzy minutes we dared to—rather than pushing ourselves into the private lives of those who'd chosen them at some shop, brought them home, worn them. We began to lose track of the meaning of what we were doing, and half a year after we'd first trespassed Mary Bendel's home we were done with our visits. We'd fallen in and out of love for the second time, virgins still, but now gratefully sullied ones.

Genuine love was not going to treat us with the same genial if curious touch. Jessica, our Jessie, dear Jess, is—as they say—a whole other story.

*T*he moon ascends, a dollop of apricot sherbet, and I come awake from a dream that I have already forgotten but for the single detail that in it I was holding someone's hand. I look at the ceiling, see a spider in one corner working very hard on a web, and then go through the moment all unseasoned travelers suffer: the recognition that my surroundings are unfamiliar.

I remember, then stand and look out the window toward the ridge across the valley and am seized—I'm wide awake now, and know just where I am—by the need to see the mountains, and I climb into my pants and throw a jacket around me and walk barefoot out onto the ruined veranda and across the stretch of grass there until I reach a coyote fence, a vertical knitting of ragged sticks, and turn to look back over the low roof of the small hacienda and see them again, way off in the distance, the Jemez of my childhood, and it seems to me as I stand in the dew-wet chill of the predawn that the mountains rise away from the earth as if from a need to be as far removed from it as possible. It's like a dream, still. Do spiders dream? Probably not, I think. Too assiduous to squander time with dreams. I draw a deep breath of gaunt air, close my eyes and open them.

The clouds begin to take on their morning colors, in the same way pigments cut by mineral spirits and poured over fine, unprimed canvas would spread in billowing shapes until the surface was all beautifully stained. The intricacy of the basin that gives into this smaller canyon, the cloud-crowned peaks, the sawtooth of trees and bushes along the horizon, the Russian olive and the tamarisk, the lilac and paintbrush, the hacienda itself whose irregular white adobe walls are covered with the fingers of creeping vines, the whole scape radiating a fragile strength, all come to me at once.

The moment is a gift. This was my home. I could resist feeling tentatively cheerful, but don't. I know it won't last anyway.

And then, I realize my feet are stinging with the chill of the night grass, and I run back inside, find some wool socks in my bag, and light the gas burner on the stove to heat water for the coffee Alyse gave me last night after dinner. Coffee beans in a paper sack, some milk and sourdough biscuits. "Just for the morning, to get you started," she said, and handed me a flashlight for the short walk back. I watch the blue corollas of flame under the kettle and think about last night—maybe as a way of avoiding today, and what it might bring.

The big house was just that. Flagstone staircases circling upward from one level to the next, doors and windows looking out every direction, southwest toward the lights of the city, eastward up the horseshoe canyon and spray of stars. All their shoes assembled by the front door, there must have been two dozen pairs, sandals, boots, moccasins. Gaslit refectory where we ate. Mission furniture mixed with Adirondack twisted hickory and painted old pine. Disarray and warmth. The pleasant, sincere mess of domesticity. They had roasted a chicken, greens, chèvre, some new potatoes with sage. It was evident that most meals here were less lavish—or, not *lavish,* but less structured—than what they'd prepared for me. Michael is an architect, so some of this unconstruction must be on purpose, I think. The wine bottle had a white sheen of dust along one side, the wineglasses were wet from rinsing. Little things gave me to believe this was something of a special occasion for them, and so I was made, despite myself, to feel welcome.

Martha is a pretty girl, self-assured and opinionated, quite a handful. Her first words last evening were, "The sky is on everybody's heads."

I thought for a moment to correct her, but then realized that she was right, and said, "How smart of you to notice."

"Thank you," she smiled.

Abandoning her earlier restraint, Alyse did ask the inevitable, and I warded it off with the half-truth—or incomplete truth—I'd thought to use if it came up. She may well have seen through it, my ruse about wanting to revisit Chimayó during the pilgrimage, clearly enough to recognize that it was no use to pressure me into giving her more. No doubt that subtlety is available to her.

"I never saw you as the religious kind, Brice," she allowed herself. I always forget how much I like Alyse. It is a satisfaction that grows, unobserved for the most part, over the years. Maybe I find her sympathetic because our contact is so intermittent and unburdened by the give-and-take experiences that become an active—thus possibly threatening—part of a true, lively friendship. She never lost her love of the West, and I admire that.

She told us a story about how when she was taking a walk out in the desert one day she came upon an old kiva that had been mostly buried under dirt and sand, and was long since abandoned by all but a colony of red ants. She sat down on a stone to rest, and found herself watching the ants go about their business, as ants do, with diligence and vigor. The ants came up from the depths of the kiva to the surface in a dark florid procession, each carrying building materials for what appeared to be a very old hill, and every once in a while she noticed that one or two of the ants would be hefting along something rather more shiny than the usual bits of sand or clay, which aroused her interest.

When she walked over to the procession to get a closer look, she saw that what the ants were carrying along were beads they had brought up from the cavern of the old kiva, and she realized that these were beautiful old beads of bone and shell from an Indian necklace or headdress. Before long, without really giving the matter much thought, she began taking the colorful beads from the face of the anthill where they'd been deposited, and soon had collected enough to make a bracelet. She said she went home that night very pleased about her discovery and good luck, and the next day strung for herself a bracelet, just as she'd planned.

But the first time she put it on her wrist and held it up to the light to admire it, she was suddenly seized with guilt that though the bracelet was beautiful, it wasn't hers. She'd stolen it from the ants.

I said, "But the ants stole the beads from the kiva, didn't they? And besides, ants don't care one way or another whether they're building their ant house out of sand or beads or diamonds."

"You've been in New York too long, Brice."

"What does New York have to do with it?"

"Anyway," she laughed. "I took the bracelet back up to the kiva site and unstrung it and threw the beads back on the anthill."

I smiled into her smile, wondering whether or not she'd made up this fable. I glanced over to Martha for my answer and Martha, rather than staring at her mother with wide-eyed wonder, was absorbed with moving her dinner around her plate with a fork. I could see that to her it was just another piece of her mother's history, not a fairy tale or fable, not a yarn, and therefore could be listened to with one ear, as it were. This happened, simply, to her mother. Not a big deal. And slowly it was coming back to me, this Western quality I had rejected and then forgotten. It seemed so pure, last night, if sentimental. It seems pure this morning, strangely unsentimental. Maybe the hand in the dream was the hand that gave back the beads? I don't think so.

In any event, her being so completely of the West is enviable to an apostate like myself. To me, Lyse is unalloyed and ageless. It has been a good friendship over the years, steady after its own manner, telephone calls from time to time, the occasional visit, an on-and-off friendship only in the sense that our lives have been led in different places. We have never wrangled. I doubt we ever will.

Need I say what happened to the two of us upon our return— or rather, upon our being returned—to Los Alamos? It was pre- dictable, in a way, that we'd be punished for our Chimayó ad- venture, but the lengths to which our parents went to keep Kip and me apart were, if not drastic, at least for a period of time passionately imposed.

—You two are not to speak, not to see each other, not to communicate with one another in any way shape or form, you hear me, William Brice? If I so much as get a hint that you two are talking, or hanging around together, your father and I . . . well . . . we have discussed what we're willing to do, so don't push it.

Were these words coming from my father's mouth, I might have allowed myself some moments' worry, but I knew my mother. We knew each other. My mother may have been furious on the surface, and was badly hurt beneath, but I guessed that somewhere buried amid her anger and hurt was a dissenter's pride in me and what Kip and I had done. She was, after all, the only one who ever bothered to ask us *why* we'd appropriated a car and driven it into a ditch up near Wyoming. Everyone else assumed it was a joyride. That element of pride was what I kept looking for in my mother's behavior those first few days back on the Hill, and I must admit I had to peer hard sometimes to find it there behind her stringent eyes. Given that I loved her, my poor mother—more than a decade younger then than I am now, standing there in her print dress with flowers, big indigo, puce, magenta, ivory flowers that promised all over its fluent surfaces, whenever she wore it, a decent and happy day—this was a nasty combination of emotions for me to admit to having provoked.

Maybe she sensed what I was thinking, and attempted to deny me. Though I knew better, she did everything in her power to persuade me that she viewed our reckless gambit as just that, an extravagant prank carried out in order to humiliate her, and little more. My father remained more or less absent from home, stayed with his work in a Tech building to which I had no access even if I wanted to talk with him, which I didn't, and as a consequence he was—to my way of thinking—less concerned than she, distant from caring, which was a kind of freedom, since if he didn't care then I wouldn't care. But the days came and went, and rather than forgiving and forgetting, my mother seemed not to want to let the matter go. She said I'd made a fool of her in front of all her students at school, students who happened to be my friends.

—If you decline to show me a modicum of respect, how do you expect them to respect me? she asked, knowing I understood there was not one soul in the community who hadn't known about what we'd done. I wondered how Kip might answer this question, and though I didn't for the longest time speak with him or risk much more than a glance at him outside the classroom where we sat in desks distant from one another, I trusted that he must have been experiencing the same feelings of guilt and disgrace as I, although leavened maybe by some residual defiance I found harder to discover in myself.

—I don't know, I said, hoping she wouldn't call me William Brice again, as she was wont to whenever scolding me.

—You don't know.

She crossed her arms.

—I guess not.

—Well, in the future you might consider thinking things all the way through before you just go and do whatever comes into your head.

Now I had my reply, but wondered whether to voice it.

—Yes? she asked. My mother did know me. —Well?

—Nothing, I muttered in a moment of rare grace.

—You're too much, Brice, she said, apparently having figured me out. —Don't even think about starting with that stuff.

Had I replied, I would have said something like, What about the forefathers of Los Alamos, the grampa progenitors of radioactive death? Talk about not thinking things through. How guilty can you *get*? Here I am trying to do something good for all of us. How come I'm supposed to feel so guilty? What is crashing one lousy car compared to scorching two entire cities?

That would have been the beginning. I'd have stretched myself out into the same arguments that had always been convenient when a subject needed changing or some guilt needed lifting from my own shoulders. For once I didn't grasp at the obvious, and it was fair I didn't. My mother was forever caught between her devotion to Dad and her own private thoughts about the nature of his work. She felt, I believe with all my heart, the same contempt as I for the plutonium and uranium devices that were birthed on the Hill—"ether ores" she called the atom bombs

once, ores that turned their victims to ether, the pun on "either-
ors," damned if you make them and damned if you don't. Make
them and you end the war with astonishing abruptness—Hiroshima, 6 August 1945; Nagasaki, 9 August 1945; V-J Day,
14 August 1945—a week and a day to terminate half a decade's
carnage. Make them and you know in your heart you've crippled
if not lost what moral supremacy you may have held dear. I didn't
launch into my usual speech for once because I *was* guilty of
hurting my mother's feelings. I hadn't thought through to the
consequences of my action. And although I was the product of a
culture that sometimes behaved no better than an inept adolescent who was intent on flexing muscles and not just climbing
trees but shimmying out to the ends of the highest branches as
if to dare the limb to break, I managed to get something from
her that day. It was a lesson I would have to learn and relearn,
but subtly I was impressed and modified.

I settled into a new life, one part of which was close to my
mother, the other devoted to wondering about Kip. They became
the presence and absence that centered my world.

My mother happened to be working on her Spanish, as always immersed in some project to improve her store of knowledge. I learned with her. That was the idea. This was to be
my punishment. She and I would stay behind after school, and
she'd drill herself as I sat with the open book and asked
questions.

Architecture, as I remembered within the first few hours of
being back in New Mexico, was one of the lessons on which we
concentrated.

If indeed memory is a function of the intensity of original
perception, so that the stronger the perception the stronger the
memory of what was perceived, these study sessions must have
been singularly intensive. Not only do I recollect with fantastic

clarity the chalkboard running one length of the deserted classroom, and the soft light pouring in from the bank of windows
along the adjacent wall, not only are the wooden desks with their
wooden tops distinct, but the sound of her voice—deep and sure,
mellifluous and bigger than her frame might lead one to expect
—I can summon at will. I would write on the blackboard with
soft white chalk the word *encalar*.

—That's a plasterer, she'd say. —No wait, that's *enjarradora*,
that's plaster—that means to whitewash, whitewash.

I'd look in the book and, yes, "to whitewash" was right.

Next, I'd chalk out *viga*.

And she'd say, —That's too easy, give me another.

—*Fogón*.

—*Fogón* is fireplace.

—Fireplace, and what else?

—You're a taskmaster, she smiled. —Fireplace, and hearth.

—Furnace, too, I said. —*Bulto*.

—Too easy.

—*Postigo*.

She thought for a moment, —That's window grating?—no,
uhm. Hold on. *Postigo*'s the small opening in a door, like a little
window in a big door.

—So what is a window grate called?

—*Reja*, she said without hesitation.

—You know all this stuff, I complained. I turned some pages,
and drew on the blackboard:

Then said, —What's this?

She said, —That isn't anything. Do it again.

—You don't know what it is, I said.

—No. I know what it should be. You drew it wrong.

—No I didn't, I said and looked at the figure in the book. I'd drawn it wrong.

She said, —Thundercloud is what you were trying to make. Your artistic skills leave a little to be desired.

—You're wrong. It's not a thundercloud. Just a cloud is all.

And I smiled a half-serious see-there smile, and she smiled an impatient smile back. —It's upside down, she said, more stern than the situation might have called for.

I was not going to be daunted; gusts, small bursts of wind soughed in the stout green needles of a ponderosa outside the window. Such solace can be drawn from little things like that breeze-song. She'd waited for me to go on.

—Here is an easy one, I said as I drew:

—Rain, she answered.

And so our sessions went until she would say, —*Bien, bastante,* that's enough for today.

Still, hard as I tried to force myself into this other life with my mother, I couldn't help thinking about Kip. I wondered about how he responded to the rebuke his parents must have given him. Was he feeling better? His injuries turned out to be relatively minor, he had a neck brace and a cast that he allowed no one to sign, and then the brace and cast came off, and he walked with a cane for a time. Did he show defiance? Yes, he must have, though I had no word from mutual friends or my parents or sister. Defiance was part and parcel of his nature. Did he feel regret, and if so, did he allow anyone to see it? Yes, again, I imagined he might have regretted what we'd accomplished, since it came to so little, and also because regret and defiance were contradictory and Kip seemed to like all things contrary. But, no—I doubted he let his regret be seen by anyone. Did he miss me? To this question I had no answer. I knew that my own feelings of warm indignation, which came on me deep in the night when everyone was asleep, and all the mountain birds were mute, and I was wide, wide awake, I knew my indignation—which I used in a way to get myself closer to him—was outdone, surely, by Kip's. I could feel his blistering hostility as if it emanated from my own heart. If he was thinking about me, what was he thinking? I had stayed with it right up to the end, hadn't I? I hadn't failed him, I believed. Would he speak to me again once these parental constraints were rescinded? Did he still consider me his best friend and true blood brother? I knew I hadn't measured up, yet one moment hoped he was thinking about me, while the next—this felt strange, like when you've lost a tooth, and your tongue keeps inserting itself in the wound, curious and persistent and disbelieving—I hoped we would never set eyes on each other again. Wouldn't a life of not having to measure up be the best?

No matter how I reasoned with myself I knew, nevertheless, we were linked. Woven together somehow. Even outside all these imaginings, rumor and derision held us in an unwelcome embrace. We were young, an amalgam of smart and stupid, like all kids. We had bolted confinement, we had gamboled and got lost, gambled and lost. And now we were doubly constricted, confined by the isolation of the Hill, and at the same time restricted each from the other.

I spent early mornings that fall studying for school, read my books at a small oak table in my room, made sure my bed was made to perfection with the edges of the bedspread just touching the floor and even all around, and was quiet as the shyest mouse throughout my classes, sat at my desk and busied myself with making pencil notes in my notebook, careful to keep my head down in the hopes of not being called on, and when I was, made sure my answer was correct. After school, when my mother and I didn't stay for our lessons, I came home and busied myself once more at my desk. I would help with the dishes after dinner, and if my father had chores for me to do, I did them, going at everything with the deliberateness of a tortoise, serenely defeated and uncomplaining.

Whenever my mother spoke to me at home, in front of Bonnie Jean and my father, I answered, —Yes ma'am. When my father spoke to me I answered, —Yes sir. Bonnie Jean I did my best to ignore, didn't hear her, couldn't see her. Her comparative triumph, the triumph of being a good girl in contrast to my bad boy, I didn't want to acknowledge. I was sufficiently abstracted that when I murmured my yessums and yessirs I probably meant them, probably didn't have during those strange directionless days the strength or presence of mind to invest my politeness with teenage scorn, although I must have fathomed that after a while this regime of abdication would break down their resolve to mete out a continued punishment. —Yes sir, I said, and went about drying dishes, or watering my mother's geraniums where they stood like sentinels in their pots at either side of the door, or sweeping the front porch that was littered with cottonwood tufts, mud cakes, pine needles, sister's almost-outgrown dolls. —Yes ma'am, I said.

Kip and I were lucky the legal actions that could have been taken against us were not. Because our parents were friends with the Wrights, there was never any serious discussion about them pressing charges. My father and Mr. Calder agreed to split the cost of repairs to the Wrights' car. Thus the insurance company was kept out of the picture, and somehow—through murky channels I have never to this day comprehended (such murkiness abounds up on the Hill, always abounded, shall ever abound)—we were never charged with anything. We were insignificant outlaws grounded by our parents. That was all our provocation inspired. What a disaster, in its way. Our act meant nothing to them. We'd risked everything, we thought, to purify them by performing a civic rite on behalf of their arrogant souls, and what had they done in return? Whitewashed our crimes, wept some, thundered and threatened some, we being too old for a spanking, removed us from each other, taken what they deemed necessary steps, then finally exonerated and so enfeebled us.

—Brice?

—Yes sir? I answer, a watched pot of sorts, not quite boiling but not quite cool, either.

—Pass me the pepper, son.

—Yes sir, I say.

A few moments ease by.

—Brice?

—Sir. And I stare at my eggs and bacon, concentrating with an almost religious ardor.

Another few moments, then my father speaks. Quiet, vehement. —You will stop this minute with this "yessir, yessum" malarkey, you hear me, young man?

Only a few weeks later I could smell my pending freedom. I didn't push it, though the temptation was strong to respond with an obvious *Yes sir*.

Manipulation: moving matter, tots, oldsters, trees, flowers, birds, emotions, imaginings, stones, leaves, all of it, all of it, all of what we can put our hands and heads to, moving it around to fit our fancy: this was what I realized we did, as people, then. This was how we imposed ourselves, and defined our presences. How we said, We live, we are alive here, this is our time on the earth, we exist!

*T*he truth is, Kip and I were a little behind. Or rather, we were out of step by being a little ahead, and a little behind. The anger we felt toward Los Alamos, anger that drove us to Chimayó, was not unjustified, in the larger scheme of things, that is, in a scheme that would take a historical perspective in a measure of centuries rather than the jot of years we adolescents had wandered through. This was not how it was viewed by those who lived it, though, flesh-and-blood men and women in the middle of it all.

To this day most of us Hill people stand by our own. Our land may be poisoned with thousands of unmarked dump sites, we may hear the stories about Indian women who continued to dig from our canyons clay for their pottery and now have all lost their hair, and we may many of us be cancerous, but look here, it is *our* land, they were radioactive toxins fabricated by *our* hands, and they are *our* carcinomas, so stand out of our glowy light that we may continue to see as we desire.

For better or worse, I recognize, in these anniversary times—the fiftieth anniversary of the founding of the Manhattan Project, back in 1943—the purity of such stubbornness. It has a charming folk cast to it. It is the pure stuff of America, oxymoron that it may be, given the country's formidable lack of purity. *Give me your tired, your weak, your hungry*—yes, magnificent oxymoron given the laudably immigrant mix, the beautiful impurity of our peoples.

Kip and I were the pure stuff of America, too. Hostile toward authority to begin with, and given to lambasting everything our parents stood for, root and branch, every filament and filigree of who they were and what they were about. Migrants in the making.

In one aspect Kip and I did diverge in our thinking about Los Alamos. I became a universal detractor, whereas Kip held an ornery affection for what we called the grand, great grampas—Enrico Fermi and Robert Oppenheimer in particular, but also Hans Bethe and Emilio Segrè, Neddermeyer and Serber and Rabi, and even Niels Bohr and Stanislaw Ulam, even awful Edward Teller (we had our demiheroes, antiheroes, and our villains too) —the original makers and keepers of the flame, the first scientists who came here for, as Kip put it, "not *totally* the wrong reasons." This fondness for many in that first generation had to do, I suppose, with a respect for naked genius, and a conviction that despite evidence to the contrary the whole community had been lulled into believing the Gadgets would never be used on civilians. It was a nice idea and had some basis in reality, however wrong it proved to be in the end.

My raving about how the bomb was evil, depraved, vicious at the deepest spiritual tier known to any of us who ever lived, how killing those hundreds of thousands in Hiroshima and Nagasaki with two quick, antiseptic atomic fires was exemplary in its perfect immorality, and about how ashamed I was of us all, each one of us who lived on the Hill where the filthy machine was devised (none of this was I able to verbalize at all eloquently, although I'm sure the passion was there)—my railing and speeches did not go over well with my parents and my sister. Bonnie Jean merely thought me boring, her older brother was "going through a phase," she told her friends, repeating some conversation she undoubtedly overheard between our parents. She was, moreover, a little afraid of me, was Bonnie Jean, and kept a distance whenever she saw me headed into one of my scenes.

There is no doubt all four of us were happier before I began to question who we were, the McCarthy family, sharing as we did that unfortunate surname that became infamous in the fifties, we who constituted such a tidy nuclear family and were possessed of all the symmetry the postwar years propounded. Father and mother, son and daughter, a perfect quincunx with the American Dream forming the dot in the middle of the square that's square as square can be. We were happier, myself included, before it became my obsession to begin connecting the dots in different ways, to begin criticizing why we were where we were.

I can remember harmony, way back when. When you have lived only fifteen years, as I had then, it's not difficult to think back over where and who you have been thus far. I remember going to church on Christmas Eve, the Communion, the wafer and the Welch's grape juice standing in for Jesus's holy blood. My mother's perfume that smelled of cinnamon, the sprigs of white fir arranged along the altar, the tapers and the choir of mothers and daughters accompanied by an upright piano whose sustain pedal was stuck. Kip a couple of pews forward, sitting between his parents, turning once in a while to make a face at me. Making a face back and getting poked in the ribs by my father, gently the first time, a little harder the second, and told, —Cut it out, the third.

Sleepiness setting in. Praying to the Lord that one of the presents under the tree back home, the one wrapped in white shiny paper, which when shaken makes no rattling sound, gives no clue as to what is inside, turns out to be the genuine desert-rat binoculars I asked for. Hymns and more hymns, and how Bonnie Jean and I would look at one another and roll our eyes in complicity. —Can we go now? Asleep in the pew, both sister and brother, then awakened. Hoping Kip hadn't seen that I couldn't stay awake. Home to bed.

I remember believing in Peter Cottontail, good Saint Nick, Wee Willie Winkie who ran from window to window throughout the town to make sure all the children were tucked in bed. I remember Old Aunt Syne who none of us ever met, though we all gathered every New Year's to sing about how she'd never be forgot, or some such business described in lyrics that to this day I don't quite understand. All the invisible playmates we invented and named and spoke to in secret languages no one could ever translate.

And there was more, much more. You have a loose tooth and you tie one end of a string to it and the other to a doorknob, and your sister slams the door, and generally the string comes loose, but once in a while it works and there is the bloody tooth dangling in the knot, and she's laughing at you when you run screeching to the sink to wash your mouth with water and salt. You put a tooth under your pillow, when you wake up there is a dime. Who can forget? The warmth of one's pajamas—mine had on them scenes with droves of cattle being lassoed by bowlegged cowboys while other cowboys stood by chuck wagons tending to broad-bellied coffeepots suspended over campfires by long sticks —flannel with feet and buttons front and back, and ginger ale and lemon sherbet and magazines when you are sick, and being tucked in tight with the sheet folded back just so under your chin. The miracle that was a paper-and-balsa kite on Saturday afternoon, bold plain yellow in the cobalt sweep of sky, rising and rising with its tail of tied strips of rag trailing, plummeting in circles when the wind weighed in too hard. A paddleboat smelling of its thick rubber band, of soap and savory mildew from the tub, and maybe the rich shore muck of old Ashley Pond. Up and down on the teeter-totter, legs extended, knees in your face, up and slow coming back down and then up again, and sometimes left dangling high in the sky if the kid you're playing with is bigger than you are and gets it in his head to keep you there, maybe laughs at you a little, maybe lets you down slowly, maybe jumps off so you drop hard on your ass with a wallop. The softball game that starts in the morning and finishes when it is too dark to see the ball anymore. Childhood. Runny noses, broken arms, leg aches, chicken pox; tincture of Merthiolate, cod-liver oil, castor oil, Vicks VapoRub.

Who could forget? It is not that these things fade away, more that they become encased, encrusted as the object—a tree, call it, for the sake of calling it something—which is your life, accretes its annual rings. When time passes and the silt settles, the trunk gets buried first. Layer buries layer. This is how it works and will always work.

—You should be ashamed of yourself, I was told, with one of the cliches that seemed devastating at the time. —Your poor father works hard to put food on the table, to put clothes on your back and a roof over your head. He's proud of his work, and your sister and I are proud of him—

At this, Bonnie Jean would reliably nod her head in agreement, and I'd think, You darned go-along, and then would think, Darn you, you love her better than I do, and I would mean my sister loved Mother better in the sense that she at least knew how to live life without hurting her, or our father either.

—and all I can say to you, young man, is if you don't like it here, you're welcome to go live somewhere else.

—But that isn't what you believe, I'd say.

—Don't get on your high horse and tell me what I believe.

—You're not proud of what he does, I know you're not!

—Shut up, Brice.

—You know we shouldn't even be eating the food he puts on our table with the blood money he makes at the lab.

—You don't have the slightest idea what your father does at the lab.

—You're wrong, you're wrong because I do.

—That's enough!

—I do, I do know what he does, and it's bad, it's wrong.

—Go to your room.

—No!

—I said *march*, young man.

These cliches could be crushing, in part because I didn't have the proficiency to fight back, and in part because within the context of my family more and more I was odd man out, and when I wasn't quick to retort, no one was there to articulate my thoughts for me. These arguments would come like prairie fire, furious and fast, and then be gone. I'd go to my room. Over and over in my head I would play out the scene I had just caused, hearing her words and mine, and thinking of all the things I could have said to make my point clearer. And then the regret would set in, and I would figure out how to apologize. I would quietly open my bedroom door and plod in blue silence down the hall to the kitchen where she was sitting with her glass and pipe, and voice cliches of my own, like —I'm sorry, Mom, it's just that sometimes I think you just don't understand, or, —I feel bad about what I said about Dad and I'm glad he's my dad and I'll never say anything like that again.

Before Kip and I left on our great expedition I would tend to capitulate more often than not in the hope of preserving some semblance of household order, knowing all the while that I could let off steam, so to speak, whenever I was with Kip. At Kip's side, where my tongue just magically loosened, I could proclaim what provisional values I was trying to work out as this personality named Brice took its form.

—Kip?

—Yeah?

—Kip, you know what they're doing in the Techs?

—Not sure, think so, though. How come?

—Never mind.

Time would wash on, the voluptuous, tardy time that children live in. We were playing marbles. Kip had fewer cat's-eyes than I did, I had more steelies than he. The ground was clean and smooth, perfect for shooters.

—Kip? I said.

There was the *click* of the marbles popping together and they sprang away at angles.

—Do a pig, he demanded, having made the shot, and I oinked. Without missing a beat, though, he answered, —Yeah?

—You understand about this Trinity junk that happened?

I shot, a tad wide.

—Yeah, so?

—Well, I mean, you know this business about the bomb drills and us having to put our heads between our knees and all?

Kip took another shot, *click*, hit another of my marbles, and said, —Make a mule.

I brayed, said, —It's bad. They're gonna blow us up, you know, and he suddenly became animated and made a very real, very effective bomb sound, silver spit at the side of his mouth, his eyes wide, his arms hugging himself as he tottered and stumbled backward and forward before falling down. I watched him. What a hambone, I thought.

—They got me, they got me, I'm a goner. I'm dying, dying.

—I'm serious, I said.

—Oh, Brice, I'm dead, farewell dear . . . friend, remember . . . me, and then lay there for a while holding his breath, waiting for me to say something, respond, get in the act with him, pretend I was a doctor come to his rescue, whatever the devil. But I didn't feel like it.

My shot now. I aimed with one eye shut and the other tight in a squint, and the marble flew off my thumb with a snap, and for once a knock, *click,* and I said, —Make a snake, and he came back to life and hissed.

Then he said, —They're gonna kill us, Brice, is what they're gonna do. Those drills where they make us stick our heads between our legs? What we oughta do is we oughta bend over a little more and kiss ourselves goodbye.

—We got to stop them.

He looked at me as if I had three heads and told me, his voice gone flat as the potsherds we used to collect down in the canyons and dry as dust, —You're just a dumb kid. You aren't gonna stop anything, boy.

I said, hopefully, —You're a dumb kid, too.

—You're right, he finished, and he would be tired of playing marbles, and we'd go off and play something else.

This was how it was when we were eight or so. We had a sense of there being something wrong, transgressive and secretive, about who we were *because* of where we came from. It was a sense that arose from how we were treated whenever we went down into Santa Fe and were first not recognized as local, but—who knows precisely how, by townie intuition, or some offhanded Hill comment that acted as a clue—gave someone to understand that we were from "up there." An abrupt shift in the way the eyes looked at us, a change, subtle maybe but definite, in the voice, a sense of now being either hurried along, or asked to linger for a while, with the obvious interest in finding out what were we doing *up there.*

Not everyone was set against us. Many were curious is all. Something powerful, something dangerous had been accomplished on the Hill, and everyone knew that having ended the war, the nasty thingamajig that broke the Japanese and the Germans was being refined and made mightier, and that a brand-new war, now a Cold War—a very cold war—had got itself under way.

The word *proliferation* assumed new gravity. Strassmann and Hahn's discovery of fission did, too. Uranium and thorium entered lay vocabularies even as world markets for them were spawned. The letter *H* became the most frightening in the alphabet. Everything was a race, a race for space, the arms race, the war between the races. In our basements we stocked canned goods, books, blankets. Dogtags were distributed among urban dwellers to make identification of the dead easier in the aftermath of what seemed inevitable. A hundred million souls had already been slain in the first half of the century, and that had been accomplished mostly by simple means, with bayonets and bullets, by privation and blitz. Carnage was nothing new—older than language, older than fire—but just think of what we could do now. Tests continued, pristine atolls in the Pacific became proving grounds for new weapons. The isle of Elugelab was vaporized by the first thermonuclear bomb, of the name Mike, the pure reef ripped wide by tritium and deuterium—isotopes that sound like books in a Bible of the Dead—and the salt water in which life on earth first was born and all the fish and coral for miles turned into blistering noxious gas that the winds might play with for a while before giving them up in the form of cancered rain. This was the month before Kip and I turned eight. From Eniwetok they watched the fireball as it rose over the Marshall Islands, and the ocean was all lit up, tidal waves, the beautiful expanding rings dashed white across the face of the sea, and the purple-white mushroom graced the South Pacific skies. The ordnance delivered by the thirteen-member crew of the *Enola Gay* was a mere candle flame to the bonfires that were to be ignited year by year in the decade ahead. The war that had just ended looked to be dwarfed by what was to come. The next war promised to be the real thing, the biggest ever waged. And if not the best, at least the brightest.

*W*hen Kip ran away again it felt as if my heart had been cored, the same way you extract the center of an apple. A yellow apple. I was yellow with fear, protected only by my thin skin, it seemed to me—and far too afraid to go out and find him. I sensed everyone was looking at me, quietly laughing at Kip's best friend who had been left behind. I suffered it all the way. The sober, stern face I put on my response was meant to keep my family and secondary friends away from that suffering. Bonnie Jean had the good sense not to tease, and Alyse came by, I remember, and just hung around with me, not saying much but willing to listen if I wanted to talk. Which I didn't. Solemn poker was better than solitaire, I supposed, and so we whiled away some days at the movies and riding trails out on Kwage Mesa past the rodeo grounds. Alyse was a skilled rider and tried to help me with my technique, but I never excelled. We rode, she with her perfect English style and me riding rugged Western, leaning way back over the horse's rump, grasping for the saddle horn, my toes falling out of the stirrups.

   —Brice, you're a terrible rider, she shouted.

   —Nobody asked you to watch.

—One of these days I'm afraid you're going to go over a cliff.

—I get where I'm going, don't I? I shouted back, and spurred my horse, galloped past her along the narrow path, in order to prove my point, while nearly proving hers.

Still, for all Alyse's friendship, I missed Kip.

—Doesn't surprise me, was how I replied to the question of what I thought about Kip's act.

But it did surprise me, it shocked me. How could he leave me behind like this?—another cliche, how they can smart. I waited for someone to tell me he had left a note that would explain why he hadn't come by my house on the sly and offered me the chance to go with him again. There was no note. I felt at loose ends, my stomach ached, it was more like feeling homesick than lonely, akin less to having been abandoned than being disowned.

This time he had defected on foot. Word was he had taken off in the opposite direction of where we had traveled before. A woman said she had seen him in White Rock, which might mean he was headed toward Bandelier, where there were many Indian ruins to hide in, countless caves and cliff dwellings, and water and berries enough to survive for a good long time. But there was no question in my mind they weren't right. He might have ventured down to White Rock in order to be seen there, I reasoned, the motive being to set in motion a rumor such as the very one that was about, but I hadn't the faintest doubt that he was on his way to Chimayó, if he weren't there already. When my mother asked me to be straight with her and tell her where Kip was, I swore I didn't know, but meantime I struggled hard between my loyalty to Kip and the pathetic temptation to send her—all of them—looking in what I thought was the right direction. To what end would I have done that? Probably to punish him, repatriate him, show him that how far he could get without me wasn't very far at all. In the end, I kept my mouth shut.

Two days, then three, then five, passed. A week went by. I sensed that I was being watched for clues, was eyed with suspicion. I suppose it made sense that if anybody would know something about Kip's latest flight, it would be me. I kept to myself as much as possible. I put an innocent look on my face, a mask that probably expressed guilt—paradoxically, the result of trying too hard. And then, one afternoon, just what I might never have wanted to happen: I was paid a visit by Kip's father. He found me sitting on the wooden porch steps of our house. A dark, elegant, slight man with a wide face and heavy eyebrows, long easy-flowing arms like those of his son, and yet a man who looked perpetually as if he hadn't slept for months from worry, so deep were the creases across his forehead and pronounced the pouches beneath his eyes. He spoke before I had any chance of fleeing.

—Your parents have been kind enough to let me have a few words with you, he said, which gave me to understand that even if I'd fled, there would have been no avoiding the discussion we were about to have.

—I see.

—Brice, would you be willing to take a walk with me down to Pierotti's?

I went—what else was I to do?—and listened to him as the lowering sun lengthened the shadows across Seventeenth. Since he wasn't going to get from me what I assumed he wanted, I told myself that this act of walking down the street, conversing with an adult, wasn't wrong, wasn't collaborating with the enemy. Pierotti's was an older-style soda bar for older-style folks, and I knew if any of our friends were around, they'd be over at the newer Baskin Robbins shop by the movie theater, the Centre, so I was safe from being spotted.

—We've never had much of a chance to get to know each other, have we?

—No, sir.

—I'm sorry about that, because I know how much Kip thinks of you.

I wondered whether he thought he knew Kip any better than he knew me, but kept walking. I didn't have much interest in eating ice cream. It was a warm autumn evening, with little puffs of cool air billowing through from time to time, like when you are swimming in a pond and the water goes from warm to cold as you paddle over a place where there's a spring. Pierotti's was dead, for which I was grateful. We sat at the counter. It occurred to me that I was too old for this.

He asked, —What'll it be, Brice? A sundae?

—All right.

—Hot fudge?

—I guess.

He had the same. We sat and watched them being made. When the sodajerk brought them over and placed them in front of us, I took up my spoon and remembered one of my mother's favorite adages: He that would eat with the devil needs a long spoon. It was a sundae spoon, long enough.

Unthinking, I took an initiative. —Do they know where Kip is yet?

He smiled, genuinely it seemed, and said, —Of course I was hoping it'd be you who could tell me where he is. On the other hand, I know you can't. That isn't how friends behave and—

—Mr. Calder, I don't know where he is.

—and I can respect that. Friendship is very important. But that isn't why I wanted to talk to you, Brice.

What was going on? We ate in silence for a while. He made an effort to find out how I was doing in school. —Your mother is a wonderful teacher, you're lucky to have her for a mom, he said. He asked after my sister.

—She's all right, I said.

After we finished he paid, and we walked back outside. Again I glanced around, hoping none of the kids I knew was there.

—Walk you home, Brice?

I sensed that by being compliant I could avoid giving him what he wanted from me, whatever that would be. It seemed the more vulnerable I appeared, the more likely he'd avoid pressuring me. I kicked a bottle cap on the sidewalk, figuring it would magnify his sense of my boyishness, youth, innocence, that sort of thing. Fifteen years old and look at what I already knew about the art of manipulation. We walked along, I kicked it again and it rolled ahead of us, and when we reached it I kicked once more. I was the very image of a good boy. What an actor. Have such powers become so ingrained that I don't recognize them for what they are anymore? Or have I simply lost them? No, I'm sure I am still capable of that much feint, and worse. After all, isn't it how I make my living, at least in part?

Kip's father was asking me something, I'd drifted, and I heard him saying, —Do the words *blue pony* mean anything to you, Brice?

—Blue pony, I repeated, knew I knew it, but couldn't put the words to what I knew. —How come? I asked.

I made the mistake of looking up at him, at Kip's father, and in the now dimming, hazy light saw the disarming thing we all carry with us through our lives no matter who we are or how far we run. Kip was there in his face, the flat tall forehead, determined lips, the austere dark irises, the gentle seriousness behind which lurked a fount of potency, of vitality. I drifted again, or rather willed myself to conjure Kip, to force his father to disappear and render in his place my friend. I stared and squinted and pulled on my memory like one might pull on the rope in a tug-of-war. Harder to do than I might have thought because for one

Kip's appearance, his countenance, was as mercurial as his manner. His eyes looked at you with multiplicity of purpose. Wideset, they had a way of drawing you in, of embracing you, even as they refused to allow you much insight into what it was they saw when they looked at you. They are dark, as I say, dark brown as raisins, and flicker with burnt gold flecks. The whites around the irises are just that, just pure white, even when Kip had been up for days. The high cheekbones almost Native American. The skin of a delicacy, a kind of thinness that made the angles, shapes, and variations of the bone beneath most immediate. And those bushy eyebrows that resembled dark clouds on his horizon.

—How come? I asked again.

As he raised his hand, began to gesticulate with the answer, he touched his fingers to his concave cheek, and I felt myself pull back. It was as if he were going to hit me, was how I thought, or rather, as if *they* were going to, Kip and his father fused into one.

—Well, it's strange, Brice. I don't know that it means a thing, but we found a notebook of his, and he'd been writing in the back of it, and he wrote *blue pony* in it over and over. I just wondered if you knew what a blue pony was.

Overcome with the sense of having experienced an important insight, I simultaneously knew, with a certainty firm as stone, that I not only didn't understand what that insight meant, but didn't even know truly what it was. Hard to describe; it was startling and had to do with the necessary rifts that come between young friends as they begin to grow into their own identities. I stared straight ahead. Kip had vanished.

—Blue pony? I asked.

—Yes, do you know what a blue pony is?

—I don't think so.

—You don't know, or you don't think you know?

These were our parents, these were logicians and scientists, thorns in the side, nitpickers and ergoists, but the distinction— a very nice distinction—brought it back, though I didn't know quite why, what happened one afternoon, what it meant. It was one day down in the peppers-game canyon, Kip and I were sunning ourselves, lying on our backs in the scant grass, naming cloud shapes. Anvils big as towns flowed by. There were monsters, many white monsters. Some like dragons with wings, others great birds like pterodactyls. The vapor trails of jets stretched for hundreds of miles across the sky and, as the high winds began to break them up, came to look like skeletons of snakes. And in the middle of an enormous cumulus a patch of blue sky appeared, an opening we watched there, entranced, as slowly it began to take the shape of a pony, a blue pony, and I'll never forget how when the pony was fully shaped Kip said, —That's what I want to ride, Brice, what I'm going to ride right out of this place, that sky pony there.

And I said, —Me too.

To which Kip responded, —No. You're an earth person and I'm a sky person.

—What's that supposed to mean?

—I think you got red blood in your body, boy.

—So what, I said. Red's the color it's supposed to be.

—That's true. But I'm telling you mine's the color of that pony there.

—Look, I've seen you bleed, boy, and it isn't any blue. It's red just like anybody else's.

—No. It's not.

—Is so.

Kip said, —You may not want to believe it, boy, but we're different, you and me.

—No we're not, I said.

—We are.

I felt sad, I remember, and said, —Not so different.

He said nothing more.

And now here I was walking along beside his father. He wasn't wrong, I guess.

I asked, —Mr. Calder?

He walked on. —Yes?

—How come Kip wants to run away like that?

—Why did you run away, Brice?

If he didn't know by now, he'd never know. And anyway it was a divisible reason, what else is new, *I pledge allegiance to the of the and to the for which it one nation under with and*—one nation indivisible with liberty and justice, my ass. Nations aren't any more indivisible than the folks in them, and I was beginning to see this. The reason I ran was divisible in at least two parts. I went because Kip agreed with me that we should go and eat the dirt Communion, and I went because I believed we had to make our own gesture of remorse on behalf of people like Mr. Calder.

—I can't say, I said.

—Did it have something to do with this blue pony business?

—The blue pony was something we saw in the sky once.

—Something you saw in the sky?

—Just a cloud picture in the sky. That's all.

Mr. Calder looked at his watch. —Well. Thanks, Brice.

—Thank you for the sundae, Mr. Calder, I said.

As it happens, I misjudged Kip and his whereabouts. Here I had flattered myself that I managed to give his father little unto nothing to work with, whereas if I had simply told him the truth about where I figured Kip had gone, I'd have steered the search in just the wrong direction. The military police picked him up hiding in a cliff dwelling in Bandelier Canyon, a quarter mile up past the Tyuonyi ruins. He was tired, dirty, hungry, but possessed

of enough spirit to excoriate his captors as they pulled him out
of his roost. Rumor had it he screamed, —Leave me alone, you
motherfuckers, at the police, and this made me happy when I
heard it, probably because I pictured myself there with him shouting and kicking. But the pleasure I took in hearing about his
obscenities soon passed. The more I thought about it, the more
I came to the conclusion there was no denying he was further
removed from me than ever. His foul language may have bound
us together insofar as I was as capable as Kip of *fuckthis* and
fuckthat. We referred to each other using the term *futtbucker* with
boring frequency in those days. —Listen here, futtbucker. —No,
you listen, buttmucker. The ritual of bonding through
expletives—toiletmouthing, my father called it—was under way
with us well before we drove to Chimayó, even though the nas-
tiness of the language we used was not as raw or transgressive as
we might have hoped. What made Kip seem so removed was that
he had failed to repeat what we had done together. He'd not
done anything the way I thought he would. He hadn't even gone
to find Fernando Martinez, as I had, in my jealousy, thought for
sure he would. —You motherfuckers, he'd shouted, and I said it
too, pretending I'd been there with him.

—You motherfuckers, and I meant it with all my heart, knowing full well how Kip's reputation as a scandalous runaway grew
and that in our conservative community, with its Western taci-
turnity, anyone associated with him flirted with catastrophe himself. But how I would have preferred disaster to my role as
rejected conspirator and failed renegade.

*T*he sky has colored pallid blue straight above, like some wax
paper sea. The morning star has withdrawn behind the curtain

of light to wait for its chance to shine again tomorrow. Across the valley, Cerro Gordo, the most perfect rounded little mountain, its reddish breast covered uniformly with piñon, offers a sort of confidence. A spotted flicker with his knife beak and red moustaches perches on the coyote fence, studies me, then flies.

Morning. Here I am. I have been offered the loan of an old retired Cadillac. —It won't get you there fast, but it'll get you there, Alyse had said. Grand and silver, it should have a set of steer horns attached to the front of the hood. Its bumper sticker reads, NUCLEAR WEAPONS MAY THEY RUST IN PEACE, which won't go over very well on the Hill. Oh well, I think, I may not go over very well on the Hill, either. Keys in hand, I lock the door behind me and head out.

It is Thursday, the traditional day of preparation and prayer before the penitentes take to the road to walk to the church in the desert, bearing their crosses. I have decided to drive up to Los Alamos to visit my mother, and also Bonnie Jean, her husband and two boys. It's been a long time since we saw one another, not to mention that I've only laid eyes on my youngest nephew, Charlie, but once, when he was just a little boy. I haven't phoned ahead to let them know I am here, in part because I figure it will be nice to surprise them and in part because this way I can back out at the last moment without hurting anyone's feelings. A half-truth and a full truth. My hapless nephews, whose birthdays I don't even know—bad uncle and bad brother—it would be the *right thing* to do, call on them, toss them a ball for half an hour if they like, I don't know, do whatever uncles are supposed to do.

The car handles like a big boat. The highway is a smooth canal of hard black water beneath it. Fins forward and fins aft, the thing is long and commodious. The steering wheel's enormous and the dash baroque. What better way to travel, I think, than in a relic that dates back to the days of one's youth.

Out the windows is a cloudless day except for the everpresent clouds along the tops of the mountains at the edges of Pojoaque Valley, clouds the colors of moonstone and rose quartz and chalcedony, with a gray-black twill pattern here and there where a morning rain is falling, far away. I turn on the radio to find a country-western station and settle in with the honeylike music of the pedal steel guitar and the homey nasal voice of a singer singing about the things country singers always sing about—how their lover left them high and dry, or how they're cheating on the one who's home with a wedding band on her finger. Banal, but I love the stuff if, for nothing else, its luscious predictability.

Up out of the wide bowl of land that holds swarming Santa Fe, past Rosario, the soldiers' cemetery, past the opera house, and into the desert now.

If something frightens you, my mother used to tell me when I woke up in the middle of the night from bad dreams, if something frightens you, Brice, stand up tall and walk straight toward it, you hear me. Walk right at it and threaten to embrace it— embrace it if you must. But no matter what you do when you reach it, that thing that frightens you, at least let it know that it is possible for you to embrace it. That way you not only know that it exists, but you understand why you weren't wrong to be afraid of it in the first place. It is not wrong to be afraid. Some of the things we fear most are phantoms and not worthy of our fear, but there are other things that merit our fear. The only way to know them and to let them know you is to embrace them.

I haven't always lived by this, but when I have, I know I've been a stronger man, a more courageous man. To know the meaning of one's fear is not necessarily to fear no more—but at least to measure its value.

I wonder how Kip learned how to use his fears to such great effect so early in his life. If it frightened him, he habitually reached out and grasped it. Chimayó and Bandelier would not turn out to be the last unknowns he attended. Bandelier did prompt his parents to take steps to rein Kip in. Especially his mother, who none of us knew well, and who in some way must have been his model, Emma Inez, distant Mrs. Calder who didn't take her husband's surname and was something of a recluse, an enigma—she came into the picture for a time after his second runaway.

It snowed a lot that December, was cold to the marrow. Gossip about what the Calders were going to do with Kip came and went. There was persistent talk of his being sent to a reform school out east—which would have been quite an irony, given that the original settlement in Los Alamos back during the First World War was a ranch school for boys who had problems of health or adjusting to society in one way or another—but that never came about. I didn't ask about him because I found myself not wanting to be asked about how I felt about it, what I thought they ought to do with Kip. I didn't think there was much of anything *to do* with him. He was going to do as he pleased. Kip was spirited, is how I saw it. He was no criminal. He was wildly alive. If he wanted to run, run he would. If he wanted to run, he had his reasons. Having used my running legs once, I remembered well the sensation of freedom seized.

Christmas came, went. Our sixteenth birthdays came and went. New Year's came and when it went I had had enough.

The night I finally resolved to break the rules and go see him was particularly snowy. A wind rode down the mountain canyons and drove the snow across the mesa in billowing sheets, we'd been inside most all day, school was closed and the blizzard kept us off the pond. As evening fell, the white world tinted to neon blue. The tracks my father had made that morning, headed back to the lab after working late the night before, were long since filled in by drifting snow. I finished drying dishes from the dinner the three of us had shared in his absence and excused myself, saying I was tired.

—But it's not even nine, Bonnie Jean said. —You can't be going to bed already.

I said, —Night, all.

Bonnie Jean rolled her eyes and crossed her arms. I thought, Bonnie Jean, if you blow this, I'm going to make you pay, one way or another.

—Goodnight, Brice, my mother said.

—Brice's weird, said Bonnie, who then uncrossed her arms and looked at Mother.

—Quiet now, Mother told her.

On the way out of the kitchen I made the devil's horns at her. Mother didn't see. Bonnie Jean made horns back and I smirked and shook my head. Unredeemable, she replicated my moves. Sometimes I found it hard to believe we were born from the same womb. No doubt, Bonnie now and then had the same thought.

In my bedroom I moved about as quietly and quickly as I could. I set about molding under the bedspread a sleeping figure, a sham Brice, of sweaters and the old Beacon blankets mother stored in the closet. Maybe I had seen this trick done in the movies, who knows, but if someone peeked in without turning on the lights, it really might have looked as if I was curled up in bed. I assumed no one would, however; my parents' trust I had regained and Bonnie Jean—for the host of other egregious faults I may have attributed to her—was honorable with regard to the sanctity of our separate rooms, and could be depended on to stay away.

Out the casement window, in the manner of the visit nights, and into the storm. As I shoved along, I breathed in the frosty air, and began to worry how I might go about seeing him without the Calders catching me, and also what I might say to Kip if we were able to talk. Gusts caught up the powder and sent it spiraling and gnarling like spectral twisters along the deserted street. Pine boughs clad in white bowed to the blue-white ground. No one was out tonight. My toes began to smart and bursts of quivering ran through me.

When our family moved from the Sundt house on the old road that was next door to the Calders', I remember how upset Kip and I were. We couldn't have been more than three or four. I wonder if I've ever forgiven Bonnie Jean, since it was her birth that made it so the house was too small for us.

The old road wasn't far, and soon enough I stood behind a row of cars, each with snow hats, and watched the house, its tangerine windows. Smoke poured from the central chimney, the rich, black coal smoke from the furnace. Jogged in place a little to keep the blood moving in my feet, flexed my fingers as fast as I could but already the icy snow was clinging to my deerskin mittens. Made more brazen by the glacial wind, I gave up my cover, pitched my way, heaved through the deepening snow to the side of the house, and looked in the nearest window.

There he was. Emma Inez was with him. He was talking to her. I couldn't hear, of course, but tried to read if not his lips his countenance. He was different, both his face and carriage were hard to interpret. I hadn't seen Kip this close-up for half a year, since mid-late summer—that is, I hadn't been able really to *look* at him—and was astonished to witness how much he had aged.

The change was subtle, sharp. What was it about him? I forgot the cold, stood there fixed in one place as I stared at that face, collecting snowflakes on my clothes and wondering whether I dare envy him still or learn somehow to master my habit of feeling a lesser boy, a dependent.

My feet led me around to the front porch of Kip's house, up to his door, on which I knocked with my knuckles, having pulled my mitten off, and Emma Inez came to the door, opened it, and said, —My god, Brice. Come in.

My cheeks, I was told later, were mottled white and matte blue.
—Brice? Kip said.

I was making a ridiculous chattering sound, all the while wanting only to apologize for intruding and just to ask them both if they wouldn't mind just helping me to warm up and let me sneak back home without telling my parents about what I'd done. She said something about getting my hands and feet into warm water. I watched them both, from inside myself, my shaking hard body, and saw Emma Inez carry a deep wide bowl of warm water to the chair I sat in while Kip removed my boots and peeled off my white socks. It felt like some of my skin was glued to the socks and I remembered the days we all used to challenge each other in the middle of winter to press our tongues to the jungle gym, and how those who rose to the challenge found that the hide of their tongue stuck and was flayed away, left clinging to the bar of steel. But I wasn't frostbitten, and was given some reheated coffee, which warmed me up. I expected Emma Inez to send me home—per the edict that our families had set forth—but instead she left the room, a tacit blessing of sorts. I had always figured it was Kip's father, and my own, rather than our mothers, who decreed that Kip and I should be kept apart for a while, and her mercy led me to believe I'd been right about that. Maybe this was all mere wishful thinking, though. Perhaps she'd gone in another room to telephone my home to tell my folks their son was somewhere he wasn't supposed to be, and that they had better come and pick the boy up. I didn't care one way or the other, or so I told myself.

—So how've you been?

—All right, I said.

Even his voice seemed older. I thought to try to lower the register of my own voice, so as to sound to him as mature as he sounded to me, but the chill that ran through me hampered my idea. —What about you? I asked, and heard the tremulousness and kidlike tenor behind the words.

—You're not supposed to be here.

I shrugged and smiled. He sat in his father's large over-stuffed chair, a grown man really, thin and long of frame, and didn't smile back. He was taking me in. Measuring, like always.

—Do your parents know you're here, Brice?

—No, I said.

—So what's up?

—I wanted to see how you're doing, I said.

—I'm all right, I guess. Aren't you worried about getting grounded again?

—I'm still grounded from before.

He liked that. That made him laugh a little. —We're too old for groundings.

—You can say that again.

Then that silence prevailed once more. Had he thought there were other reasons I hadn't come by before now to see him besides being grounded, did he think I'd chosen to stay away from him? That bothered me, but I wouldn't bring it up. I drank from the cup, and noticed that on it were Navajo squashblossom designs. It made me wish for summer. The canyons and cliffs and the mesas. The hot springs in the Jemez above us smelling of sulfur. The games.

—You done running away from home, Kip?

He glanced over toward the open door where Emma Inez had gone and shook his head no while he said, —Yeah, sure am.

That was Kip all over. While shaking my head yes I said, —Well, if you do get it in mind to run off like that again, don't count on me coming along.

—I won't, he said, shaking his yes in return.

That was more like it, I thought.

—Good, I said.

Strange, after all my boldness coming here to talk with him, there wasn't much to say. Maybe he knew what I'd been doing, through the grapevine, not that I'd been doing very much. Maybe it didn't matter to him. The fact was, our fathers seemed to have been right about one matter, wise engineers that they were. Friendships are inevitably synergistic. The energy of two friends equals more than the sum of their individual parts. Whatever Kip and I did separately was less dangerous, less provocative, less inspired than what we did together.

—I'm feeling better now, I said, though he hadn't asked. —Don't think I got frostbit.

—That's good.

What was missing in Kip's eyes? A dullness, as difficult to fathom as to describe, was dusted over them. They almost looked like somebody else's eyes. But then, I told myself, Kip's been through more than I have these months since we last talked— recovery, chastisement, escape, capture—maybe that explains it. And also, what exactly is this "it" I think I see? He didn't seem defeated. Was he the same, and were my eyes looking at him differently?

When Emma Inez came into the room, after a quarter of an hour or so, she said with her rich Cuban accent, —The snow is let up now. Time you better go back home.

—Mrs. Calder, can I ask you a favor?

She said, —I won't say anything about this, Brice. Don't do it again.

—Thanks, I said, realizing too late I'd addressed her with the wrong name. —See you around, Kip.

The edict was lifted sometime the next week. I was certain that my mother and Emma Inez had discussed the matter and made the decision; I think Emma Inez kept the confidence as promised, too, and if she didn't, my mother didn't let on that she knew I'd broken rules and gone to visit Kip. Bonnie Jean allowed she'd heard Emma Inez explain to my mother that she figured Kip was a runner, and was more likely to run when left by himself than when allowed to be with me who wasn't, all of us knew, a runner at heart. I will never forget my mother, sitting across from me at the kitchen table, tapping blackened tobacco out of her small pipe into the palm of her hand, holding my gaze level and calm, saying, —Don't blow it, Brice.

Spring and summer wafted by. The last year of high school began. We never spoke of it, but we knew we were biding time against the approach of our official home-leaving when we would go off to college, get away from the Hill. Our lives settled into routines, some old, some new. We weren't exactly outcasts, but neither were we members of clubs or teams. We floated on those months as if they were innertubes on the slowest river, and books, dances, school assignments, chores, instructors, meals, rising in the morning and undressing at the end of the day, all just came into view and laggardly were swept behind as we drifted along this time stream, dragging our hands and feet in its dream waters, and waiting for some white rapids we suspected lay ahead.

The annual Christmas party was witness to pine boughs and electric candles along the windowsills, caroling down the streets, presents in colorful wrapping and tied with shimmery ribbons under the newly cut blue spruce tree that was so prickly we had to wear gloves to string the lights and hang the ornaments, bizcochitos that tasted of anise and cinnamon, divinity candies, smiles and laughter. Small bonfires of piñon, luminarias, burned outside at corners, a place for carolers and those carrying presents from one house to another, to warm themselves. Farolitos everywhere you cast your eye, paper sacks with a candle burning inside making the most genial glow, lining our walks and rooftops, yellowy in the night, lighting the way for the pastores on their hike to church on Christmas Eve. It was about this time that we seemed to come awake again. There is no accounting for why. We did, is all.

—When do we get too old for this shit, Kip whispered, standing by the tree, eggnog cup in hand; we'd spiked ours in the kitchen with some rum Mom'd left on the counter for the grown-ups.

—Doesn't look like anybody gets too old for it, I answered. The room was full of adults talking and talking. His question brought to mind my thought that time at the soda fountain with his father. Sodas, fudge, pastores, rum—

—Where you applying?

—Columbia, I said.

My father, originally a Bostonian but a New Yorker at heart, had taught there before he was drafted to Los Alamos. New York was where my mother grew up, on Jones Street, one of the shortest streets in the Village, in a brickfaced walk-up apartment building, an only child of a lonely mother—a grandmother I never knew who had been abandoned by a grandfather whose history I also did not know. New York—Columbia—is where my parents met. She was an undergrad at Barnard and he a graduate teaching assistant at the university. Different schools and different departments, a blind date offered to both of them on the spur of the moment, there was a Halloween dance and mutual friends put them together half as a joke, since these friends—long gone, and long lost—supposed my future parents were as oil and water.

It was to be some kind of trick-or-treat hazing, all trick and no treat.

They may have been in the friends' eyes ill-matched. But they were neither ill-matched nor ill-fated. My mother and father fell in love at first sight—both still maintain this to be what happened: one look and each of them *knew*—and were seldom apart after that dance. Photographs of New York fill the family scrapbook in its first couple of years. The war just begun. My parents stylish and sage, even grim in the black-and-white images printed on glossy stock with scalloped edges. My father a chemical engineer way out ahead of most of his peers. My mother in her gray gabardine suits, a gentlewoman, formidable and exotic. An intellectual, too, and given to independent-mindedness. Sometimes I have thought it was a wonder she hadn't joined the Communist Party, though of course that would have come back to haunt her. I can imagine her, back then, seeing value in embracing its apparent humanist side, its concern for the common man, its ideological rejection of greed. It may be that God, in whom she believed—at least in an inchoate way—braked any drift in that direction. Once in a while I have thought it a shame she hadn't been a member insofar as it might have scotched my father's chances of working on the Hill.

As it was, they came directly from New York to Los Alamos and it was at Columbia University their son would continue school, there was never a question about it. I didn't even bother to apply anywhere else.

—Okay, Kip said.

I drank more eggnog. The rum was making me happy, or else just dizzy. I said, —Okay what?

Kip shot me an exuberant scowl. —Okay, he said. —So that's where I go, too. Can't break up the old gang.

This wasn't Kip, not the old Kip. I felt both excited by his declaration of loyalty and pained by the underlying defeat in it. Kip, you weren't supposed to go along with me, with Briceboy, not so readily as all that, you were supposed to direct not follow, and direct with an imperious decisiveness at that. I must have stared at him and he returned my gaze with a smirk, and then snapped his finger right in my face. What had I missed or misunderstood?

—No, we sure can't, I agreed once more, voice dropped back into a feeble whisper, more noise than melody, the words intended less to belabor the point than furnish the space between us with something, anything to drive back whatever had emerged from the depths of that look on his face. I snapped my finger in front of his eyes, and a trance was broken.

Part of me wished that Kip wouldn't or couldn't come along to New York. How different my life might have played out—not that I could have known this at the time, but I did have the sense that however difficult splitting off from Kip would be, it might be for the best, somehow. Maybe I didn't actually know this at the time; maybe that is an embellishment. It didn't matter, finally. Despite his negligences, his disobediences, his occasional hostility toward teachers—my mother excepted—and toward school in general, his grades were excellent, higher than mine. If Kip wanted to get into Columbia, he would. I dipped the glass ladle into the big bowl and refilled my cup. I drank more, tasted nothing, waited for a revelation that was never to come, or at least not that evening. My little sister we caught in the kitchen spiking her own drink with the rum, and instead of threatening to tell Mom, I said, —Merry Christmas, Bonnie Jean, to which she replied quite dryly, —You're drunk, brother. And so I was.

After that things settled down. I was determined to be happy. Alyse was almost a girlfriend, but never quite, despite how much my mother would have liked to see it happen. Bonnie I treated

almost as a brother should treat his sister. Soon enough I succeeded so thoroughly in my endeavor to enjoy these last seasons
on the Hill that the odd, temporary disturbance in the nature of
my bond with Kip faded into oblivion. We were best friends
again.

Kip came back to himself, his edge was there once more. I
don't know how it happened, it wasn't gradual. And yet he wasn't
the young Kip, cocksure and cutting. Yes, he was sharp again,
but how to put it? It was as if he had more substance to him,
like spiritual girth. His voice heavier, his walk more weighted with
each long step. Did anyone see this besides myself? I doubt it.
Possibly Emma Inez, but no one else. While he was less callous,
he was more intimidating; while less quick to state his opinion
about anything, more given to quirks such as prolonged stares,
head tilted perhaps to one side and mouth closed into a straight,
unrevelatory line.

Our games changed. What we'd loved to do once we loved no
more. Peppers was now something, Kip said, for little kids.
—Better we go jacklighting bucks, he told me and I disagreed,
—That's not hunting, and he said, —So what is it? and I answered, —Jacklighting's for bad shots and sissies, it's like some
kind of execution, and he said, —The Indians do it and they're
not sissies and they're not bad shots, and I thought he was wrong.
I mean, what kind of sport is it to shoot some poor deer, mesmerized in the night by the beam of a flashlight? I said nothing
more, and was relieved when we never followed through.

We did other things. We fly-fished. We tried to trap a beaver
for a couple of months with the idea that we could sell it to a
zoo somewhere and have money to spend. We still rode horses,
bareback and whipping the hackamore reins, rough-and-tumble
down into the canyons and through meadows, over Barranca
mesa and over to Pine Springs, almost all the way to Española,

spurring them on with the heels of our bare feet and shouting, —Giddyup, until their hides darkened with sweat and the corners of their mouths collected foam. We just wasted time, too, could pass hours together without speaking. We knew what we didn't want to do. We had no interest in football, for instance. Not street hockey, not even baseball. Nothing that had to do with teams, with balls or bats, nothing to do with keeping score.

—That stuff's kidjunk, Kip said.

We didn't consider ourselves outcasts. It was just that the others were flockers.

For a few months after our reconciliation and before we left for school, we lived for movies. By the purple velvet ropes and brass stanchions, along the carpeted path past the great double doors and into the hushed gloom of the auditorium we strode. We favored front row center the first time we saw a given picture, then for later viewings moved back into the body of the hall to cause trouble if necessary. We never saw a movie only once, not even the worst of them. The more action there was, the more we went. Newsreels and cartoons we studied, too—anything to do with Mickey Mouse we hated, Bugs Bunny was our boy, Bugs was more shrewd, knew how to get himself in and out of scrapes. Theater life was anonymous, safe, dark, cool in summer, warm in winter, scented with popcorn and salty butter, hotdogs and mustard. Here was a sanctuary where we could lead other people's varied lives, witness their adventures, travel the world with them, win the hearts of beautiful women, fight ignoble and ugly men, be spies, cowboys, riverboat captains, gamblers, detectives, heroes. Flyboy movies—about aviators, men who rode blue ponies—were Kip's favorites beyond all others. The grand silver passenger plane that carried star-crossed lovers far away from each other, crop dusters, Grumman biplanes that buzzed aerodromes upside down and then righted themselves so that goggled stuntmen could walk their wings, these were the subject of awe and cause for joy. Whenever there was an airplane on the screen he leaned forward, absorbed, even entranced. In the darkness of the theater Kip seemed to take on some of his boyishness again, let down his guard. We would fillip kernels of popcorn at unsuspecting couples whenever there was a love scene and the music ascended to violins and the lights dimmed. Most of what little money we made doing small jobs here and there went into the hands of the woman who sat in the glass booth at the entrance to the Centre theater, that winter and on into the early months of summer. We hadn't the slightest idea that we might be a bit immature for our age. The days went soft as a sumptuous fog during this last season of isolated contentment we would enjoy. It set in upon Kip first, and what came over him readily came over me as if we were one patient suffering a single malaise, one creature bewitched by a single spell.

In the meantime, Alyse wisely found another kid in whom to invest her affection.

*M*y mother. I have to be prepared that she may not know me. She threads in and out of recognition when I telephone her, has for some years. She knows Bonnie Jean but sometimes seems unclear about or uninterested in specifically identifying her, even though my sister—as Bonnie Jean herself has told me—visits Mother most every afternoon. It will be a very different kind of sadness for me to see her as she is now, as she's become, than it has been to hear her on the phone. When her monologue ranges and extends in illogical ways, I can sit there at my desk and listen in a half-there-half-not way while I study the framed photograph of her and Father I keep with other family photos, and can let my imagination modify things just a little, turn back time toward the moment she and Dad stood smiling triumphantly, having climbed to the summit of Sandia Peak, when youthfulness still was hers. I can read what she wrote on the verso of the photo— it's framed with a special window in the back so the inscription is visible—*for Brice, from his loving mom & dad here at the top of the Tewa world, Turtle Mountain (Sandia Peak), September 1967.*

Radiance and exuberance emanated from both their faces, back on that autumn afternoon in the mountains near Albuquerque, flushed from the long hike up and up through the turning aspens. Toasting their successful ascent to the summit, she lifts her flask in the air, and father waves his walking stick. Her figure is, as always, slim, her clothing smart, sensible. In her eyes is the confidence that she will live forever—and when I connect that look with the voice I am hearing, a voice that has been so influential in my life, I don't feel so awful about where she is now, and who she is. After all, she's still convinced of her immortality—and she's got two millennia of belief, ceremony, and tradition with which to back up her assertions. She borders on insanity, I think, at times. But the radiance and exuberance have never abandoned her. It isn't insanity anyway—it's something else; but if it were insanity, it would be a savant's, and a damned cheerful savant at that. The elements I can use to find the cherished *old her* in the becharmed *new her* are right there before me, then, as I merge that photograph with her present voice and perspectives.

Seeing her, though. I guess I have avoided it like the plague, without much wanting to admit my cowardice. In the past I defended myself. I have said to Bonnie Jean, —Listen, you live right there, what do you want me to do, I live two thousand miles away, drop everything and come when you want me to come? She wouldn't know who I was if I did come. I'm carrying my end of the deal.

—Your mother is not a *deal*, Brice, Bonnie Jean would say.

—All right already, you know what I mean. I'm not being irresponsible, I've been holding up my end.

And I have. I pay what bills her savings and small income do not cover. It seems fair enough. She's not yet in a nursing home—Bonnie and I've agreed to forgo that eventuality as long as possible—but when the time comes, no doubt much of the financial responsibility will fall to me.

Still, Bonnie Jean holds that my prolonged absence has made Mother sad. When she says that Mother misses seeing me, there is no escape, it makes me feel rotten and selfish and heartless. And what do I usually do but justify myself, like a fool. I am accountable for my behavior and my distance, of course, I'll say. I don't dispute that. But there is little that you could come up with, Bonnie Jean, to substantiate my inability to "face facts," as you put it two or three years ago.

—And just what sort of facts are they I'm supposed to face? I asked.

—That you've never cared about us here.

—And what am I supposed to do different from what I'm doing?

Bonnie Jean relied on an old chestnut of hers, harvested from her orchard of cliches, —Well, if you don't know, I'm not going to tell you.

—Come on, Bonnie Jean, I said. —You chose to stay on the Hill, nobody forced you.

—Well, who was supposed to take care of Mom and Daddy?

—They were perfectly capable of taking care of themselves.

—Not after Daddy died.

I thought to say, Dad didn't need taking care of after he died, but settled for, —Look, I don't think by coddling Mother you're doing either one of you any good. You get upset when she doesn't acknowledge your presence, she gets upset when you don't want to talk about her saints and angels. What makes you think, aside from doing the shopping for her and helping with the laundry, that all your ministrations aren't just a nuisance?

I was unhappy with myself for having said that. I had a way of overstating my case to my sister, and had no clear idea of what weight my words might have with her.

She began to cry. —You're the same mean person you always were.

—I'm not mean, I said.

—You just don't get it. You don't know what it's like watching her fall apart, piece by piece, day in and day out.

—That doesn't prove I'm mean.

—You're ignorant of the situation here, for one. And two, you refuse to help in any way beyond sending out checks every so often. I think that makes you mean, Brice, and frankly I don't see it as anything new.

The argument invariably came to this impasse. I promised to come out. I apologized as best I could. And after we'd hung up I had to admit Bonnie Jean wasn't altogether wrong in her accusations. There was inequity, there were imbalances, she did do more to care for our mother, hadn't shoved off like Kip and I had so long ago. But she was mistaken to think I didn't comprehend what was happening out there. I knew altogether too well.

After my father passed away, Mother married Jesus. This was how I put it whenever friends asked how she was getting along, and I wonder if such a shoddy and cynical way of viewing her zealousness wasn't seen by these friends as the wish of a son who would rather have his widowed mother marry *him*. Was my frustration with her Christianity some form of jealousy? I mean really. No, it was more a sadness as I watched her lose some of her roughed-up edges, watched my born-again mother be smoothed, planed, graded a bit by her new beliefs and hopes. She stayed with the drink and how she went about reconciling that with the faith I couldn't say, although I think many religious people manage to weave their wants into their search for *salvus*. In my own perverse way, I approved of this single paradox in her newly forming, but not reforming, character.

Rage is too strong a word, and frustration may not be the most accurate description of what I felt when I found myself on the telephone with her, sometimes letting her go on for half an hour at a time about her quest for transformation and renewal. What must have been tugging at me was that I had such a distinct memory of myself once being, by intuition, so close to the deep comfort that religious sentiment can afford a person—back when Kip and I made our midnight pilgrimage—and now hearing it again from her, well, perhaps what I was feeling was more an agitated wistfulness. But, to be fair to myself, she *could*, at times, become a bona fide drone. She went through a Rudolf Otto phase, which I thought I might not survive. This was some ten years ago, in the early eighties, when during a birthday call to her I was made to endure an exegesis of what the theologian described as "Das Heilige."

—The sacred, you see, Brice, the sacred inspires more than awe, it inspires the deepest terror.

—Terror, I said.

—Yes, a feeling of profound terror in the face of the majesty of mystery, here, let me quote from Mircea Eliade—

—Mom? I said.

—"the *feeling of terror* before the sacred, before the awe-inspiring mystery . . . *mysterium tremendum*—"

—Mom, how are Bonnie Jean and the kids?

—Listen, "the majesty—*majestas*—that emanates an overwhelming superiority of power—"

—Mother?

—*"religious fear* before the fascinating mystery—*mysterium fascinans*—in which perfect fullness of being flowers"* which is so much like the ritual the Hispanics perform with Las Tinieblas, it all has to do with darkness and light, with apocalyptic fear. . . .

And so she might go on. There was to her, still, a kind of cool, an eccentricity that could distress or nettle me but which, when in a tranquil state myself, I was able to see as admirably unique. Who would've foreseen it, my mother over the course of a lifetime metamorphosing into a handsome old bird who loved nothing better than to invite you to pull up a chair at the kitchen table and share a tumbler or two of gin while discussing the Bible? Not I, but there it is.

Now here I turn off the radio, having had my fill of "Gotta thank Mama for the cookin', thank Daddy for the whoopin', thank the devil for the trouble I'm in." Enough of "Daddy's hands were soft and kind when I was crying, Daddy's hands were hard as steel when I done wrong." Good god, I think. Enough of fiddles and twang.

All I want to hear is the sound of the wind rushing through this funky old tub. My eye stretches out in a way I haven't felt it stretch in a long time. It is no wonder that the sky is what people most mention when they talk about the Southwest; the earth is just a floor for this blue ceiling and these kaleidoscopic clouds. The sky is higher, and I don't know why that is, although I'm sure my father could have told me—there must be some meteorological explanation. The clouds are a vast scrim, frothy and mercurial as ever. The mountains blue in the near distances, violet out farther. The road broad and the air stark. A magpie overhead, its long tail black and belly white.

I'd forgotten how much I enjoy driving, out on open highway like this, the Tesuque reservation lands dirty pink bespeckled with scrub, and past Camel Rock, which way back when we used to climb—somewhere in one of Mother's albums there was a photograph of Kip and me posing as small humps on the camel's back—and along past the same souvenir shops that have been here for decades selling kachinas and corn dolls, dreamcatchers and cowhide drums, past Arroyo Cuyamungue, past the pueblo bingo hall, past boneyards littered with great piles of cow skulls, elk and deer antlers, past all the tacky bric-a-brac, past porch railings hung with tourist rugs—REAL INDIAN KRAFTS—and past the cut-rate liquor stores that now have drive-through windows so you don't even have to get out of your car before you kill the old bottle and break the paper seal on the next.

After I turn to head up toward the Jemez, Black Mesa comes into view and reminds me of an enormous dark porkpie hat laid there on puebloland, Oppie's hat of course, and anxiety begins to hew the sweetness of all these familiarities.

Mother, Mother, I think. Please answer your door and know who I am. And as I think this, Bonnie Jean begins to make sense, come into focus. Well, not so much Bonnie Jean as such—siblings, I believe, are fated never to make sense of one another—but her hostility toward me, her impatience with my distance from her and our mother. I can see it, there's some reason to it, some value. Or is this the necessary regret felt by any prodigal son? Regret that refuses to acknowledge that though the prodigal has come home, chances are good he will leave again just like he did before, shamelessly strewing the path of his exit with a hundred empty promises of a quick return.

Bonnie I will visit first, I decide, although in my paranoia I begin to worry that she may not know who I am any more than Mother. Strange, all this sudden desire of recognition. Maybe Bonnie Jean's tones of moral ascendancy about all this are at times defensible. Maybe my right to recognition here is less than

I had ever imagined, developed as it's been from the distance of an utterly different way of thinking and style of life.

Still, though, I hope my mother will know her son.

*I*t was September 1962, and within a month of our arrival in New York, Kip's disquietude began to acquire new focus. At first he tried to get with it, gave it what he could manage, tried to settle in to the life of a student, but his patience—never a long suit to begin with—wore thin with magnificent dispatch. He'd adjusted to the quickened rhythms, the babel, the pandemonium of the city with the same relative ease as I. It was not the city but university life that seemed to bother him. Restrictions, as Kip saw them, were here much like they'd been back on the Hill: odds meant to be gambled against, and beaten. He never read his books at a library carrel or in his dorm room, which was down the hall from mine, but preferred during days to linger on stoops in nearby neighborhoods, and at night in some noisy coffeehouse. He was forever wandering off campus and into the streets of the Upper West Side. Harlem, ten blocks to the north, or Morning-side Park, where none of the students were ever seen, suited him better than anything on campus. The Greentree, the New Asia where seventy-five cents got you a good lunch, Tom's Diner, these were where he preferred to eat, rather than the paneled dining hall. John Jay, our dormitory, from whose windows we stared out south and east into the hard, inviting outside world, was to him an unwelcome confinement. He devised myriad ways to avoid honoring the curfew hour of eleven, after which you were sup-posed to sign your name in a registry book. I forged his signature a couple of times, other times others must have done the same.

He was perpetually astir. Indeed, the one or two times in our lives that I saw him asleep, his eyes shivered beneath his lids like nystagmus, and his foot twitched in an involuntary mime of whatever dream he was having, a dream most probably of running.

—What're you so edgy about? I asked him one day in regard to some incident I've since forgotten.

—Edgy? and on his face was a look of genuine bewilderment.

I waited.

—Look, if I'm edgy, it's because this place is getting on my nerves. It's like a chicken coop here.

—That's ridiculous.

—It's an incubator, where eggheads come to get hatched.

—I don't see any shell around you.

—That's because I've got the good sense to chip away at mine.

Maybe he tried harder than I could see. Kip was forever full of hidden energies. Even when his spirits were low, some deep power was there, smoldering and impatient to burst back into flame. Dutiful to the degree allowed by his creeping cynicism about the value of higher education (—Like, *higher than what?* higher than a kite?), he went through the motions, bought the books, attended classes, though even in the freshman composition course we shared he managed to posture himself in his desk chair in such a way as to emanate rebelliousness and impetuosity. His entrance into Columbia was a means to an end, not for him of value in and of itself, not even finally a place to learn, but instead a crossroads—similar to the one back in Chimayó where he chose Taos over Pojoaque—valuable in that it freed him from one home he refused to accept as home, and at the same time offered a kind of solace, a transient residence that would shelter him until he could figure out how and where next to go.

For better or worse, the converse was my response to this new life. Though pride forced me to conceal my outlook behind facial expressions that ranged from skepticism to scorn, behind complicities such as —Yeah, this is no good, and —That's terrible, sorry complicities that were nothing short of lies, this life was, for me, radiant and chimeric at the same time, forbidding and spirited, a rich, promising amniotic sea in which I swam with such inner ease that it seemed everything I'd ever done before was preparatory to this moment. And, of course, I wasn't too proud to consider myself something of an intellectual embryo afloat in its albumen, in need of just the right amounts of warmth and time to gestate. I understand that I, too, was impatient in my way, but impatient about different things than Kip. And it wasn't as if paradoxes didn't await me, it wasn't as if the time wouldn't come when I myself considered the idea of a cloistered school with Ivy League pretensions, set apart from the community that surrounds it—as if you could separate culture and research and reflective thinking from the realities of adjacent communities—to be medieval. The difference between my arrival at this idea and Kip's was subtle, but as defining as anything in a dictionary.

As I say, what Kip and I shared was a quick assimilation into city life. However frenzied it could sometimes get, the city seemed familiar, and those first weeks I walked its streets with uncanny dead reckoning. I never felt lost and was often struck by a sense of déjà vu, turning a corner and seeing the facade of a building I could swear I'd seen before, walking along in the upper reaches of Central Park where I'd suddenly be overwhelmed by the odd intimacy of sights—the autumn yellows that were more varied than the llanos of New Mexico, the savannahlike yellow of dried desert grass of home—and sounds—the muffled siren off to the east, the low rumble of the streets. To me, Manhattan was like a well-worn shoe, ugly but honest, forthright about its flaws and beauties. It was comfortable with its premature senescence but at the same time was wired with a wildness and youthful energy. People here had seen and said and risked and done things I couldn't begin to guess at, and as I passed them, my speculative self—inspired by books of my childhood and movies of my adolescence—witnessed a whole new fury. There was an un-scrubbed magic in the air, a dirty charm so different from the thinner, purer air of the Jemez mountains. In comparing my new home to my old, I was as unfair as a man giddy in love with eyes for no one but his new beloved. The sins of the Hill I held tight to my heart, while the sins of the city, sins whose nature and character I didn't yet know, I forgave without question. And while I respected the fact that New York had a claustrophobic and gray, funereal firmness to it, I still came to see the city as beautiful. These were man's mountains that rose to touch the pewter sky and I welcomed the cramped cave in which we lived as much as the soot-caked brick facades out the windows. Bridges with cat-enary lights that spanned rivers wider than I could swim. Planes and jets overhead, subways rumbling below. It was a barrage of discomposure, a garden of exfoliating concrete and granite. Every window that shone with light was but a fragment of colored glass that rewarded those who would look with an endless variety of forms and colors. I was infatuated, smitten.

Kip said, —Just a couple of hicks is what we are here. All we need are cowboy boots with spurs and some Red Man chewing tobacco. We stand out like sore thumbs.

I said, —You're wrong, man, what makes this place so great is that *nobody* stands out here.

—Well, I feel like I look like a sore thumb.

—You shouldn't bother. No one's watching you.

—And you look like a sore thumb, too.

—Will you stop with sore thumbs? It doesn't matter. No-body's watching me, either.

Kip said, —I'm watching you.

I must have given myself away, despite my efforts to erase my joy, because Kip finished with something like —And for godsakes would you wipe that smirk off your face?

—It's not a smirk.

—Whatever it is, get rid of it.

The months flew through toward Christmas, the anniversary of the reconciliation. At break we took the train home, a curiously unmemorable and taciturn trip, watching the provinces flow by out the window. What was going through Kip's mind I could not know, but for my part I was suffering a reverse homesickness of a kind that made me feel less cheerful the more miles the train put between us and New York. Chicago, Denver, on through Santa Fe to the little train station town of Lamy, where all the Manhattan Project people used to arrive and make their jokes like —So *this* is Manhattan? but where we arrived to broad smiles and awkward hugs. The country somehow registered different, more flat and colossal and more tiresome, on the way home to Los Alamos than it had when Kip and I came east just a few months before. I'd begun to feel divided.

Kip, back on the Hill, painted for his parents a far rosier portrait of our accomplishments at college than I would ever have expected. Spirits were already high in town, and everyone was still talking about President Kennedy's visit a couple of weeks earlier. On a clear day, warm enough for the president to ride without his overcoat in the back of a white convertible Lincoln Continental and wave to our townspeople gathered along the streets which had been freshly swept, he was here for a hundred minutes. He inspected a new reactor, which in the newspaper photos resembled nothing more than an overgrown milk can with a diminutive space capsule attached to its top. He drank coffee with the laboratory heads, and it was rumored that he took three teaspoons of sugar and far too much cream. He gave a speech at Topper Field and heard the Los Alamos high school band play. He said, "There is no group of people in this country whose record over the last twenty years has been more preeminent in the service of their country than all of you here in this small community in New Mexico."

During dinner on New Year's Day, our two families gathered around the long table in our house, Kip and I were offered wine to drink from the crystalware stemmed glasses that came out of the cabinet on only the most special occasions, and we were the objects of rousing toasts made by both fathers.

—Columbia's lucky to have them, Mr. Calder enthused, and Kip gave me a good conspiratorial kick under the table, before making a little speech of his own about how we missed everybody back here, and how much at the same time we were learning out there. As our fathers looked on, encouraged by the wine and the fine display of admirable sentiments from my apparently reformed friend, I couldn't help but think how out of it they'd both been, when it came to understanding either me or Kip, how out of it right along, and how, now, they seemed more dazed and distracted than ever. The recognition was at once sad and hilarious. One of the remarks the president had made in his brief speech was how much he admired the kind of schools our parents were running "and the kind of boys and girls that you are bringing up." While it was a fact that in our elementary schools we began to use the typewriter in the second grade, and that by the fifth grade we used adding machines to check our arithmetic answers, there was still no way of typing, calculating, or marshaling our youthful souls. When asked to say a few words myself, I said, —I don't have anything to add.

—He certainly seems to have turned a new leaf, my mother said the next morning. The way she phrased it transformed the statement into a question. I looked at her face in the colorless sunlight that streamed through the windows. Gentle, fine wrinkles about her lips when she drew on her pipe. Her eyes were full of mischief and her comment was like a deep well into which I decided I'd rather not tumble.

—You smoke too much, I said. New leaves, tobacco. Maybe a neat evasion, but not an effective one.

—You think I'm trying to smoke you out, Brice?

I laughed, as best I could. —Kip is working hard, probably's pulling better grades than me.

—Than I, she said.

—Smoke too much, you do, you know.

—You take care of yourself, Brice. I know you find this hard to believe, but there may come a day when you and Kip—

—I am taking care of myself, I said.

—Fair enough, she said.

That was it? That was all? She was something, that morning. Another recognition. She knew that I knew that she knew that . . . and so forth. It was as if she graduated me into adulthood then and there. I remember startling her with a kiss on the cheek. Seldom had I kissed my mother before that moment, being of good Western stock, inhibited unto obtuseness. This Christmas, the shared birthdays, New Year's, were more serene than any other before or after. Not only had Kip and I come into maturity of sorts, but the Hill itself grew up that year when President Kennedy signed into law a bill that permitted the town's residents to buy their own homes. Los Alamos became a part of America, and its townsmen were finally real citizens. No longer a collective of geniuses kept like mistresses, no longer slaves and squatters at Uncle Sam's spread, everyone was finally allowed to possess the roof over his head and the business by which he made his living. It was a watershed year.

*D*ays when I was at classes, into the months of February and March and on toward when the soot-black snow began to melt, Kip continued to wander. I wasn't his keeper, I reminded myself, and so followed my own trajectory. He was the one to bring it up, his new plan for himself. For us, I should say. We were sitting on the steps of Low Library looking out over the sundial to the eight names etched above the colonnade of Butler Library— Homer, Herodotus, Sophocles, Plato, Aristotle, Demosthenes, Cicero, Vergil—which dwarfed us, just as they were supposed to, and I noticed for the first time the shadow over his lip and sweep of whiskers down from the corners of his mouth, which met at the cleft in his chin, forming an heraldic knot, palely dark. His eyes seemed bruised around the rims, deep purple. His hands moved with keen punctuation against the pattern of his words. I was reminded of Fernando Martinez.

—Brice, how're you doing?

What a ridiculous question, I thought. About to answer with something appropriately sarcastic, I opened my mouth, but he spoke first.

—I mean, I know you're doing fine.

—You all right? I looked down at my own narrow clasped hands, saw that my fingers were interlocked back-to-back and thought, I never saw that before. And Kip was speaking.

—What I'm going to do is this, I'm going to stay in school.

I said, —What do you mean? and what I meant was, Of course, well, of course you're going to stay in school because what else is there?

And he said, —During the day that's what I'll do, and at night what I'm going to do is get a job.

—What for?

—For money's what for, what else?

—I know that. What I mean is, what's the money for?

He turned to me on the steps, I can still see his face in the gray penetrating light. —I'm not made for dorms and frats and any of that stuff, Brice. But I'm not going back up to the old Hill either, no way. So what I do is I stay in school for a while, no problem, maybe even all the way to the degree, I can hack it, but I also work, get some money together, see what gives, and go from there. And as soon as the semester's done we move off campus into our own place. What do you think about that?

Triumphant cockeyed smile he gave me.

—Is that allowed? which wiped the smile away.

—First-year students are the only ones who have to live on campus. Get with it. Come May you and I are out of John Jay and into New York.

I say, —Cool, and then I say, —But what about my part of the rent? I mean, I'm willing to do something this summer but next fall—maybe you can do both, but—

—You worry too much. Look, I've already figured that out, too. You just take the money that your parents are spending to put you up in the dorm and give it to me, and I'll take care of the rest.

—All right, why not? I said, and left it there, in all its glory and ambivalence. Any implication that I was supposed to find work, make money, prepare myself for the newest exodus, Kip seemed to have left out of his announcement. I didn't want to think about it, and so I didn't.

That May we looked at apartments, including several as far from campus as Kips Bay—because Kip Calder thought that it was kismet there had been another Kip, Jacobus Kip, who'd lived on the island precisely three centuries before we got here—but finally settled on a fifth-floor walk-up on 115th Street, between Amsterdam and Morningside Drive, in an old building called the Colonial. Railroad apartment with windows on the street and windows in back that overlooked a courtyard. Ginkgo trees and ailanthus, and next door a city garden in a vacant lot, where the superintendent planted roses and hostas. A red-brick tenement across the street, and down at the corner was St. Luke's Hospital. For a hundred and thirteen dollars a month we had two bedrooms, a kitchen, bath, and common room, not to mention odd-sized alcoves here and there. Former tenants had left behind several pieces of furniture, nothing pleasing to look at, nothing comfortable to sit on or lie in, just the castoffs of transient occupants. We moved in, and Kip seemed to come to life again. No objections were raised back home about our decision—more and more I began to recognize how calculated Kip had been back at Christmastime, preparing the way for our defection from John Jay, its wainscots and the elegant sociability of its dining hall, not to mention its rules and regulations. We were, for a time, on top of the world.

His first job seemed promising, if only because he landed it so quickly. Nights after work it was like we were children again. The lock would turn over and Kip would come in well past midnight. I would be awake still, reading—bless my tractable heart—waiting up for him, and he would appear exhausted and reek of garlic and tomato sauce but have about him a determined air, and would spread his tip money—bills, crumpled and damp—on the floor in the common room. Then together we'd kneel over the array of green laid out in optimistic fans before us, and worshipfully count.

—Five, five singles, six, seven singles, and a fin makes twelve.

We were just kids, I remembered, the last time we counted money. —Not bad, I said.

—I've got wage coming on top of that. What'd I tell you. We'll be living like kings in no time.

—We're doing all right, I said.

—You call this living? This is a dump, Brice. I'm going to get us out of here.

—But we just moved in.

I don't remember what I did that summer. I was trying to figure out how to grow up. So was Kip. He became devoted to the idea that he and I deserved to live extravagantly, richly, in luxury. And when the semester began in September he led a double life, fueled by his conviction that we should share a place high above Central Park, overlooking the lights of the city, behaving like princes, a dynasty of two. Sometimes he told me that our delivery into affluence was just around the corner, other times he was despondent and told me all his dreams were either daydreams or pipe dreams and that I might be wiser to hitch my fate to another star. I wasn't offended by his pushiness. This was vintage Kip. Rampant enthusiasm or black silence was what I came to expect from him during those days, nothing in between.

We kept going. We both worked hard in our different ways. He worked days, worked nights. I don't know how he managed. We'd read our way through Western Civilization during our first year, Plato, Aristotle, Aquinas, Locke, the required classics, and had felt the same intimidation as our classmates, buried under the course load, worried about deadlines and writing papers, pulling all-nighters and discovering what five, six, seven cups of coffee can do to your mind and stomach. *The Iliad*, the Roman Empire, the Goths, Genghis Khan, epics of discord, governments lusting to rule the world, nethermen long gone to their graves—we were learning about wars other than the great one of our parents, and for the first time in my life I'd begun to see that the world was history, not just the dead and gone world of centuries past, but the world our mothers and fathers had lived in and shaped, and our own world, this very one we were breathing in now, it was history too. I can remember one night walking across campus, having read about Plato's cave, and looking up at the moon, which often you couldn't see well because of all the ambient light cast upward by the city, but which happened to be clear and full, and I remember thinking, My god, Plato looked at that same moon. And Euripides and Sophocles. It was such a revelation for me. And now, during this second year, I told myself I was going to learn everything I could. Not because I wanted to be a good boy, or get good grades. How can it be admitted in a way that doesn't sound maudlin? I simply wanted to *know*. I took courses in anthropology, economics, nineteenth-century American history. I sensed everything was valuable, and in anticipation of classes that weren't even offered to us, I began doing my own sort of extracurricular work, reading political science texts.

Maybe it was gradual, maybe sudden—it was probably convulsive in the sense that the process went in fits and starts, but we began to shed our immaturities. Like sandstone riffled by water, or flint chipped into an arrowhead or a thumbknife, Kip and I were being honed. We couldn't help it and wouldn't necessarily have wanted to stop the process even if we were able to see it shaping us. The Hill had been so abundantly secluded that it should come as no surprise we were susceptible. At the same time, it had been home to so many sophisticated minds, fine intellects, and the hardness, the severity of the high desert, coupled with these learned presences, made for a hardness that we inherited and, so, possessed ourselves. Flint, sandstone, these seem perfect analogues. Hard but soft. Soft but hard. Hard enough to hold shape, soft enough to change it. Few children have the smarts to cherish the hideaway that's home. Kip and I took every possible advantage of the splendid isolation that was ours, but the big bad world beyond the gate was what we always wanted.

One day Kip found me reading von Clausewitz's massive book on the nature of war.

—What's that for? he asked.

—It's a book. You know, they have words, you read them?

—Smartass, he said. —I mean what class?

—It's not for a class, it's just for myself.

—You're reading *that* for yourself?

—So what?

—Sometimes I just don't get you, boy.

It wasn't that I was reading outside the curriculum, but rather that Kip scoffed at anything that hinted of sociology or political science.

—Sociology is the study of the murdered and political science is the study of murderers, he said. —Knowing these people's names and their birthdates and when they kicked the can, and reading all their drivel is not going to change the behavior of one politician, one soldier, one goddamn anybody. Men fight, Brice. It's what they do. They need to step on one another's heads. They need to blow each other's brains out. You should know this by now. It gives pleasure and, besides, it's genetic. It's in the blood. You eat meat, don't you?

—What does that have to do with anything?

—That meat we ate for dinner last night was from a cow that was at war with men, and the cow lost, and you ate it. There's microbes locked in mortal combat inside your body even as we speak.

—I can't believe what I'm hearing here.

—You know how you always wanted to get away from the Hill because the Hill was a place of war?

—We both did.

Kip ignored me, went on with —Well, do you know where you're living now?

I said nothing. I didn't know.

—You're living in Morningside Heights. It has a pretty name. But you know what it is? Just another hill where they fought another battle. Washington fought right down there, right down in the street there before anybody ever thought about paving it and building buildings here.

From one war hill to another? I must have looked as if I'd seen a ghost.

—Brice, I'm not saying I like it. I'm just saying it is a fact of life and I'm coming to realize it, and I think you should, too, boy.

I argued, —Facts of life can be changed. Polio used to be a fact of life and they found a vaccine for the virus and now it is not a fact of life anymore.

—You're just proving my point. The virus fought a war and it lost, for the time being, anyway. Some things live in harmony, don't get me wrong. And other things don't. All I'm saying is that sitting around in an ivory tower, or an Ivy League tower, reading this philosopher and that theoretician ain't gonna change those basic facts.

Kip went on to do something else, whatever it might have been, and refused to acknowledge my backhanded compliment, —You're pretty smart, boy.

In a sentimental mood I might conjure the church in Chimayó and thank its god, from time to time, for how well everything was going. No matter whether I fathomed him or not, I liked Kip. He hadn't seen that I was infinitely his inferior—this was what I believed—and for that I could thank heaven, because whether I liked it or not, I was so deeply attached to him that my life seemed to depend on it. Was this the way friends were supposed to feel? I didn't know.

What I did know was that I hoped things would stay just as

they were and was grateful for what I had. But gods don't always respect gratitude. Impaired by infinite age and the lassitude that must result from attending too many grievous confessions, too many greedy requests (—Oh please, God, sir, if I do *this* will you let me have *that*), not to mention a surfeit of gushy and misguided thanks—not unlike my own—they simply don't have the holy stomach for it after a while. And for those who do, nowhere is it written they must always be grateful in turn for our gratitude. Even the lowest of the household gods, as Homer made clear and Ovid later concurred, did whatever they damn well pleased and no amount of supplication was going to alter their behavior. Kip's job lasted not quite through October before he quit or was fired, I couldn't decide which. The way he told the story, it sounded as if both happened with raw, spontaneous simultaneity. And so the thanks to heaven from a budding agnostic and even sometime atheist were premature.

—Didn't belong there anyway, Kip said.

—I thought you were doing great.

—You thought wrong.

—Why didn't you tell me?

—It's my problem, not yours. That's why.

I said, —But I thought we were partners in everything. You got problems, man, you tell me about it.

He shrugged and produced, from the depths of his jacket, a bottle of whiskey, —This is compliments of my former boss. I consider it severance pay.

—Remember the last time we shanghaied one of those?

Kip didn't accept my invitation to reminiscence. We were both dejected, but he seemed out-and-out defeated. High to low, very high to very low. Yesterday he was clear-minded and strong and content. Now he was dark and frail.

He peeled the paper off the cap and uncorked the whiskey. He drank, coughed. Looked old. But edgy still. All nerves. He held out the bottle to me.

—Hold on, I said, and got glasses from the kitchen.

—You're right, he said. —Dignity in dire straits.

—Our straits aren't that dire, I said, and proposed a toast, —Here's to new beginnings.

He didn't lift his glass, nor did he lift his eyes, which were trained on his one finger that lightly drew a circle over and over around the glass lip.

—That's redundant.

—What?

—New beginnings. It's redundant. It's like saying great big, great and big mean the same thing. Beginnings are always new and something new is always a beginning.

—No wonder you got fired.

—It's called a tautology.

—You make the goddamn toast then.

He thought about it for a moment, then lifted his glass to mine, and said, —Confusion to the enemy.

*O*towi bridge. And running beneath it, muddy as ever, the Rio Grande. Here is where they all crossed to go up to the Hill, before I was born. Kip's father and mother, mine. Like the Rubicon, once crossed you can never really turn back. Or like the Lethe which, once drunk from, makes your memory dissolve and reduces you to a person without a history or a future. But then they did come back down from the Hill and crossed the Rio Grande again, my father and Kip's and the rest of them, bringing with them their contrivance, their machine.

When the bomb was detonated down at Alamogordo, residents

for hundreds of miles around knew something extraordinary had happened. Light was seen in El Paso. A blazing flash was reported in Santa Fe. Windows rattled in their frames as far away as Gallup and Silver City. Men who were part of the Project watched from arroyos and slit trenches. Up on Compañia Hill some twenty miles away, where some of the scientists had applied sunburn lotion to their faces in the predawn dark, they saw it, and they could see it from San Antonio and from up on Chupadero Peak. Wives, too, who waited on Sawyer's Hill behind Los Alamos could see the flash and hear the rumble. A group of guards assigned to Mockingbird Gap near Little Burro lay face down with their feet pointed toward Ground Zero, and were ordered, after the first flash, to turn and watch through an oblong chunk of welder's glass the natural and unnatural disasters that ensued. On short-wave radio, by chance, the Voice of America played the "Star-Spangled Banner" just before the detonation. It was one of the greatest moments in history, great as in *of unsurpassing enormity and consequence*—some would say that what occurred that morning at Alamogordo was *the* greatest moment in history. The discovery of the wheel, of fire, of electricity—these were pale by comparison. It was the birth of a new religion, one in which the end of the world might be near but no repentance would provide for salvation. My father was there, near Carrizozo. Mother keeps the four-leaf clover he carried in his wallet that morning, pressed between sheets of waxed paper in the pages of her Bible. It was Robert Oppenheimer who gave the test its name of Trinity, and Oppenheimer who said later that what came to mind, as marl and hills were bathed in seething brilliance and the purple radioactive glowing cloud hung there over the desert, was a phrase from Hindu scripture, from a scene in the Bhagavad Gita. Vishnu, hoping to motivate the Prince to behave dutifully, takes on his thousand-armed form and says, "I am become Death, the destroyer of worlds." Many of its makers would later memorably describe what they witnessed as the convection stem of dust chased the final cloud of smoke toward the morning star. But a man named Kenneth Bainbridge, the director of Trinity, made what is to me the most indelible and peculiarly dignified comment of the day. To Oppenheimer, after congratulating everyone in the control bunker, he said, —Now we are all sons of bitches.

Winding my way up the canyon, I admire the majesty and luminousness of the cliffs, Otowi ruins with their gray sagebrush beard across the canyon from the overlook, the many different shades of brown and white and reds of the rocks that look like vertebrae, and now I begin to notice them, the roads—here and there, which trail off from the highway—gated at their discreet entrances, with small signs warning the potential trespasser away. And then I see them, hidden or not, on mesa edges—the pastel green buildings, the labs with their supercomputers and linear accelerators, the Tech buildings, off to the right, protected by the dry moats of the deep ravines. The clusters of buildings, gray-blues and earthen reds and tans, the glistening satellite dishes and radar installations pointed to the mute blue sky, the ganglia of electrical wires, the storage tanks, the nameless and faceless buildings behind lengths and widths of fences with concertina wire curling along the crests, way over there.

I breathe in deep and think, Bainbridge was right. Sons of bitches one and all.

Autumn began, autumn passed, and winter began, 1963 into 1964. The president was assassinated. My mother telephoned me with the news. She was crying and then I was crying, too. Kip said, —What's going on? and I said, —Kennedy's dead, and I could hear my mother's set on in the background, and said good-bye to her and got off and Kip and I ran from the apartment over to campus where it seemed we lived for the next few days, dazed and worried about the future, worried without really knowing what this meant, watching television in a student lounge with other students. The funeral stands in my memory more than the arrest of Oswald, his murder by Jack Ruby, or any of the other events that unfolded from the assassination. The caisson in the funeral, the cadence of the drums and sad clop of the horse's hooves that drew the stern narrow wagon laden with its simple casket draped in the flag along the avenues of Washington, the leaders of the world who walked behind the cortège in procession, the widow and the two children, the president's son with his small flag not quite sure of what was going on. For an event that had such impact on us all it was surely unreal, these black-and-white images on the screen, the hushed voices of the television commentators. It was pivotal. It was the true beginning of the sixties. Kip, I, everyone was in shock.

After black November there was a drifting that occurred in our lives, Kip's and mine. Nothing happened, everything happened or began to happen.

Unravelings, words, small occasions that seemed important and important ones that seemed insignificant.

I came home one afternoon, and he was sitting on the floor of our little common room carpeted with some material whose color it would be impossible to describe, varied between yellow and gray, but seemed to have been a lima-bean green once. Beside him was a bottle. He had been reading, but the moment I walked in he shut the book quickly and sat on it so that I couldn't see what it was.

The weights and balances of our friendship were in new throes of change. He never had the same nervous system as I. This was something I was coming to learn. He must have felt the imbalances between us. As I became more focused, he seemed distracted, but in an indescribably calculated way.

At night I had work to do, reading and taking too many notes, underlining too many passages. He'd always been reclusive, even antisocial. The year before, during dining hour back in John Jay I would sit and talk with fellow dorm residents; I would say hello to hallmates when I passed them, and though I couldn't be called outgoing, I at least tried to make the acquaintance of various fellow students. Kip forbore such behavior. But now he seemed withdrawn beyond even that. He went out, keeping the same hours he had for those precious weeks when he was working and everything was so promising. Most of the time, I had gone to bed before he returned. It was as if he had begun to evaporate somehow. He seemed never to sleep. It was like he'd become a cat with a raven-black cat soul, one that might pride itself upon crossing your path in an alley. Or an owl, similarly wise and dangerous in the dark.

—What'd you do last night? I asked.

—Nothing.

—But like what?

—Like what? Kip glanced over my head.

—Yeah, like what.

—Like nothing is like what.

I interpreted his expression to mean, Who do you think you are, my father? So I left off, saying, —Never mind.

—Just walked around, he said, after a few minutes. Yes, so catlike, owlish, aggressive and passive, hostile and amicable by turns. —Is that all right with you, Brice?

Maybe it is true that I was becoming angry, finally, despite my admiration for my friend. Under my collegian bustle I thought I'd shrouded it well and that it was hidden, too, by the simple distance our odd, uncoincidental hours created. I was mistaken. Kip knew me as well as I knew him, and his response to my silent anger was going to be anger of a different sort.

—Well, boy? he said again. —Is that okay?

I looked out the filthy window of the room, stared at the vines climbing the brick wall of the building opposite. I felt exhaustion in my head, my back, my joints. Kip wanted to wrangle.

—You be willing to share some of that?

He lifted the bottle in my direction. I pulled it up to my lips, its glass knocked against my teeth, then, drank a little, it tasted terrible, carried it over to the corner where there was a sink, some cupboards, rattling refrigerator, old stove next to our doorless bathroom. Like some prude I began to pour whiskey down the drain.

—What the hell? and he was on me quicker and with more urgency than I'd thought possible, seemed to have sobered up in an instant, at least long enough to stop me. More agile, and much stronger than I, Kip got the bottle away from me after the briefest tussle. He was yelling and so was I. This was a new one. He tore the top two buttons off my shirt when he yanked at me from behind. I saw that when I'd struck out at him I'd managed to produce a pink streak down the left side of his forehead. He threw on his coat, had the bottle clutched with one hand under it, strode past me through the common room, his face crimson, lips white, angrier than I'd ever seen him, and I stood there helpless as I watched him open the door, but managed to get out the words, —Don't you ever call me boy again, you hear me, man? before he turned, said, —I'll never call you anything again, you little bastard, before slamming the door. Our apartment had always seemed so vulnerable to noise, to the city's various voices that chose to creep in through every crevice, funnel up through the floorboards and into the plaster and rugs, glass and air, but for the next hours and days it would seem more impregnable and silent than was conceivable.

I picked up the book Kip had been reading. Thoreau's *Walden*. Why had he hid it from me? What a grand gesture for a small cause, I thought. But then I remembered that when I'd read it a few months earlier I'd carried on about how interesting cranky old man Henry David Thoreau was with his monk's shack and his crop of beans and his endless disdain for the idiotic concessions his fellow man would make in the pursuit of false comforts. He had attitude, the right stuff, like a nineteenth-century beatnik. I guess Kip hadn't wanted me to see that he could learn things from me. I was swept up in sadness that afternoon. Thoreau's best friend, Emerson, wrote in an essay that goodness had to have an edge to it, but I'm sure his own edge was never so sharp as to stab. Looking into my copy of Emerson's essays that same night—funny, Kip had Thoreau and I Emerson, but I guess it makes a kind of sense—I discovered a passage I hadn't read before: "I do not wish to treat friendships daintily, but with roughest courage. When they are real, they are not glass threads or frost-work, but the solidest thing we know."

He came back, of course, but only after allowing me to brood for half the week. He just showed up. Acted as if nothing whatever out of the ordinary had transpired. He carried a crisp brown paper sack under one arm and opened the door of the refrigerator, crouched, sniffed, said, —Jesus god, something in here's died some awful death, rummaged around until he found the offending source, an orange blotched deep green with mold, removed it, and proceeded to empty the paper bag of its contents, bottle of fresh milk, can of coffee, packet of bologna, mustard, chocolate bars. I believe he muttered, —Goodnight, before heading to his room where he lay on his bed and fell into a heavy sleep. He hadn't looked me in the eye, though if he had, I wouldn't have known, since I wasn't able to look him in the eye, either. He didn't seem to notice that his *Walden* was there on the floor in the middle of the room, right where he'd left it. The book disappeared next day and, just as I'd never seen it before, I never saw it again.

The week after that, Kip joined ROTC—the corps that had its office in Hamilton Hall, officers' training corps—just at the time when I had befriended some fellow classmen who were the precursors to the Students for a Democratic Society, and one of whom, a kid named Epstein, had persuaded me to consider coming to some of their meetings, hearing what they had to say, learning a little about the lies that are used, as he put it, to glue together the fabric of our society as it exists now. Epstein was my guide into this new world, and I was tentative about it because while I did have strong beliefs about the valuelessness and dishonor of war, I didn't yet have whatever it took—nerve? strength of will? courage?—to make a commitment. And commitment, said Epstein, was all that mattered. Commitment was consequence in and of itself.

—Make the commitment and already you will have changed the world a little bit, he told me, and I felt myself being drawn in to this idea. Epstein said, —Everything else is bullshit.

Kip's uniform lay on his bed and the manual was on our kitchen counter. Kip had set them there, I am sure, in part for himself and in part for me. I responded, as he'd have predicted.

—Rotsy? I said. —Are you kidding me?

Kip was curt with his response, —Tell you what. I'll do what I want to do, you do what suits you. Let's don't talk about it.

—Rotsy, I said. —I don't believe it.

—You hear me?

—What?

—Did you hear what I said?

—I heard you, Kip. I heard you.

Commitments were now being made. The drifting was over.

Dusty millers, petunias, and geraniums in a pot on the porch. The pot is one of the same pots that stood on the porch of the old Sundt house where we grew up. Extraordinary that it escaped destruction all these years—the pot, I mean, for the Sundts have all but one been demolished. Yet this nondescript clay pot endures. Leave it to Bonnie. Nothing new under her sun. Not if she can help it.

This is why my sister possesses the capacity to strike terror in me, I think. It is because rather than leaving, she accepted and accepted again. Then, after she was done accepting she began the process of preserving. The flowers my mother raised are those you would find in Bonnie Jean's garden. The afghan coverlet in septagonals of different colored yarns that her mother used to crochet while outside the snow fell and frost made ice ferns on the windowpanes, this was just the selfsame afghan my sister in the winter would make to spread on her children's bed. The chicken and dumplings, the mincemeat pie, the ham loaf prepared from Mrs. Norris Bradbury's recipe, with bread crumbs and brown sugar, cloves and apricot halves, she probably served to her family with the same bit of doggerel verse our mother used to recite when serving it to us—

> Some hae meat and canna' eat,
> And some wad eat that want it,
> But we hae meat and we can eat,
> And sae the Lord be thankit.

Like mother like daughter, it was uncanny how perfectly Bonnie imitated with the slightest will to *emulate* so many of our mother's tastes, her choices, her way of doing things. As I got out of the car and strode up the walk to her front porch, pushing my hands down into my pockets and then pulling them out again, I wondered whether she'd be smoking a white clay pipe and sipping a glass of straight gin.

One of my nephews stood at the screen door. Which one is he? I wondered. Their names are what?—I should have planned this with a little more care. Charlie and Sam, but which one's the younger? Shall I make a guess? Shall I really say, Hey, nephew—it's your uncle Brice? and hope for the best? I could run back to the car and be gone before he even knew what happened.

"Mom, there's somebody at the door," he announces, and saves me from either dubious choice.

"Bonnie?" I call into the darkened house through the screen.

I hear nothing, then I hear her say, "Ask what he wants, Sam."

"What do you want, mister?"

"Sam, don't you recognize your uncle Brice?"

My nephew looks me up and down. He has quite the crop of acne, doesn't he, I think. Must come from Charlie Sr.'s side of the family. We were always dry-faced and dry-footed. Eczema and cracked calluses were more our problem. How old is this child? I wonder, and calculate. Ten, eleven.

"Who is it, Sam?" Bonnie Jean calls again from another room.

"He says he's my uncle."

More silence. I smile at the boy who doesn't smile back.

"Well, tell him to hold on a minute, I'll be right there."

"Hold on a minute—"

"—she'll be right here," I say.

The boy stares at me without moving, then says, "You really my uncle?"

"Why would I pull your leg about something like that. Sure I'm your uncle. I brought you a present to prove it."

He brightens some. "What present?"

"It's in my car."

He opens the screen door and comes outside. "Let's see."

Where is my sister? I wonder. "All right, come on."

We walk to the car and I produce a Yankees baseball cap for him. "Thanks," he says and tramps toward the house.

"Hey, wait, aren't you going to try it on?"

"Okay," he says.

The cap is far too big for his head. I have another, a Mets cap, for his brother, Charlie Jr. I'd bought them both on a last-minute impulse at La Guardia, and now I'm glad I did.

"You'll grow into it, if you eat your greens," I say.

"What are my greens?" he asks.

"You know, like collard, kale, spinach."

I'm speaking in the singsong voice of an uncle. He doesn't know what I am talking about and stares at me with an open mouth.

"You know, like salad, lettuce?"

"I hate salad. You know what?"

Despite myself I look heavenward, close my eyes, say "What?"

"If I put this hat in really hot water it'll shrink and then I can wear it right now."

"You're sure that won't wreck it?"

"Yes," says he, turning his hat in his hands round and round, picturing it—I assume—the perfect size.

Then Bonnie finally emerges onto her porch.

*T*he day Kip brought Jessica Rankin over was the most momentous since our flight to Chimayó. Yet for all the consequences of her entry into our lives, and for everything we would come to mean to her, the occasion didn't seem so laden with possibilities at the time. After all, by that April—April 1965—we had been gone from Los Alamos through nearly three-quarters of our tenure at the university, and Jessica was by no means the first girl Kip had brought around. Some had been more suited to him, some less, some lasted weeks, some only a night, and I'd watched not without awe how he attracted them. A waitress, an aspiring actress, a teaching assistant. His reclusive days were over.

—You're like catnip, I said once. He didn't react to the little provocation, other than to raise an eyebrow, which notified me to keep my opinion to myself. But I couldn't resist, and a few weeks later said it again, —Just like catnip to kittens.

To which he did respond by saying, —Listen, you nun you, you lily white wimple. If you want to be purer than the blessed virgin, go right ahead, but don't be jealous of those of us who aspire to be fallen angels.

—If you'd stop flapping your wings in my face maybe I could see the light, I answered.

That April day, Kip came in, cheeks aglow, eyes alight. One glance at him and I knew he was in love with this girl who was holding his hand, a little awkwardly, at his side.

No, I withdraw the notion that the encounter wasn't fraught with potential. I knew at once that something was different, why pretend otherwise? Kip's smile was irrepressible, hers more demure but, for lack of a better image, very much alive. My mother would have said, had she seen them, that they looked sweet. She would not have been wrong. Beatific would be more like it. They looked beatific, and I looked out the window. What I saw framed there, above the vined building across the street, was a dying day, white sky, neither cold nor warming, neither wintry nor quite yet spring. A precarious, equivocal day. This was the time of year people fell in love, I supposed, but maybe the reason the meeting didn't seem too significant was because like a child I refused to admit to myself the quality of emotions I saw revealed in Kip that day. There was nothing equivocal about him. He was transformed in her presence.

—Brice, this is Jessica.

—Hello, she said, and shook my hand, a notably firm grasp.

—Hello, Jessica.

—Jess is fine, she said. She glanced at Kip. How her eyes shined.

—Jess, I said, mesmerized, and looked to Kip myself, neither smiling nor seeing him but trying to remember something, I wasn't sure what, something about her that struck me as familiar beyond her more than passing resemblance to Kip. I thought, God I know this person from somewhere.

Kip broke the lull, —And Jess? For better or worse this is Brice.

Again I brought myself to look at her. She was more worldly than we, I thought, and it was true she looked like Kip. Those wide-set eyes they shared, their depth and darkness and waxmoon shape, invited the admirer in, as I have said, drew him down, captured him in a way. Before I knew what I was doing, the words came out of my mouth, accompanied by a cough, —Do we know each other?

—I'm sorry?

Embarrassed and reddening, —No, I mean—you—

I didn't continue.

Kip left Jessica's side, threw his arm around me, —Don't worry about Brice. He means well. It's just sometimes he loses track of his manners.

—Kip's said a lot about you, Jessica recommenced, and the spell, or whatever it was, broke so that now I recognized I had probably never seen Jessica Rankin before.

—That's good. I guess.

—All good, she said.

—Don't worry, Kip laughed. —I made a few revisions.

She was dressed in a plaid shirt, baggy black corduroys, and though I have no idea what she was wearing on her feet it would be a safe guess they were clogs rather than sandals. Black clogs, with low heel, and worn in well from the first day when she walked them through the Rijks Museum in Amsterdam and along the canals there during a yearlong ramble over Europe and North Africa, by herself most of the way, a free spirit, the year before. Jessica even then was one to affirm her confidence with the resonant tap of a wooden heel. Her hair—a jostle of deep brown, with strands of auburn and premature silvers—was parted on the side, a furrow the work of a meticulous combing that belied her otherwise hearty air of unkempt defiance, and came down in bunches, graceful wild augers and coils, like a thatching. She wore several rings, which set off her fingers, which were long and strong, and on her wrists were bright bracelets of thirties bakelite, which clattered when she gestured. Her eyes were, as I say, the most dark olive brown; astute—quick but not quicksilver. Strong, clear forehead, taut but fluid skin across it and her nose, which was prominent and straight as a ruler. Wide cheeks, the narrow hips of a boy. But not a willowy woman, rather an outright presence.

She was someone to reckon with, it was clear at once. As we used to say, and sometimes still do, she occupied her space. There was a calm to her, a powerful reserve. She didn't trade in airs. Jessica insists to this day she was "almost a virgin" when I met her (what happened to her in Tangiers —Hardly counted because it barely mattered, she maintained) and that I am the third of the three men she's ever been with, but I, wary, stubborn I, used to presume there must have been others. I presumed wrong, I've come now to think. And I never succeeded in getting her to tell me the story of her Moroccan romance. Maybe one day. She is not, as a rule, a withholder of details.

—Wait till you see what we've got, said Kip, lifting high a large heavy white bag, then holding it out to me.

—Where's the kitchen? Jessica asked, at the same time that I opened the bag to see dozens of fresh mussels.

—In here, such as it is.

She rolled up her sleeves, found a big aluminum pot left by a prior tenant in one of the lower cupboards, and soon enough the scents of butter, garlic, white wine, and the salty sea-smell of steamed mussels filled the apartment. It was a feast.

We talked, the three of us, into the night, our conversation punctuated by the clatter of black shells dropping into a bowl. Kip drifted in and out of a kind of proprietorship, as I understood it, manifest by the hand on her shoulder, the many smiles, complemented by moments in which he'd jump up, midthought or midsentence, and still thinking or talking, leave the room to get more bread or a bottle of wine from the refrigerator, leave us sitting there until he burst in once more picking up where he'd left off, or where we'd proceeded. Was that a warning, that look he'd give me? Instinct proposed that his little moves were made more for my benefit than Jessica's. That was fine by me. She was interesting but didn't interest me, I told myself at the time, and still seem to want to—that is with regard to our first encounter

—though subsequent events would come to contradict any claim of indifference on my part, or intimidation on his.

We talked about music. We talked about school—Jessica was two years older than we, had graduated from Barnard with a degree in biology and resolved not to go on to graduate school as her parents hoped, hitched overseas, and returned broke to the Upper West Side until her next direction showed itself. We talked about poverty, our own but more the ghetto poverty of others. Though now, as she put it, she checked coats at a restaurant for the rich, she hoped one day to be able somehow to provide them for the poor. She, too, was an idealist, I remember thinking. After all, surely she hadn't paid for the mussels and wine any more than she had for the food her employers provided, anonymously and in ignorance, to a neighborhood shelter where on weekends Jessica worked as a volunteer.

Inevitably, as the wine bottles emptied, we talked about Vietnam and the unrest it was beginning to cause on campus.

By that spring the war was developing into an obsession of mine, one that would join, if not replace, my passion against the bomb. Kip had learned to hate it when I brought up Vietnam, much as Bonnie Jean had fled the room when I carried on about nuclear weapons. He even shocked me, some months before this introduction to Jessica, by saying, —World War Two was what brought us together, are you gonna let Vietnam pull us apart?

—Listen, I already know you're for Vietnam—

—I don't know enough about it to be for or against it, and neither do you.

—If you were against it, you wouldn't be doing those ridiculous drills with all your rotsy friends.

—They're not friends. And stop calling it rotsy.

—You bet they're not friends, man. They're the enemy.

—And so am I, is that what you're saying?

—I don't know what I'm saying.

—If you don't know what you're saying, why are you talking?

All this was the result of my urging Kip to sign a petition that was being circulated by several professors—Dean, Kahn, and Martin—which called for a "stop to the bombings" and for the parties to begin "work toward a negotiated settlement."

—I'm not going to be kahned by Dean Martin, he laughed.

I had already showed the temerity of signing, with a hundred and fifty other students, a telegram of sympathy to Ho Chi Minh: WE ARE AMERICANS WHO ARE DEEPLY OPPOSED TO THE UNITED STATES BOMBING RAIDS AGAINST THE PEOPLE OF THE DRV. WE ARE DOING WHAT WE CAN TO STOP THESE BARBAROUS ATTACKS. YOU HAVE OUR RESPECT AND SYMPATHY.

Kip said, —As if Ho Chi Minh is actually going to sit down and read a telegram from a bunch of college kids.

Whether it had to do with my father's role at Los Alamos or not, whether I would have arrived at these same convictions about Vietnam even if he'd not learned here at Columbia—over in Pupin Hall, where Fermi had gotten the football players to stack graphite columns, where Segrè, Rabi, and others had worked before joining the Manhattan Project—what he would later use in Los Alamos to make his contribution to the military industrial complex, I can't be sure about to this day. Either way, I was getting into it deeper and deeper. I'd attended a teach-in at the McMillin Theatre in the basement of Dodge Hall, eight hours of speeches, over a hundred faculty members there, from midnight until morning, a gathering sponsored by the Ad Hoc Teaching Committee on Vietnam, and whatever Kip said to the contrary I was beginning to know enough to be not just against the war but adamant in my horror of what we were getting ourselves into there.

That night, when the subject came around, I remember that Kip and I fell into debate in front of Jessica.

—Advisors? those weren't advisors, I said.

—Of course they were advisors, Kip disagreed.

—They weren't any more advisors then than what we're dropping now on the Ho Chi Minh Trail are water balloons filled with eau de cologne.

—All right, so what were they?

—What they were was scouts. Like outriders not much different from what the cavalry sends out in a bad cowboy movie, and all they were there to do was get the lowdown on the situation so the Pentagon would know how many troops to deploy.

—He's starting to sound like a broken record, Kip assured Jessica.

—When people can't hear you, you have to repeat what you've said. It's only polite, I retorted.

—Tedium unto death!

But, in fact, Jessica seemed to agree with me about the mistakes Kennedy had made committing so many so-called advisors to the conflict.

—It's a civil war. We don't have any right to be poking our imperialist noses in there.

Kip scoffed, both at the meaning of my rhetoric, and at the rhetoric itself. —Listen to you, Brice. "Imperialist noses"? Come on. Anyway, it's less a civil war than an ideological war, Communism against democracy.

Jessica said, —It's both civil and ideological. I think Brice is right, it's terrible and we don't belong there.

—Oh no, not you too.

By then I would be deep into a monologue, thoughtful if humorless. —We should have let the French fix it if it needed fixing. They were the ones who were in there profiting right along from confusion and colonialism. What use is it to us even if we do get South Vietnam under control?

—It would halt the spread of Communism, which is looking to me more and more like the same virus we had to fight against twenty years ago. You of all people don't want to see it build to that, do you, Brice? Nuclear deterrence becomes nuclear holocaust when local wars get out of hand. Am I wrong?

—I don't think it will ever come to that.

—Haven't you ever heard of the domino theory?

—That domino business is for the birds, cultures don't behave like little flat black blocks lined up in a row and toppled one against the next. Leave it to a war hero to come up with such an arrogant idea. Dear Dwight Eisenhower, screw *you*. Yours sincerely, Brice. I mean, the contempt, the kind of ridiculous superiority it takes to compare societies of human beings—people, man, *people*—with dominoes. Listen, Kip, we're the ones with dominoes clattering around in our heads, thinking that these people are yellow, rice-fed weaklings who are going to fall to Communism a country at a time, like mindless blocks of wood.

I have forgotten how the quarrel ended that night. Likely, I shrugged my shoulders and went off to bed feeling ashamed at my vehemence. On other nights the debate went on until it devolved into shouting, or simply wore itself out and meandered into silence. Though around Jessica he remained at least somewhat aloof, Kip could be brutal, especially when cornered. He might curse, he might sneer, but either way he would do everything possible to offset, if not invalidate, my rhetorical victory. He would suddenly become silent. Eyes rolled back under their lids, his tongue out and head fallen on his shoulders as—one hand grasping an invisible rope over his head—his whole body lifted, he bore himself upward by the invisible noose around his neck. The pantomime of self-hanging. Then would come forth a slow laugh.

—You win, Brice, you win, he would say. And I'd know I had lost. This mime of his never failed to invoke my deep defensiveness with regard to all things Kip. He knew me too well. No one, I expect, will ever know me better. But, of course, being known by another human leaves one open to incursion, to cast it in military parlance. Being known is being witnessed is being exposed is being made vulnerable is being placed in danger.

I can appreciate Kip's impatience. —Brice, he said, one night after the three of us had eaten dinner together and Jessica had gone home, —Brice, you've got to stop this harping about Vietnam. I want to talk about love, you want to talk war all the time.

—Get off it. If you want to talk about love, maybe it's better you talk about it without me around.

—Good idea.

—How come you're always inviting me, anyway?

—Fair enough question.

—I mean, seriously.

—Because you're lonely and love is compassionate. This was a form of the peppers game, I had come to understand.

—Kip, seriously, just leave me out of it from now on.

—Hey look, Brice. For some reason, don't ask me why, Jessie likes you.

When Jessica wasn't around, Kip and I indulged ourselves in talk, at length and in as much depth as we could manage, about her. Who we thought she reminded us of from back home, what we thought she loved about Kip and what she didn't, what her parents must be like, and so on. Who was Jessica Rankin?

She was from Ohio, a small town called Irondale, rustic little

town in a rustic little county, as she put it: —Rusty little Irondale's up above Steubenville, down below Canton, left of Pitts-
burgh, and pretty far to the right of just about everywhere else.

—Couldn't be farther to the right than Los Alamos, Kip
contended.

—He's got you there, I said.

—Still and all, it doesn't get much more mainstream than
good old Irondale. We Rankins were considered exotic because
my father was half-Sioux and even had a touch of Jewish blood
in his veins where everybody else in town was Irish and
Scottish—McEllerys and Crabbs, Barnhills and Scroggs, McYeas
and McNays. My mother and father were Catholics and still are
and ever shall be, world without end, Amen.

I looked at Kip and half-smiled. I liked his new girlfriend.

—Apple pie was invented in Irondale. I'll bet you didn't know
that, did you?

—Now hold on a minute, I said. —*Our* mothers invented
apple pie, not yours.

—Fireworks for the Fourth of July maybe, I'll give you the
benefit of the doubt on fireworks, but not apple pie. Apple pie is
from Ohio.

The better I got to know her the more I realized what I liked
about her was a simplicity, keenly Midwestern, that was and remains cut, or complemented, by a kind of hardness, complex and
finally undefinable. It's this odd combination that makes her special, to my mind. Jessica still eats Jell-O, for instance, and relishes
its goofiness even as she truly loves the way it tastes. I have seen
her make pineapple upside-down cake and then box and mail it
to a friend on the West Coast with a note that reads, "Hope this
finds you right side up." I've seen her serve dumbfounded New
York friends a politically incorrect dinner of Southern fried
chicken—dipped in enriched, bleached white flour, fried in bacon

drippings—and mashed potatoes and gravy, followed by banana cream pie and whipped cream. It's a charming perversity, given she usually lives on vegetables and water, and it is something I will always love about her. Jess and Ariel have made, on special occasions, delicacies like caramel corn balls, and fudge with walnuts, and I have eaten them without complaining even though they're so sweet they make my teeth curl.

Stories about her when she was a kid are Americana. She wore grass-stained white pedal pushers and she jumped up and down until she was nauseated on the neighbor's trampoline, whose stretchy canvas sweetly stank of mildew in the humid summer. Because her sister was ten years her senior, Jessica was the baby of the family, and was treated like an only child. She got to stay up late and "help Pop watch the prizefights," as he put it. She would see the big guys slugging it out on the black-and-white screen while her father and she ate barbecue ribs so greasy and sticky with sauce it took three napkins and a bath to come clean afterward. As the two men in the ring jabbed and roundhoused, her father would yell, —Kidney punch, did you see that? below the belt, the ref's a bum. Once in a while she stayed up to help him watch a movie. There was John Wayne besieged at the fort, cloaked in his buckskins and bravery, and there was her father commenting, —No way are they gonna make it, and against all odds of hope in her heart in fact they don't. It didn't seem fair, the honorable dead draped all over the place after the final onslaught of the enemy. How it made her cry that the cavalry men didn't win, but she held back her tears as the credits rolled.

—It's way past somebody's bedtime, her father said, and off she would go.

A good girl, was Jessica.

Then, something happened. She ironed her hair, much to the dismay of her father, freed it of its flowing waves. She stopped

watching maudlin movies and eating greasy ribs. Over the protests of her mother, the Girl Scouts she refused to join, 4-H she
begged off, junior prom and glee club she skipped, first boyfriend
was the foreign exchange student, an introverted and articulate
youth from somewhere overseas, none of her friends knew where
or cared much—spoke with an accent, wore odd clothes, what
did Jessica see in him? She became an outsider. She lived on a
tributary of Yellow Creek, could hear it below her window when
she was a girl, as it made its way along toward the Ohio River
toward the Mississippi and finally the gulf, until a scholarship
got her to Barnard and she carried her delta blues records and
rebellious attitude off to Manhattan.

—Not an exceptional childhood, she would say.

—All childhoods are exceptional.

—Exceptionally fucked up, Kip would add.

Kip and Jessica, Jessica and Kip, they were inseparables. When
I went to bed at night she was there and when I got up the next
morning she was still there. Sometimes the door to Kip's room
was open, sometimes it wasn't, and I heard the muffled giggles
of their lovemaking through its hollow frame, and caught a view
of her in the darkened apartment from time to time as she walked
past my room toward the bath, wearing a shirt of Kip's maybe,
maybe with one sock on and another off.

Was I envious? Why deny it. I came more and more toward
the recognition that yes, I was lonesome—especially when the
three of us were together, as we often were—and expendable,
from their perspective, or so I saw it, and the more my envy grew.
There was nothing to do about it, and I did nothing. I wasn't
able to conceive that my unwillingness to go out and find a girlfriend of my own had to do with a developing attachment to
Jessica. Doing nothing was if not the healthiest at least the simplest response. It seemed there was no response that would cancel

altogether my status as odd man out. When I found myself alone in the apartment, the place seemed too big, when I was there with the two of them it seemed too small. Trading roles with Kip, I now became the loner. Then I came upon the famous photograph of the Buddhist monk sitting full lotus in a swirl of flames in a summer street in Saigon and was truly radicalized. After that I would not be able to find words to voice how I felt, so fully had my horror matured beyond whatever articulation was available to me; after that I'd have to pitch my body and voice together against this thing we Americans were doing in order to make my convictions known.

The monk had taken his final step in June 1963, the same month Kip and I moved off campus. The photograph was poignant, awful, eloquent, provoking—I can to this day recall it in detail—the monk viewed from the side, seated in a lotus position with hands in his lap, his back erect and shaved head held high, at the center of a fully enveloping body of white fire. A phallic flare emanated from between his spread knees. Though his face was blackened, he appeared to gaze at a point directly before him, serene and imperturbable. At some distance in the background, other monks looked on, their robes flowing downward like inverted replicas of the upward leaping blaze that framed their brother. Dignity and strength, not a hint of agony, saturated the image. How did he do it? I wondered. How did he maintain such poise at death's gate?

Inspired, I clipped it out of the paper and taped it to my bedroom door. The photograph became a powerful presence in my life, so much so that Kip knew better than to comment. The monk's suicide and the purpose behind it worked at me, remolded me. We'd been in there with our helicopters, in the south, helping Ngo Dinh Diem put down the rebels. South Vietnamese troops in Hué had fired on peaceful demonstrators who protested a government order forbidding them to fly Buddhist flags. They raided Buddhist pagodas throughout South Vietnam, these wild troops under the rule of Diem, and arrested hundreds of worshippers. The United States complained, I guess, through our ambassador, but not with sufficient vehemence. I read in the paper that we were displeased by all this violence, and yet as if caught in a mechanical operation that disallows any change of course, as if compelled, we continued to back the regime, went on dispatching men and matériel under the presumption that as wretched as Diem was, Ho Chi Minh was worse.

Then, November 1963. A coup d'état brought Ngo Dinh Diem down. Both Diem and his notorious and rather glamorous sister-in-law Ngo Dinh Nhu, who, only the month before had toured our country to gain support for the Diem regime, were assassinated. It seemed tidy, didn't it? That happened on the first and second of the month. Kennedy formally recognized a new provisional government on the seventh, a mere two weeks before he himself was murdered. I began to understand our pattern was set and that there was a warp and woof to the larger world. Nothing thereafter, to my mind, wasn't connected. It was a lesson I must have learned from Los Alamos—the lesson that public events are masks for private determinations—and it changed me. I had come to believe that on the world stage little occurred that was strictly coincidental. The puppet-masters' strings got tangled from time to time, sometimes the lighting was wrong, too bright perhaps, and moving strings were seen by members of the audience who weren't supposed to see them, but generally puppets rose and fell by the finger actions of artists hidden behind the curtains. Diem got his threads severed once he stepped outside the painted footmarkings on the ballroom floor. I wasn't unhappy to see him tumble but wondered what manner of Punch would be brought out next, for the dance itself must go on, I knew, the dance could never finish.

Our course in Vietnam was definitive and inevitable, in my estimation. We were going to escalate, despite what we were being told, as surely as we'd intended to use all three of the bombs we had worked so hard to build back home. These early years in Vietnam were for me like the Alamogordo phase of the Manhattan Project—we were flexing, assaying, and were committed, as if by inertia, to going forward, no matter what, into the endless circle of killing and being killed. Hiroshima would, in retrospect, be cousin to the bombing of Hanoi. The macabre accomplishment of Nagasaki—which was as much a scientific experiment as a strategic act of war, a hasty testing of the plutonium 239 machine on live victims, a testing while the testing was good (they assumed it would work, but why not make sure?)—was no better or worse than the predestined, disgraceful final hours of exodus from Saigon that were ahead. Both marvelous nadirs in the country's history.

—Broken record, I can just hear Kip saying it. —Same old song all day long. Same way my father used to talk about the bomb being okay, every day, okay, now you're starting to sound like the flip side. You're both broken records.

I thought of Kip's father, remembered him walking me along toward the soda shop, insidious in that he was about to offer sweets to a child in hope of getting some information from him, and I felt upset at the comparison. Kip meant for me to feel upset, to be sure. Father's son, I thought. I said, —Listen, man, the broken record was pressed by somebody else, not me.

He moaned, —I know, I know.

—You know, you know. You used to be with me on this sort of thing, Kip.

—You're the one who's turned into a fanatic, not me. You're the one who used to be able to talk about other things besides war. But things change. And besides, Vietnam has nothing to do with the Second War.

—You're wrong. It's all the same war, first war, second war, third war, the one to come. What's going on now is no better than what was going on way back when.

He interrupted. —You know what your name should be? It should be Skip, like a skipping record.

—Forget it, I said, amazed at how hurt I felt.

—All right, we'll *skip* it.

He didn't mean to be as surly as this, I assured myself. He was still my friend, my bosom friend. There was something wrong and perhaps he was taking it out on me *because* he was my best friend and could get away with it.

*H*ere is a time warp if ever there was one. My sister on her porch dressed in a floral cotton dress trimmed in pink rayon rickrack shot with silver, smiling uncomfortably, saying, "Good gravy, Brice, why didn't you say you were coming?" and turning her son rather against his will to face me, "Sam, this is your uncle Brice."

"I know who he is."

Sam yawns.

"Well," says my sister, "aren't you going to shake his hand? Where's your manners?"

On the porch I shake my nephew's hand. We are going through the formalities of meeting twice, for the benefit of Bonnie Jean.

"Where'd you get that nice cap?" she asks the boy.

Sam looks at her and nods his head in my direction. "He gave it to me."

"Did you say thank you?"

I can feel my sister's eyes upon me, taking me in, and as a way of avoiding this scrutiny of hers I give her a brief embrace. "He thanked me fine, Bonnie. Now let me have a look at you," and I step back. She glances down. The resemblance to Father, always evident in her prominent lips and pallid skin, is greater now that Bonnie Jean's dark brown hair is graying and the half-moon creases at either side of her mouth have deepened. Her smile, seen but rarely by me, is uncannily like that of Father's; an earnest, dry, undoubtable smile. Not that she's smiling just now, of course. "You look great," I say.

"I thought you lawyers were better liars than that."

"I mean it."

"Well," says Bonnie Jean, "let's don't just stand here. Come on in, Brice."

In the house there are things everywhere, things and more things. There are little potted cactus plants, piles of magazines, there are gourds in baskets, candleholders, toys, bikes and brooms and ice skates, there are hats, cassette tapes, a Christ on black velvet, skis in this corner and archer's bow and quiver of arrows in that, stuffed bears, one chair piled high with metal clothes hangers, a Christmas wreath of plastic pine shaped like a diamond and hung with red chilies; indeed the whole place—front porch, carport, every window in the house—is hung with long strands of red chilies, mysterious bundles of dried chamisa. There is the matchstick schooner Dad and I built off and on over half a dozen summers, its masts and sails strung with cobwebs. The television plays soundlessly. On the radio, country music. Somewhere unseen, a washing machine pulses and a dryer whirs. A cat sleeps on top of the refrigerator, a yellow dog has spread himself to full length on the couch.

Sam and I have followed her into the kitchen.

"I'm sorry I didn't call, I hadn't expected to be here."

"Why doesn't that surprise me. Have you seen Mother?"

"Nope, came here first."

I'm noticing how easily I begin to slide into the lingo of my childhood. *Nope, done come here first, sis.*

"Sam, where's little Charlie?"

"I don't know."

"Go find him. His uncle's here."

"I don't wanna," says Sam.

I notice that I'd neglected to remove the price tag from the baseball cap.

"You heard me, Sam. Don't start with me now."

"But I got stuff to do."

I'm thinking, Maybe there is something wrong with the boy. "Hey, Bonnie, don't worry about it."

"Don't you want to see your eldest nephew?"

"Of course I want to see little Charlie. I just don't want to cause Sam any problem. I mean, if he's got things to do."

"He doesn't have a darned thing to do. They both got the day off from school for Easter holiday and neither one of them knows what to do with themself."

"I do," protests Sam.

Bonnie Jean says, "And here's five dollars. When you find him tell him to bring us a quart of Neapolitan."

Sam lets the screen door fly back with a hard slap into its frame, as a final protest of sorts.

"He's a good boy," says Bonnie Jean. "He's just at an age."

"I know about that."

Bonnie Jean allows a moment to gather, like a storm cloud, and I interpret it to mean, No, you don't know, Brice, you don't know the child. It passes, and she says, "What're you doing here, then?"

"What am I doing here."

My sister looks at the ceiling and says, "Is there an echo in this room?"

I force a laugh. "Well, it's a question easier asked than answered. To tell you the truth, I'm not completely sure why I'm here."

"Has somebody died I don't know about?"

"Oh stop, Bonnie."

"It took Daddy's funeral to get you here last time."

"Look, I'm sorry but I've got a family of my own and a practice that keeps me hard at it. It's not like you ever come out to visit us."

"You know what? Let's don't start, Brice."

"Good idea."

"You want coffee?"

"Only if you've already got some made."

Bonnie Jean has turned her back on me and stands at the sink drawing water into a kettle. "First time my big brother comes to visit me in how many years has it been now? Daddy died when Sam was four."

My god, what an obstinate attorney my sister would have been. "That makes him fourteen," I say, a little incredulous—the child behaved as if he were half his age.

"He'll be fourteen in July."

I say, "July ninth, right?"—not wanting to miss the opportunity of displaying to Bonnie Jean that I retained at least some bits of her family history. Not that my mnemonic isn't ridiculous and shameful. I can remember the month and day though not the year of my youngest nephew's birth only because it struck me as memorable that he was a week shy of the anniversary of the Trinity test and I recall how chagrined my sister had been at his early arrival, having told everyone throughout the course of her pregnancy that her second child was going to be born on the same day as the shot at Alamogordo. When he arrived a week shy of Bonnie's goal, I made some crack about her having a short fuse, and it would prove to be another of the various things Bonnie held and holds against me.

"—which means it's a good decade since last you honored us."

She isn't going to make anything easy for me. The cups come down from the cupboard. She asks me if I still take my coffee black, maybe as a way of showing me she can remember details, too.

I still do, I tell her.

She goes about her business of making our coffee, removes some cookies from a jar I recognize, poor vile Sambo whose smile has been chipped with time, and arranges them on a painted plate. She is waiting for me to answer her earlier question now.

"Bonnie, you remember Kip, don't you?"

"Don't tell me he's died again and you've come to bury him?"

"I thought we were going to try not to argue."

"We're not arguing," as she hands me my coffee.

"Well, your joke isn't very funny."

"It wasn't meant to be."

"I got a letter from Kip a few days ago, and I've come to meet him." There, I think, I cannot be more straightforward than that.

Bonnie Jean, sitting across the kitchen table, gives me a confused look. "You're kidding."

"No."

"But I mean he's dead, isn't he?"

"What makes you think he's dead? We don't know that."

"Well, what does it say?"

"It says to meet him in Chimayó."

"And you just up and come because you got some letter in the mail says you should?"

"Funny you'd say that. That's just what Jessica said."

Jessica was yet another contentious subject my sister and I best avoid, I remember suddenly. Jessica is, from Bonnie Jean's remove, one of the causes of my distance from the family—that is, her family and our mother—and represents to her the beginnings of my downfall, my embrace of New York, my infatuation with the false gods of contemporary culture, my loss of the innocence and dignity that are the birthrights of my Western heritage. The one time Bonnie Jean and Jessica met, indeed it was ten years back on the occasion of my father's funeral, there was such defensiveness coming from my sister—as I saw it—that I abandoned any hope of the two of them ever becoming very friendly. Jessica, for her part, recognized in her sister-in-law the insurmountable prejudice of rural toward urban, despite the fact that her upbringing was every bit as small-town as Bonnie Jean's, and early on concluded that any ambition to change her mind was energy wasted.

—In a way, I can't say that I blame her, Jessica told me after the reception at Bonnie's house. To your sister I'm nine-tenths of the reason you stay on in New York, and am a feminist to boot. A sinner and a slicker, and what's more I'm convinced she sees me as some kind of bigamist. Engaged to Kip—whom I'd bet you anything she carried a torch for when you all were growing up—and then, horrors, married to you, her troublesome but somehow perfect brother. I can see why she doesn't have any patience for the likes of me.

It was a doubly sad occasion, that funeral. Burying my father, and burying any undeveloped hopes my subconscious might have entertained about becoming somehow his replacement, and fulfilling the role he'd assumed in his last years of bridging the gaps—chasms they were, grand canyons—that had opened up in the geography of our family. Seeing Mother and Bonnie Jean together and seeing big Charlie, honest and hardworking Charles, my sister's man, and seeing too the differences between us all, my admiration for my father as paterfamilias was confirmed. He managed things I knew I couldn't. He enjoyed the diversities among those in his brood. Dad always liked Jessica, could talk with her for hours on the telephone about nothing in particular, about what was in the newspapers or what was for dinner, and often did. He also loved his daughter, and was blind to her eccentricities. My own flaws, of which there have always been many, none of which he failed to note, were forgiven as well. If he was trying to make up for lost time those final years, trying to make up to us children whatever he failed to do as a father when we were much younger and he was married to his science, I think he managed to do so. A part of my anger never abated, really, nor did my sense that his work was steeped in vice. But just like there are supposed to be many rooms in heaven's mansion, so there are many rooms in the shanty heart of any given mortal. Toward the end, some room in mine was furnished with real respect for my father.

"Well," Bonnie says. "Jessica isn't wrong *all* the time."

And, unexpectedly, my sister offers me the most genuine smile I think I have ever seen from her.

Soon enough both her boys have come into the house with the ice cream, which we take out of its frozen paper box and cut with a butcher knife in slabs, in an old-fashioned way, so that each slice has a bar of chocolate and vanilla and strawberry. We eat, and then little Charlie gets his baseball cap, which turns out to be a bit small. And then it is time for me to begin to think about walking to the cottage where my mother lives. I don't know why I feel a sense of relief and even solace here—can that much reconciliation come from one smile?—but I do. My sister has made for herself a decent life, and in that there is much to be admired. She asks me if I want her to telephone Mom to let her know I'm about to show up at her doorstep.

"No," I say. "I want it to be a surprise."

"Well, let's hope you don't give her a heart attack."

"I stand warned," I say.

—*T*ell me your worst trait, said Jessica one night. The three of us had taken the train down to the Village, and were sitting on a bench in Washington Square. Crisp evening, not cold, and overhead the stars tried to twinkle through the haze and diffused lights of the city, but only the most luminous ones succeeded. Constellations—Orion, the bear, the dippers—existed in memory or imagination. We were huddled together near the park fountain, which had water in the basin. A dog with a bandana around its neck waded there, quietly. It seemed to be ownerless, but didn't appear lost. Jess's question was directed at Kip. I remember thinking, Where does she come up with this stuff? and then listened for Kip's reply.

—That's a pretty strange request.

The dog climbed the long steps out of the basin, shook itself, and tramped away opposite us.

Jessica said, —Why do you think it's strange?

—Well. Most people want to know what someone's best trait is, not their worst.

—Since when am I most people?

I laughed, crossed my arms, looked upward again.

Quiet for a moment. Then, Kip said, —What's my worst trait? I tell you what. I'll tell you what's my worst trait if you tell me what yours is.

—Fair enough.

—Brice too, for that matter.

My gaze came back down, —You can leave me out of it.

—No, no, said Kip. —Brice has got to play too or I'm not answering.

—Brice doesn't have any bad traits, do you, Brice?

—No, it's not that, said Kip. —It's that he's got so many bad traits he wouldn't know where to begin figuring out which one's his worst. Isn't that right, Brice?

I leaned toward Jess and whispered just loud enough so that Kip could hear, —If *he* won't tell you, I'll give you the goods on him.

—You in or not, Brice?

—I don't care, I said.

—All right then. My worst trait. The truth?

—Of course the truth, said Jessica.

—All right then. He thought for a moment. —I suppose my worst trait is that too many things interest me, so I tend to get a bit scattered.

Jessica demurred. —That's it? That's your worst trait? She looked at me and I shook my head and shrugged. —Come on, you can do better than that.

—Well, I mean that's what can cause me to do things I'd rather not do, if you know what I mean.

—I don't. What do you mean?

—Brice, help me here, Kip laughed, a little hollowly.

—No way, I said.

—There's a good example of *his* worst trait, said Kip.

—Don't change the subject. Brice will get his turn. You still haven't answered.

—I did answer, though.

—What does this terrible fascination with too many things cause you to do that you'd rather not do? You haven't answered that.

—Well, I think that sometimes I scatter myself because maybe I'm afraid to concentrate on just one thing. And maybe that happens because I'm afraid that if I concentrate on one thing only, it'd be like putting all the eggs in one basket, or something like that.

—So, your worst trait is that you're afraid of failing, and so you hedge your bet? Like hedging your gambles by increasing your gambits.

—Aren't you clever, said Kip.

—Another of his bad traits is he doesn't like to be examined too closely, I offered, in the spirit of troublemaking.

—Look, I don't have anything to hide. I happen to think that serving too many masters is a problem.

—You're still holding out on us. What are some of the bad things you're talking about? Bad things you do because you get scattered.

All three of us sat silent on the bench until the words, —He runs, came out of my mouth. Jessica was sitting between us, and Kip leaned forward and his wry smile became a mask that betrayed nothing I could interpret.

—And what is your worst trait, Brice? he asked.

—I think you already said it for me.

—Let me hear you say it.

—Why?

—Because I'd just like to know if you're enough of a man to say it.

Jessica broke in, —Hey, that's it, let's stop—

—I'm not a traitor, I said.

—And I'm not a runner.

—I said let's stop.

Jessica was on her feet.

—Wait a minute, Kip said.

She was walking away from us, without a word. We were both up and following her now.

—Jessica never told us her worst trait, I said as we caught up with her.

—I'll tell you what my worst trait is, she said. —Hanging out with you two.

*T*he time had arrived for me to agitate. It was a form of falling in love, my commitment. It was inevitable and necessary. My tongue and fist wanted to collaborate. Signing a petition against the war and arguing with Kip in the privacy of our apartment wasn't enough. Dilettante radicalism seemed the worst kind of hypocrisy. There were moments when talking Vietnam with Jessica I felt like a fool. She agreed with me in principle but I felt I could see in her eyes the question, Who are you to have this information and these sentiments but not the conviction to do anything serious about them? The time had come to get off the fence and begin to walk into what was unknown territory. Safe for the time being from the draft because of my college deferment, it was my duty to go with others into the streets to bring this immoral business to an end so those who were stuck over there fighting for no good reason could come back home. I felt full of life and my commitment to activism was, for me, a rejection of death.

Posters on walls and bulletin boards were by 1965 becoming ubiquitous on campus and off. The riots of '68 were already in the air; faint, perhaps, in light of what was to come, but *there*. Meetings were open to students, faculty, anyone who wanted to come. The gatherings at first were small and we began to know each other in stuffy basement classrooms under the dry humming white light of fluorescents or out under the plane trees off to the side of Low Library. We got together at noon at the sundial in the center of the quad, maybe just a few dozen of us, some members of the SDS, others just undergraduates interested in helping to organize, to build support. The talk was of war, deceit, the patterns of the military industrial complex, of pigs, genocide, and imperialism. Our demonstrations were small at first, but soon would grow.

Epstein had become one of the student leaders by then. I can still hear his voice, ardent and clear, —If they're going to act like demons and traitors, it's up to us to be the demons' traitors.

—Right on, we cried, and our words echoed off the smooth facades of Dodge and Low and Hamilton and John Jay and the library, reminding me of the drum that echoed back at San Ildefonso when the Indians performed their corn dance. It had a holy quality.

—Demons' traitors are demonstrators.

—That's right, we shouted.

He must have been about twenty, a year younger than I, though he looked much older, commanded more and more respect from those of us who were working in the movement. He had been arrested, it was said, a dozen times, which was a considerable record for those days, was one of the protesters with whom any personal association meant you were added to a secret list in Washington, became the subject of a closed file. He wielded real moral authority, to my eye. I admired his guerilla instincts and directness of approach, and even if he could be overbearing at times, Epstein was a likable, decent guy. He appeared to have no life distinct from the stratagems involved in bringing the war overseas to an end and condemning the establishment that deceived its people into fighting it. He spoke of little else, and managed to get enough work done to stay in school, but was often absent from class; the sole exception was that he was devoted to the university basketball team and sat in the bleachers with the SDS contingent—we radicals adopted the basketball team back then, and of all the jocks on campus the basketballers seemed to get along with us best. He wore the same tired jeans and black sweatshirt to every gathering and game. His deeply sunken and dark eyes bespoke the insomnia of an obsessive or a saint. When he found out that I'd grown up in Los Alamos his mind moved quickly to an idea.

—Is the place as spooky as it's supposed to be? he asked me one afternoon.

—What place?

—You know, Los Alamos.

It is and isn't, but I knew better than to say no. —Spooky enough, I said.

—A lot of that shit started here, you know. It was called the Manhattan Project because Fermi conducted his fission experiments right over there.

—I know, I said.

—You ever been in Pupin?

I hadn't, and it was meaningful I hadn't, since Pupin Hall was where my father must have spent most of his time back in the forties when he went to school here, when he first met Emilio Segrè, and saw his first cyclotron, which they used to generate high-energy protons. It was here his interest in chemical engineering was coupled with a fascination of physics, the combination of which would get him the job offer to go to the Hill.

—You got a minute?

We walked up from the quadrangle, along the brick pavement and to the north end of campus, where the physics building stood.

—Come on, he said, and I followed him through the front doors and down a flight of stairs and then another until we were in the basement, which was a long hallway with rows of parallel ducts and conduits hung precariously from the ceiling and with discarded desks and chairs, antiquated electronic equipment and other ditched junk in the corridor. The lights blinked and hummed as I followed Epstein down toward one end. —Look at this, Brice, he said, pointing to a small sticker on the metal door, yellow and black. DANGER, RADIOACTIVE MATERIALS, it read. —Did you know that Fermi once looked out his window on the seventh floor and said, "Imagine, a little bomb like that would make all this disappear"?

I said I did, but I didn't. Not really.

We walked upstairs and found his old office, the door locked.

—You know what I think we ought to do someday?

—What?

—I think we ought to blow this place up.

—You're kidding, I said.

He slapped my back and said, —Maybe so.

Pupin Hall did become his prey for a while after that, though. We rallied in front of its doors, hassled students entering and leaving, told them to wake up, urged them to cut class and join us. Epstein was eloquent about the nuclear deterrence charade, the world sitting on a bona fide time bomb, how there was no such thing as conventional war anymore because of what had happened up at Los Alamos, how we were headed on a direct course to Armageddon in Indochina because we weren't going to win and when the hard-liners down in Washington finally saw that a ground war wasn't going to bring us victory they would have to trundle out the bomb. —They threatened to use it in Korea, didn't they? Hanoi is the future Ground Zero, he said, and went on to say how Hanoi would be the third and last city we were ever going to get to take out, because after that every intercontinental ballistic missile in every Soviet silo was going to light up in retaliation, and we would have to put all our birds in the air, too. —Hiroshima, Nagasaki, Hanoi, he said. —Those'd be the three cities kids would read about in their history books, the three cities America burned down clean with the bomb, except that there won't be any history books and there won't be any kids to read them, because it's not 1945 anymore, it's 1965 and we're not the only bastards on the block with a mean streak and an inflated sense of self-worth. To quote from the SDS position paper, the "Port Huron statement" of three years ago, "Our work is guided by the sense that we may be the last generation in the experiment with living." We can wish that this weren't the situation, but it is. And if you and you and you and I can't change it, then nobody will. That's our challenge, and this is our time.

We had not been to the barricades together yet, the thousand police it would take to quell us several years hence were not even imaginable. Our major initiatives were still ahead of us, up there in our future, our soon-to-be past. I was untried, and potentially untrue, but I was willing and able. One could feel the sides becoming more entrenched even though Vietnam was, in the wake of Johnson's continued expansion of the war effort, still a relatively unheralded adventure. Informants had begun to abound on and around the campus. An atmosphere of ferocity tempered by paranoia settled in upon all of us. Epstein, whom we naturally followed during his season (others would rise and disappear, some jailed, others disaffected), was as ascetic a guru as I would meet during those months; ascetic and potentially violent. He was bright and alive, and made those around him live more vividly or else move on. It is this aspect of the antiwar movement I remember as well as the occupation of buildings, the riots. The soldiers had their comradeship, we had ours. When all was said and done, I wondered whether we activists weren't closer in spirit to the soldiers off in the field than those same soldiers were to the politicians who conspired to send them to Vietnam in the first place.

My life developed into a duplicity. Or rather, a triplicity. There was my new life among fellow activists. There was my life led at the edge of Kip and Jessica's romance. And then there was the life I led with myself, by myself, often at odds with myself.

Brice—me, myself, and I—Brice living his own life was a person who wrote from time to time letters to his mother, letters that may have distorted the truth about what he was doing in New York and at school but did so only in order to insure her happiness. This is what he told himself. "Dear Mom," this Brice would write, "things are going so well here, I can hardly tell you, learning so much each day, Kip doing all right too, both of us have made some interesting new friends, I think you would approve. Of course I miss you and I miss our beautiful mountains and the clean air, which I'd trade any day for these gray skyscrapers and brick canyons and the putrid stench that sometimes settles in on the island, but it is good to be here, and many are the times I walk down the streets and think of you and Dad here, back before I was born, and it makes me happy to think of that. I love you and send you hugs, Brice."

Maybe my letters weren't quite that maudlin and stilted, maybe they were somewhat more cunning—Mother probably still has them in a shoe box somewhere if I ever wanted to know for sure—but the mistruths they attempted to convey were at least this venial. Sometimes, when I wrote her, I would reread what I'd written and then, nauseated by my shallowness and insincerity, crumple the paper into a tight ball and bury it deep in the garbage, down under tea leaves and cantaloupe rinds, both out of a sense of personal disgust and in the hope that Kip would never find it. Travesties, I would scold myself, nasty horrid vain pathetic travesties. Most of the time, though I knew she deserved better, I went ahead and sent them anyway. Surely she didn't believe half the words I wrote, but her return letters were equally cheerful and more cheering since less artificial. And her hand, that of a schoolteacher's, gave me great comfort to look at. She represented home at its best.

Indeed, the only times I could read the words *Los Alamos* and not feel my stomach begin to sour were when they were part of the return address on the envelope of her letters.

I am thinking about her as I walk. The town has changed and grown. And she has grown old and changed with it, though towns don't grow old as fast as the souls that build them. I am here in Los Alamos, I think. Here I am in Los Alamos, poplar hill.

The Hill, I think.

"The fucking Hill," I say.

No one hears me and I walk on.

"The motherfucking Hill."

No one there, no one responds.

What am I doing? Chants, chanter, chants is what you are up to. You're trying to incite your own little riot. But it isn't happening, you aren't able to multiply yourself into many selves, like

Vishnu, and then storm the barricades. You're just Brice. Just
one William Brice, eldest son of Mr. and Mrs. McCarthy, brother
of Bonnie Jean, once best friend of Kip Calder, husband of Jessica
Rankin and father to Ariel Rankin, daughter who carries her
mother's name rather than that of her father because that is the
way things go in this world where everything is physics and physics proclaims everything to be nonlinear, of fractals and fuzzy
logic and chaos, and chaos theory proposes that the universe is
subject to a dynamic known as the butterfly effect—if a butterfly
flutters its wings today in Tokyo, it will affect the weather next
month in New York. All is elastic as warm taffy, all is connected,
nothing is independent. They have people up here working on
this stuff day and night. Chaos management. I can almost hear
the computers humming under my feet, because they're there,
tunnels and subterranean laboratories with sleek equipment—
nothing medieval or Frankensteinian—rather postmodern, values
and numbers conversing among themselves across the placid faces
of microchips. Nine hundred million dollars a year put in here
still. There's a reason the streets are so clean and the sidewalks
so tidy, why the businesses are bustling. Los Alamos seems as
friendly and normal a town as you'd ever want to visit, and in so
many ways it is. With street names like Peach and Nectar, Iris
and Myrtle, how could one expect it to be otherwise?

Her cottage is just that, a cottage. An adobe box is what it is,
with flat roof and copper spouts to drain rainwater at either corner. The windows are armored with decorative black grilles. The
small yard is fenced and its grass is patchy. The adobe is in need
of fresh whitewash, though I thought I had paid a bill just last
year to have that job done. On the porch, in a wooden trough-
box, not geraniums and dusty millers, but a phalanx of golden
chrysanthemums. Something new. The latch on the gate is
locked, and so I walk around to the side, but neighbors' chain-

link fences do not permit me access to the back so I brace my hand on the lintel of one of her fence posts, which comes to above the hip, and leap over into her yard, feeling altogether the intruder that I am.

Bonnie Jean might have been right. Probably I should have let her phone ahead, given Mom the opportunity of not being shocked by my sudden, unannounced arrival.

I needn't have worried. She opens the door before I make it halfway across the hard lawn, and says, "Brice, how nice of you to come over."

"Hello, Mom," I say.

She smells of pipe tobacco, which gives me a sort of comfort. Her rooms are small and tidy. Maybe Bonnie hasn't replicated her mother with such slavish perfection as I'd thought. Mother is frailer, and her eyes have that milky glaze of incipient cataracts. But she is a strong old lady who gives me a hug. My fear that she would not recognize me was time wasted. I also notice the fresh lipstick and powdered nose and realize my sister had done as she pleased. For a moment I'm angry, then think, This is their world, their rules apply here. And the anger is gone.

"Let's have a drink," she says.

Her bottle of Tanqueray stands on the table next to a glass, and her clay pipe is beside it in an ashtray. There is her Bible, opened to the First Epistle of Paul to the Corinthians. Her flowers out front may have changed but little else has, it would appear. For the next several hours I will act as audience to a rambling, provocative, even inspired discourse on the history and nature of the Pauline epistles. From aspects of Aphrodite worship in Greece to the escape from Damascus, from the troubles with heathenism and Greek asceticism to Paul's thought about the role of women in the church—I listen to my brilliant, balmy mother range her fields of interest. The gin flows and the room fills with smoke. She pauses from time to time to ask about Ariel ("Does the poor girl ever see the inside of a church?") and then picks up where she left off, sometimes stopping to ask me what did I think about *that*—what did I think about the theory that Saint Paul suffered from epilepsy, for instance? When I tell her that I haven't given the matter much thought, she tells me I ought to read the Bible more often.

There is structure to her dialogue, but it works its way along through a complex series of stitches, thinkings and rethinkings. The gin makes no obvious impression on her, neither speeds her up nor slows her down. She has matured into a splendid character, perhaps not as sad as I'd thought, and by the time evening comes I find myself thinking, I am glad I have come here if only for these couple of hours with her.

The telephone rings and I answer. It is Bonnie Jean. "How's it going over there?" she asks.

"We're having a wonderful reunion," I say.

"Are you going to want to stay here tonight or with Mom?"

I haven't thought about this. I'd thought, in fact, to return to Santa Fe for the night. But given that tomorrow's the day, there seems no reason to circle back to Michael and Alyse's when I could just as easily leave from here.

"Does she have room for me?"

She's overheard, and says, "Plenty of room here, Brice. You stay here and tell your sister if she and the rest of them want to come to dinner, it's fine with me."

I begin to repeat to Bonnie Mother's offer, but she cuts me off. "You two go on with whatever you're doing," she says. "Is she still in Corinthians right now?"

"She is."

"Corinthians Two?"

"One," I say.

"I'll talk to you later, Brice," she says.

"Later."

Mother, lovely wisps of white hair curling about her ears and shoulders, is telling me that though the speeches of Apollos might have been more elaborate than those of Paul, there was something to be said for the power of crudity and plainness. Apollos was the lesser orator because he could only be articulate, whereas Paul could be both elegant and unpolished in the same breath.

She has some pasta in the cupboard. I put on water to boil. I tell her to keep on talking.

"It *is* interesting, isn't it, Brice?" she asks.

"It is, Mom."

"What are you doing?"

"I'm going to make us something to eat before this gin sends us both to heaven."

She is relighting her pipe when she says, between draws, "If you could get to heaven on gin, I'd already have booked passage a long time ago. But Brice?"

"Yes?"

"Did you know that Corinth was the home of Sisyphus?"

And she was off into her bedlam of mythology once more.

*H*ow it came to pass that I have no photographs of Kip is beyond me. Certainly photographs were taken. I can easily imagine one when our families visited Mesa Verde together during the summer of 1957. Kip and I at the foot of a long, lashed ladder, our arms over each other's shoulders, straw hats. Watches, I believe, with flexible silver bands that dug into the wrist, matching watches whose faces caught the sunlight and flashed back at the

camera, making it look like we held small suns in our hands. We
two browned by summer stood against the blanched stonework
of Cliff House. I envision him now as possessing marvelous and
intricate crow's-feet spreading like fans at either edge of his eyes.
Maybe some smile lines, maybe not. The skin under the eyes
would be limpid, possibly sallow. He was always stronger than his
size might convey. Narrow shoulders, indeed the shoulder blades
were pronounced and his chest was rectangular. Kip had long
arms, which swung with characteristic ease at his sides when he
walked, and his wrists seemed if anything too thin for his hands,
which were as large as those of a workman—veins standing high
between and behind the knuckles that, when we were kids, were
often bruised, or cut, from the extravagance of our activities.
Wide feet, and long, too—and if I remember right, yes, ankles
thin just like the wrists.

Kip was as fragile as he was sturdy. As for myself, I have always
been less fragile, less sturdy, and even now live in the commodious in-between. I look at my wrists and hands and see that they
are of a more harmonious (or, rather, common) symmetry; I see
that my fingers are neither too long nor short, but average and
proportional. When I study myself in the mirror—something I
seldom do, by the way; makes me feel uncomfortable—I see a
man of certain purpose and energy, right there on the pivot point
where youth is behind but old age is still ahead. I am in good
health, good form. Lord knows I don't do anything to keep myself fit.

—In the genes, my father'd have said if he could see me, and
no doubt he'd have disapproved of my easygoing inertia. He was
always the active one, the winter skier, the spring hiker, the summer rider. I'm more like Mother, I suppose, given to bursts of
mental activity combined with stretches of physical indolence. My

father liked to work standing in the lab, read and wrote standing—just as Karl Marx did when writing *Das Kapital,* as he was fond of reminding me.

—The Reds stand, we can stand, too, he'd say.

I tend now to the sedentary, and when I walk in the city I prefer to amble. Jessica has long since given up walking with me. I hold her back. She and Father would have gotten along famously as walkers if they'd ever had the chance. The stroke that brought my father down was enveloped in its own ironies. But though his regimes of exercise didn't save him from his own dying heart—given where he lived and worked, I'm surprised cancer didn't find him first, in the way it found so many of them who worked up here on the Project, playing with radioactivity before its effects on the human cell were fully known—I don't fool myself into believing that by taking a different approach to diet and health (my approach is to ignore such matters) I have any better chance than my father had of tricking death into some delay.

And as for Kip? There is no telling what his genetic fate had in store for him. His parents' death in the accident precluded our ever knowing how long a natural life they might have enjoyed.

I remember the night Kip was orphaned. Why does it come to mind just now? Because they were in the same car the night they died as they'd been in when we caravaned to the Four Corners and Mesa Verde.

Like all the accidents that descend upon us, this one seemed inadvertent, though maybe more cruel in its timing and circumstances than any I had known before, harsh and meaningless. And yet it is so meaningful in its absence of valuable meaning. So long ago and still rife with paradox. It was catalytic. I speculate that his father had suddenly diagnosed what Kip's blue pony meant, figured it out in a deeper way than I had, and hoped to dissuade him. This may be a romanticization of their purpose in coming east, however. The engineering department at the university had been the recipient of significant grants from the Atomic Energy Commission and had begun to expand its nuclear science programs. The dean was recently quoted as having said, "Technology is liberal arts." Maybe Kip's father was thinking of leaving the Hill for academia, just as my father threatened to do every so often. Of course, I will never know. But I do know that it seemed to me at the time they were doing nothing else but being parents who loved their wayward son, and were on their way to be supportive of him, on their way to New York to visit him. They were coming, and though Kip had been a model skeptic, he had not been able to betray—by my sights—his subdued joy at the prospect.

They were in Pennsylvania or New Jersey or somewhere. They talked to me when they telephoned, since Kip wasn't in. I found myself wondering what they would look like in New York, as opposed to on the Hill, but try as I might I couldn't picture them here.

—How's the weather there, Brice? Emma Inez asked me.

—Okay, I said.

I wasn't sure how the weather was, nor why it mattered.

—When do you think Kip'll be home?

—Pretty soon, I said.

I wasn't sure at all when Kip would come home. I was never sure when Kip would come home.

—And how you doing, Brice?

—I'm doing fine, Missus.

—That's good.

Some Western habits don't die hard, they simply never die. Yes, I did say *missus*. I'm sure of it, same way I still put *melk* in my coffee and know the opposite of weakness is *strainth*. I waited for her to speak next. All this was beginning to make me a little angry with Kip. Where was he and why wasn't he here to take care of answering all these questions his mother put to me?

—Brice?

—Yes?

—Would you tell Kip we're looking forward to seeing him? And you, too. And his girlfriend Jessica, too.

—I'm looking forward to seeing you, too, and I'll tell Kip what you said.

—Goodnight, Brice.

—Goodnight, I said.

It was I who got the next call, too, and though I wasn't told what had happened, I knew something was wrong. The man wanted to locate Kip. His voice was more sour than curdled cream. There was boredom behind, or inside, his constraint. Voice of an official. Made me indignant in the same way virtuoso bureaucratic behavior still provokes me. He was an intimidator and tease, this man who called, with his dismal inquirings. Yes, I would find Kip right away. Yes, this was where he lived. No, he's not here right now, I already told you. I already told you my name. Yes, that's with an *i* not a *y*. Can I tell him what this is in reference to? Well, all right, his parents are coming in this afternoon and so he's bound to show up sometime soon. Yes, that's our address but—

Kip did turn up, not quite sure how to take this visit from the folks, on the one hand nervous that his father intended to ride him about his drifting lifestyle, on the other excited—as much as he could allow himself to be—to see Emma Inez. He had been over at Jessica's, so I supposed but didn't ask. He had a composite dreamy and astute look to him, difficult to describe yet nothing I hadn't seen before.

—Some man called looking for you, I told him.

—What about? as he wandered into his room, unbuttoning his shirt to change into a relatively fresh white one.

Wasn't sure. —How's Jessica?

—Was it about a job?

—I don't think so. I don't know.

—Did the parents call?

—Last night, your mother did.

Rummaging through the chaos of clothing piled on the floor of his closet, Kip finally drew forth a tie, a wide conservative swath, and said, —She say when they're showing?

—You're really going to wear a tie?

—I wish you asked the guy for a name at least.

—He knew our address, I said, watching Kip knot the tie.

Nothing more was said, at least that is how I remember the day, until the police arrived and broke the news to Kip. Something of an emotional smear or haze thereafter. Kip left on the tie. To this day I am ashamed I wasn't able to piece together the quite simple puzzle the man on the telephone had provided me. Those weeks that followed the accident were unmoored—and I cannot help but think that if I'd been discerning, I could have softened the blow. But maybe that is the worst sort of wishful thinking. We were helpless. What can I say? Jessica and I went out with Kip into the night, walking together, stopping for a drink here and there as we went, and she cried, and I came very close to crying myself, and Kip changed as he walked, got darker and darker, but never cried. Not even when the sun came up the next morning and we decided, all three—if for no other reason than to keep going for a few hours more before Kip and I faced returning to the apartment and the responsibilities that death in the family brings to the living—to take a ferry out to Liberty Island.

We somehow found the ferry, and bought passage. We were

all sick during the short windy crossing. None of us had the strength or desire to take the circular stairs up into Lady Liberty's crown, from whose vantage the downtown buildings and bridges could be seen. Instead we sat on the scant, colorless grass and watched the brown waves build their own white crowns and carry them for a little and then lose them in the muddy harbor swells.

*D*ear Brice, Kip wrote from New Mexico, "Dear Brice, strange it is to be here again, and to see the old place. Staying at your house, thought I could hack it at mine, but I was wrong. Your parents are being nice. Nice, listen to me, no, they're being more than nice, they're being family. Your mother is looking after me like a hen, and your father came with me over to the house, my house, I mean, to help me sort through things. The authorities wanted to come by to go through Dad's papers, make sure there wasn't anything that might breach security. As if the old man would ever break their rule about engineers not keeping notes outside the Techs. He wouldn't even have thought to bend one, let alone break it. I started to go into a tirade over it, them combing through what's private property, but then I remembered what it was about this place that always drove me, and you too, Brice, drove us nuts. They still think it's 1945 here, some of them anyhow, the questions, the secrets, the poking and prying. Can you imagine these people wanting to go through Dad's stuff? What can someone like me do? Nothing is what. So I kept quiet and I certainly didn't let on that I managed to get his diary into a safe place. What do you think of that! I wanted to read it the other night, but I couldn't get myself to do it. Maybe someday, who knows, it may be interesting. Instructions on how to create a neutron shower in the privacy of your own home? I doubt it. If anything, it's probably pages of worrying about his son and wondering what he did wrong as a father to have a child like me—or is that just self-centered of me to think that? Am I just so narrow that I believe the world revolves around Kip? I don't know. But I do know I couldn't face reading it now. Maybe I should have handed it over, at least that way I'd know that no-body would ever see it again. But anyway, Brice, as far as pos-sessions go there's not much here I really want. Your mother says to put them all into storage because someday, she says, I'll have a family of my own and I may want these heirlooms and all, but to me it's junk, most of it, just junk. Is there anything you re-member in my house you want? Give a call if there is, because I don't know how long I'm going to be able to stay here. I go from being bad off, to getting these strange moments of feeling positive about the future. I know I am alone, and that's bad and okay too. What does it mean when you feel like you don't have a history? That's how I feel. I know I do, but I can't touch it somehow. I keep thinking Emma Inez is hiding around a corner somewhere and she is going to pop out of nowhere and say, Sur-prise, surprise—we're still here, son, and we know it's pretty harsh but we wanted to teach you a lesson in appreciation. Child-ish thinking, eh? Did I tell you your mom put me up in your old room, that's where I'm sleeping. Brice, she's kept it like some shrine, just exactly the way it was when you left. Creepy. I don't know how well I'm dealing with all this business out here, if you want to know the truth. Or did I already say that? The stars are out the window right now, I'm looking up at them, and I think it's new moon, real black outside. . . . Later same nite. So this is what I'm doing, I decided. Went out and walked over to Ashley Pond and thought about stuff and what I want to do is go by your mother's advice and not think about any of this junk, there's some money by the way, more than I thought they had, but while it's true I wasn't that close to them these last years I'd sure trade ten times, a thousand times the money to have them back safe and not gone, sounds soft but it's what I'm thinking. Something like this happens to you, like I was saying, you realize how alone you really are in this world. I got you, I got Jessica, and that's not nothing (backhanded compliment). What I have in mind to do is throw everything in storage, like your mom was saying, then come back to the city for a little while and do this. Don't tell Jessica what I'm going to tell you, promise me or else. And don't give me any shit about it either, because I don't need that kind of thing right now and you're my best friend, and I won't tolerate it, all right? Okay, so this is it. I've decided I'm going to ask Jessica to marry me. I'm not a child anymore, and if I was a month ago, I'm not now. Of course, I want you to be best man. You are the best man, so you can be best man. Then what I got to do, what I am going to do Brice old best man Brice, and I want not to hear one word out of you about it because I just don't, because I know what is right for me, what I want to do, and so lay off on the advice and especially the politics that are so important to your intelligentsia elitist shitfilled head, I say this knowing I like you better than any brother I would ever have had, as you know, asshole, what I intend to do is to go ahead and join the air force. I want to do something, and this is the only way that makes sense to me to do it. I know you think Vietnam is a bitch. I'm not even saying you are wrong, all right? I'm not saying that. What I'm saying is that it may be right for me. That's all. I remember you telling me that you and I had the same blood, when I was telling you that no, we've got different blood in us, and maybe you'll believe me now. So that's it, it's what I want to do, and if you're my friend, you won't say word one about it, and if you're not my friend, you can protest and lecture till you're blue in the face and Brice it won't make a bit of difference. What else—not much, I suppose. All I can say is I feel strong, given the situation, and that your parents are good people, Bonnie Jean's got a boyfriend, a nerd but all right, and I went way out of my way to tell her that her Charlie is the living end. Predict nuptials. Okay, that's it. I miss Jessica and I miss your sorry ass every so often. Please destroy this after you've read it.

"Keep the faith, Kip."

I read the letter only once, folded it, slipped it back into its pale blue envelope, then hid it at the bottom of my desk drawer. The letter gave rise to polar sentiments in me, yet incongruous as my two responses were, both directed me to bury it deep, under paper, under wraps. Not destroy it, as requested —for what reason, I couldn't begin to guess other than that such a request was typical Kip—but rather cache it. On the one hand, the letter was precious, this private treasure that displayed Kip's intimate fraternity with me. Here was an old, familiar voice, the voice of youthful friendship. On the other hand, the letter aroused in me rich animosity toward Kip, which made me want to get it out of my sight. Surely, the sanguine tone seemed out of place; maybe it was meant to mask deep discouragement.

I couldn't destroy the letter, no, but neither could I fully cherish having received it. I didn't want Jessica to marry Kip, but I did want them to be happy; I didn't want Kip to go off to Vietnam, but I did, didn't I?

Kip and I created our own games, as I've said. I still don't care about baseball one way or the other, but I've always liked the quote of Yogi Berra, "When you come to a fork in the road, take it." Having arrived at a crossroads I decided to look both ways and, as best I could, take them.

*W*hat is conviction? It is different from *a* conviction. Conviction when followed with strict, unveering resolve, can lead to arrest and arrest to conviction. Convicts are sometimes convicted because they took their convictions out and did things that might seem crazy to people who did not share those convictions, or at least didn't share them to the degree of intensity that might carry them away into action. The word comes from *convictio,* proof. A person who has proof can therefore believe and can be compelled by belief to act with conviction. And I began to believe, I had proof sufficient to compel me to believe, and so I took my convictions with me, and I acted upon them and with them.

Misery acquaints a man with strange bedfellows, says the jester Trinculo in *The Tempest.* In the same way Los Alamos was a motley of different temperaments, the Movement—and I capitalize the word if only to show how much it became as formulative as the Hill had been—brought me in contact with more contradictory souls in the period of several years than some might encounter in a lifetime.

Epstein was one of many who disappeared into the swirl as the Movement grew; the last time I heard about him he'd become one of the Weathermen, had slipped from radicalism into the nebulous world of pacifist terrorism. Someone told me he'd been shot and killed, someone thought he was incarcerated for having taken part in a bank holdup, an action to liberate capitalist monies to redistribute to the cause, but I discounted these latter stories, since I thought I'd have read about it somewhere or heard about it in law school. The Columbia University Independent Committee on Vietnam came into being to "unite all those who oppose the war regardless of present political affiliation." Five hundred of us from the university marched in Washington on the seventeenth of April one year, the cherry trees white and pink in bloom below the majestic monuments of the capital, which I thought were beautiful even as our chants, twenty thousand voices strong, drowned out the spring songs of the birds overhead. At the end of that month, we sent another telegram to Ho Chi Minh: THE STUDENT LEFT WING AT COLUMBIA IS STILL A MINORITY, BUT IT IS AN UNCEASINGLY PERSISTENT GROUP AND AN INCREASINGLY VOCAL ONE AS WELL. I had no sense of being to left or right, just knew what I knew was wrong. And then came the protest of May seventh against the presence of the ROTC on campus. I was there because I'd stayed with it, got deeper and deeper into the rituals of the Movement. Rancor and keen mistrust of authority pitched themselves at the center of some minds. From others I witnessed the same conundrums I'd never reconciled back on the Hill. Calculated violence—limited and specific—to force peace to come about. It was more than I'd expected, to be in the middle of a riot. I could have stayed at its edges but for once didn't.

I threw rocks. I threw bottles. I threw gassing canisters back at the pigs who'd launched them into our ranks. I threw fists and kicked hard as hell when they tried to get the cuffs on me. I went limp when they carried me to the wagon. I made it so that it took three of them to get me where they wanted me, and by doing that I won a small and fleeting victory by taking three of them away from their positions in the melee.

This happened when Kip was still in New Mexico, on leave from school, putting affairs in order. In the same way the death of his parents freed him to make certain decisions, to begin acting on his convictions, Kip's absence from New York freed me to act upon mine. History is not a backdrop to our lives, I came to presume, but is an agent, interactor. It was in my hands.

Jess bailed me out. She took my arm and walked me down the street.

—It's in the newspapers.

—Good, I said.

—Your shirt is torn, she said.

—As well it should be.

—I think you're a fool to have done this.

—If you think I'm such a fool, why did you bail me out?

—Don't be dense, Brice. You know I'm proud of you, too.

—You should come with me next time.

—Who'd bail you out of jail?

Gently, I removed my arm from hers and we continued along in silence. After a while, I said, —Don't be proud of me, Jess.

—Why not?

—I don't know exactly. Just don't.

*W*hen he came back to the city, closeness and distance between us began an interplay. He brought presents. For me, a Hopi ceremonial sash his father had kept draped over the back of his reading chair, its strict geometric patterns woven with vegetable-dyed wools of dark green and bright red, eggplant purple and black, all on a sheep-white ground. It was long, with fringed ends, and I put it over my shoulders like a minister does his tippet. I thanked him, embraced him.

Jessica was exuberant. —Sweet Kip, she called him, presenting him an armful of irises and tulips. When he handed her a small, squarish box with white string around it tied to look like ribbon, I knew what was inside and about to happen, but didn't know why Kip felt it necessary that I be there to witness. The ring was modest. Navajo, old, a silver band with just a bit of ornamentation to set the little oval of deep-green turquoise.

—I hope it'll fit, he said, and it did fit her little finger. —My new family, he said, then, his right arm over Jessica's shoulder, his left up over mine.

She moved in with us, some few days later, and when she did I was seized by the desire to leave. Kip argued, —This is where you live, Brice, you're not going anywhere, we're kin here. For her part, Jessica, whose side Kip now seldom left, was—so far as I could fathom—not less enthusiastic than he about my staying on. Once more I drifted in a wobbling ellipse around them.

It wasn't a horrible existence, this our brief experiment in Fourierism; it had its rewards. They made me feel at home and even as I felt that they were children and I the guardian, Kip and Jess no doubt looked on me as their ward. For weeks that accumulated into a month, I basked in the reflected glow of their sexual warmth. And it was true, wasn't it, after all, that we were kin?

Jessica took it upon herself to find me a "companion"—her word for it. She had not told Kip about my participation in the May seventh riot, or about my arrest. I saw it as an act of complicity, and withheld the story from Kip as well, in part because I didn't want to hear his comments, in part because I saw the shared secret as a declaration of her separate intimacy with me. More and more I could see how all things might lead to Jessica. How nothing I saw didn't have her face in it, nothing I felt failed to bring me back to thinking about her. It was another conviction, and one to resist with a far greater strength than I'd resisted my first arrest.

—I've got someone I want you to meet.

—I don't want to meet anybody, I said.

—Come on, don't be stubborn.

—Jess. You know that line, You can't push the river?

—You're not a river.

—And what is *that* supposed to mean?

—She's really great, I promise. Her name is Marisa.

Pushable river, I said, —All right, already.

And so entered Marisa, for a time. It was true that she was great. She straddled the two subcultures of beat and hippie. She had been present when Ginsberg, Corso, and Orlovsky read to an audience of over a thousand at Columbia back in 1959. She was one of a handful of students who protested former president Truman's presence on campus that same year, when he came to deliver a series of lectures, and I liked her for that. She was possessed of a wryness toward things around her that was endearing. She read *Mexico City Blues* and *The Dharma Bums*, she read *Howl* and *Kaddish*, and the hash was burning one night at our place, soon after Jess had made her introduction, and the incense—Marisa's aura was the color of a patchouli blossom, she told me—too, and the room vanished behind a willowy scrim of sour-sweet smoke as Marisa intoned, ". . . who bared their brains to heaven, waltzed by, tricked us" as only words and the music of words can trick you, and made us realize how holy we were indeed and in fact, and the toke pipe went around again and though it made me cough and turn crimson I smoked with the others, tried to keep up, and though I had doubts about the value of what Marisa was reading, I listened to her read on, "who got busted in their pubic beards returning through Laredo with a belt of marijuana for New York, who passed through universities with radiant cool eyes hallucinating," and I began to feel unleashed despite myself, and yes, sexed up and very much alive in my body, "with dreams, with drugs, with waking nightmares," went the poem . . . and in my delirium looked over to Kip, watched him while he lay back on the pillows, big floppy pillows Jessica'd sewed together using some old curtain fabric, and saw that they were kissing while Marisa kept reading, "whispering facts and memories and anecdotes" . . . and I thought, Brice, this is two things, this is easy on you and this is not easy on you, it's easy because these are your two best friends on earth and not easy because you want, you've always wanted, to be Kip, or at least the Kip that's kissing Jessica. And you simply cannot have her and you cannot be Kip. You must be Brice. You are Brice. For better or worse, in sickness and in health, and so it is you are married to yourself as if there were an undetectable wedding between you and yourself that occurred at your birth. And I am thinking, That is genius—isn't it? the idea that you are married to yourself, a shotgun wedding, with your progenitor's penis as shotgun. Then I realized that I was not thinking with my straight mind, and I came back into the room there to join the others, such as they were.

". . . grandfather night," the poem ribboned forth, Marisa transfixed in its sonorities and beautiful impudence. She looked at me and smiled. She laid her head in my lap and held the book above her face, her long brown or was it black hair flowed over my thighs. She meant every one of those words with a fervor that suggested more than just that she believed the poem, but believed she'd even written it, out of her own pain and hipster wisdom, and she kept going, she was too much, exotic and authentic, wise in her way, and as I listened to her I understood she wouldn't hate me if I kissed her forehead, would not resist if I lay my hand on the flat curve of her shoulder, began to move the tips of my fingers across the toffeelike skin of her neck and down underneath the fabric of her blouse.

And so it was I lost my worthless virginity.

*O*ur days and nights were lived without much distinction made between one and the next. Marisa left, but seemed to return when she pleased, sometimes wearing the same clothes, in different clothes other times. She would drift in, a sack of groceries cradled in her arms, and proceed to make a deep dish of lasagna and a great salad of lettuce and sprouts. Once she arrived with two large pair of fresh shad roe, said they'd been a gift of a friend of hers who'd been on the Hudson fishing and who though it was late in the season had caught his limit that day, and proceeded to fry them with rings upon rings of onion in bacon grease.

—I thought you were a vegetarian, I said.

—Not when the shad are running, said Marisa.

I liked her for her inconsistencies. She kept erratic, nocturnal hours and yet seemed always to be the first person awake and out of bed in the morning, to have chicory black coffee made—she detested herb tea—and set out for her daily constitutional of some ten miles or so. —When you wake up you get up, that's what my great grandmother says, and she is closing in on a hundred years old, so she ought to know. Marisa was hard and quaint at the same time. Plain and strange, giving and parsimonious all at once.

Did I love Marisa? Kip wondered.

I loved her, I supposed, in my own way, just as she probably loved me in hers.

When she vanished, at the end of the summer, I was disappointed though not surprised. I was disheartened less because Marisa had run away—no, not run: faded away is more like it— than because her absence left me free to begin weaving my fantasies about Jessica again, an exercise I resisted as best I could, with varying results.

Jessica is maternal. Not smothering—mothering with the s of squeezing, or suffocating, or short-pantsing in the fore of it—not maternal in a mama kind of way, just warm, and kindly disposed, especially toward the hurt. She wanted me, in her Jessica way, to be somehow more distressed by Marisa's leaving than I was.

—I knew she was out there, but I wouldn't have expected her to just up and go without saying something to you.

—But that's Marisa for you. To be fair about it, she never promised anything different.

A frown from Jessica. Studied her lips, despite myself. All these shades of brown and red.

—Brice, she said, flat, undirecting.

Some part of me saw it was a moment to feign discouragement. —I mean, I guess I never expected her to stick around for too long . . . this was more or less what I managed to concoct. But what was I doing? that is, I did have feelings for Marisa, but I wasn't so very sorry she'd left, and I did have feelings for Jessica, but wasn't so happy about her being there, right in front of me, so near, asking me about Marisa.

—I'm sorry it didn't work out. I feel responsible.

—Well, don't.

Jessica must have said something. What she said I can't remember, yet what I knew, at that moment, was that Marisa meant so little to me by comparison.

The best offense is defense, they say, and was I defensive about Jessica. There was no coming to a solemn peace with those days. My imbalance was secure, a pure fragility consecrated by the emotional stupidity of early manhood, crowned—or haloed, if you will—by the bright innocent light of inexperience, and made powerful by the sheer and unavoidable reality, to use *that* word, that I was in love.

*L*ittle by little the bird builds its nest" is a folk saying, one of my favorites, from way back, that resides in my memory along with smatterings of this and that, nifty ditties and speculations picked up along my way from the heaving tide of verbal flotsam that never ceases bobbing by, and probably never shall. Like most folk wisdom it is true, I think. What it proposes is obvious, but what it doesn't account for is upheaval.

There was a year when things didn't go little by little, an exponential year, and it began with the infamous flight down to Chimayó. The last year of the fifties, the last year of a decade of outrageous optimism. Kip and I ran away, were brought back home, then Kip ran off on his own, failed again, and by autumn we were like a pair of whipped pups, neither members of the litter nor fully weaned, neither immature nor matured.

—Brice, what's gonna happen with us? and I couldn't believe that this was Kip, my strong and belligerent Kip, speaking.

—What do you mean, what's gonna happen with us, what's gonna happen is we're gonna go away to school together and leave the Hill behind, and everything will be fine.

—Everything will be fine? Why?

—I don't know. Because.

—Because why? he asked.

—Because because.

—Because because why, boy?

—Because we're going to make it fine is why.

I didn't know what I was talking about, of course. *Why* is the most enigmatic word in the language. Never ask why. We can know what, we can know how, we can know when. We never know precisely why. I remember thinking that, and may have made a significant advance toward weaning myself away from childish ways and thoughts. And besides, Kip was having fun at my expense, and that too had become newly tiresome.

Little by little the bird builds its nest. Here was another exponential year. Kip was sure things were going to turn out great. Graduation, then on to flight school, the service, then home and marriage, then happily ever after. What makes you think it will all turn out like that? I wanted in the worst way to ask him. Why will doing things like that be so great?

Because, he might have said if I'd asked.

Because why?

Because we're going to make it so, he might have answered.

But I failed to ask. Instead, whether motivated by ripening resentment, newfound lust, plain confusion, or all three, I hurled myself into a sea of women in the hopes that I, like the legendary brand of Meleagar, might be quenched. There is a poem by Ezra Pound that proposes Meleagar's carnal sea was composed of six lovers. How many I managed to have, if *have* is the word, might've been more or fewer. Now, I'm not sure.

There was Rachel, with her biblical name and her square build and heavy breasts, matched by her equally heavy, squarish sweaters. Jane smelled of coriander and clay soaked by hard rain. There was Margaret, whose hair was redder than any Pre-Raphaelite model's, who spoke with intelligence far superior to mine on every topic, and in such measured tones, was both graven and grave, and who was more my friend than any kind of lover—our lovemaking was neat as the proverbial pin. There was Sam, short for Samantha—gray-green eyes and a Southern accent. She and I went for walkabouts, began in the morning, no itinerary, and took off into the streets to see what there was to see. We would piece together lunch from one grocer and another, as we marched along, side by side, saying whatever came to mind. Willa remains, in my memory, my dearest ally. Willa embraced the many grievances I held against this and that aspect of our society. She might not have been so interested in these matters when we met, but after some hours of listening to my passionate talk about not just the war, but all the maladies of our world, as I saw them then, she too became an advocate of some new order—or positive disorder—and together we would sit, try to write, try to think, and I would stay over at her place some nights, sleep with her, try to kiss her and I know she'd try to kiss me too. Willa over-lapped with Amy, Amy whose lissome strength was formidable, Amy who lived in jazz clubs and carried an abundance of rebel-lion in her heart. Amy cut all her hair off one night and I was, if taken aback, left to be supportive of this gesture, because what it signified to her was liberation.

And surely there were others. I wonder where they are now, who they became, and imagine that they might recall me in the same vaporous detail as I them, or perhaps they don't remember me at all. But what it came down to, back then, was an abiding, a living along. We all walked hand in hand, slept together when the night came, we taught one another a little this and that. We tried with each other, we were kind. We drifted in. We remained for a while. There was true warmth. And then, we were gone.

These liaisons, these breakneck infatuations, came to as quick a conclusion as they had commenced, and all the while who was most in touch with my somewhat disembodied sexual meander-ings but my mother? Kip swore he did not betray to her whatever it was I was doing. She simply knew. And didn't disapprove, not altogether. She wrote me one of her letters, and swathed in obliq-uity was her opinion, though it took me some meandering of a different kind to come to it. She wrote, as a throwaway, hidden in the company of many ideas, many anecdotes, "Brice, never forget what I used to tell you about what the tortoise must be thinking during his marathon with the hare. 'Slow and steady wins the race.' Slow and steady, Brice, is what I say. Forget the race. There are no winners. But just think slow, steady."

All roads led back to Jessica. There was another poem I recall from those days, "Mr. Housman's Message," by the same poet who wrote about the brand of Meleagar. It ran, thick with irony,

O woe, woe,
>People are born and die,
>We also shall be dead pretty soon
>Therefore let us act as if we were
>>dead already.

I knew who I wanted, was unable to hear any message that would suggest I relinquish even this fragilest, pipemost of dreams. I was not ready to act as if I were dead already.

*B*y 1968 Vietnam was Vietnam. Vietnam in the sense of Viet*nam,* man. Vietnam qua Hades all our own.

Even those who had denied we'd been at war, waist-deep in quicksand war, war with casualties, more and more flown home in spartan boxes every week, were forced to admit now that we had lost over a thousand men in Ia Drang right in the dead middle of the decade, battalions of enemy mastering our Air Cav with shocking agility and resolve. Ia Drang brought Command to the recognition that it might take a few extra months, yes, maybe as much as a year, to get this situation under control. But it was like trying to push that river. Nineteen sixty-eight was the year of the Tet Offensive and that same burning winter the hilltown of Khe Sanh was besieged, fatigued marines dug in, shooting back when the fire came in, some looking to catch the next transport out, if there was a next transport and if the Viet Cong in the surrounding hills let them out, some looking to kill back. Names like Giap and Con Thien entered the language. The black-and-white images on television saturated our visual memories, the airlifting of wounded by dragonfly choppers, the length of jungle erupting into flame after one of our jets passed by, low and lightning-fast. Vietnam had become Vietnam and it was Vietnam in-country and it was Vietnam here at home.

When Kip finally shipped out to Saigon, Jessica and I kept our distance from one another. It was my doing at first, but she soon enough followed suit. The apartment never seemed more cramped with just the two of us knocking around in it. Routines that never felt intimate before now felt most intimate. Dinner together was inhibited by self-consciousness. Her clothing hung on the hook of the bathroom door was charged with some fresh meaning now, and it made me weak with discomfort. When around her my breath narrowed, every sound I made seemed too loud. Without discussing it with her, I found myself a small studio apartment and moved out. She expressed little surprise and didn't make any effort to dissuade me from going. There was no resentment, no animosity. I left many of my things at the Colonial, and continued to pay my share of the rent. The studio was on a month-to-month lease.

And there was other business to attend. I read the Selective Service Act in search of the definition of conscientious objection, and what I found was that the lawmakers who'd drafted the act had foreseen every exigency. While it was written that nothing in the act "shall be construed to require any person to be subject to combatant training and service in the armed forces of the United States who, by reason of religious training and belief, is conscientiously opposed to participation in war in any form," it was further stipulated that the term " 'religious training and belief' does not include essentially political, sociological, or philosophical views, or a merely personal moral code."

A merely personal moral code! Here the country was sinking under a plague of immorality while its congressmen wrote into law a depreciation of the value of having a personal moral code by which to act? The word "merely" I stared at in disbelief before reading on. Further in the same paragraph there was a final sneer, in the form of a provision for the lucky Quaker whose birthright exempted him from having to conceive his own morals. The provision made it possible for those who fit the prescribed definition of conscientious objector to be placed "in appropriate civilian work contributing to the maintenance of the national health, safety, or interest." I thought, Great—if that is what they're supposed to do, contribute to the country's health, safety, and interest, where they should go is straight into the front lines of the next march, endure a little tear gas along with the rest of us, or a guardsman's buckshot, in the interest of their nation.

Knowing better than even to apply for conscientious objector, I went about avoiding the draft another way altogether. When I entered Columbia Law School my military deferment was in default. I had considered leaving the country for Canada, and believe even now that what prevented me from following that course was a desire not to leave Jessica behind.

In the end, I went the basest route. President Carter would later pardon those who fled the country in protest against Vietnam. But there'd never come a pardon for me. At the time, I viewed the lie as a guerilla tactic. One lie mandated another, was what I told myself after procuring a 4-F—unfit for service—by means of false data worked up by an upstate physician sympathetic to the cause. It seems a tawdry nightmare, looking back. Bad heart was what his report said. Complete with someone else's electrocardiogram.

Bad heart. While it wasn't true, it wasn't altogether false. Medical deferment for a very bad heart.

Kip left. Having given me a handshake, looking askance—he knew what it meant for me to have come to say goodbye to him, that I was betraying myself—he'd embraced Jessica. Then he turned and climbed onto the bus, silver with a lean leaping dog logoed on its side, so polished I could see my reflection next to Jessica's as it pulled away for the cross-country trip to San Francisco, where he would catch his flight to operations. I recall thinking, Probably I will never see him again. I also felt peculiarly diminished, for all my moral superiority with regard to the conflict into which Kip was about to hurl himself; an odd experiential diminishment that arose from the certain knowledge he was about to see things—blood bleeding into soil, napalm tingeing jungle green—and hear things—mortal screams, the rocking power of helicopters' blades, the hollow *clack* of rounds being launched into the dark—that I would never see or hear. It was a perverse jealousy I felt, envying him sensations no one should have to suffer.

That bus carried away in it a distorted mirror-image of my own experience. The eyes, dark and confident, that looked out at me and Jessica from behind the glinting windows (Kip didn't wave; Jessica did; I did not) were in many ways my own, insofar as they had seen much of what I'd seen. I felt something akin to the tender hatred one can sense when staring hard at a photograph of oneself. Love and disgust wrapped themselves like caducean snakes weaving in neat opposition up a sword that neither cuts nor comforts. And only after Jessica and I had left Port Authority and gone to have a coffee in Chelsea somewhere did I begin to understand that I'd probably lost not just one but two friends that afternoon.

Kip was gone, he'd never be the same, whether he came back from combat or not. Gone with him, or so it seemed to me at the time, was Jessica, since my affection for her grew almost at once in his absence, and pathetic as my moral fiber has sometimes been, I could not see myself pursuing the object of this affection. Jessica would be so easy for me to love. If Kip had stood in my way, if he had recognized how I felt and demanded that I stop, then I might have been free to pursue her. But if he'd recognized it, he had managed to conceal his response brilliantly. Nothing, he gave me nothing in that regard. Unchallenged, there was no way for me to contend.

That night when I kissed Jessica goodnight on her cheek, and smelled her hair—a smell of chestnut, and butter, maybe of sage, certainly of warm earth—and sensed more than ever the danger of myself with her, I came as close as I ever would to wishing someone dead. Why was she so tangled up with him, what did she, as a woman, see? I knew him as a brother and a man, and knowing him thus had somehow come to see him as someone a woman might do well to avoid. Whether it was true or not, I doubt there was much merit to whatever reasoning stood behind such an opinion. And yet, I knew that to wish him dead was to all but wish myself the same. He'd said something on the telephone from San Antonio, Texas, that made me understand his thinking was not unlike my own.

Aviation cadet Calder on the phone to antiwar activist Brice, —You know, sometimes I think worse things could happen to you than getting your silly head bashed by some cop's billyclub out there during one of your demonstrations.

—That's charming, I said.

—Might knock a little sense into you.

—Right. And when'll you see the light? When they shoot some antiaircraft fire up at you?

—Fuck off, Brice. We can't talk about this subject anymore.

—Did we ever?

—Hey, I listened to all your palaver for years.

—A lot of good it did.

—About as much good as what I had to say to you about the topic.

—This is a dead end, Kip.

So it was. Thenceforward when we did speak we spoke of anything but the war and politics. We talked about the Hill, we talked about my mother sometimes, or Jessica in a superficial sort of way. And now he had finished training, and was gone to find his fate on the other side of the world.

After moving out I didn't call Jessica for two weeks, and when I did it was to tell her that I had to be out of touch with her for a while. She knew why without my having to explain. Her response to this was to be ashamed of me, and she didn't hold back.

—Just when you should stand by me and Kip, what do you do? It makes me so mad, Brice. What gives you the right to think you're in love with me?

—I can't tell myself who to love and who not to.

—Why not?

—It just doesn't work that way. You know that. Why are you making me say such stupid things?

—I'm not making you say or do anything. You were the one who moved out. You're the one who's abandoning me—

—Most of my things are still there in your place.

—See. You even call it *my* place. And all because you think you love me. But you don't love me.

—How do you know?

—You just think you love me because if Kip loves me then you've got to love me too. Isn't that the truth? Well, isn't it?

I searched, against her tide of words, for an answer. But Jessica'd hung up. First I was dumbstruck, afterwards what could be described as a slow panic—sharper than dread, duller than fright—came upon me. It was inevitable, I thought. It had been coming for a long time, this argument, but it hadn't gone at all the way I might have hoped it would. Though I'd never had Jessica, I didn't want to lose her.

The silence stretched into two months, in many ways the most disturbed, disturbing months I'd ever know. Filled with precious paradox, they slipped by slowly, switching back and forth from violence to catatonia. From melancholy to odd euphoria. From sensitive if witless clarity to the numb stupidity of the proverbial dumb ox. What was consistent was that I was very alone. Even in the midst of the crowds that would come to define that period of history, which over the years that followed would swell from hundreds to tens of thousands, I was isolated.

My arrest record as an antiwar protester meantime became longer and longer, memorably long in fact. This business of radicalism was incremental. One day, back when still an undergraduate, you elect to help write a position paper instead of finishing an essay on *Macbeth*. You tell yourself that Shakespeare would approve, and so would Macbeth. Nights and terms and years pass, then suddenly you are sleepless wondering whether to burn your draft card, wondering what it would mean to give up your whole life here and leave the country rather than participate as a peon, a hod-carrier of its policies. When I chose to throw a rock or a sidewalk brick, when I took the next step and forced myself down into the thick of a riot and actually drove my fist into the gut of a policeman who was just as surprised as I about it but who didn't move fast enough to catch me when I dove back into the crowd and got myself lost in its storming sanctuary, when I tossed buckets of blood—often just red housepaint deepened with a bit of black to give it the right blush, but sometimes the real thing (I never found out where or how my friends came into possession of this blood, putrid and serous, whose weight and odor one does not forget)—on the front doors of government buildings, when I made these decisions they were like steps. One and then another. Nor did it occur to me to meditate too deeply on the fact that some of these were activities that no self-possessed pacifist should engage in. A step, then two, three.

Restrained pacifism, however, was not a trait I could claim for myself during that time of my life. I found it impossible to accept that everyone was so naive about the direction our government was taking us in Indochina, and had been taking us all along. I did my best to ignore Kip and the steps he had chosen to take.

Who said walking is a series of recovered falls? Jessica haunted me now. With her or not, little failed to remind me of her during the course of a day. I was becoming the very exemplar of the fool in love. There were moments when I found myself deviating toward hating her. Love her, hate her, love her—recovered falls.

It was like trying to waltz a mountain, though. She redefined the term *stubborn*. She gave me no reason to hope, and the integrity that fueled her principles only made my position worse. There were so many times I considered calling, or going by, but was blocked by that mountainous candor of hers. I wanted to apologize, I wanted to try to move back in to 115th Street and see if we couldn't live together as friends, as we had for so long. With every week that passed my own fears became foggy and it became less clear what I'd done to deserve her enmity. What was the crime in falling in love with Jessica? Was it possible Kip left without knowing?—no, it was not possible. So what, so sue me, I thought. And it wasn't as if I proposed to do anything about it. Why couldn't she perceive my affection as a compliment instead of an affront? Through dubious logic I was able to convince myself that love, in certain controlled situations, could remain harmless to both lover and beloved. There's inexperience for you. Love and logic, as is well known, have nothing to do with one another. But surely Jessica'd gone too far, and I wanted to tell her so. There was no viable or valiant purpose in this separation. Why couldn't I be allowed my little infatuation, so long as I never acted upon it or asked her to reciprocate? My need for some time to digest what was going on in my life: I was unable to view this as an abandonment.

Silence is not golden, never was golden, never will be golden. You put someone in exile, you turn them into a cartoon, you dismiss all objective referents, you relinquish your right to review realities that are there, alive and available to you, at the end of your upturned nose, at the tip of your admonishingly wagging or accusatorily pointing finger. While we have words to speak with, let us talk. Emersonian as it may sound, this is what I now came to conclude, after hours of circular pacing in my downtown room. I made up my mind to risk going over to visit her, but sat for some days, inert. I stood up, I sat down. And, ultimately, it wasn't I who broke the silence.

She was so hysterical I didn't at first understand what she was trying to say. There was something about a telegram, I got that much, and my heart sank. Telegrams are death when your country is at war. But there was more.

She said, —I'm pregnant. Brice, I can't be pregnant.

When I arrived, she was a study in nervous calm. Jessica the mutable. Kip was not dead, as it happened. Nor was it a telegram she'd received, but a letter, the first from Kip since he'd arrived in Vietnam. She put it in my hand without a word, and I read a few lines, no more. Wild place, sick puppies fighting over ghost bones, hate it but can't imagine being anywhere else, I may be assigned north into the fray, or deep south, one is doom the other monotony I don't know which to prefer, no one's coming out of here with anything of use—was how the letter began, or with words to this effect. A disjointed, wise, mad Kip. One who seemed even farther away than on the other side of the world.

I folded the letter, careful to crease it only where it had been folded before, handed it back to Jessica, and when she moved forward to take it from me she kept coming until I found her in my embrace. Some feeble phrase like, —It'll be all right, was all I could manage, but what I felt was unambiguous and more immediate than a slap. Although it was too early in her pregnancy for such things to have developed, I could have sworn I felt her belly was expansive, firm and warm, with the fetus inside. My cheek molded, awkward but exploratory, into the curve of Jessica's head.

—I'm moving back in, I said.

And once more our lives began in the midst of war. Except rather than it being someone else's war, this time it was our own.

PART II

THE FOREVER RETURNING

New York and Long Tieng

to Chimayó,

1968 – 1993

A willow tree grows down by the river that runs between the field and the small park—an open-air chapel, really—behind the church in Chimayó. Willows grow fast, especially when near water, and I would imagine that this one was nothing more than a sapling back when Kip and I first came here half a lifetime ago.

Now, this tree is aberrant in that it has two trunks. At the base of the bole, where the willow emerges from the powdery pale clay of the riverbank, the tree is an individual. A crease in the bark begins just above the ground and the trunk divides into two distinct extensions, one growing thick and straight, the other ascending out away from its counterpart, then flexing back toward it about halfway up. Whenever I have walked in the woods, whether back east or around the Hill, these crouchjobs, as foresters call them, have always been more abundant than one might expect. Nature embracing freakdom, I guess. The aberrants' limbs and branches tend to plait one another in such a way that a double-trunked tree often becomes a threat to itself, with boughs strangling each other, leaves thick and casting too much shadow, so that it becomes choked and diseased.

This willow doesn't seem to be like that. Its bright yellow pendulous boughs have begun to bud, and its contours give evidence of a healthy plant. It has matured, though, in a unique way. Its angled trunk twists back to meet the straight one and I can see even from where I am standing that the two have actually merged. Fused just above the leaf line, they are, so that if you look at the tree straight on, what you see is a single willow crowned with a head of sprouting greenery over two stems that form an elongated triangle. The trunk looks like a pair of legs, back leg upright, front bent at the knee. You squint, and for all the world it looks as if the willow is about to walk.

Kip is sitting under this tree.

He is different and the same. He sees me and stands. There are pilgrims all around us, the second Station of the Cross of the morning having just concluded. Were I trysting with an old lover whom I hadn't seen for a long time, I would not feel more awkward or unnerved. As I work my way toward him through the congregation of Good Friday worshippers, who mill about under the twelve magisterial cottonwoods (one for each of the stations) around the cement pulpit there, and the rustic benches that fan away from it, I wonder what does one say in circumstances such as these—circumstances I as yet don't fully fathom—what does one do? Do I smile? Do I say, Kip, it's good to see you again? Do I wait for him to define the character of the meeting, or what?

Different and the same—eyes as dark as ever, capacious space between them, magnetic as ever. He is wearing an old leather jacket, black jeans, midnight blue sweatshirt. He has a cap on, which he removes. He is thin.

"Thank you for coming, Brice," as he shakes my hand.

"It's good to see you," I say.

"I didn't know whether you would or not."

"You knew I'd come," and his hand, firm and powerful, lets

go of mine. To him there is an ineffable compressed seriousness. His cheekbones are more prominent than before, his forehead wrinkled with lines fine as thread, and thread-fine wrinkles fan at the sides of his eyes. He is brown, not quite as deep as mahogany. He has been in the sun. In the whites of his eyes, jaundiced to saffron, ocher like antique ivory, I recognize something off. This is my first impression.

He smiles his curious lopsided smile and in it I see immediately my old childhood friend. "Do you believe how many people make the pilgrimage now?" he says. "Not like back in the old days when just a few eccentrics and a handful of true believers would come out. It's an occasion now. But you know what, I've been watching them and I swear most of these people are believers still. Even now, after everything that's gone on. I envy them."

"You look well," I say.

Kip narrows his eyes at me and it is as if I am being looked through. Another of his traits I'd forgotten, a singular mannerism to forget, since it was one he displayed often when we were growing up together. It wasn't the evil eye but was unconscious, I always felt, on his part. Something he did when a person made a statement he wanted to *see* better.

"A quarter century, can you believe how long it's been?"

Despite everything I might have demanded of myself, despite my knowledge that to keep one's own counsel is wisest, not to reveal but to read the revelations others make, I seem unable to suppress the complaint that's inherent in my question. I can hear my voice as the words come forth, can even regret the indictment that's there, subtler than I think perhaps, but apparent enough, and I can only be dismayed with myself. Already scolding him, Brice, already forcing a conversation at cross-purposes; it is as if some part of me has dreamed of this moment when I could finally let him know the extent of my hurt.

He says, "Did you notice this tree? It's my favorite down here."
I grasp he has revealed something to me.

"Not for that long, but the past year or so. I walk down here,
listen to the water when it's running. They regulate the flow. I
never knew how much until I started coming every day. Even in
the wintertime they'll slow it down to a trickle and then suddenly
open up the floodgates. It's really more an irrigation ditch than
a river."

"You've been living in Chimayó?"

"I never much missed this place until I got sick. Then, when
I knew what was wrong I thought, Oh well, where do I go from
here? And then I remembered the santuario, and it seemed like
the right place to come to."

"What's wrong, Kip?"

"First things first. Should we sit?"

"All right," and so we sit and what we begin are several hours
of tales from his last decades and from mine, and when I ask him
what is wrong with him, and what the meaning of his letter is,
he puts it off, rather casually, as just another part of the story, a
natural consequence of what he decided to do with his life after
the war. "I'm telling you," he would say, a little exasperated at
my wanting to hear the end before I have been told the middle.
His stories wander backwards and forwards, just as he did. They
begin with a question he asks me, however, about whether I ever
heard of a form of meditation practiced by the Buddhists where
you set off from the bottom of a hill, a rounded hill chosen just
for the purpose of this meditation, one like Cerro Gordo over in
Santa Fe for instance, and walk in absolute silence to the top? I
say I don't know about it, and he says that the meditator walks
along a path that ascends along a spiral around the hill. Every
time you reach the place you began you are a little higher up,
and from dawn you walk along all morning until finally you reach

the summit, from which you can contemplate all the surrounding fields. This would be midday, if you've timed your climb just right. And then you turn and follow in your own footsteps, around and around again, all the way back down the hill until you reach the bottom that evening.

He tells me he used to do this as recently as last year. The first time he did the walking meditation was at Nam Yao.

"Where is that?" I ask.

It was nothing I might have guessed. Nam Yao was a refugee camp along the Mekong River, in Thailand, just across the border from Laos. He was young still, then. This was after the war was over and the Americans had given up on Vietnam and abandoned their allies in Laos. The Pathet Lao swept into the cities and those who had fought on our side fled the country. Thousands of them together in wretched shanties along the banks of the big brown slow river, families broken, orphans walking like little blind men, their mouths open, their eyes having seen more wickedness in the few years they had been alive than most people witness in a lifetime. In Nam Yao the tops of hills were deforested, and the few trees left standing were as skeletal as the refugees who stood in their gaunt shade. Seven lengths of barbed-wire fencing prevented them from straying deeper into Thailand. There was no going forward for them, and no going back.

These refugees in Nam Yao used their hill in the way their ancestors had decreed. Their dead they buried at the summit in order that their souls find the path to heaven more easily. Below the burial grounds they disposed of their garbage and had their latrines—their refuse they kept in a place above them because, Kip was told, in this way on hot days the smell would rise away from where they lived and be carried off by winds. Below the garbage they'd built a shantytown. It ringed the hill in a disarray of misery. And finally, where the land flattened at the foot of the rise, away from the river, was a cistern—deep and wide—which they had dug by hand to collect rainwater.

When Kip first arrived a terrible thing had happened. The week before, a monsoonal deluge had swept through the river valley. The rain had come down not in sheets but walls of water and had, as if under the influence of an evil spirit, floated the bodies of the dead from their shallow graves, and carried them down through the garbage and human mire into the town of huts and hovels, on the crest of a river of death and filth that finally made its way into the communal cistern. It was a scene of inexpressible horror.

"There was nothing I could do but help them rebury their dead and then try to persuade them to move their dump. It was then I started doing this form of meditation, walking around the hill and up it. I didn't really know what I was doing at first. I just walked. Sometimes I'd stop, if there was someone I could help. But then I'd go on until I reached the burial ground from where I could see across the Mekong into Laos in one direction, and out across the beautiful green hills of Thailand in the other. It didn't take too many of these walks before I figured out what to do."

There was a tributary creek that ran about a quarter of a mile from the encampment. Kip persuaded the Thai authorities to let him run a pipe, two-and-a-half-inch PVC pipe, from the tributary, along the ground and up the hill. He got his hands on an old generator and a pump. It took the better part of a month to accomplish this. "The day we switched on the generator and the sump pump, everybody was standing there waiting, watching. It seemed like the water would never come. All you could hear was air hissing out the pipe, like a gurgling sound, then hissing, then silence. It took forever but when the water finally came, and all these faces that I'd never seen smile suddenly began smiling and laughing—if I never did another thing, it was worth living just for that. It was the greatest moment of my life."

He looks at me and I can feel that I, too, am smiling. It is suddenly quiet, incantations and volley of song are over and the priest has moved to the concrete pulpit to say the third station. I notice that the last segment of Kip's little finger on his left hand is missing. The greatest moment of his life: after all these estranged years the same possessiveness in me toward Kip is brightly viable. I sit beside him and wait for him to continue.

Nothing's more fertile than a secret. Secrets father secrets that in turn father more secrets. What is known is barren and marks the end not the beginning. But secrets lust to make more of their kind. Kip is delivering his own inverted sermon, it occurs to me as I hear the priest intone, "*Como era en el principio, ahora y siempre.*"

Secrets brought him here, not to Chimayó as such, but to this place he was describing to me as the morning went along and the congregants had gathered for another of the hourly devotions, and it would be through some kind of secrecy that he might get back out. The air is scented with smoke still, and the smoke in this valley in New Mexico quite soon becomes for Kip the smoke from a fire in another time and place. It is as if I am with him in Laos as he tells me that he dare not move. He dare hardly breathe.

From one secret to another he had journeyed. It was as if his life were bound together into a single iridescent winding sheet of stealth, so that Kip was always hidden inside a shroud. From one covert place on earth to another. It was second nature to him, though there was nothing secondary about it—more his first nature, this will to move in such clandestine ways. His life was being lived inside an integument, like one of Mary Bendel's pupae. I remember she called us both chrysalid, once, and though we didn't understand what she meant, we were wise enough to fear she was onto us. Chrysalid? we wondered, feeling like fools and looked it up in the big dictionary in the library. Chrysalid came from chrysalis, *a protective covering, a sheltered state or stage of being or growth*. It was an apt image, and I believe the term remains applicable to Kip. Yet even the chrysalis—this quaking life potent yet helpless, wrapped in its own protective cloak—is driven to reveal itself, and once the impatient butterfly bursts forth to take flight and show itself to the world, gaudy as a courtier, it is no longer a secret, but tempts death on its bright wing, and often finds it. Kip shared these penchants.

But how had it come to pass that he was in this clearing, on his side, breathing as quietly as possible, stifling his need to scream? None of our riskiest games might have prepared him for this. All through the night he discovered then rediscovered how far from home he had managed to come. He did not want to dream. He did not want to hallucinate. Was this the distance necessary for him to feel that home was home? Was home what this was all about? Just the kind of questions he did not want to ask himself. Not now, not here. He had never been much of a sleeper in the past. Insomnia would stand him in good stead in this expanse of knee-high cover. But was he awake? Hard to know.

The elephant grass whispered. It told him how exposed he was out here. It told him it was grass, and grass could hide only so much.

Maybe he and the other man should have stayed back in the trees and tangle, but they had understood that their hope of avoiding quick capture was to put as much distance between themselves and the wreckage as they could. They also understood that if they were to be evacuated, it would be possible only from the relative flatness of this rolling field. None of the friendlies would have been able to see let alone reach them under the dense canopy where they went down. This is what Kip thought, and he hoped the grass would understand.

I'll do my best to help you, the grass promised.

Where was his companion? he wondered, and no sooner had he considered that than he forgot. Have you gone crazy? he asked himself. What did the grass think? And what did the ant in the grass think?

Had he been concussed? Had his helmet failed, or had he not secured it? Too many questions. He could not be sure whether he'd even worn his helmet. He touched his skull and his helmet was not there. Maybe he had lost it when running away from the fracas of metal and hollow clacking of gunfire. In war people died more often from the little mistakes than the grand errors of judgment. A false step, a forgotten detail.

Now he was trying to think of what he had just thought. Hell met, oh yes, the grass had asked him if he'd *hell met*.

—Talk forwards please, he murmured.

Then he slept, then he woke.

—Yes and no, he told the grass. It was an answer, but of course he had unremembered the question that invited it.

His colleagues had his coordinates, he was almost certain. It was a matter of who found him first, his people or their people. He had nothing to eat but a granola bar, and nothing to drink, and though he was not hungry, he was thirsty. Maybe the ant would bring him something to drink. Ants know how to carry heavy loads. A thimbleful of water, sir? he asked the ant. The ant wiggled its antennae, the grass rippled.

—Forget it, he said.

Maybe he had a toothpick on him. That would alleviate the thirst and help the time along. His fingers worked through the pockets of his flight vest and touched one by one his possessions. They weren't numerous. His medical kit, his map, his survival knife, his Colt .45 automatic, his bartering gold, his blood chit —a piece of silk folded into a wad with a message printed on it in several languages asking whoever could read it to help the pilot. And here was his pointee-talkee, the phrase book the air attaché had given him back in Vientiane, a bad joke really, the *Yeah Right, Dream On* book he called it, using the same name he once used, upon his discovery that God was dead, for the Bible. The pointee-talkee had English phrases printed on the left-hand pages and Vietnamese and Lao translations on the right, phrases like "I am hurt, please get me to a safe place, you will be rewarded," phrases that were likely never to save a single soldier. It was common knowledge the enemy did not bother taking prisoners in Laos. Not a matter of sadism but rather convenience, as there were neither contingencies nor facilities for prisoners here. It was understood that if you went down and you were captured, you would not be officially recognized as having had anything to do with Laos. Your biography would be rewound to point of departure from Vietnam and odds were that you would just flat disappear as if you had never existed. Were someone to suggest you'd been fighting in Laos, he would find out just how obtuse our government can be when it wants. Field command wouldn't know of you. The ambassador is terribly sorry and denies any intelligence of your activities, and would take the opportunity to reiterate that this was a neutral country and we were not engaged in any military operations here. Maybe you were a mercenary, he might suggest, or maybe you were mad. Maybe there was some mistake. Your parents would get a little note saying you were missing in action and that's about all it would amount to. So much for the pointee-talkee and the blood chit.

Overhead the beautiful stars flickered and aligned themselves into patterns. Kip lay like a child on his back and began to count them. He tried to think of all the different worlds at war up there in the black spaces between the twinkling suns. He wondered if someone were lying in a place foreign to them on one of those worlds, looking out into the universe too, wondering what his fate would be, counting the stars to while away the long, long night. This idea pleased him. Stars were ever-wonderful medicine. As a boy, when he was sick in bed, he would do this, count the many white grains of light in the heavens above his window. The stars had always been our friends. Soon the early mist would dampen them along the horizon, then put them out one by one.

Was there poetry on those distant worlds? Blake had never seen these constellations, had he? More questions—or was that the grass speaking again. No, it was he who was thinking. He thought, It wasn't Blake but Milton who went blind. Milton had two or was it three daughters and they wrote down his poems as he dictated. And Blake? How many daughters did Blake have? And what was it like to have daughters? Kip didn't care, not really, not then and there. What would Thoreau have done in the same situation? Answer, Thoreau would never have got himself into this situation in the first place. Kip didn't smile, but were he in less pain, he might have smiled. He was trying to stay awake and alive, pushing his consciousness along as if it were the Sisyphean stone, up the long hill, and up the long hill again when it rolled back down, as it did over and over.

He slept, and then he woke.

The ant had brought him water and as he drank the ant spoke of Urizen and Lucifer. I never would have thought you'd know so much about such things, Kip marveled. The ant demurred. When Kip thanked him for the water, the grass laughed a little, and the ant began to laugh along with it. You're drinking air, fool, the grass said, finally. When Kip reached out to crush the ant, it was gone, of course. And when he looked at the blades of grass he saw that they were only blades of grass.

Impudence and imprudence landed you in this mess, mother-fucker, he scolded himself. But what passion was there in a life lived with prudence? It was Blake who wrote that only Incapacity would fall in love with Prudence. The line, could he remember it? *Prudence was rich,* it began. No, it went *Prudence was a rich, ugly old maid courted by Incapacity.* Yes, he could draw it up from memory—his tenacious, slipshod memory—and this meant that the accident hadn't robbed him of that part of his mind, but what book was it from? In a moment the answer to his question would come. All he had to do was wait and it would rise to the surface like a message in a bottle carried by obedient waves to his tempested beach. He wondered how could he remember such eccentric fragments? Surely, he reasoned, this was the first time in history that someone lay wounded just here, in this particular wild field of hissing grass, hissing like surf over sand, who conjured a line from the English poet William Blake to anesthetize an evil night. His incapacitation promised to be temporary only, and given he had tried never to court prudence he wondered whether the time to begin was now. An old maid, perhaps, but what had Prudence accomplished to get rich? Pondering this would occupy a quarter of an hour, if not more. Keep out the bad thoughts for fifteen minutes because fifteen minutes was eternity. He closed his eyes, having realized that he'd forgotten which star was the last one he counted.

They had assured him he would never make it through the night up here if he were downed. In most ways it was worse to be shot down over Laos than North Vietnam. There you became a prisoner of war and were reduced by interrogation, torture, humiliation, the gradual destruction of your ego and your will. Here, when you went in you could cry "Mayday Mayday" over the radio for as long as you liked but chances were you were on your own. They might well hear your cries, but often there was nothing they could do. He could still see the long face of the man who, with a rheumy wink, told him that, back in Vientiane. He'd said it without inflection, —Not even a posthumous medal for those back home since officially you're no longer a member of the service. . . . No, I tell you sir, the best advice I got for you is don't get hit.

Where was the grass? He rolled on to his side again. Here I am. Good, the grass was again articulate. Where was the ant?

Fifteen minutes, Kip. One–one thousand, two–one thousand, so the seconds crept just as they had when we used to play hide-and-seek down in the summer canyons. Say, how did Prudence come by her fortune? Hard to guess, quite a question. Three–one thousand. He thought about it not because he cared to know the answer—he decided there was none, Willy Blake had erred —but because given all the reasons there were to abandon hope, you still hoped, and you didn't want to hope, and so you blocked out hope by answering impossible questions. But hope seeped through and stained you anyway. You still pressed your defiant ear hard to the sky to hear the signs of your salvation.

So what happened here?

Before the catastrophe he had stretched forward in the cockpit to landmark his position, note the coordinates on the inside of the windshield with his grease pencil in case the crash would knock him witless. If he could still read and if his UHF survival radio—the field radio that was his "hope chest" (he liked naming these things)—were functional, he could call in his latitude and longitude and try to summon a rescue chopper. The impact had mangled the plane but not caused a fire. They'd already made their run and were on their way back, so fortunately the fuel was low when they took the hosing. He knew where he was. Lima Site 21, Sam Thong, he could make it on foot, if he were lucky enough not to be seen and taken, in two days, three at the outside. Dear Prudence would dictate staying put and waiting for air to come and retrieve him. He would make the decision to move but didn't. He resolved to wait, not be cavalier, and the line from Blake began to persecute him again.

Kip had never been shot down before. His aircraft was, he estimated, half a kilometer north of where he lay. He couldn't remember exactly how he got from the jungle to this field, the adrenaline must have powered his legs. Neng Kha Yang, his Hmong backseater, was conscious on impact, more than conscious, had helped him out of the fragile, broken Bird Dog. They had sprinted together through the thicket until they reached a flatland. Neng Kha Yang had gone out to patrol the area, not to secure it but get a better sense of the immediate topography, while Kip lay in this shallow cover, awaiting morning, not daring to sleep but also oddly doubtful whether he even was conscious. He wondered what was next. Would a Spooky gunship appear in predawn before the enemy found him? the enemy who he heard now and again, as close as a few hundred yards away, having fanned out from the downed aircraft in search of its crew? Would our people bring in one of those Psyops soundships to hover, and broadcast at full volume to point of distortion the music of breaking glass, or women weeping, or bagpipes wheezing, or babies screaming? We did that to torment the enemy in Vietnam, in the theater east of here. Psychological combat. Nobody knew whether or not it worked but we derived a certain pleasure from the savagery of the gambit.

No, there was no such backup in Laos. A bat drove peeping through the dark. Bats here, he thought. Was that acrid stink cordite, or just the stink of fear pouring off him? Or was it napalm. No, that could not be right. No nape here. It was terror and nothing more he smelled.

He could remember a first lieutenant, thin peaked fellow with dilated pupils, who once threatened to cut off a prisoner's nose back near Can Thó. The boy had sneezed in the lieutenant's face during an interrogation. Prisoner stank of terror. Smelled like this present stink.

—Leave him alone, Kip said.

—Fuck off, the lieutenant said.

—He's sick, look at him.

—He's about to get a whole lot sicker.

Kip had learned to turn away from situations like this. They never had happy endings. The kid's fate was sealed and Kip knew that arguing with the lieutenant was a waste of time at best, and at worst could turn into something ugly between himself and the marine.

—You soft on slopes? the lieutenant pushed.

Kip said nothing.

—I tell you what. You like his nose so much, I'm gonna make you a little present.

The prisoner, understanding nothing, sat with his mouth open. His eyes darted back and forth between Kip and the lieutenant.

—You're cracked, man, and with that Kip backed away toward the door of the hootch.

The lieutenant had shouted after him, —You know what. You're right. I'm gonna leave this bastard's nose right where it is.

Kip did not reply, and it possibly cost the captive his manhood because no sooner had he turned his back on the lieutenant than the marine started sawing away at the poor fellow whose agonized cries about his penis Kip understood from his knowledge of Vietnamese slang. Hideous screaming followed him for days after that, screaming and the stench of fear. Soft on slopes. He thought if he could have one thing now, it might be the tongue out of that lieutenant's foul mouth. But that was elsewhere, another time. This was now. He tried to get his mind straight, hold his bearings from veering off further. He listened, he pulled himself with considerable ardor into time present.

Laughter. What he heard was laughter. Dry, emphatic laughter. It irritated him to hear it, and if he was imagining he heard it, he was irritated, superbly and profoundly irritated anyway. Pathet Lao and some Vietnamese troops, the NVA, who were no more supposed to be operating inside Laos than we were. A taunting, chill laughter toward which he was meant to react with hostility. Grace notes, kind of giggles, or sniggers. Sneers, deliberate and calculated to provoke a response that would betray his position. He was up and running, bent over so as not to be seen or shot, and Kha Yang seemed to be running with him. Then they stopped at the far edge of this same field and Kip went down to his knees, keeled onto his side and curled into the fetal position, which he knew not only gave comfort in the maternal grasses but was the posture that least taxed his drumming heart. He clutched his gun, dear teddy bear, to his breast.

He woke up, having slept.

The laughter may have ceased, replaced by a silence intended to inspire dread. Or it may not have ceased, but rather not have been heard by Kip who had bundled his consciousness into a protective coil that mirrored his jackknifed legs, rounded back, head cradled in his own bent arms. His palms locked him in from the jeering world.

Was this perspective enough, *Tan Kip,* as his Hmong

associates—the backseaters who flew missions with him every day, sometimes as many as four between sunrise and dusk—addressed him, perspective enough, Mr. Kip? And though the only perspective these Hmong were concerned with had to do with distances between their spotter plane and enemy movement below, Kip might allow himself to wonder how much farther from the Hill he might have to travel before he could see himself as he had in the ocotillo-framed mirror in his parents' den. He might, on bad days, indulge himself in reveries—some unkind, some kind—about me and Jessica. But such daydreams were reserved for bad days, and bad days were days that saw no action, and the need to assure himself of ceaseless turmoil, a clutter of missions so perpetual that waking nightmares would crowd daydreams right off the mental stage, was satisfied by volunteering for covert duty here. The option was to figure out how to join the grunts up on the incursion points, some of whom had gone berserk, homicidal, who trashed their memories, their futures, any interest in survival, whose sole purpose was to take out as many gooks as they could on their fast descent to hell. For all their madness they had a purpose and a commitment. But gruntdom was not, for whatever reason, an option. Kip was a runner, not a suicide. And so this program in Laos, about which he had kept hearing rumors, suited him.

Prey to memory, he didn't want to be. Not now, not here. "No memories no regrets." He had chalked those words in yellow on a bomb casing before an operation near the tricorner, an early run up the Trail when he was still over in Vietnam, growing bored and anxious. Message in a bottle, again. A form of farewell for his victims, but also a philosophy for himself, one that he knew he could never embrace given the persistence of his memory.

What was he trying to justify? And where was his companion, who went down with him just now, into a sprawl of vegetation?

He should have been back from his patrol by now. But no, hadn't they just been running again? Yes, after the laughter, or?—well, maybe not. It was hard to say. Kip's sense of time was all skewed. Kip should never have let Kha Yang leave in the first place. Mistakes were compounding. It was not good.

Tigers, he remembered. They had smartassed about it back in the capital of Vientiane. There were many tigers out here in the mountains. It was a joke among the pilots, what more brutal irony than to survive a crash and escape capture, only to be eaten by a tiger out in the jungle. Tyger, tyger, burning bright, he thought. In what distant deeps or skies burnt the fire of thine eyes? On what wings dare he aspire?

The grass had sharp edges. Either that or his skin had thinned during these last hours.

Predawn was quieter than ever. He licked his finger, which was wet. He couldn't taste whether it was dew or blood. It didn't matter. He held the finger aloft to check the direction of the wind. The eastern sky was just beginning to brighten, however dully, and the stars had begun to fade under a thickening cover of clouds. It threatened rain, he could smell the moisture. The breeze freshened. His finger tingled most when its damp flesh was pointed south. Wind from the south always boded evil in the old romance novels. Soon enough it began to sprinkle. Weather would keep the rescue choppers grounded, that is, if there were any rescue choppers. It was time to get moving. He didn't move. The clouds continued to lighten. Someone quite nearby coughed. Kip's stomach began to grind. He didn't breathe. A caterpillar of some sort climbed with mechanical vitality over a spear of crushed grass several inches from his eye. His finger tightened on the trigger.

He waited. Nothing happened. Had the cough come from his

own mouth? Perhaps he had drifted off to sleep yet again, despite his efforts, and despite his unwonted anguish—anguish more than fear or dread, almost a form of sorrow or a kind of regret, regret because in his progressive delirium he had come upon the hard fact that he was here because he had put himself here. —What the fuck, he said. The ant was there again and seemed to hear him. It wiggled its antennae, like a rigid semaphorist. —Tell it to me straight, Kip beckoned. The ant did not reply. He was mildly surprised it seemed not to have the power of speech. Blake had written about a fly—"For I dance and drink and sing till some blind hand shall brush my wing." Had he ever written about an ant?

Kip, stop flowing, man, he thought. Keeping his mind steadied was like trying to nail a raindrop to the wall.

Then it happened. The hand on his shoulder was real, very real, and grasping him. It was strong.

The cough and the hand came in lightning succession despite the intervention of observations and ideas. The moment felt excessive. It was as if the amount of time that passed between the cough, then the occurrence of the hand touching his shoulder, and his response to the hand on the shoulder was not enough to accommodate the emotions and thoughts coursing through his imagination. The time should have been doubled or trebled to hold all that occurred within its temporal borders. Regret didn't feel right. No, regret wasn't enough. It was more like revulsion. Arrogance had brought him to this. He was so angry with himself. His skill, his training, his native intuition should have precluded this ever coming to pass.

As the fingers tightened he resigned himself to the worst. He knew what would be in the man's other hand. And in his own he held nothing with which to protect himself but a gun whose two spare clips wouldn't give him even two dozen rounds. —The last bullet's for yourself, the pilots always joked. Shoot, get it on, get it over with.

Then it was all movement. He twisted around toward the one who had him in his grasp, and let out a guttural, weird howl. Ire, terror, frenzy, an elaborate weave, no language, just noise, or this cluster of such unlikely noises, bound into a single cry, and though it was not loud (terror imprisoned much of the air in his lungs), it was compelling because so peculiar.

Neng Kha Yang locked his hand over Kip's mouth, and whispered, —You no shout, no shout.

—What the fucking, goddamn it, Kha Yang.

—Quiet, you be quiet, Tan Kip.

Kip's finger eased forward off the trigger. His barrel was at Kha Yang's temple. He stared with wild eyes at Kha, and said, —Where the hell you been?

Kha Yang's English was a little better than that of many backseaters but he still communicated with gestures and the few dozen words necessary to his job. —Here, he said.

—It's almost morning, argued Kip.

The Hmong hesitated.

Kip pointed to his watch, then to the brightening sky.

—Where you been all night? All night you've not been here.

Kha Yang shook his head and frowned. —I here, night. You here, sleep.

—Where are we? he asked.

—We here. They know.

—Who knows? Bad guy knows?

—No, they know.

—Our people know.

—Yes, our people.

The downdraft began to buffet through the grasses and a gust now and again carried with it a light spray of rain. Our people might know they were here but so did the enemy. He was out there, the enemy was, and Kip had learned to think of them as him, as not the *bad guys,* which was what everyone called them —not Viet Cong, not VC or Charlie as over in Vietnam—but the enemy, one body made up of thousands of youthful enemies, boys and men and women and girls, and to Kip melded as if into a single organism, regenerative and apparently ineradicable. Having grown up where there were no mangrove channels or tidal pools, Kip had only read about the sea star and how if it lost one of its rays, it simply generated another. He was like that, the enemy. And he was out there now.

The first time Kip had seen him dead up close, his youth and beauty were arresting. He turned the frail body over not with the tip of his boot but with his hands, less an act of reverence, more curiosity satisfied, because yes he wanted to *touch* the thing. It was featherlight, this corpse, and upon its visage, astonishing tranquility. Genderless, the delicate neck, his eyes moist and contoured like a sunflower seed, the cheeks pronounced and lips apart, the look on his face of modest, languid surprise. As if to be no longer alive was unexpected.

That was not quite a year ago, and Kip had seen so many of the boy's comrades since then that their beauty and adolescence he had come to take for granted.

And, yes, he was out there now. Kha Yang, whom he watched in a very loosely focused sort of way, betrayed no nervousness about their vulnerable situation. He was armed but must have known as well as Kip that if the enemy wanted to take them, Kha Yang could not prevent it.

—Why don't they move? Kha Yang's comrade asked.

Kha Yang looked into the south skies and listened for friendly air. The sun was coming up, or had already come up, and the heavy mists wore a pearlescent glow. The earth was fragrant, smelled of sweet feces and of jism, fecund as the scent of intercourse. The grass rattled and sang, but it was just dumb grass now. Where was everybody? What was going on here?

—Why don't they move? he echoed himself.

—You are hurt? his companion asked.

Kip couldn't tell. He must have been, mustn't he, but it was beyond knowing.

They hunkered down, silent, and waited. No sooner had it begun than the rain seemed to end. Kip may have dozed again, he could not tell wakefulness from dream, and didn't care to distinguish them. No point to it at that moment. He knew that should the need arise for him to burst into consciousness, he would.

Kha Yang clicked his tongue then. Kip admired his adjunct for these tics. Kha Yang was simple, in his way, readable. Kip listened, too, for that's what the clicking tongue was meant to communicate.

Air was off to the south, very low. And he heard now, from another direction, up above the cloud cover, a T-28. No, not one but two of them. In the southern air was what sounded like a Jolly Green Giant. It was about to happen, it was going to happen, Kip thought.

Popping at every periphery. Resistance from the ground had begun. Tracers lit up the fog like a false dawn. Flak fire from the gunners' nests on the near hills. Blasts, and snapping from a gatling gun festooned the soft wind. The enemy had not bothered with Kip and Neng Kha Yang because the enemy wanted more from the situation, wanted to take out a chopper if one arrived to evacuate pilot and his spotter from where they were pinned down. This tactic was nothing new over in Vietnam but the enemy here was often too disorganized and dispersed to employ sophisticated strategy. But here it was, going on. The T-28s were pounding positions just north and east now, plummeting forth from the cloud base to rain fire not a quarter kilometer away. Kip and his backseater hugged the earth as their own position was strafed. High and wide the barrage poured in so that it appeared they would be cut off from the rescue chopper, but then there was a break in the action. The lead T-28 had swung around to unload the balance of its ordnance, and after a series of profound explosions, punctuated by secondary blasts which indicated to Kip that an unfriendly position had been hit, there was first a riveting flash of silence, then the conspicuous, horrid sound of engine trouble. Kip took the chance of divulging his location to some sniper who might just be waiting for him to make a mistake by raising his head to see the plane forfeiting altitude, veering in a lazy course out away from the heavy forest toward this open pitched field, and before long a parachute burst into view. Most of these T-28s flown by the Hmong were antiquated and had no ejection system, so it was a promising sign that the pilot had managed to pry his canopy open and scramble out. At least he wasn't dead yet, though floating under his idle chute, he would be easy prey in the gunsight of anyone who wanted to pick him off. The second T-28 dove through on a final strafing run, and hell broke loose again from a more distant enemy perch. The parachute disappeared over a rise downfield.

Time fractured. The grass was flattened by the density of the downthrust wind off the chopper blades. There was shouting, and he was lifted by several arms, carried to the platform, and no sooner were they aboard than the chopper dipped, then banked hard, rolling him over on his back. A medic was asking him what was wrong. He shouted over the din, —Forget it, I'm fine. Kha Yang sat on heels next to him studying the quick landscape that tumbled behind, and knew better than to contradict Mr. Kip. He understood, too, why Kip had warded off medical attention. Having worked so hard to get detailed up in Long Tieng, he didn't want to risk being medevaced down to Udorn or worse yet, out to the Philippines. The breed of soldier who sought out an injury by which to rotate home was not one who ended up in Laos, and certainly not as a member of the Raven outfit. Just the opposite. These came to work. Kha Yang knew that if they got out of their present situation within the week, Kip would be back in the air, back on mission.

The fire was more sporadic now. The chopper dropped, hovered. The door gun was rattling away all the while the Hmong pilot from the other plane was hauled in, unceremoniously, by the collar of his flight jacket. He was breathing, but his leg was a mess, must have been hit on the drift down. Kip and the man—both on the metal floor of the chopper, a chaos of vibration, its floor violent, which now was taking on velocity—locked eyes, and seeing the other give him a thumbs-up just before he passed out, Kip managed, —I owe you, then himself closed his eyes to retreat back into his head.

Sometime before they reached Long Tieng it came to him. That line. Came to him in the midst of a litany of promises he was making to himself that he would never be downed again, and that if he did, he wouldn't call in help but get himself out of the jam on his own. What came to him was he remembered that the contemplation of Incapacity and Prudence was one of Blake's proverbs. *The Marriage of Heaven and Hell.* A proverb in fact from hell.

His eyes opened and he saw his finger caked with blood. He should have known it wasn't dew he'd tasted back there lying on the grass. A broad smile broke across his face, and he thought, Proverb from hell, wasn't that just too perfect for words.

Kha Yang looked at his partner and shook his head. —Tan Kip, he said. —What so funny you laugh?

Kip closed his eyes and said, —You are funny, Kha Yang. You are making me laugh.

—Tan Kip, Kha Yang mused. —Tan Kip, he crazy sometimes.

*T*heir engagement might have been made more formal, might have been expressed with more resolve, she thought. They might as well have gone ahead and married, if they were as much in love as they told one another they were. Even before her pregnancy was confirmed she found herself regretful at not having been more direct with Kip about her dread of his leaving her with this promise, his proposal, and nothing more. Or, if not more direct, more sure *herself* of what she wanted to do, because wasn't it true that she had resisted the idea of making an "institutional commitment" as much as he? Wasn't it true that even now, as she thought about it, she couldn't with confidence remember whose somewhat cynical definition of marriage those words had been?—"institutional commitment," like being committed to an asylum for the romantically insane? And which of them had proclaimed, with all the studied naivete of a lyricist writing a mushy Broadway musical, though perhaps without the lyricist's understanding that most musicals are by definition cheap fantasies expensively staged, that they "needn't a piece of paper to keep their love together"? Another question for them: why bother with these ridiculous French terms—fiancé, fiancée, past participles of *fiancer,* to vow, promise, trust—and all the wicked weight of history and tradition they conjure, if neither she nor Kip had the mettle to carry that weight to its proper end? He had come back from

New Mexico after the death of his parents and proposed to her, had he not? And she had accepted. There was the valid excuse to delay the marriage because air force regulations stipulated only unmarried men may enter pilot training school. Training stretched over months into two years or so. But things drifted after flight school, Kip left for his tour of duty, and now, here she was, into her second trimester, this fiancé of hers on the other side of the world. Jessica could with the authority of experience shake her head at the thin innocence she and Kip had shown regarding all this. But couldn't she at the same time be grateful, if that is the word for it, that the piece of paper did not exist, given how things seemed to be evolving?

Jessica reminded herself, when these regrets crowded her head, as they did more and more now, that wartime romances—at least as she had understood them through the movies—often were fraught with problems. She remembered the Preston Sturges picture *The Miracle of Morgan's Creek* that was supposed to be a comedy but which she didn't find funny at all. It was a campy classic, and she had gone to see it by herself, in fact with the thought that it might cheer her up, or at least distract her from her own problems.

A room full of newspapermen has heard the report of a miracle. Mayhem, pandemonium, everyone talking at once. The telephone lines are singing, —Miracle down at Morgan's Creek, there's a miracle down at Morgan's Creek. What was it, what was the miracle? They all want to know. Jessica settled into the plush violet velveteen of the seat to enter into the world of Betty Hutton and Eddie Bracken. Flashback to 1943, late spring or early summer, a time when Jess was only a year old, the foliage full in the black-and-white print, the war storming overseas. The sweet patriotic youth of Morgan's Creek looking sharp in their starched uniforms, under orders to ship out early next morning, determined to have themselves one devil of a farewell ball. Betty with her bright smile and coquette's manners, and Eddie whom the service rejected because whenever he was nervous—which was almost always—he began to see black spots before his eyes. Here is the problem. Eddie loves Betty, Betty loves the boys. Betty's father refuses her permission to attend the dance, so Betty arranges to go to the movies with Eddie. But Betty is just using the date with reliable Eddie as a ruse to trick her father. Once she's left the house and is safely out of sight, she ditches her nervous suitor—tactfully telling him she will pick him up after the movie is over, and borrowing his car in order to drive to the dance. Eddie, poor fool, complies. Hands in pockets he disappears into the moviehouse.

The party. Many drunken and happy faces. Betty dances and dances the evening away with one anonymous, dashing soldier after another. Somehow during the night a group of them, boys and girls, reeling with the spiked punch, gets it in mind to drive to the nearest justice of the peace, and all get married. It is accomplished in a haze. Betty, in the morning light, still plastered, swings by the moviehouse to pick up loyal Eddie, who's been sleeping on a concrete bench. The front fender of his jalopy is bashed and the seats are bedecked with paper ribbons, decorations from the dance. Eddie, ever patient if a bit nonplussed, drops her off at home. It is only later, when Betty is recounting to her younger sister the hilarious events of the evening, and her narrative comes to the part where a bunch of them blindly drove off to get hitched, that a shadow of dismay crosses her face. She glances down at the ring on her finger and nearly faints. She can remember getting married but cannot remember her husband's name. What a fine mess. And that's not all. She soon comes to believe she's pregnant. How can she keep her father from finding out that she went to the soldier's dance after all? What is she to do? It doesn't take her long to figure out the answer. Why, she'll get Eddie to marry her, of course. Eddie will have to take the blame for this unfortunate pregnancy, but Eddie's enough a swell kind of boy to agree to a little thing like that. Eddie will understand.

Jessica left the theater before the film was over. She didn't stay to find out what the miracle was, because if she believed in miracles before she saw this movie, she certainly didn't believe in them now that she had. Miracles were fools' fiction, panacea for the thick, the dim, the stubborn. Betty disgusted her because Betty was selfish, and Eddie disgusted her because Eddie was selfless. No, she thought, there was no more a miracle to be celebrated at Morgan's Creek than there was in New York. The deep insolence of patriotism was what irritated her most about the movie, that the boys shipping off to their uncertain fates on the battlefield should be exonerated—if only for a night—from responsibility for the bedlam they leave behind.

It was hot in the streets. Thick humidity clamped down on the night people, of whom there were many, couples here and there just ambling along, individuals sitting on stoops. Jessica didn't want to go home yet and found herself walking toward Central Park. Haze hung in the trees like blurred gray webbing. She drifted without purpose until she found a bench. Images from the Sturges film replayed themselves on a warm, low screen of mist for her, and she had no trouble summoning an image of the boy who stood before the justice of the peace with Betty and said, "I do," in a slurred voice, "Ahy *thoo*," like a solemn sneeze, and as she did she changed his face to that of Kip. The imaginary portrait was more disturbing than she might have expected. It wasn't that his countenance was distorted: she hadn't twisted him into a monster. Quite the opposite. It was simply Kip she saw projected against the sheet of night haze, Kip neither smiling nor frowning, not quite looking her in the eye but not looking away either. She wanted to ask him something and he looked at her in such a way that she knew he had no answer for her.

—Damn you, she whispered at his miasmic face.

When she came home I was awake. It was as if she left one movie and walked straight into another.

—You all right? I asked.

I followed her from the front room to the doorway to her, or rather, *their* room. She pulled out a suitcase from the closet, theirs. There was a domesticity established between Jessica and myself that allowed me to trail along behind her without giving much thought to her possible desire for privacy. If she wanted to be left alone, it was understood that she'd simply say so. She hadn't answered my question.

—Well?

—Well what?

She was staring at the chest of drawers as if shocked by it, somehow, as if it were most unfamiliar.

—I said, Are you all right?

—No, I'm not all right.

—You mind if I ask you what you're doing?

She'd broken whatever spell had come over her and begun to pull clothing from the chest. A heavy white cable-knit sweater was packed, then unpacked.

—Jessica? What are you doing?

—I'm going over there. She didn't look up at me, was on her hands and knees now in the closet rummaging through a clutter of shoes, both Kip's and her own.

—Over where? I asked with some innocence.

—Vietnam, she said. —To Saigon, that's where.

—Saigon, I said, voice flattened by the variety of responses I felt. How I envied Kip at that moment. Who was he to deserve this devotion, or deference or homage or passion or allowance? I managed to say, with broader voice, —He's not in Saigon, Jessica.

—I'm going to find him and he's going to know.

—You already wrote him, give it time. He maybe hasn't even got the letter yet.

—I want him to know.

—He'll know without you going there to tell him.

She said, —It's hot in Saigon, right?

Summoning the presence not to say something catty, I said something silly. —Don't you need some kind of special visa or something? You can't just pack a suitcase and go to Saigon.

Silly or not, this slowed her down. She appeared forlorn and frail in the yellow light that gave from the closet in a downcast column, and my eyes underwent a strange sea change of sorts. Rather than gazing on her with the lonesome empathy of an unrequited lover, I found myself staring at her with open anger.

—What?

—I said you can't just get on a flight to Saigon, just like that.

She looked at me for the first time since she'd come in. My voice must have produced the words in different timbre. Her pupils expanded toward the edges of her irises, were so commodious that I felt as if I might fall into them if I stared at her long enough. —Are you all right? she asked.

I ignored this and said, —There's a war on, Jessica, remember?

She laughed, but soundlessly, and I will never forget the shape of her lips, turned outward into a wave neither frown nor smile but with elements of both, her whole face broken into a contortion, her forehead furrowed with drifts of parallel lines, her eyes welling into tears, which never flowed easily with Jessica.

—Jess, I said, helpless as a scolded child.

It was as if she drew the tears back into herself; she would not cry, nor laugh. Her face was once more hers. —South Vietnam's our ally, isn't it? I'm sure citizens can go there. Tomorrow I'll get a visa, and then I go. I can't live like this.

—You can't live like this, I echoed, but she didn't hear me, or if she did, she wasn't able to detect my irony.

Nothing more was exchanged that night between us. I left her to her preparations and craziness, and back in my room, behind the closed door, made a pact with myself to move out again—this time for good—when she was gone. Withdrawal was the only path toward sanity here, I assured myself. To persevere in the face of her attachment to Kip seemed immoral, I assured myself. This time I would take all my belongings with me. She could find someone else to cover half the rent, it wouldn't be so hard to do. Left as is, the roles we'd assumed would lead us to unavoidable sadness, and I told myself I didn't want to learn to loathe Kip any more than I already had. It wasn't right. I had to give all three of us a reprieve. I was sick of being ashamed at all my gestures of duplicity. And I could sense that now I was at the outer bounds of my patience with Jessica, too. Though I might not want to admit it, I was on the very verge, myself, of exploding. God knows, if I were a shrewder man, I'd have abandoned this mess a long time ago. It had to end.

That night, despite the droning mosquito that drew a vortex in the darkness of my room, despite the ponderous summer heat, I slept a dreamless and benign sleep.

Back in Long Tieng he would sleep too, sleep for several days in the Raven hootch. When he awakened he got up and that seemed to be the end of it. Kha Yang was ready to fly again as soon as his partner wanted. They went up later that same morning. Kha

Yang noticed that their experience on the ground hadn't made the American more reserved or cautious. If anything, the good-luck star over his head was brighter than before, and he proceeded with greater grace and accuracy and abandon. He would be back to his sixteen-hour days within the week.

So how had he gotten there? I want to know.

The stories come fast, and to me they are so singular in their way that I find myself forgetful about how awestruck I should be at the fact that their narrator and protagonist is here in the person of my oldest friend, my daughter's father, my wife's ex-lover, a man I thought I would never lay eyes on again, someone better forgotten, it often seemed to me. But we are here. And what Kip is telling me I am envisioning with a kind of charged clarity that is hard to fathom, and harder to explain. Spring light, desert air, the valley filled with believers, the magic of Chimayó and its inexplicable purity—these contribute to my own sense of the deep importance of this meeting between two men who have been strangers to one another and at the same time intimates, even counterparts like gender-same yin and yang, like the light of *chiaro* and dark of *oscuro* that characterizes an old master painting.

We sit, we speak, we listen. We do this with unwonted urgency. I want to remember everything. He wants me to remember, and I know that though I would try, I might never hold on to all of it. It dawns on me that I am hearing the history of the other half of my life for the first time. The only time. It seems, too, that by giving me that other half Kip senses he will survive somehow, intact and fulfilled. He says, "I was discouraged beyond any concept of discouragement I'd ever had before. There aren't words for it. Demoralized is too optimistic. Depressed is too cheerful. Bored to tears, bored to death, beyond death even."

Deeply, unutterably discouraged. Before Laos and Long Tieng, existence was an unexpected grind. After all he had gone through to become a pilot, here he sat bored as bother in the sultry sun and the deep humidity, on a pitted concrete slab that may once have been a tennis court, next to the remains of a small building—some sort of clubhouse, or garden shed—that had rotted down to its stone chaff of a couple of broken walls. Southernmost South Vietnam. Here he lay back in his own private getaway on a decaying mattress and listened to warped, scratchy records and tried to get himself to learn Vietnamese, a language that but for a few words and phrases evaded him, and perfected his tan. Some might envy his position down in Ca Mau, precisely because nothing was happening. But it was different to wish for calm and to be caught in calm. Kip was tired, exhausted not from physical exertion or mental stress, but from inactivity. Enervation had set in like rust, or mold.

Can Thó, the nearest major military base, was some two hundred kilometers to the north. Between Ca Mau and Can Thó were rivers and jungle and fields. Hong Dan and Go Quao were the only villages of any size you might overfly between them. Compared to the north there was little activity in this region anymore and command wanted it to stay that way. Hence the strategic value of peaceful Ca Mau, at least on paper, on maps. But to be stationed here was, for Kip, a terrible detention. Already he was softening. He drank too much with the others. He slept too long. He'd even taken up smoking—a habit he had always despised in the past, perhaps because his father had been a chain-smoker, and anything his father had done was to be avoided. The cigarette occupied his hands, the pouch and papers, the expertise involved in rolling one's own. The burning in his lungs, which bothered him, was even deemed somehow valuable in breaking the deathly dragging boredom, in that it gave him something to concern himself with—should he stop smoking, or not, and if so when, today or tomorrow? Well, it was a problem he would have to think about.

The detachment set up in what seemed to have been a monastery, or an old French hotel—rundown now but clearly once a place, if not of splendor, of certain amenities. Architectural details there were few and those were the worse for wear. The balustrade leading from lobby to the floor above was of ornate molded wrought iron capped with a teak rail. A chandelier in the dining room collected dust but still threw off translucent reds and purples and blues through its many glass prisms. Guest rooms where the officers bivouacked had small balconies, each fitted out with more of the same fanciful wrought iron. The original furniture must have been stolen, Kip figured, before we got here. Now, but for tables in the bar and some chairs whose fabric was haggard and cushions fatigued, the place stood pretty empty. What furnishings existed were standard-issue Army gear. Cots in the rooms, drab olive blankets meant for another war in another climate, folding chairs. Radio and other communication equipment had been set up in what used to be the manager's quarters. Like Kip, all the current residents of the hotel were American military, and like him most were unhappy about the noncontact assignment they had drawn. Morale was low, frustration was high. The couple of men who weren't upset by all this stasis had already seen some action, already been through shooting incidents, and could speak with authority, had stories to tell. They considered the hotel a nice respite, a place to fill out papers, drink in the evening, relax. A tropical country club fallen on hard times.

—Hey, one said, what's the rush? You're gonna see more than you ever wanted to see in no time.

—Not at this rate I won't, said one of the new arrivals.

The first man continued, —Over in the U Minh forest, over

there west of Ca Mau, over toward the coast? Over there they got a war on. U Minh's a triple-canopy forest, doesn't get more dense.

—Triple-canopy? asked Kip. This was a story he hadn't heard before.

—Trees peaking at three levels. Short trees, medium, then your top cover of tall trees—triple canopy. The forest is so thick, you can't see what's going on down on the ground, which makes it perfect headquarters for the bad guys. So one day there's a bunch of us talking about this damn triple canopy and how we got to find a solution to it and we come up with this scheme, see. What we're going to do is, we decide the best way to handle this situation is to burn it down.

—What?

—Burn it down, from a triple- to a zippo-canopy forest. So we get together with some C-123 jocks we'd met at the Can Thó O Club and one Sunday we get some old condemned jet fuel and we load it in drums, bring it down, and we fly over and dump barrels and barrels of this jet fuel, and set it on fire. Let me tell you. That was one fire. Beautiful bitching old mother of a fire, beautiful. But what happens is we light it so good that it starts making such an updraft, it causes a thunderstorm to start in the humid air, unstable air there, a freak rain, and what happens but it rains so hard, it puts out the goddamn fire!

The man laughed, and the others joined him but none of the neophytes felt differently about their wretched lot in life. Kip, who neither laughed nor asked the man any further questions, in fact knew that forest. Whenever he got tired of sunning himself out on the concrete at the outskirts of town, whenever he wearied of his thoughts and the same old songs on the plastic portable turntable, he would take one of the planes up and just fly around looking for something to do, all the time monitoring the various ground radio channels—calling in to command posts to see if they needed anything checked out.

Once he had flown out in that direction and there was a Coast Guard ship whose captain wanted to fire his guns at something, get in some activity on the day, and Airborne Command radioed Kip and asked him if he had any time available, and Kip said, —Sure, sure, while thinking, What else do I have available? and they gave Kip a frequency and a call sign to contact the ship, and this captain asked him if he had targets, he had some boys on board who wanted to shoot their guns.

—You want to shell anything in particular? asked Kip.

—Put us on whatever strikes your fancy, sir.

The collection of huts whose coordinates Kip gave the captain appeared to be abandoned, two of the three were roofless, but of course he couldn't be dead sure. He banked to make a second pass to verify the farm was deserted but the captain called all clear, and so he had to make a fast departure from the airspace so as not to take a hit himself. Maybe there were people in there, maybe not. He tilted his wings to a vertical and bore away. —All clear, he said, long before he was all clear. Out of the corner of his eye, down by one of the shanties, something moved. With luck, an ox. He didn't want innocent blood on his hands already and for no good reason. Wasn't that the tragedy inscribed into the very words, *Los Alamos*, that designated home? He didn't need to repeat such things here. No, he decided; nothing had moved. A shadow was all it had been. The sun had caught a wing strut at just the angle that would create an illusion of ground movement.

—Okay, he heard the captain say.

All clear . . . okay, funny kind of death sentence, wasn't it? He hadn't been in Vietnam three months and already he understood one crucial aspect about its character, that certainties weren't part of the landscape. If you cherished waking up to the same world in which you'd fallen asleep, you would soon find your reason stretched to a gossamer thinness, stretched and twisted and maybe just broken. Somehow Kip had got that within the first month of being in-country. You have to stay loose and strong at the same time, you can't get stiff—you've got to remember that in heavy gales the stiff branches of a tree are the ones that break. And when he banked away to let the artillery barrage come in, he recognized the shadow of a doubt about that third hut and the possibility of there being some civilians inside, so he told himself, Stay loose. It was afternoon, wasn't it? What kind of farmers would be hanging around in their hut on a hot afternoon like this? And as he watched the scene, not a thousand feet below him and out toward the north, boil in orange and then black, he recognized at once what you do with such doubts is to lay them to rest right down there at the epicenter of the flames, to see them for the stiff dry tinder that they are, and place them so they incinerate themselves rather than scorch *you*. This was how he learned to stay limber.

Kip passed over the site and saw the structures were collapsed and on fire, as were several acres of the surrounding tract. He may or may not be seeing figures in the paddies just east of the hamlet. They couldn't be there. He saw them, he didn't.

The captain was requesting assessment.

Wake up, he told himself. And what he said was as outrageous as it was common. He wanted the captain to feel good; he wanted to feel good. He said, —Your BDA, sir. We got three bunkered command posts destroyed here.

BDA, bomb damage assessment. Lies, as often as not. It is what they also called a WAG, a wild-assed guess, the sheerest sort of fiction. But Kip wasn't guessing, of course.

—Thanks much, said the captain.

—See you, said Kip.

War. A WAG's war. And Kip would fly himself back to base and the hotel and there would be some small satisfaction in having at least seen a pantomime of action from the air. By the time he touched down, those figures would be gone, if not from the rice paddy at least from his memory. And before they were gone they would be altered. They probably weren't children, or women, or innocent rice farmers. They might have been water buffalo. Or else they might have been nothing more than phosphenes, those little squirming lights that can crawl across your field of vision when you are fatigued.

Two weeks after that, Kip had his first real experience, and would discover that the process of mentally revising the war to fit his own spiritual needs might be harder than expected. One of the army personnel came into the hotel and reported that they had troops in contact at a certain coordinate—TIC as it was called, an antonym to TLC—and he asked, —Can you go over and take a look? Here's the radio frequency we're working with in there.

Kip flew over the coordinate and was told by the man on the ground, —Some bad guys over here about a hundred yards, can you get some air?

—We'll see what we can do, Kip radioed back, got on another channel to the Airborne Command Post and asked if fighters were available. At any given hour there were aircraft aloft on combat air patrol, killing time, waiting for orders. As it happened, two Phantoms were nearby, and were ordered in.

—Where do you want it? the flight leader asked, and Kip gave them geographical coordinates, went in, launched his marking rockets, and radioed, —Okay, hit my smoke. From eight thousand feet the two-ship descended and once again the earth metamorphosed from stable green to cascading reds and blacks.

Kip watched the pyrotechnic display from the window of his slow craft. This wasn't artillery practice, and he could physically feel the difference, the heavy low thud impacted his chest, like a sonic boom, a profound thump, the tightening of the shoulders and neck, the punch and ferocity of the bombing below, the stunning detachment of those voices coming into his ears when one of the pilots announced he'd taken a hit. Kip meantime flew over the target to assess damage. The pilot who wasn't hit had simply stepped up his focus so that now he engaged at the same time with the ground, with the other fighter, and with Kip as well. The man's voice could not have been more calm. On the ground there was evidence of continued activity about a quarter mile to the east. —What've you got? he asked Kip, and Kip told him, gave him the landmarks and some estimated meterages. The crippled jet, leaking fuel, headed back to base. His wingman banked, made a second run over target, and a new salvo rocked the earth accompanied by a fresh concussion of flame and rolling smoke. Then they were gone, both of them. Kip heard the jargonized acknowledgment of thanks from the calm man, but it made little impression upon him. That is, there were so many other thoughts going through his head that the five, six, seven words signing off were just so much background noise to the percussive din, the heavy cacophony of voices that troubled him just then.

He circled the burning fields both at a lower altitude and more times than he should have. He knew very well that under fifteen hundred feet he was vulnerable to small-arms fire. Maybe he was inviting someone to play a game of peppers with him—a tactic that forward air controllers did employ here sometimes, it was known as trolling—offering whoever was left down there to send up some fire, and give away their hiding places. Like fishing, with yourself both hook and bait. He was drifting along low to the earth, carving such a lazy circle, not making an erratic flight pattern that might protect him. He himself didn't know what his intentions were. He even ventured close enough to get the vaguest sense of what one of the faces of the dead looked like, charred but not so burnt that its features weren't still evident. The burned body woke him up from his aerial stitching. He took on altitude, and set a course toward Ca Mau. So this was the war, he thought. He never found out whether or not the disabled plane made it back home. He cared, but he didn't care. He'd never felt so far adrift from the world, and when he landed he remembered thinking how spongy soft the soil under his feet seemed. It was like he wasn't much anyone doing anything anywhere. And rather than being a strange moment, memorable for its spectral, delusory augur of the void, the void for a while took a fancy to him and decided to move into his heart and head, take residence in Kip. He could fight an enemy, but not this undefinable emptiness.

The charred face came back to visit him during the nights that followed. He almost welcomed it, this odd recurrent nightmare, because it was something that was palpable, more concrete than half of what he experienced during the course of a given day.

In the dream the charred face spoke, saying, *Tên tôi lá Kip. Mây giò rôi? Xin cho tôi zem bán thúc don?* Vietnamese from his primer. Black teeth and black tongue moving, black lips quite near, saying over and over, My name is Kip. What time is it? Can I see the menu, please? I like that. How much does that cost? And a black finger would then point to Kip's foot. The dream always ended the same way, with Kip failing to find the words in Vietnamese to tell the charred face that his foot was not for sale.

These were climaxes, then, blessed crises that shattered for the briefest hours the prodigious, overwhelming ennui that ruled the routine of Ca Mau.

They weren't enough. If anything, they served to intensify the boredom by providing a comparative. For Kip, highs and lows were tolerable. It was experience of the middle he found unbearable. That middle was where the void dwelled. It had to leave, this had to stop, he begged himself.

One morning, before dawn had spread its tropical whiteness through the maze of the hotel-monastery, Kip rose, had some coffee, and drove himself out to the airfield in a jeep loaded with radios and sprouting so many antennas it resembled a metal insect. He had been down here for only eleven weeks and three days, not counting the day that was just emerging, but he knew it was time to make a move. He preflighted his plane, fired it up. The runway had upon it a light skein of mist, and he sailed through it and up into the high air. Over east the yellow sun brimmed while along the western horizon the purple lip of night still clung. He set a course north toward Can Thó.

During his first in-country briefing, the operations officer in Saigon had paused in the middle of the lecture about rules of engagement and procedure, had fixed the new men with a peculiar, wicked look and said, —If any of you gentlemen don't get enough excitement where you're going and you want to jump things up a notch, then you come on back after your tour and there are some people here who'll be happy to talk to you about a program we got.

—What kind of program, someone asked.

—Steve Canyon program.

—What's that?

—As I say, it's for those of you still intact and wanting a little adventure in your life.

Get off it, Kip thought at the time. Where do they get these people? Dropouts from drama school who had learned just enough about theatricality to make a nuisance of themselves. The briefing had continued without further definition of the program.

But it had come up elsewhere. Others mentioned it, but weren't quite sure what was the nature of the enterprise. Around it was an aura difficult to define—some scoffed at the mystery in which it was shrouded, others sensed it was too dangerous even to consider—but to Kip with each day wasted in Ca Mau, the Steve Canyon program became more and more the focus of his thoughts. He assumed the designation for the program was an ironic smoke screen meant to disguise a serious agenda, despite the briefing officer's insipid delivery. Steve Canyon, a comic-strip superpatriot and ace flyer. Just the kind of marginal folk hero they would go and use as a mascot. Kip remembered Steve Canyon well, and how after the war he founded his own one-plane firm, Horizons Unlimited, used a Navajo double-eagle design as his emblem, and traveled around the globe on perilous missions. Steve once was one of Kip's heroes, too. But time had passed. Now he thought, Steve Canyon—give me a break. It was resonant of the absurd, Milquetoast term "the Gadget" that Oppenheimer used whenever referring to the bomb. "The Gadget" was meant to make it easier for those on the Hill who were involved in building the bomb to talk about it and not feel quite so guilty about its intended destiny. Just what was "Steve Canyon" meant to mask? he wondered.

Up in Can Thó it was overcast and getting sticky. Still morning but the day was heating up. He found himself referred from one officer to another until, in a cool room whose ceiling fan purled the air, he encountered the group operations officer he had been looking for. After half an hour Kip was surprised by a sudden forthrightness from the officer.

—I'm going to take you into my confidence, the man said, and the deep vertical furrows at either side of his mouth deepened. The program was "over the fence," outside Vietnam. He wouldn't say where but he would say it was the most secret operation in the war. More paramilitary than military, more maverick than paramilitary. —The loss rate is high, quite high, he said. —That's the downside. The upside is freedom of action, nobody tailing your kite and dragging you down. Rules of engagement there are, but like I say, freedom of action, if you get my drift. No boredom and no bullshit, guaranteed.

—What do we do exactly once we're there? Kip asked.

—Does it matter?

Kip supposed it didn't.

—Anyway, that's privileged.

—How are you supposed to know whether you want in or not?

—Did I ask you to come here?

—No, sir.

—You want in?

—Yes, sir.

—Then you don't need more information right now, do you.

—No, sir.

A week dragged by before Kip heard from Can Thó that he had been accepted into the program. He was ordered to present himself at the base the next day. Having no friends in Ca Mau made his departure a simple business. He packed his single bag, left his Vietnamese records in the dining room, and hitched a ride on the daily courier flight. In Can Thó he was given a final chance to change his mind about volunteering. This was called a back-out briefing. Kip did not back out. Once that was settled, matters took a turn toward the peculiar.

In a hangar at the edge of the airstrip was an old high-wing monoplane whose identification markings had been stripped away so that it looked more like a private craft than a government plane. The officer said, —Got a dollar on you?

Kip went along with what he took to be a travesty, or like the first line of a joke. —You want a dollar from me, he said, playing straight man.

—I do. And I want you to sign this.

It was a scrip that transferred ownership of the airplane from the government to William Calder Jr. for the consideration of one dollar. The scrip seemed authentic.

—All right, said Kip, more unwilling than ever to request some explanation for such abnormalities. —Where do I sign?

His destination was Udorn, in Thailand, and he flew there the following evening, still in the dark about what to expect. He tried to empty himself of hope or presumption, knowing that whatever he encountered would then be free of useless comparisons. Instead, he worked on bundling together in his mind his experiences in South Vietnam, and began to fold them again and again just like he had his first combat frights (while folding, the word went from *frights* to *fights* to *fghts* to *fts*) until they were reduced to a very small wad, and once he felt he'd accomplished that, and was sure there were no stray moments that might return to stalk him down, he forced himself to bring that wad of experience out through his forehead into his fingers, where he clutched it and then tossed it out, just before crossing the Mekong, which divided Viet from Thai.

He landed at night, and was met at base ops by a lieutenant colonel. The deference displayed by his superior—not deference so much as brusque respect—disconcerted him, as he sat across from the man in an air-conditioned office on the second floor of a building in a remote part of the base. The officer, however respectful, was at first no more informative than anyone else had been. Kip began to believe that the men back in Can Thó who had inducted him into this secret society didn't in fact themselves know what the Steve Canyon program was.

—So you're going to be a Raven, the colonel said.

—That's what they tell me. Whatever a Raven is.

—Tomorrow morning I want you to report to the office—we got a place for you to stay tonight—and there we'll want you to surrender your dog tags, your uniform, ID card, all your personal belongings.

—Can you tell me where I'm going? he finally asked.

—Up-country.

—You mean China?

—I mean up-country.

—What happens with my airplane?

—What airplane?

—The one I flew over here, the one I own.

—You don't own any airplane, sir. You ferried a private aircraft over here is all. Forget about it. Now, we'll give you some money to get some new clothes, some jeans, shoes, that sort of thing. Get yourself a jacket of some sort, but low profile, and not a word to anybody. Take a few minutes, write your parents a letter and tell them you're on a special assignment, tell them not to worry. You'll be just fine.

If Kip's father were alive, and if he were here, how strong a sense of déjà vu would he have experienced hearing the lieutenant's instructions? Was he running away from or toward his childhood? He concluded that he was probably doing both, and that these questions had no value at this stage of the game. The directive to write a farewell letter of sorts begged several other questions, too. Given his continued ignorance of pertinent details, what could he betray even if he wanted to? Which he didn't. He said nothing, kept his possible riposte as cards firm to his chest. Treated with respect, he accorded respect as best he could in return.

The transport left early morning the day after and it wasn't until they landed at tiny Wattay airport where he was met by a civilian man in a jeep and taken in along the brown, lethargic upper reaches of the Mekong into Vientiane, the capital of Laos, to an American compound, that all the veils of intrigue would begin to lift—but not before one final conundrum was set forth.

Vientiane was a city more slumberous than the wide river that drifted along, mute and laggard, at its southern limit. Stupas and shacks and centuries-old wats with their swooping roofs and gold-leaf doors stood here and there, bicycles and motorcycle taxis called tuktuks moved in the streets. Girls walked arm in arm, in threes and fours, along Fa Ngum, the road along the river. A teenage boy sat in the shade of a doorway plucking the feathers off a lifeless duck and smoking his cigarette with dignity. An air of calm seemed to have settled with the dust in every corner. What was most conspicuous here was the absence of war, even any hint of war. It seemed on first impression a dreamy, pleasant, backward, uninspired place, steeped in a blend of French, Chinese, Thai, Lao. The city was neither prosperous nor populous. This was not Saigon.

Kip arrived at the address he was given in a deeper state of confusion than before. Vientiane was civilian in the extreme, at least upon its surface. It would take a long night with the modest, subtle whores in Les Rendezvous des Amis, a complete induction the morning after into the purgatory of the secret wars—which here were numerous and quite diverse and altogether unknown to those on the outside—as well as a wild flight the day after, with its unauthorized side trip over the Plain of Jars, to convince Kip that he hadn't made the mistake of going from a dull war to a duller nonwar. He need not have worried, as he would come to discover. Whether or not he knew it, Kip was about to find what he had always been looking for.

*W*e stand, we walk a little. My stories have begun to twine into his if only because I had my war to fight, too. From a grassy flat in the chapel park I can see the church above us, and the dormer window over the sacristy glints and stirs the memory of a night I hadn't thought about for a good long time. Not the night when Kip and I crawled through that window on our way into the church and what we presumed would be a new life. I remember the darkness of the nave, leaping down into the candlelit sanctuary—but, as I say, that isn't the memory it has shaken loose now.

I see the window and am transported back to a young man among hundreds of other young people and we have just marched from a construction site in Morningside Park, where we'd gone to protest the university's plan to build a gymnasium on public property there, a gym that was to have lavish facilities for Columbia students and a separate, much smaller gym for Harlem community residents. Racism and the war were the two prominent issues of the day in the country, and we abhorred the implications of this project. We'd torn down a fence around the excavation site, one of us was arrested, and we marched back to the sundial on campus to figure out what next to do. The anger and spirit and fever had never been higher. I knew that this day something significant was going to happen. Whatever rules there were surely would be broken.

The university had a policy that prohibited indoor demonstrations. In the spirit of defiance we decided to take Hamilton Hall.

We were together an organic gesture, a tumult and turmoil inspired by what we believed was right. Idealism, rough élan, a spirit of tough good spread through us. It was our moment to seize. The SDS leadership walked side by side with the leaders of the Students' Afro-American Society, the SAS, and several hundred of us marched with them.

Events unfolded with a manic slowness at first. The dean of the college challenged us to leave, but was instead held hostage in his office well into the next day. In the middle of the night we splintered into two groups, the blacks asked us to leave Hamilton Hall, said Hamilton was theirs and would remain theirs until the university agreed to discontinue work on its racist gymnasium. They told us to do our own thing, take a building for Vietnam. The blacks had a problem with Vietnam, too, but they had this other problem to work with first, and we heard them, they were brothers, we were behind them.

We caucused. Eighteen hours we'd been at it and here we were with nothing to show for our trouble. What we decided to do was take Low Library. Not just Low, but the office of the president of the university. That was going to be ours before dawn broke.

When we advanced together in the darkness—it must have been five in the morning—up the steps in the quad, we hadn't an idea what would come of our action. We pried loose a red brick from the walkway, which were laid out like latillas, broke the window of the heavy door down at the southeast corner on the first floor of the building, and we were inside, our cries echoing through the vaulted marble corridors. Dim oil paintings of presidents and college dignitaries long since deposited into their tombs lined the hallways above our heads, the grave faces in the portraits staring down at us with inanimate horror as we streamed along. A frightened security guard was allowed to leave, but not before we informed him that this was the beginning of an all-out strike, that President Kirk could telephone and make himself aware of what were our objectives and demands if he so chose.

—He'll know the number, someone said.

The president's suite was located, as it is now, on the second-floor corner of the massive, ornate, colonnaded library. It faces out toward Dodge Hall, across gracious grounds of hedged walks and great plane trees. The suite was possessed of baronial detail, it emanated wealth—there was a Rembrandt on the wall—though I remember thinking how seedy some of the appointments in the office itself really were.

How we hated him. Hated what he stood for. We urinated in his wastebasket. We opened the humidor that was on his long desk, and with delight passed out his cigars, lit them up and smoked them.

—Not bad, someone said.

—Cuba libre, someone said.

We barricaded the door to the suite. We began rifling through his personal correspondence, and looked around in his file cabinets for documents that might incriminate him. What we didn't crumple we tore in half.

It was the beginning of a siege that would last a week. By the end of the day administrators were forced to order all the buildings on campus closed, but this didn't prevent seizures by some graduate students of Fayerweather Hall and later of Mathematics Hall. A group of counter-demonstrators took the old gymnasium and demanded that the administration do something to stop all this or they would take matters into their own hands.

Below our window, members of the faculty formed a human barricade to prevent the antiprotest forces from climbing the heavy black iron grates and entering our headquarters from the outside. Just beyond the faculty queue were the jocks, themselves shoulder to shoulder, their backs to us except to turn every so often and shout some imprecation up at where we sat on the window ledge, defiant and decided. The jocks lined up to keep any sympathizers from joining us. Beyond the jocks many people just milled, some heckling the jocks, some trying to toss food up to us—sandwiches, bananas—most doing nothing, only watching and waiting for something to happen. I knew that Jessica was out there somewhere in that farther crowd, and I can remember spending time looking out across what used to be the epitome of an Ivy League campus, with its stone plazas and polished white stone benches, marveling at what we had prompted.

During the night, strikers managed to sneak in and out of the building. The administration had shut off electricity and water in the hope of forcing us out, but they underestimated our tenacity. We slept on couches or on the floor. We weren't budging until our demands were met, among them that the university end its association with the Institute for Defense Analyses and that all work being conducted in Pupin Hall on the electronic battle-field cease. Our position was simple. It was black as night at new moon and white as frost at first light. If they wanted to have their university back, they would have to make just a few changes, reorganize it in such a way that its students could attend it without shame. Civilize it, acculturate it.

Rumors ran like light, faster than the sounds that carried them, it seemed. What we demanded was rejected. We demanded that every student who took part in the protest be granted amnesty. No, word came back. No amnesty. We demanded that the police not be allowed onto the campus, and that the leaders of the strike not be made into scapegoats. The answer was no.

On the sixth night I decided I had to slip out. Failure of nerve, concern that another arrest was going to ruin my chances of being admitted to the bar, exhaustion, worry about Jessica, there were a host of reasons behind the decision. Several of us ducked out under cover of darkness, even as others arrived. I walked past the chapel and over toward the law school, curious about the rumors that upward of a thousand police were gathering there.

The rumors were true. Wielding blackjacks and nightsticks, the cops thrashed their way through a phalanx of students sympathetic to the protest, bloodying noses in their progress toward justice. Once inside Low, they broke down the door to the occupied office and arrested all the strikers within. Elsewhere on campus, matters got even worse. Fire broke out on the sixth floor of Hamilton, then too in Fayerweather. Police swarmed through tunnels under the campus, emerging to arrest protesters in one building, and taking axes to break down the doors in Mathematics, where they discovered students chanting "Up against the wall, motherfuckers." Students who had soaped the steps to prevent the cops from climbing them were now dragged, face down, out of classrooms and down those same marble stairs. Thousands had built barricades, thousands had torn them down.

I wandered, for days, from College Walk to South Lawn. I tried to get back into Low, but couldn't. I felt that I had let myself down, my principles. I thought of Kip—he was over there fighting as he believed, and here was the closest to warfare I would ever experience and somehow I had failed. Some three weeks after the strike had begun, I got what I'd been looking for. Standing on South Lawn with a number of others, heckling a group of officers, we were suddenly rushed by plainclothesmen who'd been hiding behind bushes at the perimeter of the lawn, such as little children playing games do, and though everyone around me scattered, I stood dead still and looked into the blue eyes of the one cop who had set his sights on me. He came, slowly it seemed, running. I kept thinking, Brice? Why aren't your feet moving? It was a dream, I was sure. And I remember that the look on his face, as he bore down, fifteen, ten, five feet in front of me, expressed the same thought. Why aren't you running?

Together we buckled backwards onto the ground, there was an audible snap. Others were on me before I knew it and the handcuffs were in place. I made no resistance whatever to my arrest. Only later, at my arraignment downtown, when the charges were read to me, did I find out that he had broken his collarbone.

What marginal satisfaction I had felt upon hearing that the plainclothesman had hurt himself when he slammed into me was erased when I was made to understand that the charges included resisting arrest and assaulting a police officer.

—Your Honor, I said. —I did not resist arrest and I did not assault the officer in question.

—That's fine, said the judge.

—But sir?

He raised his eyebrows, waited.

—Sir, he assaulted me. I was standing, as any student ought to be able to stand, on the South Lawn of the campus at Columbia University.

—Minding your own business.

—I was minding my business.

—And would you care to tell the court just what was your business there?

Go forward, I thought, unleash it. I spoke up clearly, —I was there to protest the war in Vietnam, the illegal war in Vietnam, the unjust and idiotic war in Vietnam, sir. But, for what it may be worth, I did not assault the policeman in question. He assaulted me, in fact. I did not commit any crime.

—You're a law student, I see here.

—That's correct, Your Honor.

—I assume you understood that a crime of the nature you are accused of would make it difficult for you to be admitted to the bar.

—I was minding my own business, sir.

—Answer my question, young man.

—I am aware of what you're saying, and that's why, although as I say I strongly oppose our involvement in the war in Vietnam, I removed myself from the protest.

Painful admission. The judge eyed me, then studied the brief before him, commenting on the fact that it seemed to him I hadn't always been quite so becomingly circumspect, given my record of arrests over the past several years. No sir, I told him, but it was hard for me to harbor such strong convictions about the mistake I felt our nation was making while at the same time studying the law and developing my knowledge of its importance and intricacies.

—Catch it and see what it eats, said the judge.

This is what I thought I heard, at any rate.

—I'm sorry? I said.

The charges were eventually dismissed for lack of evidence. Catch it and see what it eats. Ketchup and see what meats. Catch up and seize the meet. To this day I've not been able to figure out what he really said. If he were still alive, I suppose that after all these years I could look him up and ask him. He seemed a decent-enough sort of man, had seen a lot, had cultivated some sense of balance and distance. He retired a few years after my small episode before his bench, and I read in the paper that he died soon thereafter. No voice, no remembrance. Which brought me back to Kip.

*W*e knew where he was, Jess and I. We tried to know. We knew where Ca Mau and Can Thó were, down toward the very bottom of the country, and we knew the famous sites like Bien Hoa and Khe Sanh. She had hung a map of Vietnam on a wall in the apartment, a vast operational navigation chart with many markings that meant little to us but to a pilot would show where were aerodromes and vertical obstructions, floating villages and pagodas, rice fields. I complained that a map of Vietnam on the living room wall was morbid, and while we could refer to it I didn't see the need for its display.

—Morbid? display?

—Look, can't we just keep it in a drawer? I asked, to which she rejoined, —Listen, Brice, my map is nowhere near as morbid as your burning Buddhist monk, the one I've had to walk past each and every day for how long now?

—That monk is, was, principled and noble.

—And Kip's not.

—Not in the same way.

—I tell you what. You put the monk away, I'll put the map away.

They both would stay up for a while yet.

We were, Jess and I, still hanging in with each other despite the clear difficulties. She shared with me the several letters from Kip that followed that curious first he'd mailed, and what he wrote me I shared with her. Although it is possible he hadn't intended I see hers or she mine, Kip divulged nothing in either correspondence that was so private as to be exclusionary, nor so uninnocent as not to be potentially manipulative. A statement like "I assume Brice is still throwing time and energy into protesting the war, what he needs is love from what I can tell, that would be time and energy better spent, when *will* he find his own woman?" was sufferable because—to my credit or shame?—I had kept my hands to myself, but it would also serve as advice, if not caution, to me, were the letter to be seen by me, which, as I say, it was. I read it as advice to stay away from Jess. Similarly, when I sensed Kip was making inquiry about Jessica's fidelity, he tried to manage it in such a way as to make it more endearing than provocative. Jessie deserves better than an absent fiancé, he might write. Or else, I don't know why any of you has anything to do with me. Rather than interpret these observations as something that might indicate Kip was beginning to lose what center he had, I saw them as quaint rhetoric meant to prod from me some report about her doings, her state of mind. I took it all for false naivete. And again, astute enough to know Jessica might wind up reading my letters, I sensed that he guessed right in thinking her response would be sympathetic.

—Forgotten him? Sometimes I don't understand him. Brice, do me a favor and make sure you let him know—

—I know what to let him know, I said.

When she received his final letter, the letter that came before the telegram that announced he was going to be incommunicado for the length of a tour, she came to her senses about Kip's precariousness. It would come to be called the Last Letter, as if a miserable holy document.

"Dear Jessie," he wrote, "I'm going insane in this place. What I described in my last letter is basically what is going on now. Boredom incarnate, that's me. Nothing doesn't bore me about where I'm at. Same beat-up old hotel, same bored comrades, not that they're comrades since how can they be when we don't do anything together. It's like a morgue but no dead bodies. Maybe I should be grateful but I'm not. Most of these guys are happy not to be up north where by all accounts the world is coming to an end (for the thousandth time, right). There have been moments I even thought about getting up in the air and going straight toward Da Nang and just forcing myself into action. From what I hear, things are out of control there enough I almost think I could get away with it. But not quite. My other infatuation is the Gulf of Siam. Swear to god if the plane had the range I'd be tempted by Malaysia. It won't, so point moot. This is just ravings. I have to do something soon, though. I'm here and don't let Brice see this or know, but I'm for the first time not so sure why I'm here. You can get out of doing this if you want out badly enough and are willing to sell part of your soul to do so. Look at Brice with his artificial pardon from service. I don't know. And another thing is these South Vietnamese don't seem worth all this effort, they don't seem really to give a fuck one way or the other out in the villages. Just those in power want to keep their hands on the reins and in the tills. The whole exercise seems futile from down in the toilet where I'm positioned. I'm not sure what I'm going to do about it, but something—and soon. Sorry to be pissing and moaning. Most letters written from the battlefield are brave boys addressing beautiful worried girls back home, right? Harrowing dignified documents of courage. Like, My darling, we beat back the enemy today and took many casualties but the cause has advanced and Victory shall soon be Ours! I shouldn't even send this bit of drivel, but the frustrations are closing down on me. Or that is, closing me down. And your work? It's all right? And Brice—he's okay? If he's in jail tell him I'm proud of him, and if he thinks I'm being facetious tell him I am being serious. I'm sorry for everything. Love you, Kip."

Jessica and I happened to be at the apartment when she received the letter and she read it aloud—there was no hiding it from me. It wasn't all that strange to hear. High, low: Kip. He was low—*way* low. No mention of her pregnancy was my first response, but kept to myself. "My other infatuation is the Gulf of Siam" prompted my second: onward Kip, and away? If his airplane could fly over the moon like the cow in the nursery rhyme, would the moon be regarded as beckoning him? Kip, I thought. God, man. What are you doing and who are you?

Jessica was saying that it was clear he hadn't received her letter. Couldn't be that selfish. That wouldn't be Kip, would it? She took a pushpin and stuck it in Da Nang. Red marked places he mentioned, blue places he'd been. And what color would mark where he died? There were plenty of black pins in her little canister. I asked her if she wanted to talk but she said what about? There wasn't anything to talk about.

Then, the telegram.

Jessica had been aware the chances were about one in ten he'd not come home alive, those were the official probabilities. That Kip might be killed or injured she and I had understood. But neither of us was prepared for this. I read the few sentences printed in purple on the leaf of pale yellow paper. The message was remarkable for its marriage of curt precision and inexplicitness.

Capt. William Calder, it disclosed, had volunteered for special operations from a position which was secret. She should not expect to hear from him for at least six months. She should not ask questions. She was respectfully requested to keep the fact he is on special assignment to herself and her immediate family. The captain was in good health and would be back in touch with her when circumstances allowed.

That was all. After the telegram, the few pushpins she'd used to mark Kip's locations in Vietnam seemed sad and vain, and the map was transformed into worthless colored paper. His trail was no longer traceable. I don't think it was a week before the map came down. Jessica, in a rare moment of crooking her thoughts, explained that for some reason she considered it bad luck to leave it up. Maybe so, maybe not. It wasn't my place to agree or dispute. I didn't miss it, though, nor did it occur to me to reciprocate by removing my monk from the door to my room.

Obviously she had not, in the end, gone overseas. Nor had I withdrawn from the apartment again. We persisted. Our lives as individuals and as mates (loaded word, but this is how we began to think of ourselves) began to deepen. How could they not? Jessica Rankin was pregnant, and I was her best friend. Morning sickness, maternity dresses (—Tents is more like it, she said, —tutu tents), what pediatrician and what hospital—these problems and questions we attended to as a team. She refused to rely on anyone but me and above all refused to let her parents in on the pregnancy until the last possible moment. Our world became circumscribed. We were alone with the glorious adversity of it all. We couldn't and didn't allow for any direct comment about what was going on between us, but our discrete intimacy—not to mention our *discreet* intimacy—we allowed to grow. It was treated like some plant in the garden that is not watered by the perverse gardener, but from a biological stubbornness of its own refuses to wilt and perish. Like a tenacious weed with a deepening taproot. And lots of succulent spiny leaves.

What stands out most about that summer is the heat. An *Old Farmer's Almanac* would show just what the weather was truly like, measured by more objective instruments than myself. For all I know there may have been cool showers, unusual chilly nights and days. But I doubt it, because heat, ungodly heat, heat sweltering and heavy with humidity, is all I can conceive when remembering those months.

There was no flowering between us, just the unstated promise of responsibility between one friend and another. None of this was difficult, there was no work involved. We did not *work* on our relationship any more than we tried to discuss or define it—or, for that matter, any more than we called it a relationship. It became understood, in the purest sense became a tacit agreement, that I would help her through the pregnancy and the birth of the child. It was Jessica's idea that if it turned out to be a boy, it would be named William, and mine that were it a girl, she'd be called Ariel.

I never asked why she changed her mind about going to find him, assuming that if she wanted to discuss it with me, she would, given Jessica's penchant for discourse rather than strength through silence, but the morning after she had packed and I had slept so well, she went about her business as if nothing out of the ordinary had taken place just eight or ten hours before. Her eyes were clouded and dark crescents impressed the skin beneath them; otherwise she seemed surreally self-possessed. Sometimes over the years, when I allowed myself thoughts about her slow arc away from Kip, I have wondered whether this wasn't one of the crucial moments in his career of losing Jessica. She left for work—she'd taken a job at a halfway house for troubled children (they call them "at-risk children" now, shifting blame from the runaways and child-vagrants to the society that bred them)—and I indulged myself in a look around her room. The suitcase was back in the closet, as were her clothes. Nothing need be said. She had made her decision. Life went on despite the languorous heat and the silence from abroad.

That September I began my final year of law school.

*T*he first time Kip flew over the Plaine des Jarres, back in his fledgling week as a Raven, so much came back to him from that other part of his life. There was a karst, a tower of limestone that rose from the lush flat, and this reminded him of the volcanic tuff cliffs and great tent rocks that stood like giants in canyons back home. There was an old French colonial road cutting straight as a horizontal plumb line through the bush that put him in mind of Route 502 leading from the Pajarito Plateau down across the unpopulous desert, across a similar beautiful if barren stretch from one place to another—the very road I traveled last night to get from Los Alamos to Chimayó. The Plain of Jars itself was much like the Valle Grande near Redondo Peak, the verdant flat valle caldera, an earthen pan, the remains of a collapsed volcano. Then there were famous and mysterious ancient stone jars, scattered everywhere, broken and overgrown with wild vegetation, which made him think of the equally mysterious ruins of the Anasazi, still charged with potency, and reminded him of the ruined cliffside houses in the dry valleys back in New Mexico, of the Tyuonyi circle with its ratlin of stones in Frijoles Canyon, pueblo fragments now fallen into disarray, but which once meant everything to the Indians who piled them into place. Laos, Kip could see at once, was another land of enchantment.

He and the pilot who was ferrying him to Long Tieng were not afraid. They would not have got to this place were they the kind to be afraid, or the kind who would admit to fear, either to themselves or any other.

They weren't cleared to be up here. The area was reported to be thick with antiaircraft installations. Back in spring of 1964 the Pathet Lao and North Vietnamese had launched attacks on the neutralist Laotian forces and installed antiaircraft guns in sixteen sites around the plain. Later the same year we would order a series of secret attacks on installations near Xieng Khouang, with results of a sort we hadn't anticipated or desired—two planes down, a pilot captured, rescue efforts thwarted by heavy flak trap fire, and the whole fiasco brought to the attention of the media through reports from the New China news agency in Peking.

Nothing but trouble ensued. We weren't supposed to be operating in Laos, neither were the North Vietnamese. Laos was neutral. Laotians were supposed to be here. Instead, everybody was here. It was like a big wink among us, like everyone signed the treaties with one hand, knowing that all other hands were hidden under the table, fingers crossed.

The Plaine des Jarres had proved to be hexed tract, and if it weren't for the sudden escalation of bombing over North Vietnam, which drew the media's concern away from Xieng Khouang and environs, they wouldn't be flying—Kip and the other man —over these urns this morning. In the rush of events things are often lost and forgotten. Neglect settled over the violations and wreckage here once more, and Laos again became a part of the map less observed by the watchful back home.

Kip had remembered, though. He had heard about it back in Vientiane, maybe at the des Amis, maybe elsewhere. But he'd heard it was a sight to behold. He knew that the Plain of Jars was not only dangerous but off the course to Long Tieng by an hour or more. He thought he would ask anyway. It was as if he wanted to test the laxity and freedoms of waging war up in here. And the Air America man piloting the twin-engine Baron had said, —Why not? after Kip asked him if they could manage a pass over the valley. Mysterious strew of funerary urns. He had to see it. It seemed to him of ritual importance.

They flew low, often below the mountaintops, in and out of overcast, then the plain emerged dotted with the hollowed stones.

—Beautiful, Kip said.

Taciturn, Air America banked them away to the south. Nothing untoward had happened. Indeed, it was understood between them, without their having had to discuss it, that nothing had happened at all. They were not in Laos. They were not about to land in Long Tieng. They had not been over the Plaine des Jarres.

Long Tieng—or Long Chieng—means *clear valley*. However, that afternoon when they finally came in, fog hung in the fissures of the karsts, and they dropped down through patches of obscurant white. There was the one strip, one approach only. They flew from the southeast toward northeast, buffeted lightly by some crabbing winds. Two karsts, of limestone and violet, drove into the clouds, like dark fins up into sea foam. Kip took note of the airspeed, the length of the runway, the landmarks.

Spook heaven they called this place. The twin karsts at the end of the landing strip were known as the titties. Long Tieng, referred to as Alternate, the heart of our quiet operation out of Laos, would come to be recognized as the most secret place on earth at the time. As at Los Alamos where men went by names other than their own—Enrico Fermi was known as Henry Farmer, Niels Bohr was Nicholas Baker, Segrè was Samson— here they assumed code names: Hog, Black Lion, Mr. Clean. In the same way that everyone on the Hill was simply called an engineer—the word *physicist* was not a part of speech—here, along with the discarding of uniforms, the usual hierarchies, formalities, niceties of military rank and behavior were eschewed. Everyone was simply a Raven, and that was that. Like Los Alamos, Long Tieng was nicknamed Shangri-la. Like Los Alamos, it was cradled by mountains and hastily built in order to win a war from an odd angle. Shangri-la, poor James Hilton, the memory of his Tibetan or was it Nepalese mountaintop utopia was once more dragged through the muds of irony. Though Alternate perched in solitude and was powered by what was considered a worthy wartime cause, its conditions were less than paradisiacal. As with Los Alamos, Alternate was no Shangri-la.

None of this was lost on Kip. Los Alamos, the most secret place in the world when he was born. Long Tieng, Laos, the most secret place on earth during the Vietnam war, his war, now that he was a man.

The words had something eerie in common. What was it about them? *Laos, Los Alamos.* He wrote them with a marker on the back on his hand as the plane taxied to a stop. *Los Alamos, Laos.* And he saw it there, so perfectly apt. The word *Laos* was hidden twice inside the words *Los Alamos.* Islands in the sky. Laos, Los Alamos.

The place was a chaos of enterprise. Transports in and out carrying shipments of rice that were dropped into remote villages. Beautiful chubby T-28s with their engines that sounded like old gas-powered washing machines, everywhere Bird Dogs with their single prop and ironic fragility, helicopters rising and settling, and the ever-present Pilatus Porters with their buzzy turboprop engines. Alternate was a wall of sound (he would discover that at night it was just the opposite, totally serene, no movement, only the distant cry of a refugee baby awakening its mother). Kip drew his eyes down from the luminous dark green peaks that ringed Long Tieng. Again, Los Alamos, the Jemez mountains. And like the Hill, here people of such different backgrounds were tossed together into one grand ferment.

Movement, exuberant, greeted him on the ground. Boys chewed and smoked opium in the small open-air market, sold cucumbers and onions, blue eggs and small tomatoes. People lived in makeshift huts fashioned of petrol drums and torn parachutes, of wood, tin, and rice sacks. There were piglets and chickens, pet Himalayan black bears—two of them—in a cage; there were children playing in the shade of parked jeeps. Along the runway there were refugee shacks and hovels that constituted the saddest, most pitiful provisional borough anywhere on earth, with a populace driven here by the war, driven into what was nothing less than a political leprosarium. His heart broke as he walked along, his heart broke but it also beat to a memory of such a familiar rhythm.

What is this place? he thought. Who are these people? Familiars, so different and the same. Secrets, he thought, beget secrets, but also remind us of what we know too well.

On one side of the runway stood a pretty bouquetière dressed in jacket and grand hat trimmed with silver French coins that chimed when she moved. Men with stick crutches and armless waifs hung around on the other. He had expected this. The stories about this place he'd heard back in the capital lent it mythological glamour of a depraved cast. A forward staging area, a transient town of soldiers and refugees, of displaced mountain farmers and guerillas, another nonexistent mountain village in which Hmong, Kmhmu, and Lao blended—by an exigency of war—with faces of white attachés and advisors who, insofar as they did not exist, might as well have been benevolent ghosts.

A Hmong maquis aide-de-camp in white pajama pants and loose khaki jacket greeted him with a salute first, then with a *whai,* palms pressed together prayerlike before his grave face, both of which respects Kip returned. An American, his face bathed in shade thrown by a bush hat, noticed Kip and came up to introduce himself. The Hmong nodded to the other man and went his own way. It was clear that Kip had misunderstood in thinking the Hmong and this American had come out especially to greet him. They were each busy doing something else and happened to encounter him is all. It was an informal place, wild with activity. A helicopter rose off the runway, some supplies being airlifted out. Noise of engines was a constant in the days here. Dust lifted in whirlings.

The man asked, —New Raven?

—What? he leaned toward the man's shoulder to be heard over the chopper.

—I said, New Raven?

Kip squinted, nodded.

—Raven hootch is back over here against the mountain.

—Thanks, said Kip, and hauled his light duffel over his left shoulder.

In the military, one who was involved in covert activities was known as a spook, and there were loose cadres of spooks working these regions—*isolatos* and bushmasters who gave up dogtags and identities in favor of taking it to the enemy like a virus might, quietly as possible—and Kip, there on the airstrip, realized he too now was one of them, one of *l'armée clandestine,* a spook come to join these mountain people in fighting the *Tchaw Gee,* "eaters of gall bladders," as the Hmong referred to the enemy. He was now an invisible man, a lethal specter.

And as he walked along past the orphans and the clan children giggling and running back and forth, chasing a dog with a stick, or a gourd that had been converted into a ball, he found himself thinking thoughts he had come a long way not to think. Maybe it was seeing the dog there that prompted him to recall the proverb, "The wolf is kept fed by his feet," which meant that the wolf was always on the move, a migrant on the prowl for prey. That, it dawned on him, was what he was becoming.

This was as near the edge of the world as he could ever go. And still it might not be far enough. What did he finally care about the Viet Cong or the Viet Minh? This was not his war. Maybe it was just that which attracted him to it—that it wasn't his, so that if he lost it, he lost something he hadn't possessed in the first place? No, that seemed too much of a dance. He felt suddenly very sleepy. He who always found it difficult to sleep.

He'd been up for the better part of three days and nights, traveling from Vientiane to Luang Prabang—hitching rides with others who had their own peculiar agendas—and now to Long Tieng.

By morning the next day he was already on his first mission. Kip's job was that of a forward air controller, an FAC, and though his work was not as wrapped in obvious glory as, say, that of a member of a fighter squadron, it was far more dangerous. A forward air controller was the avant courier, the scout. He did not himself kill, but engineered strikes. He would fly out over unknown terrain and make that territory known, mark it with smoke, call in assaults from the fighters stacked in the skies above. He carried no significant armaments, he flew in antiquated aircraft, not in formation, but low or high as he saw fit, tracing erratic patterns against the sky.

Kip was assigned a plane, a backseater, a flight time. The backseater told him where Vang Pao, the Hmong general who directed operations here, wanted them to go. And they went there, or else they went where he, Kip, thought they should go. His independence was almost consummate.

On that first flight, they found evidence of troop movement, and before Kip had so much as got his bearings he found himself laying down white phosphorous smoke rockets on a camouflaged encampment, having called in a flight of Phantoms and watched the flames bubble up off the edge of the jungled ravine. A fuel dump. Another pass over the blackened patch of double canopy revealed that the bad guys had been greased. If the bombing hadn't got them, the moisture-sensitive white phosphorus did. When you fired the rockets into the land below they would blossom like beautiful flowers, and the flowers would drift in the air, willowy and fragile and changing shape as they went. Then, if the flower found you, you'd be burned. Willy Pete—even chemicals had nicknames—turned to terrible poison the moment it came in contact with skin or was breathed into lungs. Moisture burns was what you got. Don't be sweating and don't tongue your lips. And for godsakes do not cry. You cry, you die. It was interesting, Kip thought, that napalm was what all the folks back home thought was the worst stuff we were using over here. Not that napalm wasn't terrible. Jelly gasoline. Gets on your skin and you can roll around in the mud and throw yourself into the nearest river and the burning will not stop. But the phosphorus was even more devious, because the white phosphorus was a gas that could find you down in your subterranean hideout. There wasn't much talk about Willy Pete rockets, but the Ravens would use them when the enemy had dug in too deep to bomb.

Some things went right, some went wrong. What else was new. The Hmong with whom they worked had radio equipment that was corroded, antique, unserviceable. You have a good radio and a bad radio and you may as well have two bad radios. It would have been more efficient to give the pilot a tin can, give the field command officer a tin can, string a wire between them, a very long and flexible wire indeed, and hope for the best. But they made it work. Cases of filet mignon from Central America were traded for watches; the finest prostitutes were not as valuable as a British Sten gun or a couple of working nine-millimeter pistols. This was barter, the most primitive capitalism, and this was what we were fighting to protect. War, Kip noted once more, brought out the best of the worst in people.

And then back to Long Tieng for a beer and sandwich in the hootch and to sleep.

The next day was essentially the same. Different part of the terrain was visited. Different individuals marked with the white smoke. Different route back home perhaps. But the same urchins along the walk from the strip back up the rise toward the quarters, the same characterless sleep. After a few weeks of this routine madness you'd fly down to Vientiane for rest and relaxation in the villa there. Eat, drink, find a girl.

This was how it worked.

Insofar as you didn't exist, the duty was far superior to what he had been doing before. Moreover, there was something about the people here—they were, for want of a more specific word, *good.* The Hmong had been displaced from mountain to mountain for centuries, the Chinese had herded them south, the Vietnamese had pushed them west, they were reduced to vagabondage, and wherever they would settle they knew they would be able to remain there for the briefest period of time before someone strong would come to ward them off. Kip felt kinship with them. He embraced their plight as best he could. They were outsiders, too, and he determined he would stand by them as long as he could.

*L*ast night, while walking back to the old Cadillac, hands in my pockets, my nose was sated with the powerful scent of mothballs. I borrowed from my mother one of my father's old jackets. The chill in the air caught me by surprise, a sharp mountain night breeze. Rather than feeling uncomfortable in his clothing, a kind of congenial rapture spread through me. The fit is a little tight, the sleeves short, but I was grateful to wear it not just because of the physical warmth it provided, but because of the fatherly smell that lives on in its fabric.

The smell reminds me of his patience when I used to ask him a question about the bomb when our family would take a Sunday drive up into the mountains to see the first spring flowers or the last of the fall colors. His answers were patient because my question did not accuse him of anything. I was just old enough to know about what he had helped to accomplish, but had not yet reached that moment when a child begins to separate himself from his parents and to see that his perceptions may, for a thousand reasons, differ from theirs.

I remember how I asked, —Did it look like *that* cloud? pointing out the window at some formation that is not uncommon here but which elsewhere would appear to be a miracle.

—No, my father said.

A week later, or a month, I asked, —Did it look like *that* cloud there?

—No, not really, son.

A month later, or a year, —Did it look like *that* cloud?

He hesitated. I sat up straight, wherever I was, in the back seat of the car, on a hiking trail.

—That one?

—Yeah, did it look like that one there?

He said then, quietly, —Maybe just a little like that one, yes.

—Like that one there, I verified, my mouth ajar as I memorized the massive white cloud with blue-gray shadows.

—It must have been something, all right, Dad, I said.

Silence followed.

—It was something to see, he said, finally.

When I might have looked at him I didn't. I looked up only.

Another time I asked my father, —Did you ever stop to think how weird it is we live on this lava-flow mesa that was made by a big old explosion when this volcano blew up and that you made a blowup just like it?

He said, —I did.

I waited.

He said, —But you've got it wrong, Brice. The explosion of Jemez volcano made the Trinity blast look like nothing.

I believed him at the time because he was my father and what he told me was to be believed, but I was at the turning point and soon enough everything that was accomplished in the labs would be, by my sights, against the laws of nature and man. As it happens, he was correct about the Jemez eruption being greater than Alamogordo. They found ash from the volcano all the way over in Kansas. Man had not yet bested nature, but a rivalry between them had commenced.

For all that, I loved my father, do still. My fingers feel for buttons along the front of the jacket, but they are gone. Knowing my father as I did, I search the side pockets for the missing buttons and there they are, a decade later, waiting to be sewed back on. If I have to do it myself with my ten thumbs, I think, I will make sure they are back on by the time I leave for New York.

The coffee had cut its way through the gin. Good thick black coffee. Mom keeps as furnished a house now as she did when we were children, her pantry stocked with just enough of what is needed to live quietly, in comfort. Her grace has abided by her, it seems to me, and her quirks may spin like curious weights tied to the ends of the threads of a mobile, but the center does not change—she, as a whole, remains in balance. Queer balance, but balance.

I have promised to come back tonight. I was surprised a little that she didn't take me up on my offer to drive her to Chimayó for Good Friday services, but it is possible she could tell that I was hoping, in fact, she'd decline the invitation. On the other hand, she well may not have needed any hints from me in order to decline. She had her own theories about Chimayó.

"I don't believe in dirt, Brice," she'd said. "I went down there once some years back and saw where they piled it, over by the latrines, and that was enough for me."

"What do you mean that was enough for you? I don't get it."

"The hole with the sacred dirt? I thought you were a pundit on this topic. The hole is supposed to refill *itself*, Brice. That's the miracle of Chimayó, that the posito is self-replenishing. When I saw the mound of yellow dirt next to the toilets I went into the church and got some soil from the hole. I saw they matched and that was it. To think they store it right next to an outhouse."

In the old days, I would have interpreted her skepticism about Chimayó as a barb for me, an innuendo meant to repay me for the ordeal I put her through way back when. I didn't say a word, though. She's allowed. And besides, I admire the distortions that can come about over the course of the years—that is, how we can come to believe whatever we need to believe in order to survive. What a luscious irony that I, the sometime atheist, would believe to this day that Chimayó remains a sacred place whether or not they bring in a little extra earth to help the miracle along, while she, the believer, is able to endorse things infinitely more far-fetched than what is proposed down at the little adobe church, but scoffs at the healing powers the soil is famed for far and wide. For me, the archbishop and church elders could excavate their sacred soil straight out of the latrine and I would still have the firm faith that there is something special and healing about it. And yet, I can look at the colorful carving of Christ on the cross above the altar at Chimayó and see nothing more than a folk artist's rendering of a man who defied the establishment and met with very harsh punishment for his dissension. That a religion would arise in his wake, a religion with the magnitude of impact Christianity has had over the centuries—*that* seems the miracle to me. But still, I don't know—I waver.

I waver because whenever I approach the valley an ineffably compelling joy comes over me.

The feeble heater in the car cranked up all the way. The wind whistling at the windows. A draft of cool air seeping in around my feet and calves. The old bucket humming along the road under the stars. On the road down to the desert, past San Ilde-fonso pueblo, across the flats toward Pojoaque—Po-Su-Way-Gay, if I remember right, which means the watering-drinking-place where three rivers come together. Toward Nambé and the bad-lands beyond, not sober but not drunk either, me at the wheel and this time all alone. No Kip, no Martinez, just me and my sensation of profound unreality coupled with crystal clarity. I turn the radio on. Crank the big knob over and run through a series of crackling stations until I happened upon the old Hank Snow song, "Keep On Movin'."

Along the way, even at that late hour, I saw one ghostly figure and then another, walking along the shoulder of the highway, serious pilgrims who have set out early to be there for first light and Communion at the santuario. I slowed down, didn't want to hit anybody. Coyote fences and grand cottonwoods that looked like giant puppeteers along Rio Nambé. Many more settlements, houses and trailers, side roads disappearing into the dark, than there were years ago. Horses behind barbed-wire fences caught in the headlamps. And then the settlement of Nambé fell behind and once more the open desert. Sandstone formations stood out there in the blackness, shaped like bishops and circus bears, and while I couldn't clearly see them as presences—see them rather as negative statuary blocking out the stars—I knew their color and in some cases knew what it was like to climb them. I came to the place in the road where you bear left to go down to the valley of Chimayó. Long gentle curves as the asphalt clefts the wilderness. Way off in the distance, over my shoulder to the south, the amber lights of Española shined as I descended into the town with the same ease as if I did this every night of my life. I parked by the old cattle guard and walked down to the church.

The plaza was almost the same as when I was fifteen. There seem to be more walls and fences than before. The church was open—it would remain open to pilgrims all night long, but I didn't go inside. I walked instead its perimeter, the collar of my father's jacket turned up around my neck against the dewy cold, and tried to connect this man who is me to that boy named Brice who no longer exists. Stars sharp, the moon low to the west. The trees are taller, and the two biggest cottonwoods out front by the gate were gone. These wooden picnic tables were new, and what appeared to be concrete benches down in the outdoor chapel behind the church I didn't remember. The town was less quiet for the hour than I thought it would be. The church-run concession was open, selling coffee and hot chocolate. It would be much livelier with throngs of penitentes later in the day, they say as many as twenty-five or even thirty thousand people this year, walking across the April scratchland. Back in the fifties no more than a hundred pilgrims congregated here, some of them having walked great distances, maybe carrying a heavy homemade cross in honor of their Savior all the way. Before that, back before the turn of the century, you might have seen zealous members of the Penitente Brotherhood, come to dramatize the fourth station— *El Encuentro*—when Christ meets his mother—and to enact a *Procesión de Sangre de Cristo* complete with Christ's three falls, his flogging, the ministrations of Veronica and Simon the Cyrenian, culminating in an actual *Crucifixión* (rope was used rather than spikes, but the effect must have been devastating to these true believers). The flagellants and extremists may be gone, but the desire to walk some miles across the desert as a way of sharing with Jesus the tribulations of the Via Crucis remains. All night, all day, they come, in wheelchairs and pushing baby strollers, some hobbling behind canes, others on crutches, some barefoot with sackcloth robe, some wearing Nikes and gaudy Day-Glo sweatsuits. Military fatigues are donned by quite a few, and there are those in solemn groups with their MIA/POW flags aloft, black background with white lettering, THEY STILL WAIT, their own warrior cross. Low-rider chariots with rap music blasting, silent horseback riders. By the end of the day some will be somber, others festive. Many will fast and pray and, having touched the sacred soil, walk back home. For others the tailgate parties will begin, with tamales and fresh burritos and posole, with thick lemonade and lukewarm beer.

The moon last night, past full but still heavy with light, was setting over the long measure of hill, sinking into the scrawny bush up there when I heard a pigeon coo in the eaves. The forsythia bushes at the back of the santuario yielded a delicate, sweet scent in the dewy air. I couldn't see the hands on my watch, but it must have been about three-thirty or four. Contentment welled within. Whereas most people were in their beds asleep, there were a few owls who understood the pleasure of darkness. We were alive, terribly and completely alive. I am not always an owl but for this one night I was among them, just like I was that once when Kip and I slept in the depths of the church here.

The creek trickles pleasantly, carving away at the pale loam. There is the heavy smell of burnt leaves, or scorched soil, which hangs in the air—as I suspected, the fields have lately been burned to clear the ground for the new shoots of meadow grass to grow. I remember that smell—indeed, I remember everything in this place—with much more ease than I might have expected.

It is far too late to get a room at the Rancho de Chimayó, and too early to wander and wait for sunrise, so I decide to get a little sleep in the rear seat of the car. The chill filters down through the starry night and edges under my skin. It hurts, in a way, and is also exhilarating. My back aches—a tart, sharp flame—my punishment for having jumped over my mother's fence. I rub it as best I can and think, Pathetic, Brice, you rickety corpse. Then I think of calling Jessica. There must be a pay phone somewhere. But what would I say?

I cradle my head in my arms and try to find a position in which my back doesn't throb. My eyes are open and out the window I see a shower of shooting stars, watching them trace quickly their way down the heavens one after another over a period of several minutes. Soon the shower is over and I huddle under my jacket, wondering will I ever get any sleep at all, wondering whether I'd have been wiser to have stayed at Bonnie Jean's house or my mother's, like they asked, and for once have been accommodating and sociable. Despite the pain, however, and the knowledge that I'd have been a better son and sibling for having remained on the Hill, I know that being here is somehow right, for the best. Like my mother herself used to say, —I'll sleep when I'm dead, tonight I dance. I'm not dancing, but there is to this a kind of dance. You're not that old yet, I tell myself. Lay some claim still to what youth is left in you.

Dawn lights the valley. A neighborhood rooster crows once and then twice and then falls silent. Some dogs are barking. I must have slept a little. I look up and see the faces of five or six children in the windows of the car, their dark eyes looking me over, their hands and noses pressed against the glass, peering in as if I were some strange saint enclosed in a casket. For an instant I am overwhelmed by the thought that I might be home in New York, dreaming a dream of having come to New Mexico to meet my childhood friend once more—but then I begin to come to and remember. They don't move, those kids. And they don't smile.

I run my hand over my forehead, and when I sit up in the

back seat they take off kicking up dust as they go. I have an urge to yell out at them, but what would I say and why yell? The sun is not yet dry and baking, but it will be. My shoulder and neck ache now as well as my back. I cough, and notice how every sound I make inside the shell of this old car is amplified, so that my breathing, my moaning and swallowing, my shifting about in here to find a comfortable position, is deafening.

Brice, you old dolt, I think. Vaulting your mama's fence like you were ten years old, sleeping in the back of a car like some vagabond or runaway. *Viernes Santo,* Good Friday, man—penance for the apostate. Your pains are not inappropriate.

Everything seems possible in the morning. The day is before you and you have done nothing as yet to foul your lines, you've uttered nothing regrettable, you've heard nothing you'd rather not have heard. Your senses are coming to focus but are not so sharp as to allow the world without to enter you, pollute your personal environment, convert you into the man you become during the course of the day. I feel indescribable peace alone, awake, in the morning. Sleep has intervened, however subtly, and I'm born new, no matter that the sun has come up to show me for the wearied assayer that I am. The photograph of the two prospectors.

Día de la Cruz, my Spanish comes back to me. I step out of the car and draw myself up slowly to height. Pilgrims are everywhere. Smoke reaches up past the shadows, rising from where bread and chilies will be baked to offer the visitors today, some of them the very walkers I passed along the road under the stars. They made it, and will be among the first to enter the church, as they'd hoped, to receive the Communion wafer and the wine —*Tomad y comed todos de él, porque esto es mi cuerpo . . . tomad y bebed todos de él, porque este es el cáliz de mi sangre*—as strange a rite as exists, to enact the cannibalization of their Messiah, and afterward be granted the privilege of entry to the small room where the sacred healing dirt is available to each repentant believer. Several women and a man stand before the open wooden gates of the courtyard of the church. The very first of the processioners to arrive.

I begin to wonder, as I have off and on for the past few days, what Kip will look like after all these years, what he will sound like. My stomach grumbles, perhaps responding to all these lariats of smoke rising from ovens in the village. I decide to get coffee and something to eat. I pat my trouser pockets for the keys to the car, find them, and begin to lock the doors. Then I think better of it. Why worry about such matters. I have nothing worth thieving, anyway. Moreover I believe, perhaps naively, that even if I did, there's no one who would want to steal from me. Not here, not this morning.

*T*he strangest letter my mother ever wrote me, back when I was in college, when Kip and Jess and I lived together, opened with the words, "Let me tell you a story. It is a kind of parable. The parable of the cowbird and the hermit crab."

I resented the letter at the time, but later I learned to prize it for its impossible fusing of directness and obliquity. This is what she wrote.

"There is a species of bird known as the crown-headed cowbird that thrives in the eastern part of the United States, and this bird has developed a most eccentric way of perpetuating itself. Unlike most birds, the cowbird builds no nest in the spring. Instead, it lays its eggs in nests of other birds, and depends on others to hatch and raise its young. The cowbird is neither fastidious about habitat—deciduous woods or conifer, farmland or suburban garden, its preferences are broad—nor particular about who will wind up parenting its young. A yellow warbler will do just as well as a vireo, a spotted thrush as well as a song sparrow. The cowbird lays her egg at dawn. Sometimes she has removed an egg from the nest of the poor host bird the day before, sometimes she throws out the host's own egg the day after. A few birds, the robin and catbird for instance, won't tolerate her frightful and parasitic conduct. Either they'll abandon the nest, or build themselves a new floor of twigs and leaves right over the cowbird egg. Or else they'll simply throw the unwelcome eggs out. But these ladies are the exception. Most of the victims fail to fight back, and rather than incubating, hatching, and feeding their own young, they wind up raising a brood of orphaned cowbirds.

"There is a kind of crab, the hermit crab he is called, who occupies the shells of tulip snails or conches, lives in periwinkles or whelks. The hermit crab comes in many varieties—the long-clawed hermit, the hairy hermit, the star-eyed hermit—but all share this characteristic of moving into somebody else's home and calling it their own. As the hermit crab grows it has to change shells from time to time, and it does so whenever it comes upon a shell it fancies as better than the one it has already appropriated. In it moves and on it goes. Often the hermit is joined by others, the parasitic parasitizing the parasitic. A funny sort of animal called the Snail Fur—pale pink and whitish—has been known to colonize the surface of the hermit crab's shell, and will contentedly go wherever it is taken. The Fur is made up of several kinds of tiny polyps and as it's carried into new waters it can use its stinging cells to get its food. As spongers go, the Snail Fur is a decent companion, and often protects the crab itself from being eaten, by stinging this predator or that and making them wish they'd never got stranded in the same tidal pool as the hermit.

Others are known to join the mooching hermit and his furry adjunct. Sometimes you can find a Zebra flatworm sharing the snail shell with the hermit crab. And there's another, the little Say's Porcelain crab, that will work its way into the shell, too, and live right there—cheek to jowl, so to speak—with the larger hermit crab. The hermit is a sloppy eater who shreds his food into bits and pieces, getting some into his mouth but leaving much afloat. And this is why the Say's is there, to snag the leavings for himself. The hermit crab, the Fur, the flatworm, the Say's: they're a veritable ship of fools.

"Masters of leftovers, all these fellows: why do we view them with contempt, not admiration? Isn't it true they're economical, and awfully ingenious? Isn't there even a bit of whimsy, of the black-humor kind perhaps but whimsy nonetheless, that is evidenced in their manners and mores? The chickadee can find itself a hollow in an old tree and there lay its eggs and raise its brood without so much as a how do you do. The little wren does the same and is shy but smug in her self-reliance. The hawk circles until it finds a hapless mouse in the field to bring home to its young for food—it would never consider letting another bird near its chicks, let alone leaving the task of child-rearing to someone else. And shrimp and lobsters can swim along, nestled in their own exoskeleton, proud of their autonomy, triumphant in their godlike wholeness, just a bit superior for having an existence that neither depends upon the kindness of strangers nor forces them to annex the property or products of others in order to make their way through the world.

"But the cowbird and hermit crab can make no such claims. They have other fates to realize. And though the hawk is magnificent in her way, and the lobster is king of what he is about, who is to say their lives are superior to those of the crab and cowbird?

"I wrote this down, son, so that I could answer that question. My answer is, Not I. What's yours?"

She had made her point with as light a touch as she could manage. It was a good try, but just as the cowbird is one with her habits, I seemed to be one with mine.

I think of that letter now as I begin to look, in the morning sunshine, for Kip.

*A*riel was born in the earliest hours of the first day of March. Her maternal grandparents had come to New York for the occasion. Aware of my peculiar status there at her birthing, but unable to suppress my real excitement about the event, I behaved in many ways as if I were the child's father.

By then, Jessie and I had developed into some kind of couple, however unconventional and undefined, however unconsummated was our affection, and so I didn't even attempt to disguise my elation about the baby being a girl. —That's what I'd been hoping for all along, I said, shaking the hand of the newborn's grandfather with both my own.

—I'm delighted you're pleased, he offered with a slight smile, rightly convinced that my passion was ingenuous and that at worst his daughter had a good friend in me, even if I was a little touched.

Seeing that response, I wondered, just for a moment, whether Jessica and I should have gone ahead with the idea that all this might be easier if I'd pretended to be her husband, Ariel's father, the whole bit. It had been her proposal, so to speak, a few months before she was due to deliver.

—There'd be a lot less explaining to do, she said.

—Maybe for you, but what happens when Kip comes home?

—You and I—I guess we get divorced.

—I still can't believe you've never told them about Kip.

She tossed her head, —And what precisely was I supposed to tell them?

—That you met this interesting guy, that you're seeing him, that you decided to move in.

—I could never tell them *that.*

—Why not?

—Because I don't want them prying into my life.

—So what's with the pretend marriage? Aren't you contradicting yourself? Here you are keeping them at arm's length about who the father is, but then you want to fake up a marriage to make them feel better.

She said, —It isn't for them, the marriage. It's just another way to keep them from prying. One less question for them to ask.

—There's a point when independence becomes so much work that it turns into a form of slavery.

Jessica gathered her hair with both hands and turned the length of it at the back of her head until it formed an impromptu bun.

—This isn't logical, anyhow, I continued. —You want to keep them from prying by falsely assigning me the role of husband and father but at the same time are afraid they'll pry if you tell them the truth about Kip? I don't get the difference.

—They know how I feel about Vietnam.

—So what?

—So they'll say, what're you doing getting engaged to a pilot who's going off to war, having his baby and all? It won't work, is what they'll say.

Many possible responses to this that came to mind, and I discarded them. I said, —So we're married and Kip comes home. What do you tell them's the reason you and I are getting a divorce?

—Irreconcilable differences, she said.

—Irreconcilable differences. All right. And what kind of alimony do you intend to pay me?

—What alimony.

—A good lawyer has to think ahead in these situations.

—Never mind, the marriage is off.

—So's the divorce.

What quaint, peculiar flirtation, I thought.

—I guess you're right. Just tell them the truth, Jess finally said.

—They're *your* parents, not mine.

—But what do you think?

—I'd rather not think about it anymore.

The parents received the news of Jessica's pregnancy complete with an accurate description of her romance with Kip and a firm recommendation that if peace were to be kept in the family there should be no insults, no sarcasms, no denunciations. If they wanted to be supportive, she would welcome their support. If they found they couldn't in their consciences support what she was doing, then that would be legitimate. Her parents—I think to her surprise—hadn't the least interest in argument or anger.

Ariel Rankin, then. If Jessica considered using Kip's surname, she never mentioned it to me. It seemed to make sense that Ariel would take her mother's name, at least temporarily.

Through the fall, through winter, until we stood at nascent spring, neither Jess nor I had any word from Kip. On one hand, it seemed extraordinary, it seemed unforgivable. On the other, Kip had proceeded only to do nothing more or less than what he indicated by proxy he would do. His telegram must have crossed her letter, and Jessica and I both thought that the only viable explanation for this prolonged silence was that he'd never received her news of the pregnancy. Still, it seemed inconceivable that Kip's mission could be so clandestine and his separation from the outside world so hermetic that he wouldn't be allowed by his superiors, whoever they were, to reply to his fiancée in light of the news he was going to become a father. Even the most obsessively secretive military administrator would see a way clear to allowing a man to respond to such tidings as that, we'd agreed, and back in early October Jessica had written again, and again there had been no reply. I took it upon myself to telephone some armed forces administration office—or should I say offices—in Washington and explained the situation to whoever would hear me, and while each of the people I spoke to was sympathetic and concerned, each with unerring obtuseness passed me along to someone else at one extension or another until I recognized that there was nothing whatsoever to be learned in this bureaucratic labyrinth. Even now, I don't think it was that they were purposely trying to keep us from finding out William Kip Calder's whereabouts; instead, I think it's possible the lower-level functionaries with whom I talked just didn't know the answers to my questions. And long ago I forgave myself for not pushing a little harder. It had occurred to me, of course, that the threat of legal action against them might have prompted some more lively assistance. I knew more than one law professor at school who was hostile toward the military and would have been all too eager to figure out a way to litigate, or at least cause them a little trouble.

But I held back. I was torn in two directions and rather than try to force matters one way or the other I thought it best to let fate seek its own resolve.

What was happening to me was that I was falling deeper in love, and now my love wasn't only for Jessica but for Ariel, too.

Paterfamilias. That had always been a rich word to me. Truth to tell, I found myself infatuated with the idea of family and the creation of this new home.

*H*e started going, he said, and he kept going. And after the crash he found that rather than withdrawing or recoiling, he pushed even harder into his work there. Three- and four-flight days again became the norm for him, more hours above the earth than on it. When he was up in the air he was engaged, his spirits prospered and his intellect was keener than a needle. When he was back on the ground he mostly slept a deep, free sleep—no demons and no dragons. The only American there he felt a kinship with was an older guy who was from the Four Corners area, and also happened to be madder than a March hare.

The first time Kip met Wagner, he said, his expression brittle and serious, without so much as a twinkle in his eye, —Hey, Calder, were you there the day they crucified the Lord our God?

—Weren't we all? Kip answered, affable and in stride. He was crouched over his map pack before taking off on a mission and this man ranged over him, casting him in shadow.

Wagner said, —I thought you looked familiar, and walked away.

Kip had made it a practice to stay off on his own for the most part, but this Wagner intrigued him. Like many of the Ravens, he was outgoing in a quirky way. He was known for non sequiturs and off-the-wall commentary. He also had been on more missions than just about anybody here, and above all seemed to have an unusual rapport with the Hmong. He'd mastered the language better than any of the others, a language whose meanings were often carried by intonations of words rather than the vocabulary.

Lao was tonal, and its grammar seemed flexible as gum. The tones were high or low, and they might rise and fall from a midrange, or they might start deep and in the same syllable arc upward. The Hmong were called Meo by their American comrades and other foreigners—an unintentional derogatory, means "barbarian" in Chinese—and indeed it sometimes sounded, when a group of them were talking together, like a meowing of articulate cats. Wagner was also said to have embraced the animist beliefs of the Meo, whom he called Hmong, while at the same time not abandoning his Baptist background or the Buddhism he picked up while serving his first tour over in Vietnam.

Kip asked him once, regarding this animist belief of his, —So you think there's a god in every bush?

—If a devil didn't get there first.

Another time, when Kip asked him about how he could reconcile one creed that held there were guardian spirits in most every object with another that quite clearly disavowed such things, Wagner said, —If I could reconcile everything, I'd lose my faith, wouldn't I now. And when Kip asked him what religion he was, saying, —Like a pantheist of some sort? Wagner looked at him and answered, —I'm not anything but if I was something, I'd be a devout potpourrist is what I'd be, and potpourrism would be my religion. You've heard the phrase, Spread the wealth? Well, I believe that it's also a pretty good idea to sample the wealth. Sample and spread, spread and savor. I've never met a religion yet that I couldn't learn something from, and when I believe in a cause I do something about it, you know?

Kip observed this Wagner from a distance at first, watched where he went and when. None of the other Anglos stationed at Long Tieng ate with the Hmong as did Wagner, none seemed as well connected to Vang Pao, the Hmong general who ran operations here. In a community of eccentrics, Wagner became, in

Kip's eyes, a kind of guru. But a quasi guru, given he refused to accept any such role. —Places animate people, people animate places, he told Kip once.

—So?

—So you're from Los Alamos, right?

—Who told you that?

—Pajarito Plateau. I've flown over there once, very beautiful the way the tuff has flowed out in fingers away from the rim of the volcano skull itself.

—Who told you I was from Los Alamos?

—But what I was saying about places and people, I'll bet you didn't know about old man Pond and flying, did you?

—Old man Pond?

—You know, the man who founded that boy's ranch there for frail kids, boys with respiratory problems and flat chests, Ashley Pond? Don't you know about where you grew up?

—I know who Ashley Pond is—

—And there's a pond there named after him, Ashley Pond. I think that's rich, don't you? Strictly speaking, it should be called Ashley Pond Pond, shouldn't it?

—What about him?

—He was a dreamer, was Pond—not at all unlike Robert Oppenheimer in that respect. The place draws dreamers in. But you've got a little of Pond in you, too. Did you know that more than anything in the world Pond wanted to be a combat pilot in World War One?

—You're making that up, said Kip.

—It's true: 1918, he left Los Alamos and wanted to go to war, but he was told he was too old to get his wings. So he worked for the Red Cross in France, instead.

—Then he never did become a pilot?

—He was almost sixty, but he finally got his license. You see what I mean about places animating people?

—No, said Kip.

Wagner said, —That's too bad.

My love of law is almost equal to my aversion to lawyers. Even now, despite what good I have managed to accomplish over the years through my practice, whenever I read the words *Attorney-at-Law* beneath my name, a part of me withdraws—recoils, even. There are lawyers who are proud of their craft, and get defensive at the mere mention of lawyer-bashing. The joke that asks how do you tell the difference between a dead skunk in the road and a dead lawyer (there are skid marks in front of the skunk) will irritate many of them, and though I maintain a distance from most of my colleagues, I can respect their sentiments.

But still.

Benders of the truth, sculptors of sorts, was how I first began to think of attorneys. Cajolers, shaders, subtracters, adders— adders as in those who augment and those that slither and bite. A breed of men to whom truth was open not just to minor revisions and nice distinctions, but to management. Truth management. And though such assessments were not altogether wrong, they were cynical maybe, precocious perhaps too. Children of scientists learn early on just how relative everything in the universe really is.

Yet the law itself, like any law of physics, is as beautiful as the workings of a clock, immutable and always in motion. And practicing law—I like it that one *practices* the law, and thus never fully *masters* it, as such—has given me the chance to witness its balances and intricacies, to come to appreciate it, especially when it functions just as it should. It is flawed, of course, as are most beautiful artifacts, but is often so precious, it seems a crime that law is the province of lawyers.

My practice started small, after I graduated from Columbia Law School, and has remained as small as I could manage to keep it. My success as an attorney I chose early on in my career not to measure in fees. I still care most about getting an acquittal for my client, especially when I'm defending idealists—people who range from saints to the scurrilous (never think that the spirit of an idealist doesn't sometimes live in the body of a scoundrel, it happens all the time).

Flower children and insurrectionists never had money to compensate lawyers, and more often than not, no matter that public opinion about the conflict in Vietnam had swung from pro to contra in the early seventies, conscientious objectors were still being jailed with regularity, and boys were in exile in Canada and Sweden and elsewhere even though the lottery had come into being and the unwinnable war was grinding down. So these were my clients, and because I worked for barter or a pittance or often pro bono, Jessica supported us through those years—a special-education teacher, a halfway-house worker, an English-as-second-language tutor; the jobs were various and many—and only sometimes doubted her sanity. When I stopped to contemplate her sacrifices, her towing Ariel from place to place, I never doubted Jess's sanity—she loved me and believed in what we were doing—but I did doubt, from time to time, whether my activities were entirely responsible. There is nothing worse than a self-doubting ideologue. Guilt and virtue make for uneasy partners—and so for a while it was, with me. The virtuous defender of the rights of all oppressed but myself and my foursquare wife.

More than once, more than a dozen times I have been tempted

to try my hand at another profession. As late as age forty I'd toyed with the idea of going back to school, getting a degree in history, becoming a teacher. There was a time when I thought of opening a bookstore. Few city dwellers haven't considered giving it all up and moving away to a farm with a big red barn and a trout pond at the margin of a fresh-mowed field, with an apple orchard, with warblers in the treetops and deer grazing beneath the boughs heavy with tart reddening fruit. There are few who haven't dreamed of a pristine desert island and days of endless repose on white sand beaches against whose edge an indigo sea laps. I dreamed of country or island sometimes, but I stayed with law, stayed with New York. I can remember how revolted Kip was when I told him where I'd decided to go to graduate school, and to what I wanted to devote my career life. —The anarchist turns a legal leaf, he laughed.

I confess that I laughed along with him, from habit as much as anything, before coming to the awareness that his comment wasn't all that witty.

—Anarchy's just another field of law, I said.

It gave him pause, but soon enough he had his own retort.

—Yeah, right. Like the fourth branch of government.

I liked that. I said, —Yes, that's right. Like the fourth branch of government.

—*H*ey, Calder? said Wagner one evening. Monsoon rains had them pinned down all day and the night darkness was little different from the day darkness except the generator came on and there was electric light in some of the windows, and your watch told you it was nineteen hundred hours instead of seven hundred hours, and people were drinking beer rather than coffee.

—Yeah, said Kip.

Wagner was the only person who ever called Kip by his last name, and once when Kip had asked him why he used Calder instead of Kip, Wagner had a ready answer, —Because here in Laos the money's kip and I have enough respect for you not to refer to you in those terms. Kip had said, —If you say so, Wagner, and Wagner had said, —I say so, Calder.

—Listen, Calder, you remember once when I told you that when I found me a cause that was a good cause I got to work and tried to help that cause?

—Yeah okay, so? he said.

—You don't remember when I said that?

—What do you want, Wagner?

Wagner smiled across at him from where they sat together out of the thick rain on barrels in a sandbag bunker.

—We're kind of friends, aren't we, Calder?

—Sure, isn't everybody?

—Well, you know what I'm doing here. I'm here because I'm against the war, and I don't want these innocent people slaughtered.

Kip had heard him rehearse the grounds of this argument on three or four occasions and still felt that he hadn't understood what Wagner meant. It seemed contradictory to him, and if he didn't in fact like this guy Wagner as much as he did, he'd long since have written Wagner's Paradox off as a bit of absurd denial—denial of a variety he had seen before here in the war, not to mention the other war he knew so well. He let it drift; Wagner accepted into his heart religions whose gospels were all but mutually exclusive. If Wagner could reconcile his fighting in the war with his belief in pacifism, then more power to him, Kip figured.

—What's your cause here, Calder? That's what I want to know.

—I don't have a cause, said Kip.

Wagner demurred. —Oh, but you do. I'm just not sure what it is. And I'd like to know.

—What makes you think I'd tell you even if I did? Which I don't.

—Because we're friends. And you do.

—I'm telling you, I don't.

—Who's Jessica Rankin?

Kip stood up suddenly and took a couple of steps forward and then turned around and gave Wagner a burning look. —What are you talking about?

—Nothing, said Wagner, a light smile playing at his lips in the murky cool.

—You been going through my stuff, Wagner?

—What's your cause?

—Fuck you, Wagner.

Wagner said, —Is it because you're afraid of something that you wind up going to a place like this where the only thing that could possibly count is your courage?

—There you go again, man, with your nonsense. I don't have anything more to say to you, Wagner.

—I didn't go through your stuff, Calder. What d'you think I am, some kind of creepy motherfucker?

—I couldn't have put it better myself.

—Well, you're wrong. And you know it. You know old Wagner wouldn't do that.

The wind changed direction, as it often did up in the mountains, catching Kip at the back, and he stepped into the shelter again. —How do you know about Jessica Rankin?

Wagner reached into his flight jacket and pulled out a letter —*the* letter, in fact—and handed it to Kip.

—Where'd you get this?

The letter was unopened. Kip could see that Jessica had written her name with return address on the back of the envelope.

—Guy gave it to me in Vientiane the other day, knew we was both up here, asked me to pass it along. I guess it's been following you around through three countries.

—How come you didn't give it to me before now?

—What am I, a postman? You've got the letter, don't you? Give me a break, Calder.

Kip tucked the letter inside his shirt. —I got to go. I'm sorry, Wagner. I hate this rain, all right?

—She your lady?

—See you later, Wagner, said Kip, who walked out of the shelter into the hard monsoon downpour.

—I want to know, Wagner shouted after him.

Kip waved his arm down, without looking back.

—I want to know what your cause is, man. What's your cause, Calder?

Givings and misgivings. And then when it happened it was so abrupt, I hadn't enough time to scold myself for having drifted into such profound spiritual slumber. I was so content as to be completely unprepared for the obvious eventuality of his return. Denial is what a psychiatrist would designate my selfish armor. Wishful thinking, purblindness, blissful ignorance, the dumbness of a doorknob. Given just how far from any real center of gravity I had allowed myself to lean, enjoying the foreign perfumes and breezes at my furthest reach, it is a myope's miracle that when the time came I didn't fall even harder than I did.

The givings were mutual between myself, Jessica, and her newborn girl. Whatever selfishness, whatever foolishness, whatever faults I had shown before Ariel's coming into the world surely must have been diminished by what her presence inspired in me. Jessie's girl changed my life. I gave myself over to helping in any way I was allowed. Her crib, a late Victorian flamboyance of spindles and finials, I found in a secondhand furniture shop on 125th Street, brought back in sections to be wrestled up the stairs and into the apartment where I scraped, sanded, repainted it ivory white. When mother and daughter came home from the hospital and my parents-in-law-manqué left New York, I learned how to boil diapers, and had strung a line in my bedroom on which they dried. I helped with bathing and powdering her—Jessica and I would both be drenched and dusted white as the baby with talcum. I rocked Ariel in my arms and even tried to sing her little improvised melodies.

It is true that Kip was present in Ariel's face, the dark eyes and wide set to them. But the child, as I could see her, was most clearly Jessica's (I know the judgment was prejudiced: Ariel defied my every attempt at objectivity). Her warm head, smooth and fuzzy with first hair, pulsing with life, I cupped in the palm of my hand. Her mouth, forever wet, full and plump like Jess's, I adored. Her perfect, complex ears caught the sunlight in a hundred ways. Her olive irises—more Jess—presented unplumbable depths. She smiled at me and I smiled at her. All three of us cooed like arrant fools. Ariel was ecstasy.

An intimacy Jessica and I conceded to was holding hands. In the middle of the night, Ariel having awakened us both with her crying, Jessica and I sat with her in the common room, side by side on the couch we'd pooled resources to buy, and cradled her, and by the time the baby had gone back to sleep we found ourselves holding hands. All the breathing in the room, hoarfrost on the windowpane and the stray flake of snow corkscrewing down toward the street where it would soon melt into part of a puddle where the morning would find it bearing iridescent motor oil, all the fondness in the small world there where we clasped hands conspired to send us off into sleep as deep as the baby's. And when I awoke some time later, and got Jessica and Ariel back into their room and beds, I kissed them both on the forehead and smelled them both.

Trading fingerprints is what we named it, the handholding. It was sweaty and innocent at the same time. From the distance of over two decades of marriage I can still affirm its sexual power. Hands are among Eros's greatest instruments. The sensitive tips of our fingers, the bawdy palms, the kneading thumb. Curious, but the trade in fingerprints was and remains as erotic and un-immaculate an intimacy as I have ever known. Misgivings came with it, to be sure. Yet it continued. Givings and misgivings.

Nor had I ever understood how quickly babies developed through their phases; I read about it, I'd been told, but nothing compared with the occasion itself. Before my—our—eyes Ariel was prospering. She reached out and clasped in her tiny fists air and it was as if she were pulling the whole world toward her. —There is a time and a place for everything, my mother used to say. For Ariel it seemed as if at every moment, this was the time and the place. She grasped at the world, and Jessica and I were delighted by her willfulness, extended our fingers for her to clutch.

I shouldn't have forgotten that the world moved along outside this domestic bubble, because indeed I was finishing classes, soon would have the New York bar exam to study for, and my participation in the student antiwar movement continued. The world did, however, continue to spin, and if I'd somehow managed to suppress it—sleepwalking in the arms of this domestic dream, stepping through the craziness as if it were not there—the telephone call from Kip slapped me into a quick wakefulness. He had completed his second tour and had to decide whether to try to extend again or try to reenter civilian life. He had thirty days coming to him. They offered to fly him anywhere in the world; it was one of the perks of being a Raven. Jessica's letter was bringing him home. He was at Clark Air Base in the Philippines, would be in California the day after tomorrow, next day at the latest, it depended on what flights he could manage to catch. Then on to New York. He was happy to be coming home, he said. And his silence? He would explain as much as he could, but he had to go now, there was a long line of homebound soldiers waiting to get on the phone to make their own calls.

And he did. He showed up at the apartment. My thoughts, his thoughts, her thoughts, all chaos. There was a look on Jessica's face—it was mostly in her eyes—when Kip took her into his arms and held her (she held him back, in both senses of the phrase) that is both inarticulable and indelible to me. Never have I seen before nor ever will I see again such pain merged with such elation.

—Brice, he said, and he started to shake my hand but instead stepped forward to embrace me.

—Kip, was all I could say.

Givings and misgivings. Some taking and leave-taking. I can't think of another time in our lives when so much was crosscurrenting, pushing and pulling us. We were damned well forcing each other to live full out. The life of the heart and life of the mind were constantly confrontational, it seemed—the movement resembled the heart's, diastole and systole, expansion and contraction, what was without was pulled within, what was within was pushed without. I could by now admit to myself, and in no equivocal terms, that I was totally in love. It wasn't that I might be falling in love, it wasn't that I sensed I might be falling and should resist falling because it was inconvenient or hurtful. No, I loved Jessica Rankin now, and I loved her daughter. I watched Jessica for signs of hope, and I saw them, or began to think I did, less in how she acted toward me than toward Kip.

—What kind of name is Ariel? he asked. —Ariel is a boy's name.

—In Shakespeare maybe, but not in real life, she said.

Shakespeare *is* real life, I thought. If Kip hadn't been standing there in the room with us, I would have said it aloud and Jessica and I'd be off, suddenly, into a romp of words over the statement. But Kip was in the room, and he was an agitated Kip, a different Kip, yet another of the Kips I've known.

—Brice put you up to this, and then he turned to me and said, —Didn't you, Brice?

Jessica cut in, —Nobody put me up to anything. Ariel's a beautiful name, and it's her name, Kip.

When I heard the baby cry during the night it was everything I could do to keep from getting up and going into Jessica's room, lifting Ariel into my arms, rocking her gently until she went back to sleep. Instead, I lay awake and listened hard—listened shamefully—to the sounds that came from the adjacent bedroom, heard Jessica cradle Ariel until the baby stopped crying, heard the soft resonance of Jessie's voice as she spoke words I could not quite understand, heard the creak of the springs as she herself climbed back into bed. I listened for the appalling sounds of lovemaking, and only fell asleep again when I had assured myself that Kip and Jess were no longer awake. I didn't hear lovemaking. What I heard instead was my own inner voice. What a rude, deviant character you've become, I would reprimand myself. Is there a rock big enough for you to crawl under, that you might hide your prodigious shame?

After a week Kip asked me if I would take a walk with him. We walked toward the natural history museum.

—What happened between you and Jessica, Brice? he asked. His voice was dark with accusation.

—I knew this was coming, I said.

—Spare me the prophecies and tell me what happened.

—Nothing happened between me and Jessica.

What hate I felt for myself when I said that; though the words painted the truth, plain and simple, they betrayed it, too. Some wounds cannot be remedied with an act. What could I do to appease Kip's pain? Only to offer words that were as false as they were true. Nothing happened; everything happened. Kip wasn't having any of it anyway.

—Liar, he said. —Let me ask you another question.

We walked on. He wasn't going to manipulate some reaction from me by calling me a name; he'd done it a hundred times in the past—and indeed I'd done the same to him—and it wouldn't work now.

Kip said, —I appreciate your helping out with Ariel, Brice. You've been at least in some ways all that a friend could ask for. But I want to ask you to move out. Will you move out as soon as you can? I can help with the money if that's a problem. They pay me pretty well.

—You can keep your money. You don't need to insult me.

—I don't mean to insult you.

—"Helping out with Ariel" isn't an insult?

—No, why should that be an insult?

I said, —Let me ask you a question.

—Ask.

—Where have you been, man? Where were you? Why didn't

you get in touch with us, with Jessica, when she wrote you about Ariel?

We crossed Central Park West and walked through the grape arbor, whose old-fashioned bough roof was teeming with sparrows.

—I can't tell you where I've been.

—Come off it, I said.

—Someday, when the war is over, I'll tell you, Brice. But you of all people, you're the last person I'd discuss it with right now.

—Why not? I'm your friend.

—You are, are you?

How can I put this remembrance into words without saying how tired and tumultuous, how terrified Kip looked, to me, at me, looked, just *looked,* just then?

I said, —I'm trying to be your friend, man. I'm trying my best.

—Maybe your best—

—Ain't good enough? Are you really going to say that?

—What happened between you and Jess?

—I like Jess, all right? I love Jess, just like you. But nothing's happened between us.

—But you wish something would, don't you?

—Listen, Calder.

Kip laughed. As well he might. What was I doing? Threatening him?

He said, —No. You listen, Brice. You admit to me what happened between you and Jessica and I'll confide in you where I was. Is it a deal?

—I told you nothing happened, and thought, Do I go ahead and make it clear, be blunt, tell him that nothing happened despite my thoughts, my intentions? —Get off it, was what I said.

Kip said, —She's different. Jessica is different.

—Of course she's different, what do you think.

—You've made her change is what I think.

—It's you who's made her turn away from you if that's what you're talking about.

What were Jessica's feelings? Even now I can't trust my own conjuring. Picture a shallow pool with a glassy surface, and in the pool picture minnows fluttering their tail fins but otherwise stationary. Now throw a stone into the water—see them scatter like lightning? brilliant flashes beneath the surface disturbed by ringlets that distort your view? Any question such as this about Jess's feelings, or Kip's, or even my own, is like that stone. My thoughts dart away no matter how hard I concentrate, dash in opposite directions. The fact is, no one had a plan—neither Kip, nor me, nor Jess.

—You're the one who invited her to change, not me.

He said, —I did nothing of the sort.

—Well then, no one did. If she changed, she changed. She's got her own mind, I said. And then my thoughts couldn't stay with the pain of this and disappeared for a moment into Mary Bendel's bedroom and a remembrance of how Kip and I had latched onto her nightgown, the one we knew Mary would wear to bed later that same evening once we had fled her house. Kip had found the nightgown hung on the hook of the bathroom door. —Brice, my god, he'd said. —Brice, this is her. I ran into the doorway where he was standing with his face smothered in this whiteness. —Let me too, I said. And he let me. We both pushed our faces into this cotton that had Mary's scent inside it, a scent of neither sweat nor sex but of something ineffable: the person Mary Bendel hung in that piece of cloth. Then I was back with Kip, walking.

—What about the letter? I said.

—I got the letter just before the tour was up. Tour's over and here I am. Are you moving out or not?

I said, —You think it's fair to just show up out of the blue after all this time, and ask me to move out?

—Not really. But I think that's what should happen.

—Why don't you move out?

—Don't you wish I would.

—I wish you would, yes, I said. —You know, I really don't understand what's with you.

—How could you?

—I'm willing to try.

His gait, his voice, everything about Kip suddenly altered. I felt afraid for him at that moment, when he said, almost as an aside spoken by someone else, —You know something? There's no sense in trying to understand. You don't even know that you're insulting me by offering to try. You can't understand, Brice. I just realized that I'm the one who should go. I don't even know what I'm doing here. I don't belong.

—Belong to what? I faltered.

—I don't belong *here*.

—Of course you belong, man. Look, all right, I'll move out. I'm sorry. I don't mean to insult you.

He glanced sidelong at me and said, —No, no. It's your place in every way, Brice. All of it, it's yours.

—And what's that supposed to mean?

—It just means I don't belong here, that's all.

—Well, where do you belong?

Diastole, systole. This was the bottom, the moment I realized that I had *won*. My heart never was heavier, every beat seemed a waste somehow. We strolled at one another's side from force of old habit now, not desire to continue with our fragmenting talk. What else was either of us to do but walk on. I am certain he must have thought the same. There was a sadness, formless as a skein, enveloping us. We walked on. —No, I don't belong, he said once more, quiet as shallow breath, and I couldn't think of any rejoinder. We just walked.

It wasn't the full four weeks before he left. How dishonorable was it of me not to have budged? I didn't. A demoralized atmosphere saturated the apartment. It was stunning, benumbing. Kip pretended to apply for a job, perhaps did go out and look for work, but his efforts seemed to me faithless, hopeless, and his attempt to come back home seemed without heart, somehow way *off*. How else to put it? Like he was now a circle that wouldn't fit back into his former square hole. A triangle against a circle. The hole triangular, and he a mismatched square. His frustration he tried to keep to himself but it hovered about him until it shaded and finally swallowed him. In my ignorance, I thought to myself, Get with it, Kip. The narrowness of my behavior toward my friend should appall me even now, shouldn't it? I saw him struggling but felt helpless in view of his pain. I considered proposing to him the reason he felt he didn't belong was that he was suffering from the moral guilt of having fought in the war. If only he would come with me, join us all in protesting the abomination that was this war, then the balances of his conscience would be set right again, and he could feel that once more he belonged. But I knew that would be foolish audacity at work and of no help either to him or me or Jess. Pity was too vertical an emotion for me to display. He'd be right to resent it. But empathy, or sympathy, horizontal feelings as I imagine them, seemed beyond my reach. Our timing was more off than it had ever been. We, who once walked step for step in perfect cadence, saw and did every little thing together, could no more stride in synchronous calm than leap hand in hand over the moon.

And as much as he was out of step with me, he seemed inept with what used to be our world. I don't know what Kip had expected, but this was not it. Many were the times, in the years that came after, that I rethought my moves, reconsidered my conduct toward my friend during that awful season. I don't think I am cheating truth when I say that he was beyond me, and that even if I had wanted to reach out to him and help bring him back, haul him like you would a drowning sailor aboard a rickety, risky skiff, I would have found him resistant. But this, once again, may be the defensive conclusions of a naif, of someone who was opposed to the war without having the least idea what *his* war really was. I wonder how we lasted through those weeks. It is hard to know anymore. Certainty is the province of youth and the faithful. And, for me, the former is gone and the latter beyond my reach.

What occurred in the third week that brought everything to its crisis was that Kip, against all evidence to the contrary, became convinced that not only had Jessica and I cheated on him, but that Ariel—named by me, often cared for by me—was also fathered by me. A tragic absurdity that would resemble a cowbird come to clean out the nest of another bird in order to make room for its eggs—but then, through haste or craziness, forgetfulness or knowing perversion, throws its own eggs out, and leaves those of its intended victim safely in the twig cradle high in the branches.

Ariel, as I say, was possessed of Kip's eyes from her first day in the world. To me, his argument and accusations had to be the fruit of a terrible blindness, because all he had to do was look at the girl to know she was his. But Kip could not look. And Jessica would not bow to the madness of it anymore. She took Ariel one morning and left for her parents'. She gave me the telephone number and told me she was sorry to be such a cause of strife. It was insane, all of it. And what about Ariel? What kind of devastation was she suffering with all this mayhem around her? —but this was, of course, why Jessica decided to leave. I asked her if she wanted me to go with her to the airport. She said no.

—Isn't that tender, I thought I heard Kip say, when I carried her suitcase down to the street. No response from me. I left them, Kip and Jessica, alone in the apartment, and sat downstairs for the long minutes of their goodbye. Guilt taunted fear, fear undermined desire, desire deplored my apparent failure to stop any of this from playing itself out.

My imagination flew scattershot through those spiraling moments, and ranged across a broad spectrum of delusions: at the farthest periphery of possibility I believed, for a moment, that Kip might even consider committing a fratricide of sorts. Why not? —it wasn't as if he hadn't been betrayed, I by then was willing to see. What grandiose lunacy, though. Feeling preposterous, I sat and waited. Then I began to worry for Jessica's welfare—but knew at once that it was more inane phantasmagoria. It wasn't until I came upon the thought that Kip might be prodded by all this wreckage into an act of self-destruction—an act that could just well touch his taxed soul—that I woke up. Jessica was standing next to me in the street. Ariel was crying in her mother's arms. Jessica had tears in her eyes, too.

—I'm sorry, she said.

The driver had lifted her several bags into the trunk of his cab and was back behind the wheel.

—What does that mean? I asked. I wanted to tell her that I was going to miss her but instead I shook her hand and hoped that she would recognize it as some sort of fingerprint trade.

—I'll call you soon, she said. All I could do was kiss Ariel on the forehead and turn to go back upstairs.

Kip, too, was leaving, it was clear. The same duffel he'd arrived with was now out on the floor and into it he was pressing clothes, a couple of books, odds and ends. —Where are you going? I asked. He was all concentration; I was fully excluded. I asked another question or two, said something to the effect that he should take it easy, he was bringing all this down on himself and on us with-out thinking things through. —Kip don't do this, man, I said.

He said nothing to me. I looked at Ariel's ornate crib there just next to the bed and felt utterly emptied of thought or feeling. I left the room in silence, walked to my own, paced the few possible steps its small size allowed, then went out into the com-mon room. I sat down by the door. Soon enough he carried the duffel out of the bedroom.

—Where are you going? I asked.

—Brice, he said. —I love you like a brother. And I love Jess, too—

What? I thought.

—But I've got to go.

—Where?

—Goodbye, Brice.

—Where are you going?

He extended his hand down to me and I grabbed it and he pulled me to my feet. We shook hands. He left. And I thought to follow him, catch up to him and tell him to come back with me to the apartment where we could rethink everything, sit and talk, give it all more time. I'm sorry Kip, I thought. I'm sorry for my intransigence and covetousness and my callow feelings of ri-valry, I thought to tell him. But I did not follow him. Sorrow moved in and through me, but I myself was unable to move. I haven't any idea how long I stood there staring at the shut door.

Hay las sierras debajo de los llanos, as an old New Mexican saying had it. There are mountains below the plains. Kip always liked that expression, and sometimes in response to a question from one of the neighborhood kids he might not want to answer, a question like—Where'd you guys find those arrowheads? he'd pull a straight face and say, —*Hay las sierras debajo de los llanos,* then turn and walk away. It never failed to work. Dramatic and cryptic in equal doses, it left our friends scratching their heads, puzzled but somehow impressed. What's more it would leave their question unanswered. Where we hunted for arrowheads and the little shards of Anasazi pottery we collected was our business.

On the other side of the world there were mountains above and mountains below, too, just like back home in New Mexico. And like back home, in Laos—perhaps even more than in Vietnam—things could seem upside down and inside out.

The Geneva Accords were seven years old, and for seven years both sides had broken the treaty. Laos had been declared a neutral state but the highlands had been trampled by Pathet Lao and Royal Lao, by so-called neutralists and Viet Cong, by all manner of covert American forces, businessmen and spooks, mercenaries and vagabonds, from the day of signing to the day the Ravens were born. Not that it stopped when the Ravens came in; the converse, in fact—it only got crazier. The one thing all sides honored was a general distaste for the press. Let us fight in privacy—*privatim pugnemus*—might well have been the axiom for this place and time, sealed with wax and signed in blood. Leave us alone and let us get it on. This wish, for the most part, was granted. While the accords were most specific about the prohibition of foreign troops and bases in Laos, the North Vietnam negotiators knew as well as their adversaries in the dark gray suits sitting across the polished mahogany table that the topography of Laos was rugged and sparsely populated and was therefore ideal for clandestine infiltration by either or both parties. Deep valleys, mountains with multiple peaks like spades shoved skyward, lush forest green with succulents and scented by exotic flowers, and jungles whose floraed floors raindrops never touch for all the leaves that intervened between the clouds and the earth to intercept them. No, there was no need for either side to withdraw troops upon the signing of the treaty, they had but to deny their presence, and did so in the grand tradition of tactical fraud. The statesmen wielded their subtle mistruths—"subtle mistruth" being the everyday white lie that throws people off, say, for just long enough to get a covert problem squared away, and a good excuse readied for public consumption—with calm. They colluded, in their way, knowing that their fraudulence was in fact too big to believe, because logic would dictate that deceit on such a grand scale could never be sustained. And would therefore not be risked to begin with. But, as the phrase has it, there is a time and place for everything. And for Indochina this was that time and Laos was one of the places.

By 1964 Vietnamese and Pathet Lao troops occupied the Plaine des Jarres, in the heart of Laos, and when Hanoi continued to hold that none of their men set foot on Laotian soil, it was a lie of sufficient boldness that it ossified into a truth. Who was in a position to protest or accuse? You tell people the sun is yolk and the moon is cheese, tell them over and over with a straight solemn face and eventually some of them are going to believe you. There isn't a politician on earth who hasn't read this basic law in his unwritten handbook on human nature. Given—surprise, surprise—that we were building up our own presence within the country's borders, any allegations leveled by us at Hanoi might have a ricochet effect we could ill afford just then. Wink, don't blink. And besides, those who were being displaced, those whose ancestors had eked out an existence and maintained tribal cultures there for some four thousand years only to be killed in crossfire and cast into exile, those people weren't cause for worry. They had no diplomatic skills and no means of communication with the outside world. The ethnic groups who lived in the mountains of Laos could hardly communicate with one another. They would work well and hard for us, because if we lost, they lost even more. The Hmong, we employed them for a few dollars a month in supply support and trained them to stalemate our mutual enemy. If they failed, they would lose a war perhaps—an inexpensive one, compared to the hundreds of millions that were being spent over the fence in Vietnam—but we would lose only a battle. Cynical? It would be a pity not to win, but should that happen, it would come to be considered no more a problem to see them cut down than it was for Catullus's indifferent ploughman to leave the flower after scything the field. And we could still claim we were never in there waging an illegal war. The dead may not verify the presence of infiltrators, friendly or otherwise.

From the first, the Hmong who lived in those wild mountains reminded Kip of the pueblo Indians of his birthland. They planted their crops, raised their livestock. They were given to deep spiritual attachment to the earth beneath their feet, which was bounteous when respected, and the heavens overhead, which could be cruel or lenient depending upon how perfectly the ways of worship the ancestors had ordained were followed. In the highlands of the Hmong the orchids swelled in the misting mountain fogs of the morning, and the bamboo grew and pine scented the high air. In the mountains of the pueblo Indians hummingbirds attended the dark, fluted flowers of the sacred datura, the jimson weed, and the children walked out into the dry calm flats populated by all manner of cactus, from prickly pears to green-flower hedgehogs. Just as the Jemez Indians called themselves *people*—Jemez comes from the Tewa word *hemish,* meaning "people"—so do the Hmong, whose name for themselves means "mankind." Both had been the prey of vicious interlopers and their wars. Both moved from place to place when it rained too little or too much.

Both were possessed of a trenchant taste in color and angle, of an aesthetic that was clean and wildly brilliant at the same time. Look at Chimayó weavings, look at a Hmong needlework technique *pa'ndau* (means flowery cloth, or flowers from the mountain, the *phou*). The zigzags, ecstatic colors, the silverwork. But being unfettered in art and life are different matters. The Hmong and pueblo Indians were pushed from mountaintop to mountaintop or plateau to plateau, were made captive in their own worlds. Both, Kip believed, were like bamboo and barrel cactus and would survive no matter how harsh the adversities. The spirits that animated the heavens and the plants and the rains and the earth that quickened into life under those rains, the spirits could be trusted. The ancestors would watch over them. But it was forever a struggle.

Kip spelled backward is *choose*. And he made his choice, though I never knew this at the time of its occurrence.

It took a little doing to get back to Long Tieng. The military goes into the populace and seeks out boys who would be warriors, but when those same boys are trained and taught all the ways of combat, are given their jets to fly and ordnance to drop, and are sent out into the dangerous air to complete their tours of duty —when those same boys keep wanting to fight some more, and ask for a third tour of duty, or a fourth, then the air force pulls a curious reversal. Two tours as a pilot, or about a hundred missions, is considered the most that can be expected. Less than that and the pilot's training time was a bit of a waste. More than that, well? A pilot who wants to keep on flying, wants to go up and up again and again—after a time, he is considered a little mad. He becomes suspect. Why you want to go back up? they ask. You've done your duty, your service to the country has been of distinction, and your nation is grateful to you. Now reenter civilian life and pick up where you left off.

Kip wanted in again. War was home; or else, this place that war infected, this place was home. Not fragile disintegrating Vietnam, but Laos, and the Laos of the Hmong. This was where he felt he had some chance. And his record was quite unimpeachable: over three hundred missions, and one downing. Granted it was a bad one, lost the plane and gave the enemy a chance to set up a flak trap. But he'd got out alive, and so had his backseater and rescuers.

And as I look at Kip now, the shadows beginning to lengthen in the park below the santuario, I can see on his face a somber serenity that begins to bring him into intricate focus for me.

"What're you staring at?" he asks.

"What?" I respond from down in my daze.

"You look like you saw a ghost," he says.

"I apologize," I say.

"Don't," says Kip. "Maybe you did."

And so what happened; where did things go after that?

Laos was at the edge, like a prophetic precursor to what was going to happen over the border in the main theater, and Laos wasn't going well. The Plain of Jars had been occupied by the enemy for some time—to the dismay of the Hmong who considered this high valley their ancestral domain—and though it had been retaken by Vang Pao's forces toward the end of the year, by early 1970 the North Vietnamese took it back, pushing deeper and deeper into Laos, threatening to advance as far as the town of Muong Soui, and when it did overrun Muong Soui, Nixon could no longer keep our activities in Laos a secret affair performed by proxies and the idiot savants of Long Tieng. The first B-52 bombers ever to enter Laos on an offensive sortie pummeled the Plain of Jars and by the end of February the secrecy that three administrations including Kennedy's had managed to hold intact was finished. In March, when I read the Nixon admis-

sion in the newspapers, I knew, at last, where Kip was. I saw the
same thing he had seen, saw Laos hidden inside Los Alamos.
And I thought then, This won't go on forever. Either we will
wind up burning Hanoi into glowing cinders with a single
detonation, drop the bomb that would light up the world, or we
will pull out. It wouldn't hold together much longer. And where
would Kip come out, tiny piece that he was in that massive
jigsaw? Le Duc Tho and Henry Kissinger kept talking in Paris,
and in the meantime the North Vietnamese army advanced
on Long Tieng. And those of us opposed to all that was happening advanced on Chicago, on Berkeley, on Washington, and
on university campuses—and our protests spread across the
capitals of Europe as well. And when men like William Calder
came home, they more and more discovered that the hostilities
they'd experienced in war were only half of the traumas they
were going to suffer. This is history now and known to all,
but when it was occurring the disbelief that fueled their rising
frustrations was thicker than Mekong fog. How could it be that
they'd been pressed into fighting an unwinnable war only to come
home to a vindictive reception? It was cold. Very cold. And
Kip had, for a few weeks, felt that cold—as it emanated from
me, and even Jessica, without our fully knowing it. He fled from
it, me, her. But that was not all. This time he ran toward, not
just away.

   He was allowed one more six-month tour. After that, he was
told, he would be on his own.

I possess few keepsakes from my childhood on the Hill; for all
my ambivalence about growing up where I did, I treasure them
with a reverent enthusiasm, and keep them in a marquetry box

of honey and ebony woods that my maternal grandfather, an amateur carpenter, a man I never met, had crafted when my mother was a little girl. When times are rough, I can close the door to my room, look at the relics, and feel a kind of solace. It would be a frivolous practice if it weren't so effective.

One of my favorites is a photograph of my father and me with Enrico Fermi. I am in Fermi's arms, all of several months old, and on his face is a passionate, clear smile. My father wears a smile, too, standing next to us. He is looking at his boy with eyes that reflect both love and distance. The photograph was taken at Edith Warner's house down at Otowi, I have since confirmed, which stands on the banks of the Rio Grande at the foot of the Hill, where the old Chili Line used to come through on its narrow-gauge rails. My parents had just attended the corn dance at San Ildefonso pueblo, when Fermi met Maria Martinez—no relation to our sometime companion Fernando—the famous potter. It must have been a wonderful occasion. The image is saturated with vitality. For years I swore I could remember the sound of the Nobel physicist's voice, but no one believed me. —You were too young, Brice, my father stated. I have never given up on this fancy of mine, even though Fermi left the Hill before my second birthday and was, by the time Kip and I were ten, dead of a cancer probably brought on by his experiments in the thirties in Italy, when he bombarded with neutrons everything from arsenic to iodine to copper to water.

Another is a postcard from Truth or Consequences, New Mexico. My mother and father, who were on vacation driving around Texas and the southern part of New Mexico, sent it to Jessica and me on our fifth wedding anniversary. On the back, in my mother's hand, is the message, "Dear ones, happiest of anniversaries from this dusty old place, from your dusty old folks who want you to remember that Love is the Truth and Joy is the

Consequence, many such consequences and truths to you both, Mother and Dad." My father wrote out, "And don't forget to have fun every so often"—as if he knew whereof he spoke— beneath her philosophical admonishments.

In the box is a dried rattlesnake tail that gives off a percussive hiss when shaken in the air, and never fails to conjure the fear I felt when I killed its bearer with a camping shovel back when I was a kid. There is a fossil ammonite I found near Nambé Falls in a shale bed, remnant of the days when that whole wilderness was a seabed submerged under a branch of the Gulf of Mexico. There is a petroglyph made in school using a hammer and nail on small flat riverstone. The image is the best I could manage of the plumed serpent. Dry things fluid with memories.

Kip's letters are here, too, as are some baby pictures of Ariel, and my father's wedding ring, which Mother asked me to keep for her after he died. —Shouldn't he be buried with it on? I asked her, when she pressed it into my palm at the funeral home.

—He's not married to any mortal person now, Brice, and I hope one day you'll come to understand that.

—Whatever you say, Mom, I answered, knowing that I could never bring myself to wear it. I have his wristwatch, too. It keeps perfect time, though I seldom wind it and have never worn it either.

The things are talismanic in their way. Whenever loneliness sets in, or nostalgia, or even insecurity of some kind or another, I will look at these several objects, and often I can find something that will work a little sorcery on me and make me feel the deeper rhythms or balances of my life. A metaphor for it would be a sailor in moorage who, feeling adrift, must weigh anchor every so often to make sure the cable is still firmly attached to the ring, and that shank and flukes haven't corroded away.

For the weeks that followed this exodus from the apartment, I lived a hermit's existence. My marquetry box held fewer talismans then, but I opened it over and over again, as if there were some answer to be found therein—which, of course, there was not.

I remembered another of my mother's aphorisms, Never try to make crumbs into a cake, and put the box away.

Graduation exercises had come and gone. I hadn't attended. I took the New York State bar exam in a bloodless daze. I knew the material backwards and believed I would pass, but hardly cared if it turned out otherwise. I could always try for a clerkship, I figured, and keep up with my activities against the war in some legal frame even if it meant only watching from the sidelines.

I read. And what I read darkened my already-deep depression. Masuji Ibuse's *Black Rain* was published that year, and every page of its account of the life of the young woman Yasuko, who survived the bombing of Hiroshima only to be slowly poisoned by the black radioactive rains that fell on the city afterward, every page moved me. I read, "In Sorazaya-chō at the northern end of Aioi Bridge, I saw two women seated on the ground amidst piles of broken tiles, weeping silently. They were both about twenty, and looked like sisters." It brought to mind me and Kip, and the strangeness of Kip's name once more being woven into these histories bothered and awed me, *pika* being the term survivors closest to the hypocenter used to describe the heat flash that converted their children into boiling char; *a kip,* then, asserting my estranged friend's innocence, was just the opposite—a benign dark, rather than a destructive light.

When what I read didn't make me sadder than I already was, it tended to make me more angry about what our blessed country was mixing itself up with only a quarter century later. The wars kept getting merged in my head. Napalm, orange rain. Atomic bomb, black rain. We kept showering the East with insidious rain. Ibuse's novel mingled with my law books and legal outlines. And I was as porous as I might ever be. It soaked into me like ink into dry white cloth.

I read other materials. I read the Constitution. I don't know why, except that maybe it was the search of one adrift for grounding—the same way some people turn to the Bible for solace, I turned to legal briefs and legislation, statutes. The Treaty of London caught my interest, and soon I was back in the Second World War again, but rather than meandering, a peculiar weave began to evidence itself to me. Was I forcing my father's war to connect to my own? I'm not sure. Even now I don't know whether coincidence is the result of simple luck, or whether it is brought about by someone unknowingly forcing two elements to come together as if by means of a kind of spiritual gravity. I drank water from the tap, I ate scrambled eggs and fried cottage cheese and the occasional raw carrot. What is there to do in solitude but read, dream, doubt, drink water, and eat the occasional carrot?

During the trials in Nuremberg, after the conclusion of the Second War, the United States prosecutor Justice Jackson set forth a simple tenet regarding equity in the making of rules of conduct between states. He said, "If certain acts in violation of treaties are crimes, they are crimes whether the United States does them or whether Germany does them, and we are not prepared to lay down a rule of criminal conduct against others which we would not be willing to have invoked against us." In other words, what's sauce for the goose, and so forth. Given the circumstances, his impulse to invoke decency and fairness was admirable. Victors are not always so principled. I copied the sentence out onto a sheet of good paper and it went up on my door beside the newspaper photograph of the burning monk.

It was prophetic, in its way. The Treaty of London would be

ratified in August 1945, making all "wars of aggression" illegal. I doubt our fathers, when hammering out the details of the treaty and solemnly affixing their names to it, could ever have foreseen how it would come back to haunt them. But it did, and in no time at all. Only a generation later the words *war of aggression* became a buzz phrase of the sixties antiwar movement. In our commendable labors to make sure that the War might never be repeated, we established doctrine that we ourselves could not— could never—hold to, so that the very articles of treaty we held in such high regard in the wake of the collapse of Germany and Japan cast a longer shadow than we'd expected, and sank our clay feet in deep, dark shade by the time Kip and I came of age. Who is angel enough not to be fond now and then of a righteous bitter irony? Mine may have been black laughter, but laughter is laughter.

Soon after I'd entered my first year of law school, I had read through some of the testimony and decisions made in Nuremberg, not just because *that* war tugged at me—our final nuclear acts were, to my mind, crimes against humanity sufficiently heinous as to have merited prosecution no less severe than that to which the Germans were subjected—but because I had begun following cases of citizens who for legal reasons refused to participate in Vietnam, and I came upon *Mitchell v. the United States.* It was a wonderful case. Mitchell would lose as a defendant, then again as an appellant in the second circuit court, and finally see his case thrown out in March 1967 by the Supreme Court, which avoided dealing with the material problems raised in the defense by finding Mitchell's claim injusticiable. I thought, Hey, wait a minute—the Supreme Court can't just walk away from this without so much as offering an opinion. But they did. Only Justice William O. Douglas dissented, and in his dissent raised, to my mind, the touchiest legal issues surrounding all such cases. In a way, his dissent was Mitchell's triumph because it opened up the eyes of some of us who came along a few years later to challenge the war in the same courts a little more efficiently. Though most of our suits fared no better, the executive branch and Congress surely began to feel the heat from all this litigious activity. And Justice Douglas, pressed by that final appeal, did connect for me some of the immoralities of my father's war to my own.

It seems David Mitchell was called up for duty but refused to report for induction. He would have nothing to do with the selective service system because it was his contention that the war in Vietnam was being conducted in violation of various treaties to which the United States is signatory—primarily the Treaty of London, in which an individual is not exempted from responsibility for participating in a war of aggression just because he was ordered to do so. Just as the claim made by German officers in Nuremberg that they were following orders was insupportable, so the American soldier is responsible for his decisions in battle because, no matter what, a person is always accountable for immoral, unethical, criminal acts, war or no war, orders or no orders. If a war is waged in a manner considered unlawful by the community of nations, the individual caught in its mesh cannot later say, I was just following orders. A soldier is still possessed of reason and is obligated to use it. Such was the argument.

The more I read, the more I began to admire this guy Mitchell. He was impenitent, an absolutist, resolute and cocky as hell. There was an Old Testament stubbornness to his approach that awed me. It was true that he registered with his local selective service board back in 1964, but when he started to inform himself about our doings in Vietnam, he took a stand. He didn't run and he didn't lie. He sought no relief in any of the various administrative remedies the service is empowered to grant, such as community work. He didn't make a claim to be a conscientious objector. He didn't flee across the border into Canada. He acknowledged receipt of the notice that ordered him to report for induction on January 11, 1965—didn't burn his draft card, didn't allege that it got lost in the mail like others did—but simply refused to report as ordered. That was that. His was civil disobedience of the purest kind, I began to believe. He would not do what he was told to do because, he held, to do so would be to defy the laws of the land. With the spunk of a born contrarian, he sought nothing less than a declaration in court that the selective service immediately cease to function, making—under his lawyers' aegis—a pretty good argument against the legality of its existence in the first place.

The reasoning went as follows. One, the Constitution avows —Article 6, clause 22—that treaties our government makes with other nations are a part of "the supreme law of the land, and that Judges in every State shall be bound by them." Two, the Treaty of London is a treaty within the meaning of said article in the Constitution. Three, the conflict in Vietnam is a "war of aggression" in the sense defined by the Treaty of London. Four, our waging of a war of aggression in Vietnam violates that treaty and therefore makes that war illegal. And, five, a citizen bound to act according to the supreme law of the land cannot rightfully participate in the Vietnam war. So that, six, as a law-abiding citizen of the United States of America, and an individual responsible for the morality and lawfulness of his conduct, he was obliged to decline the selective service system's invitation he report for active duty. This was insolence in a class of its own, was brass-balls reasoning, and I admired him for it.

The only problem with brass balls, however, is that they lack the capacity to produce semen. Nothing, unfortunately, *came* of all this. It was a shame. The court of appeals affirmed the original trial court decision. In March 1967 the Supreme Court denied

him his petition for writ of certiorari and tossed the case. I wondered whether Mitchell was aware of the futility of his honest
approach. I also began to wonder whether it wasn't the courts
that were becoming the ultimate dodgers of the draft issue. It
seemed unconscionable that they would refuse to consider this
case. At least find him guilty and offer a written decision.

But, as I say, in his dissent, Justice Douglas touched upon
points that would shape me as a man and, soon enough, as fledgling lawyer. By late 1969, for better or worse, this was what I
was—almost. The exam had been passed but the conduct committee decided to hold up my final admission to the bar while
they reviewed my arrest record, and weighed whether or not my
behavior as an activist would jeopardize my ability to protect and
defend the Constitution and the laws of this land. Hearings were
scheduled, took place, and then months would go by with no
word until I'd receive a letter to inform me that another hearing
would have to be arranged so that the committee could cover
some points that had not been addressed during the last hearing.
Et cetera, et cetera: I knew I was being punished, and guessed
that eventually they would have to grant me admission. In the
meantime, while they were making up their minds whether or
not to admit me, about whether my conduct would or would not
bring shame onto their lousy association, I had taken work with
a lawyer who was an active member of the ACLU, and whose
practice was an ideal model for what my own would be: devoted
to civil liberty cases, and vis-à-vis the war, dedicated to getting
protestors out of jail, not to mention out of prison, to filing dis-
crimination suits against my alma mater, to acting as legal counsel
to any members of the antiwar movement who needed such help.
My sham discharge from service in my pocket, I set forth to assist
anyone who had acted similarly, burned a draft card, needed the
telephone number of a psychiatrist who opposed the war and

would produce an evaluation—after a battery of tests and a session—that spoke of a suicidal disposition or homosexual tendencies, who in other words would create a written deceit that would cause the recruiter to deny the subject admission into the military.

Months grinding along, the deepness of my depression got silted in, slowly. The country was caught in its own agony, and given I'd chosen which side I was on in the general argument, the work for me to do enlivened me again, despite myself.

Jess would call and I didn't know which was worse: the pleasure that came from talking with her, or the melancholy that blanketed me afterwards.

—How's it going with your parents?

—Sometimes fair, sometimes not.

—Why don't you come back?

—I will, she'd say.

—Great, I would answer. —When?

—I'm not sure.

—Well, you have this place, you know, and it's yours.

—I know, she would say in a voice so low I could hardly hear her.

And then I would say, —Well, in as cheerful a voice as I could manage, and she'd say, —I assume they haven't let you in yet or I'd have heard about it.

—You assume right.

—How's the work going?

—Nonremunerative and labor intensive. Kind of the perfect thing for me right now, I guess.

—You eating anything?

—Fingernails and carrots.

Which would make her laugh the laugh I loved best from Jessica. It was immersed down in her, and then almost against some demure will, just rose into the air, just like that, innocent and really exuberant. It was her best laugh, the kind that would make me laugh right back. Jessica is your friend, I'd think, when we did hang up. And I'd begin to think of reasons to call her later that same day, or early the next.

I heard the word *inexpiable* used in court on the afternoon of our birthday—mine and Kip's. It is one of those terms my father would call a five-cent dime. It means unforgivable. Would I ever be able to forgive Kip for doing what he'd done? would he be able to forgive me for what I intended to do? Then Jessica called me that night to wish me a happy birthday, and I asked her once more, —When are you coming home? and when she said, —What about tomorrow? I said, without missing a beat, —Tomorrow would be just fine. And though she didn't return on the next day, it was the beginning of her coming home to me.

*T*here was a canyon up in the Jemez so backland we could only reach it after half a morning on our horses, followed by another hour of tricky climbing. It was our discovery, this place. The horses tethered below receded until they became dark stains on the pale green floor of the head of the canyon cleft. We pulled ourselves up the face of the warm semivertical cliffs, finding footholds and niches as we went along. Sometimes the indentations in the stone seemed of such accommodation to our progress that we sensed they had been carved out by early settlers, Anasazi climbers, pueblo people who scaled these sheer slopes with the same ease we walk a level path to the market. Weather had worn away all evidence of tooling, though, so we couldn't be certain.

The cliffs projected in different directions as we reached a midpoint toward what appeared to be the first summit—we were nowhere near the peak of the mountains that rose away, horizon after horizon, toward the farthest clouds—and just when we thought we were too tired to hoist ourselves upward farther, the rock gave into a flat, and we lurched forward and lay recumbent, breathing hard in the thinner air. At the time, we never considered the peril in arriving here. If one of us had, no doubt it wouldn't have been mentioned for fear of prompting the contempt of the other. We rode, we climbed, we lay face down for a minute to catch our breath, is all. And then we stood on top of the world, or nearly, and then strode forward on this miniplateau, this stone table that, again, was smoothed to something of ballroom glaze, as if by thousands of bared feet. The first time we'd come here we didn't know what lay at the interior edge of the long shelf of rock. The first time we just meandered, balmy pioneers. Thereafter, we knew what was ahead.

Some stands of aspen and fir. An Abert squirrel with rabbit-tall ears scurrying away, annoyed. Some mountain sheep droppings. And always the hawks, broad-winged and red-tailed, and every so often a bald eagle.

It was like looking down into the sky. We reached the end of the plateau and the rock broke off from its easy horizontal plane into a straight vertical drop of about thirty feet. At the bottom was an irregular oval basin, a sink of water. Its surface was serene, as if asleep, and it mirrored the passing clouds with such verisimilitude, detailing every shadow and wisp in its dense glass, that in the right light the pool looked as much like sky as the sky did.

Kip let out a shriek when he was pushed, and his voice followed him down, already resounding in the stone bowl, until he hit the even surface of the water with a thick splash.

He disappeared underwater.

When the top of his head appeared, a good distance away from where he had entered the pool, the surface shattered with foaming white and green bubbles. He howled with laughter.

—It's freezing, he cried out.

Without a thought I leaped out into the dry emptiness and when I punched through the skin of sky's reflection the walloping, hard water pulled my flesh upward on my face, and my feet braced for the bottom of the pool; I didn't know how deep I had plunged but it seemed leagues before I kicked not rock but cold water, and paddled quickly back to the surface. Kip was already out and ascending a quite defined path that curved back toward the crest.

Games never stayed simple, it seemed, with us. This one developed in the following way. The object was to watch as the clouds passed, and wait until there was an opening of blue, a patch moving along the face of the pool, judge its direction and velocity and dive, headfirst or feetfirst, it didn't matter, straight into the center of the target. You named your target right before you dove.

—Elephant, we'd shout, or —dragonfly!

—Hedgehog, we would shout, then dive.

—Blue pony!

Then down into the elephant's eye, the dragonfly's wing, the hedgehog's belly, the blue pony's mane.

Kip was smiling when he reminded me of this. They were good days, I knew it. What he told me then was that he used to do the same thing with the Hmong kids. They had found a place, up in the dangerous hills above Long Tieng. The water was not nearly as deep, and the jump from the cliff was possibly longer —it was as if you hung in the air endlessly before your body slapped into the cold water—but otherwise was much the same.

It was like a second chance for him, he thought. But a second chance at what?

"There are words to describe what had happened to me," Kip is saying. "They're meant to be derogatory. What happened was that I'd gone *bamboo*." Like going crazy, perhaps, if viewed from the outside. But from inside the experience, a seductive alternative to going crazy. The lunar New Year came, and by the time it did Wagner and Kip were remarkably integrated into the community. They had made many friends, not only among the children, but their parents. Kha Yang was there, with his wife and two young boys. There were a few other spotters, joined by farmers and refugees—all distinguished by their hopeful will and strong capacity to survive. Kip and Wagner sat with their friends and drank *lao lao*—white lightning, rice whiskey—they watched the game of ball-catch between the girls and boys. Black iron pots of sticky rice stood on fires and the smells of roasted meat wafted over the three-mountained bowl of Alternate. When you eat with the Hmong you must always finish the food you accept from your host. Kip knew this. Hmong feasts were always served the same way, with woven bowls and wooden or silver platters laid out for the guests. Many were the times when you weren't quite sure what was being offered you. Kip knew this, too, and tended to favor the vegetable dishes, which at least he felt he could recognize. A bean looked like a bean, but with meat—you could never tell. The banquet was well under way, the *lao lao* flowing, when Kip and Wagner, guests of honor, arrived. Each took the broad leaf of plantain, as was the custom, and went to the feast table. Roasted chicken flavored with lemongrass, *larp*—a cold minced pork or fish that tastes of lime and garlic and onions—tiny fried birds—hummingbirds, Kip was told—that were crunchy and eaten beak and all, a kind of ratatouille seasoned with hot spices that reminded Kip of Chimayóan red chili. There was a dish they served that looked for all the world like tomato aspic. Wagner urged Kip to give it a try, which he did.

—How's that taste? asked Wagner.

—Not bad, said Kip.

—Take some more, it's good for you.

Kip spooned some more onto his green plate, and continued on.

Their hosts were congenial and never were their earthenware cups of *lao lao* allowed to become empty. There were stories told by various heads of the families gathered, but though Kip's command of the language had improved, they tended to talk too quickly for him to understand much of what was being said. Wagner, from time to time, would lean over and fill Kip in on the gist of the story. Sometimes Wagner would warn him, —Don't smile, this is somebody's cousin who witnessed a torture, or other times ask, —You following this? we're supposed to laugh at the end of this one. Wagner helped him with vocabulary whenever he could, as well.

Dinner was far along when Wagner, a mischievous twinkle in his eye, turned to Kip, nodded at his plate, and said, —I'm proud of you, son.

Sensing that something was wrong, Kip refused to ask why. He had another spoonful of the tomato aspic at his lips, but laid it down and simply turned to look at his colleague. Wagner ignored him. Kip, by turn, ignored him and finished eating.

The festivities continued. A gift of an amulet for protection in the field was given to Kip by Kha Yang. A silver necklace with a dark stone image of the Buddha set in a triangular silver base.

—I don't wear jewelry, said Kip.

—You wear this all times, you never will get hit, said Kha.

—What happens if they shoot straight and true, right at the plane? Kip asked.

—The bullets will not find it.

—What happens if they hold the gun right here in front of you and shoot? he asked, a little high from the *lao lao*. He held an imaginary gun and pointed it at Kha Yang's heart.

—The bullet will go around, yes.

From where they looked out into the evening that now came over Alternate the karsts at the northern periphery gathered violet light so that they seemed to glow, like two enormous tapered bulbs, and the milieu radiated a quality of home, a contentment that Kip hadn't experienced since early childhood, perhaps not even then. What strange sweetness, he thought, expecting it to leave him, but it did not pass away. He held the amulet before him in the dusk, saw that the Buddha did not reveal himself, and then slipped the amulet necklace over his head. As the heavens purpled and captured black so that the first stars began to pulse, Kip imagined forward to when the war would be over, projected himself toward an evening much like this when the advisors began to be gone, the USAID workers were on their way, the field officers, the ambassador down in the concrete bunker war room in Vientiane, the hundreds of thousands of protestors who had come to Washington back in October to signal the beginning of the end of our commitments here were finally going home too, the North Vietnamese Army who would soon enough begin their annual fall offensive and the negotiators in Paris now began to be gone, the irregular forces out in temporary bunkers under the emerging stars, the capitalists and Communists, hawks, doves, all of them would be gone from where they were now. As he willed them home it was as if all of them seemed just to float away into the ionized ether of dusk light. Kha Yang asked Kip, —You want ball play?

—With the children? Kip asked.

—No. We football, play.

Wagner said something in Lao, and asked Kip if he knew how to play soccer. —Not really, said Kip.

—Neither do I, but I guess we're about to find out.

By the light of two bonfires on a field down near the airstrip, a group of men ran back and forth. The green body bags that were laid out in a nearby morgue, delivered earlier in the afternoon from out in the mountains in order that their contents be identified if possible before burial, were for the briefest moment forgotten. Wives, daughters, widows sat along the edges of the field and watched all the other stars come out, and fed the bonfires, and dared to talk contentedly among themselves while the men played on.

The next day Kip finally asked Wagner, —Okay, so what was in that tomato aspic?

—What tomato aspic? Wagner retorted.

—Come on, man, said Kip.

—I don't know what you're talking about, Calder.

—The aspic, you said it was good for me?

—Oh, that. I never told you that was tomato aspic, did I?

—Wagner, said Kip.

—Congealed water buffalo blood, said Wagner, after a pause. —Hey, don't worry. I like it, too.

Once I knew in my heart Kip was never coming back, my burdened view of Jessica was free to change. He was gone now, and he was going to be gone if not forever at least long enough that Jessica's heart—were she to save it from being broken—would have to learn to elude him.

The danger for me in all this was less that Kip might return to make some new bid for her and the child, than that Jessica would keep on loving him in the way people have of coveting absent lovers. But I could see at once that this was not how Jess was going to behave in the wake of Kip's desertion—desertion, yes, to call a spade a spade since it was as much an abandonment as a being pushed out—no, in fact, it appeared she was going to act in quite the opposite way.

—Everyone has the freedom to make whatever choices they want. I couldn't expect him to try to be somebody he's not.

—That's a pretty generous outlook, I said.

She said, —So, I'm generous.

—I mean it, though. You aren't angry with him?

—I was, but I don't see what the point would be to stay angry anymore.

—It's not a matter of whether there's a point or purpose or something, I just meant—well, *I'm* angry at Kip.

—Why?

—Because—

—Because he isn't doing what you want him to do?

—It's not that.

—If it's not that, it's something close to that.

—Maybe so, I said.

—Kip has the right to run away. You yourself said it that night when we told each other our worst traits. Being mad at Kip, when you take a couple of steps back and look at it objectively, or fairly, being mad at him for running would be like being mad at a bird for flying or a rabbit for hopping.

—You still love him, don't you.

—I don't see why I shouldn't. But it doesn't mean that I have to throw myself and Ariel away just because he's doing what he's got to do.

—I like you, Jess.

—I don't know why.

—You're a good person. That's why.

—No, I'm not, she said. —I'm just trying to be a sane person.

Our domesticity reestablished itself with an easiness that should probably have alarmed us. Or at least alarmed me. I liked Jessica, I loved Jessica. Bird meant to fly, rabbit meant to hop, Kip meant to run, I was, I thought, meant to love her. What was new was that I didn't much care whether she wanted me to love her, didn't want me to love her, whether she was indifferent to my loving her, or any other configuration. I just lost whatever self-consciousness had plagued me before; a lesson taught me by Jessica herself—and if she didn't care to love me in return, who was I to reproach her? who to presume more?

And my love for Ariel grew so spontaneously and fully that there were moments when, I believe, if Kip were here again and asked me if I were her father, I would have to ponder hard for an accurate answer. I forgot with such thorough, unhurried forgetfulness, that Ariel did become my true daughter and I her true father. Day and week and month, Ariel was my girl. I played with her, I read to her, sometimes I even overcame Jessica's jokes about my voice and sang to her: —Froggy went a-courtin', he did ride, to which Jess rejoined, —When Brice starts a-croakin', even froggies hide. And while the process may have been slow, and so many of its individual details lost on me, Jessica learned to love me, too. Our incipient family, always hitherto on the brink, always *almost,* subtly branched into fulfillment. I do, in fact, remember.

It came in an embrace. Both of us standing, me and Jess. We were on the street.

A nothing day. Nothing romantic, neither serene sunshine, nor evocative rain, nor a pretty snowfall around us. Overcast, drab. Ariel was with a baby-sitter and Jess and I had decided to take a long walk somewhere, no particular place in mind. She was wearing a dark blue velvet djellabah-like dress with a wide Navajo belt strung with silver suns around her narrow waist. She smelled of lilacs.

I forget why it was we embraced, but we did. We held each other with impassioned strength and my hand moved up her back until it reached her neck whose flesh was so warm. My cheek was against hers, my fingers tangled in her fine hair, I reveled in that flowery smell of her with one deep breath after another, and without another thought we were kissing.

We slept together that night and most every night ever since.

*W*agner had a little book whose Sanskrit title was, more or less, *Ka-ka Chareetra.* It was a tract on the behavior of ravens and crows, and a lexicon of their language, the language of ravens. In the foreword, the translator mentions that there are "expressions in the language and behaviour of ravens and crows which accurately convey messages and portents. These can be interpreted, if observed and understood correctly." It was a guidebook to the cawing of ravens, a map to the meanings conveyed by these black, intelligent, and, according to the book, helpful creatures. Wagner loaned the tract to Kip. One night, without preamble, he put it in Kip's hands with the words, —Here, check this out.

Kip read the book by flashlight that night. Wagner was one weird puppy, he thought; maybe a genius, maybe just plain nuts. But the book was fascinating—itself genius, itself nuts—translated by one Mahapandita Dhanasheela at Yalung Thangpoche Monastery in the province of U in the late eighth century. It was very small, unlike the birds it hoped to interpret.

It said, There are Brahmin ravens, Kshatriya ravens, and there are Vaishya and Sudra ravens. Those that like yoghurt tend to be Brahmin, the red-eyed ones are Kshatriya, the stocky ones Vaishya, and the lean-bodied who sup on leavings, like ordure and carnage, refuse and trash, are the Sudra. Mentioned here are the utterances in the language of the ravens that hold equally true for all householders. Then there was a colon. And then Kip turned the page and entered into the language of the ravens.

When a raven caws in the early morning, just at first light, and his sound comes from the south, it means friends are on their way. When the cry comes from the southeast—just the opposite. It means your enemy is coming for you. If the bird makes its noise at midday and from the northwest, a king will be dethroned. From the northeast, a quarrel will take place. In the afternoon, should the raven caw from the west, you will know that a woman is coming to you. And if from the northeast, something will be burnt by fire. If the raven makes its cackle directly over your head, you will find the means to please the king. In the late afternoon, it is often best not to hear the raven. If he is overhead, hunger and famine are in your future. If his cry comes from the west, a storm is brewing, and if from the east, there is something greatly to be feared. Similarly, at sunset, ravens might best be avoided, for if you hear one cawing in the east, it indicates that enemies are on their way, and approach you from the road. Southeast—you will suffer a wretched loss. South—death from disease. And almost as frightening, if the raven flies overhead in the evening and calls out to you, you will attain whatever you have in mind.

Kip put the book down more than once and extinguished the feeble light, to think. His mind would race and ramble, and then he would turn on the light again and read more.

The next morning Kip was preparing to fly. He stood by the left wing of his plane while two Hmong attached a white phosphorous rocket to its underside. The book was in his flight jacket pocket, there with his pointee-talkee. Wagner came up behind him.

—Caw caw, he said.

Kip turned to him, looked up at the sun, calculated direction, and said, —Praise and raise in status will be received.

Wagner walked away, smiling. Said, —Have a good day, soldier.

*L*ife broadened and narrowed. I was finally admitted to the bar after two years of hassling with the conduct committee. Admission was anticlimactic after all the legal maneuverings, the delays, obfuscations, petty grievances. After working with the civil liberties lawyer for a time, I served as a judge's clerk to make ends meet. During all this, I'd made friends with a couple of young fellow lawyers whose beliefs were parallel to mine, and so once I was allowed to practice law, we naturally drifted together, shared a part-time secretary and a downtown office space, cramped and with windows looking across an airshaft to a wall of darkened brick and other windows in which people not unlike ourselves labored away in their own small cubicles lit by bald fluorescents. Yet for all its lowly lack of charm, I was content to be content, and took every case that came my way that could be deemed socially responsible. Our collective was modestly successful and soon enough we formed a firm.

Ariel was growing. Jessica was a good mother, more protective than I might have imagined, nurturing and reliable. Kip was dimming on a daily basis from our lives. One year we three took a vacation as a family, went out to Montauk to escape the city.

We walked down along the sea and I took Ariel into the

sizzling waves for her first experience with the ocean. Jessica was worried that I was carrying her out too far, and called from the shore to come back in, to watch out for the undertow. I swung Ariel around and we bobbed upward with incoming surges, and her face was radiant with fearlessness. Seeing that she was un-afraid, I waded her back toward the long beach.

During the train ride back, Ariel had fallen asleep in my arms, and I turned to Jessica and asked her to marry me. I told her we were already kin, why not make that final step.

She said, —I love you, Brice. You know that, I think, by now. But I can't marry you.

—We love each other, Jess. You want to be with me, don't you?

—Of course I do.

—Then why not let's get married?

—I don't have anything more to say about it. I just can't do that, not now anyway.

—Then when?

—Brice.

—But someday?

—Maybe someday.

Then we were both quiet and the question and its reply passed like a little rain shower.

There is a term I have always liked: *bundling*. It comes from colonial times when men and women slept together, side by side, in the most intimate of circumstances—there is little more inti-mate than falling asleep in the same bed with another person, sex itself can be less intimate—but bundled up, each in his own bedclothes, untouching and not touchable. One night, later that same fall, we were bundled together in a bed laden with many blankets. The window to the bedroom was open to allow the cool night air in. I was fast asleep, peaceful, when Jessica woke me up and said, —Brice? Will you marry me?

I would, and we did. Ariel was in Jessie's arms during the short ceremony down at city hall. A modest gold ring. Her parents we visited during our honeymoon drive out toward the West in a rented car. Mine we stayed with on the Hill for a couple of nights before we drove on toward the painted desert. Jessica, looking at the map one night, determined that we had to visit Bryce Canyon, my namesake. And we did, after wandering from El Morro to Gallup, up to Shiprock and down through Canyon de Chelly. Several summer weeks later we were back home and settled down in a new apartment we'd rented downtown. I did what I could do not to speculate about my oldest friend.

Nevermore . . . until tomorrow. This was the Ravens' motto. Their literary godfather might well have appreciated the blunt irony of the declaration. On their company patch, the one they had sewn on the shoulder of their leather flight jackets, the legend crowned a heraldic image of a fierce black bird perched on a white skull over crossbones. Where its talons attached to the skull bright red blood poured forth. The whole was set on a midnight blue background.

Nevermore, each day you would come back and this is what you would think. Never again should what happened that day be repeated. Fury is what they felt as they saw what they were doing was losing momentum, losing ground. Some month-old editions of military newspapers still found their way out to the frontiers where Kip and Wagner hung on with the other hinterlanders, having gotten further extensions by pulling strings and altering dates on records, and in these newspapers hidden as if in shallow graves covered over with optimistic rhetoric were all the signs that this struggle was coming to an end, and that no matter what oratory was used to scumble the fact, it was clear we had lost our war.

The edges fraying, the center seceding—these they could deal with. But trying to work after the secret had been blown was all but impossible. And now word came that they were about to be ordered out.

The hootch, a different kind of night than any before. The nevermore looked for all the world as if it would have no tomorrow. They were drinking. They had been drinking from early in the afternoon and they were still drinking late into the evening.

—Happiness is a warm gun, some sang.

—Bang bang, shoot shoot, others answered.

Why, if not to save his own scrawny behind, did the president blow their secret? Nixon's obfuscation about our presence in Laos had been perfectly in line with the tradition set forth by his two predecessors, had it not? But the introduction of bombers into the war in Laos, the massive bombardment of enemy positions on the Plain of Jars back in February 1970 changed, in the course of two turbulent days, the nature of their lives and mission here just like that. Covert was overt, and overt was the beginning of out. They would fly their devastating sorties for the next several years, burning climax forests and ancient jungles wholesale, leveling who and what had the temerity to try to stand. But they were worried about credibility gaps back home, back in the highest offices, and the disclosures that now had begun to come through from Laos to the people of America, many of whom had lost heart—if they ever had it in the first place—made the tangled war untenable.

And here were the Kips and Wagners out at the farthest end of it all, about to descend into freefall.

—Happiness is a warm gun, bang—

—Bang, shoot shoot.

—When I hold you, in my arms.

They scuffled. They were very drunk.

—Shoot shoot.

—And I fill you with all my charms.

—Bang bang, shoot shoot.

Le Duc Tho ran circles around Kissinger in Paris, and as he did General Giap and the NVA stepped it up in the center of Laos. First they took Sam Thong, a civilian base. Then they set a course for Long Tieng. They knew, even if the rest of the world hadn't known, that one of the roads to Saigon was through Alternate.

March, and the battle raged. Refugees fled again, swelling the camps on the outskirts of Vientiane. Many of the Americans were now evacuated. But though Long Tieng held that time, it wouldn't hold forever. Betrayals were about to occur here. There was a peace agreement that would be negotiated, and a cease-fire was to begin, February 1973. We were to withdraw with honor, we had had enough of our boys dying over here.

—Bang bang, and they all broke out slapping each other on the back, chuckling so hard their teeth and gums were bared. Their laughter was blistering.

—You know what we are? said one.

—Singers, man. We're *singers,* said another.

—We're just the singers, not the song.

—No, man, said Kip. It had been Kip who asked the original question.

Some ignored him, some didn't. One who didn't said, —So what are we, man?

Kip said, —I tell you what we are. Lizards, man.

—Bang bang, said another.

—That's pretty good, said the drunkest of them all, who got down on his stomach and said, —Watch me go.

—You've got it, said Kip, calm. —Slithering away on our bellies like lizards.

They calmed down a little. The drunk man lay on his side to catch his breath.

Kip continued, —And you know what else?

Silence, or almost. There was some laughter still in some corner of the hootch, apparently unrelated to the parody of lyrics, unrelated to the announcement that we were looking to pull back from the conflict, in order—as the wording went—to allow the indigenous forces to seize control of the destiny of their own countries: to leave in other words, as Kip saw it, the Hmong high and dry, the Hmong we had encouraged and funded, however meagerly, over these last years in the attempt to stop the domino flow. —What else? someone asked.

—We're not done yet.

A Raven, one of the younger men, said to Kip, —Don't talk that way.

—Why not?

—Because we are done. We're done here.

—No, said Kip, swaying. —No, listen. You're done here maybe, but I don't have the stomach for slithering.

Most of the men agreed with Kip, and soon enough a song was struck again when one man sang a capella, —Living is easy with eyes closed, not understanding what you see.

Then another, —I have to admit it's getting better.

—Bang bang.

—A little better all the time.

When he woke up some hours later Kip's first thought was,

where was Wagner during all this? He crawled to his feet, stood unsteady, and left the hootch. Others slept here and there. He was reminded of the sweats the pueblo elders used to enact down in their kivas on the reservations. Or in the long houses—which Vang Pao's communal bunker was said to resemble—close quarters, considerable foreign substances introduced into the body, all men, crazed with the ritual of testosterone, so forth, as he stumbled—tripped literally—into the hard light (as Kip tells me this I remember our first venture to Chimayó and how firm morning sunlight can be when caught by the eyes of an enfeebled mortal)—tripped, then regained his footing.

—Wagner? he called out.

He forced himself to walk a straight tack.

—Wagner?

The airstrip was lifeless. Kip walked over toward Vang Pao's compound and asked the first man he met whom he recognized, —Have you seen Wagner? The man didn't know but asked him in Lao, Do you need help? In pidgin Lao Kip said, —I need Wagner. The man asked another Hmong something, and Kip could see that the news of the withdrawal was spreading through their ranks as well and that confusion was to be the order not just of the night but of day.

—Wagner? He go Luang Prabang.

His head felt like paste as he lifted off and the bowl of green mountains seemed especially beautiful as they lapsed below him and behind. A thought that had often come over Kip in the past came to him now as the vertiginous horizon with its subtle curvature loomed out beyond the scratched plastic of his windshield. The earth, its long curve way far away out there: it was too old for this lunacy. It was far too magnificent for this madness. It deserved to house better than the likes of us. Kip'd never thought about it before, but what did we do but take from it our fill and offer in return little more than our own dead bodies? The sun off his right shoulder rising into the low mist. The power of its whiteness. The depth of these valleys and the cold purity of the rivers that traced their floors. The flora stretching forth from every peak and furrow. It deserved so much more than what we'd given.

Landing in the royal capital Kip was in a state. His spirits were in such turmoil that he had to dead reckon his descent, the same he would as if it were night. But he didn't notice. He had to talk with Wagner. Wagner would have some thoughts about what they should do next.

*A*riel, Aerie, Ellie—my daughter the airy sprite, the *Tempest* queen. Jessica, Jess, Jessie—court Jesster, Jess of the D'Urber-villes, Jess passing through. Nicknaming, shameless nicknaming, has always been an impulse of mine, and Ariel suffered through more than her fair share in her time with me. —Get *real*, Areal. —Don't be airy, Ariel. One might have thought she'd have grown impervious to the potential sting by the time she entered school, but in class, where the renaming of friends and foes is prerequisite in the process of growing up, poor Ariel got stuck with the nick-name Eerie. My attempts at condolence, after she came home crying one afternoon, didn't work. Eerie, or Eerie-oh, it seemed, had metamorphosed first into Oreo, then veered into Weirdie, from that into Weirdo, and finally crystallized into a ditty, sung by several kids at recess that day,

> Hey ho, what do you know?
> Miss Eerie Weirdee Ariel?

I told her that back when I was a boy, there was no end of jokes about my initials. Fighting back was futile, I told her. I was a bum, a bowel movement, bum muck.

One of the playground songs in Kip's honor went,

> Kippy Calder,
> Who is he?
> His friends all say
> He's a double-you-see.

but I didn't tell her that one, instead told her one of mine,

> —Little hungry baby Brice
> Eats the tails of rats and mice.
> And though they screech and squeak and cry
> He'll eat them till the day he—

Hey, you're not listening, I said.

Ariel remained mute. I thought to say something about doggerel being a means for people who liked each other to express their affection in an ironic way, but knew enough to see when a deaf ear was about to be turned toward me. It was something she would simply have to wait out.

—Just consider the source and rise above it.

Ariel said, —Thanks for nothing, Brice.

I wanted to tell her not to call me Brice, but she'd left the room by then and I lapsed into one of those rare but inevitable moments when parenthood observes itself with a little cool distance and asks, Now let's go over once more how I got myself into this particular tangle, what do I think I'm doing trying to be somebody's father? And distance or not, the voice of putative reason would speak, and say something to the effect, Listen, she no more asked to be a daughter than you a father—you're doing fine, you both are doing great, just keep it up, keep on going.

Ariel, the next morning, would hardly remember the trials of the day before. She wasn't a holder of grudges. In fact, as she worked her way through the grades, through high school, and on to college, she reminded me of no one more than my own mother, at least in certain respects. She was enamored of learning things, not just from books, although she was a prodigious reader, but from whatever source presented itself. Whenever we traveled together, the three of us, Ariel would never fail to engage people in conversation, make immediate friends. I think this was less the result of gregariousness than simple, but willful, interest in what was going on around her.

Knowing this about Ariel only made more difficult Jessica's and my decision not to tell her about her relation to Kip until her twenty-first birthday. In a way Ariel was beyond us, or so we felt, in that she most probably would have taken the news in stride, would even have seen it as *cool.* —But Brice, that's so *cool,* I could just hear her saying it, and then imagine what inevitably would follow: —Are we absolutely sure he's gone? I mean, we should find out about MIAs, shouldn't we, there's an organization or something. We have to find out for sure.

It was this eventuality as much as anything that kept me in dread of the day the revelation would be presented. To be sure, fear that she would reject me, that I would be exposed as a genial imposter, terrified me. This is why I've always been more resourceful than Jessica in finding reasons to prolong the status quo, and keep Ariel in the dark.

—You'll always be her mother, I once said to Jess. —Whereas I'm never going to be altogether her father.

But fear of my own heartache surely was not the only thing that prompted dread at the prospect of letting her in on the secret: to witness all the disappointments Ariel would suffer in any quest for her other father would have been devastating. There is no question that she would want to find him, nor was there much hope that anything would come of it.

Missing in action, absent without leave, something had happened to him. For the longest time I resisted looking into it myself but a long while before the birthday approached, I decided to run some checks on William Calder.

Inevitable disappointments were just what was experienced at every turn. He was not listed as killed in action or POW, I found, nor was he registered as MIA. When I made the next logical step to find out if he'd deserted, absent without leave, I was astonished to discover that no studies had been made of AWOL soldiers— a claim I considered as silly a lie as I'd ever heard. Over the course of weeks of telephone calls and letters I came to realize that it was no lie. The Veterans of Foreign Wars office could not help me. The Veterans Administration archives and its public affairs office possessed no such list. The Department of Defense was not of assistance, nor was its public affairs office, nor was its Southeast Asia archivist. The personnel office press agent could not help me and the National Archives did not have a catalogue of AWOL soldiers. I approached the National Personnel Office people in St. Louis and met with resistance. The Washington National Records Center maintained they knew of no such document. The end of it came for me when I was told by a gentleman at that center, —Try the library.

I didn't. Instead, I told Jessica what I had done, and though her habit was not to want to discuss Kip, she too experienced— by proxy—some sort of catharsis: Kip wasn't less absent or more than before, but an effort had been made, a serious effort. Is it possible that both of us intuited, deep down, that one day an answer would present itself? I think so, yes. But after that, Ariel's birthday seemed far off in the future, and once more the weeks began to stretch themselves out, not so much like teaspoons laid end to end, but in the form of a quilt with images of a family eating supper in the evening, of the daughter sitting with her cat doing homework, of the father arguing some case before a doubting jury, of the mother reading a story to a group of children who could not read it for themselves. A quilt of plain cloth, simplest pattern, basic colors, and one that would keep you warm on a winter's night. I read somewhere that too long a sacrifice can make a stone of the heart. The same is clearly true of holding on to a hope or guilt.

The most prominent event after that was the sudden death of my father. I had no right to be as upset by it as I was. Bonnie Jean would have the audacity to make note of the fact some months later.

—You acted like you and he were the closest father and son that ever existed, Brice, she'd come to say, and she wasn't wrong. I was broadsided by it. Patresfamilias weren't supposed to die and furthermore *mine* needed to go on living so that one day, when it suited me, when I had left childish cares behind, I could come to terms with such matters as the ambivalence I'd always felt about his life's work, so that one day we could attend to the business of understanding each other, even admitting to a certain attachment for one another. He wasn't supposed to die yet. Who knows?—maybe he harbored similar ambient dreams of having that talk with me, the one we always avoided with such splendid success, the one where we'd finally see eye to eye. And so, broadsided. I'd become the child who failed to speak up in time.

My mother's serenity in the midst of this was disconcerting, as well. When she gave me his wedding ring as a remembrance, I felt embarrassed, resistant, curiously obtuse. It was as if the world knew what to do, how to behave, while I had, at least for a time, tumbled off into a strange ignorance.

—One of the things we'll all miss most about him, the minister whom I'd never met said at graveside, —was his love of knowledge. Know thyself was his belief, his guiding light, and it is a trait hard come by, but it was a trait that defined him above all others.

He was talking about my father? and I looked at Jessica, then around at the faces of fellow mourners for some confirmation that surely this fellow had got his eulogies mixed up. I mean, I loved my father, did I not? But he knew himself no better than I know myself, which means he didn't know much. Then I thought, Christ Almighty, Brice, these are the last rites of the man who engendered you and listen to yourself rave as if you knew him, as if you ever knew who he was. I told myself, You'd best shut up and listen, you might learn something.

But it was over, too late, the little tribute had concluded and my mother approached the open grave after the four men had lowered his casket into the ground with tatty ropes, two on either side, not straining as much as I thought they might. I thought, What is he, a feather, my father?—then suddenly remembered thinking *but my father was not so tall as that,* recalling that cowboy song he loved to sing about his head in Colorado and his feet in Montana when he lay himself down to sleep, or was it the other way around, and my mother bent down and gathered a handful of soil from the mound of displaced earth beside the grave, and gently cast it over the lid of his coffin. Bonnie Jean went next, in tears, gathered an ample handful of dirt and followed suit. Finally, it was up to me to make the few steps forward, take up a bit of dust into my clenched fingers, toss it into the sunken rectangle, and after I did what was expected of me I walked away from the mourners—and the men with the ropes also left, coiling them into lassos for the next occasion.

During the trip home I found myself thinking about Ariel (whom we'd left in the care of her grandparents Rankin), about patrimony, about fatherly responsibilities, and before I knew it was speaking to Jessica about what had been preying upon my mind—wordlessly, unconsciously—since we'd arrived for the service.

—I owe him.

Jessica placed her hand over mine. —Your father?

—For letting me do things I had to do he probably didn't like. When I was arrested those times, when the bar admission was held up—all that antiwar business must have hit him right where it hurts.

—That's probably where you were aiming, wasn't it?

—But he never let me know whether it hurt or not. No criticism, no chiding, no rebukes. I can't believe it never occurred to me before. Let me ask you a question.

—Ask away.

—Do you think I've gotten complacent?

—About what?

—You name it. About you, my work, whatever.

—I don't think so. Why?

—It's like, the things that really used to bother me—it's not that they don't bother me still, but I don't believe as much as I used to. I mean, the world hasn't stopped ordaining rogues and bastards to run it, there are more wars going on now than when I was out in the streets protesting, aren't there? And what do I do? Not a damn thing. I'm completely inert.

—No, you're not.

—I am. Probably because I'm inured to it all.

—If you were inured, you wouldn't be thinking about it. You

might be less involved than you once were, but it's not like . . .
Look, no one's stopping you from doing anything you want.

—I'm not being complacent about Ariel?

—What are you talking about?

—Do you think I'm a good father?

—Brice.

—What I mean is, I know it's been more me than you who's
wanted to put off coming clean with Ariel. Maybe you've been
right all along, about not waiting until she's an adult to tell her.
That's what I'm trying to say, I guess.

—I don't think that it's a matter of coming clean—you make
it sound like we're some kind of obfuscators.

—Ariel'd want to know. She's old enough to handle it.

—The question is, Are we?

—No, it's more the question is, Am I?

—When do you want to tell her?

—Maybe we should talk to her now. I'm just thinking what
did my dad take down into that hole with him that I could have
known, or should have. Maybe nothing, maybe some wonderful
things that he was afraid to tell me that I'd have loved to know.
Not just out of curiosity, but to understand who he was.

—If you want to talk with Ariel, I'm right there with you. If
you want me to tell her, that'll be fine, too.

Ariel was the very image of youthful dignity when we arrived.
She'd talked her grandmother into buying fresh flowers, and had
made a sign, which was taped to the mirror in the entrance hall,
that read, WELCOME HOME MOM AND DAD I MISSED YOU!—and
when I gave her a hug she whispered in the most earnest voice,
—I'm going to take good care of you from now on, Brice, because
you're the best father anybody could have and now that you don't
have your dad anymore I'm going to be your dad from now on.

I smiled, heartache flustering my efforts to maintain a calm veneer, and said, —You're already a good daughter, you don't need to be my father, too.

—But I want to be.

—All right, I said, and when I glanced up at Jessica from where I was crouched holding the flowers Ariel'd presented me, I saw in her eyes the very look I knew must be in my own: a look that declared that the time to talk with Ariel about another father had once more vanished, come and gone with the same precipitateness as that wartime apparition on temporary leave from battle who had visited us so many years back.

Life settled again afterward, but settled in a way subtly different from before. The incompleteness of my kinship with my father worked at me for days, for weeks. I continued to bristle about the eulogy. Know thyself, was this ever the true formula for improvement? Aristotle thought so. Yet knowing hardly guarantees acting on what is known.

I got to know myself in the weeks that followed my father's funeral maybe more than was salutary. Or, not well enough; either way, off the mark.

One of the pitfalls of being a temporary anarchist is that your conscience is wise to you, can see right through you. Even as the tear-gas canisters used to dance and rattle hollowly at my feet, and began to cloud the air thick with the perfume of acrid chemicals, even as our cohorts were being chased by guardsmen with definite orders and live ammunition—Kent State was in the minds of we who were in the thick of it, and the colloquialism "getting busted" shone for us in its full spectrum of meaning—even as all this happened, as I ran and cursed the pigs and chanted, —Ho! Ho! Ho Chi Minh, and —One two three four, We won't fight your fucking war, and even as I lay face down as I was being taken into custody yet again, and still couldn't believe the weight of a man's wide knee on my back as he got my wrists together behind me, thought he'd break my arms like a chicken's wishbone, and locked on the cuffs, a voice inside me spoke, and what it informed me was, This is all a fake, Brice. It's a sham and you are a sham, too.

It wasn't, though. Neither was the instance sham nor was Brice, that *he* who was me. Strange how it sits in my memory, one of the defining moments, just like when my father died, like now—like when Kip wrote and has come back. You get older, you go along, you are diluted by many labors and loves and necessities. And then, if you are awake and lucky enough, your rigorous complacency is challenged. And this is it. Third time, the charm. You try, you fail, and then either you try or else you don't. Third time is the definer.

Which brings me back to one last thing. So many of my best moments were spent with Kip, and the unconscionable pang of jealousy I'd felt toward those refugees when he'd described engineering water up into their shantytown comes over me, jolts me, out of the blue, once more. Had I mythologized everything, carved it in marble, or framed it in gilt? No, hardly. But while the finest moment in his life might not be the finest in mine, I wonder if the worst moment in his was still the worst in mine. Probably not, probably no longer and yet I can still picture the look on his face when he broke attention during drill back on a flat field at the edge of campus, and began to study the crowd of hecklers to find if I was there among them. A hundred of us to the twenty ROTC men in dress uniform. We were protesting their presence on campus, the university's tie with the military, and the inevitable had come to pass, where Kip was on one side of the fracas and I on the other. We chanted, they continued their marching drill as if we did not exist. My focus was on my friend and I was exactly divided that afternoon between crying out so loud that he would have to hear me, maybe even rushing forward to assault him with my bare hands, and withdrawing altogether. Torn in two, my instinct was to conceal myself from Kip in the throng yet stay with the demonstration until we disbanded into the early autumn dusk after their training session had concluded.

How does one compromise when what he believes and who he loves are at utmost odds, without losing one's integrity and wholeness?

I walked home that evening, my breath forming mirages in the frigid air before me, and faltered between hope that Kip had not seen me there and hope that he had. Neither of us raised the issue that night, the next, or any other night. I thought that this was the worst moment in my life, just as I'd think later when he came back from Laos and left again and Jessica left too that *that* was the worst. Just as I'd think when my father died, that was the worst. Whether or not I've been fortunate in being able to cite these as the worst is hard to tell. On the one hand, the cornucopia of hardships available to any individual has forever been overflowing with variety.

Laotse wrote, "A good runner leaves no track." Here is another question I've never been able to answer: had I been a good runner that October afternoon when we were growing into different men, Kip and I, and were going off in opposite directions, or was Kip's the silence of a master runner? Had I kept to my course, held my bearings, and managed to elude the one obstacle I didn't want to encounter? Or had Kip seen me and out of courtesy or perversion chosen not to challenge the tracks I was making? Whatever the truth might have been, the tracks seemed long since to have been lost. And here, now, they risked once more being uncovered for both of us to see. Well, I think, let us look. Let's see what there is to see. Who knows but that Kip and I are building what we could both come to believe was a day purer than clean water in droughtland.

*J*ump-cut time to mid-decade, bleed space from Luang Prabang to Luang Prabang.

Kip was walking with Wagner as he did on Saturdays, every week. Other men walked the streets with them, all going to the same place. Luang Prabang was no longer the royal capital. Royalty now had no place in Laotian society, not since the Pathet Lao assumed power after the American retreat. Jump-cut time and bleed space, because Kip had found Wagner that day some years before, and he'd been correct in assuming Wagner would have thoughts about what they must do.

They had finished out their tours of duty as gentlemen should, but had not rotated home, as obligated. They simply declared themselves private citizens, not bothering with the niceties of discharge, and took up residence in Laos. Neither clung much to where they'd come from, but were absorbed in how they might stay where they were. Laos had given them each their first opportunity to act in a way that might be deemed responsible and honorable. They found, after the others had gone home, that they were not required to forfeit their United States citizenship, but did have to attend these weekly seminars—*seminahs,* in fact, was the word the Lao used for these annoying symposia, taking the English word straight into their language. And so now they were walking to the seminar run by the government and mandatory for all who had during the war shown sympathy for foreigners who'd backed the previous regime. A man in a uniform stood before an assemblage of some four hundred seated citizens, and declaimed for the entirety of the afternoon. He spoke of communal farming and mass ownership. He derided all forms of economics and governance that veered from the simple truths of socialism and communism. He abhorred private greed and extolled the virtues of hard work toward common good. His khaki cap he removed from time to time and shook it before him to punctuate a particularly important idea. He frowned, then laughed, was warm and then darkly serious. He paced. His energies seemed interminable.

When he finished, Wagner and Kip rose with the others and left the square at the center of the city to walk back to their storefront house near where the Khan and Mekong rivers merged, along a road where buffalo and cattle jostled among the occasional car and playing children, across the way from a row of beautiful wats whose layered roofs swooped low toward the ground and whose doors were decorated with hammered silver. The seminars were a necessary nuisance, but far better than the reeducation camps, where many of the anti-Communists were taken for periods of time that could range from months to years to forever.

Some Saturdays were work days, not lecture days. The men were assembled down by the river and given scythes and hand sickles to mow with. Work was regarded as important a part of their reformation as listening, and so on these work Saturdays Kip and Wagner could be found along the shoals laboring side by side with other citizens of Luang Prabang, some of whom had become their friends, cutting the long grass that grew there in the soft mud.

When they learned why the grass was being cut, their resolve to create a secondary business to the tourist business they'd begun was galvanized. The vegetation was being mowed in order that government soldiers would find it easier to spot people attempting to flee the country at night, across the Mekong, as they hauled their ramshackle boat or raft down to the bank and set forth across the dark, muddy water, toward the refugee camps awaiting them on the opposite shore. It was not the government officials Wagner and Kip stayed behind to live among, it was the very people who were sometimes taken away to camps deep inside the country, those who defected in the hope of settling one day somewhere else. Just as they felt they ought to be able to live where they wanted, these people should be allowed to go as they pleased.

All right, they thought. We will mow, and we will conduct our business by the rules during the day. And at night, we will get out of here those who want to go.

The two did not begin to identify how many cross-purposes they were working at. They were now reduced—or rather, extended—to living by intuition, wits, guile, impulse, spirit. It was Wagner's potpourrism become political, and Kip rolled with it like a colored chip in a kaleidoscope.

Now they were finding their way, but back in the beginning, at the end of the war, it was clear they had a lot to learn. Neither Kip nor Wagner was much the entrepreneur. And so, before they began their tourism outfit, there came the misguided bicycle shop. The bicycle shop began as a repair shop.

Kip never rode bikes when we were growing up—he rode horses or walked. He never understood how people managed to balance themselves along those narrow central horizontals forged of metal and supported by tires thin as sausage. But in Long Tieng he not only learned how to ride, but taught himself how to repair them, and made friends with some of the Hmong children there through this skill. The bikes in Long Tieng were rare assemblages made up of different sizes and kinds, not one unadulterated. Kip, on a day when weather kept him grounded, might repair a frame with junk metal left behind by construction workers or other pilots, glue rubber to the inside of torn innertubing, and come up with an object that acted like and resembled a bike enough to make some child happy.

In Luang Prabang gas was expensive, cars exorbitant, and since even the few roads that existed between major towns in the country were damaged during the war, or difficult to negotiate during bad weather, bicycles were the principal means of travel, aside from walking. "It all made such sense. We thought we'd hit on the perfect way to make a living."

As it turned out, there wasn't a bicyclist in the city who didn't know how to repair his own. The business went under before it was so much as up. It was then they struck upon the idea that since they knew how to fly, knew the terrain, they would go into the tourism business. The enthusiasm they felt about this maverick new venture erased all sense of failure about bicycles. They came up with a name, not imaginative but earnest, Laos Tours, and began again.

None of this capacity to keep themselves in-country came without compromise. And this is where life got most complicated. The new Republic, founded in the last month of 1975, and headed by Kaysone Phomvihane, the chief of the Lao People's Revolutionary Party, badly wanted Americans to live in Laos. When we pulled out of the war, leaving our Hmong allies, and open to revenge of the victorious Communists, very few of us had the interest or audacity to stay on. It was difficult, even dangerous for any American who had lived in Laos even as a neutral businessman to continue on after the fall of Saigon, but for an American who had worked with the CIA during the war, served with the Hmong in an effort to defeat the very people who now constituted the membership of the ruling party?—this was precarious ground being traveled. Wagner and Kip would take the risk. Why not? they figured. This was where they wanted to be, and the compromise asked of them was small.

To wit. Every year, in order to renew their visas, each had to write a short statement and submit it to Kaysone's people at the local office of the foreign ministry. The statement was always the same. "I regret the actions that the United States of America took against the people of the country of Laos. I will never bear arms against the people of the country of Laos." They believed that what they'd written here was true and represented their feelings. By compromising themselves just this far and no further they felt a perfect independence from any outside authority. They were their own state now. They were citizens of their own country.

Of course, having done this, they burned bridges. Never again could either of them be granted the security clearance necessary to serve as a pilot for the United States. That was out the window. At the same time they could imagine wholly sinister things in store for them from Kaysone if they ever refused to make their annual statement—and perhaps even if they didn't. It was easy to imagine being detained at any moment, for no legal reason, or deported. A morals issue could be fabricated, a situation in which their ethics could be questioned, nothing was impossible.

"So, like I say, when we saw the bicycle shop wasn't going to work, Wagner and I put our heads together and decided that we would run this tourist service. And it worked. We opened an office, hung out our shingle, and began to employ people, friends of friends, whoever wanted work. And we began to take visitors up the river to some famous caves where you could see hundreds of carved Buddha images, the Pak Ou caves that you explore by candlelight, or to take them into the interior by plane if they wanted, up to the Kuangsy waterfall where there's this water-driven rice mill, or even over to the Plain where they could look at the solid stone jars, to ferry them around and show them how beautiful Laos was. And it was beautiful, Brice. Nothing like it have I ever seen since New Mexico. Green rolling hills punctuated by these karsts, winding rivers like endless silver snakes in these vast stretches of grass. And the people, no one like them anywhere in the world. Gentle and decent. Good working people. People who deserve so much and have got so little."

As time passed, he tells me, Wagner became more involved in running refugees across the river to the limited freedom they might hope to find there. The long flat-bottom aluminum canoes they used to outboard up the river to the caves began now to be employed in the middle of the night, during new moon or when the sky was overcast, to transport émigrés to the far shore. Neither Wagner nor Kip went along on these nocturnal excursions—their situation was tenuous enough, they knew, and were they caught, it would be the end of everything for them—but they allowed their motormen, who had family or neighbors that sought to make passage, to use the boats, which they launched with paddles so as not to make noise.

The tourist business went better than might be expected, and the government, seeing that people were being brought in from the outside, did nothing to block their efforts. Indeed, they would fly members of the ministry from place to place when the occasion presented itself, and that same night they would come back and meet with people at a designated place, down by the river, where they'd give instructions and what money they could manage—hoping that the Thai waiting on the other bank would not confiscate everything they took with them—and hand them over into the care of their boatman, trusting that their nighttime lives would never come in contact with their days.

They walked a sharp new edge, and yet, for all the risks they now were starting to take, Kip tells me, "I can't speak for Wagner but for me I was at a real high point in my life, like when you and I crashed that car way up on the border of Wyoming." This is what he says, and all I can think is that Kip never did stop, he did keep going. When we first left the Hill on our way to Chimayó, and went on to Taos and onward up into Colorado, and when in my youthful imagination we continued to Montana and Canada and became cowboys and later built a noble house of stone where we were going to live as lifelong pals, it turned out that Kip made it there. Not exactly where I'd thought he would go, west not north, westward like the course of civilization rolling.

I think back to my own favorite line from Kip's Thoreau: "Nature abhors a vacuum, and if I can only walk with sufficient carelessness I am sure to be filled." By then he'd become a vacuum, I could see, and was walking with more than sufficient carelessness. All that was left for him was to be filled.

*U*ncanny how we can anticipate the implausible. It was November, New York, a few years ago. Darker early, the lights in windows coming on along the streets. Sun cool, gusts crisp. Ginkgo nuts and yellowed leaves still clinging to their branches, but many of the other trees looking skeletal, shedding themselves for winter. Christmas was already in the air, and shop windows had been transformed from colors and themes of autumn, of Halloween and goblins, oranges and blacks, to the stock Xmas imagery of Santa and elves, reindeer and sleighs, of greens, reds, silvers. Garbage set out in molehills of dark green plastic didn't stink so under the frost, and for that we were grateful. Out came the heavier clothes, my proven tweed jackets, mufflers, the thicker socks. Jessica would already begin to wear her gloves and hats, her sundresses and light camisoles put away for winter.

How I loved this time of year. When we ventured forth to walk through Washington Square our faces blushed in the bracing wind. I swear I could see and think more clearly at day, and slept better at night. August was but a bad dream with its weighty wet dead heat, its ruthless air-conditioning and allergy headaches, its sweating sleepless nights that give way, with cruel seamlessness, to work days marked by nothing but drear exhaustion. August, like a tightening belt around one's head. Everyone suffering. City of sleepwalkers as the strangest of the strange come out to prowl and the murder rate soars and the streets teem with the maniac cast of a lost, dark carnival. The streets are sunk under haze, and the haze itself is sunk under wan wen of sun. Hell weather, the dog days. It is a punishment, a curse, just as late fall is a blessing, is the most prodigal, most congenial season, even preferable to spring with its mere buds and foul mud.

It was after Thanksgiving, and I was at the height of content-ment. Ariel had come by and indulged me in celebrating my favorite holiday just as we had when she was a little girl, rather than a young woman who would be graduating from college, third-generation Columbian, the following year. So it had been an old-style Thanksgiving. She and I went to the parade, com-mented like we always did with mock scorn at the gaudy floats and mammoth balloons, elbowed each other with shameful delight when the majorette dropped her baton, and just generally misbehaved so thoroughly that Jessica had long since given up coming along with us. Then back home to feast. The celebration of Thanksgiving had become such a ritual in our urban house-hold, it seemed left over unrevised from the folksy postwar forties, or the more desperately traditional fifties. Here was the turkey browned just right since predawn in the oven, drumsticks proud as cannon at his sides, brimming with spiced sausage stuffing. Here were bland white crumbly biscuits that collapsed when spread with butter, the floury gravy crunchy with crisps spooned from the drip pan, the sweet cranberry sauce, the unskinned buttery mashed potatoes, the musky sauerkraut from my mother's old recipe . . . pork strips, salty and mushy, drowned in brine and laid beside the string beans. Ariel's friends sat and ate with Jessica's and mine. It had been an afternoon that left me buoyant for days on end.

The first snowfall of the season, a dusting that lay like parchment along the walks. When we went to bed, flakes here and there were trailing down through the lamplight outside the window. Jessica in my arms felt smooth and feral, her back firm against my front, both her breasts cupped in my palms, my face buried in the pale heat of her neck. The cat in a pleasant heap in the crook behind my knees, my knees pushed into the crook behind Jessica's, our legs parallel like our lives, and the whole scene as miraculous as it was mundane, the way we lay, the way my hand moved down the plane of her belly, and how my fingers pressed inside her, the joy of growing deep into her, and the gentle delirium of orgasm. Family and home and life going along, so that, when I drifted into sleep, I might never have expected what I would find there.

The nightmare was this. Jess and I were seated on a grassy knoll and we were holding hands and facing each other and she was beautiful, her hair wafted by soft wind, a fond glow in her eyes as she gazed at me. She cherished me and I her. Nothing was spoken, but the air was charged with sex, the smell of sex—briny, lush, dense—flowed from her skin and mine. Now I looked down the hillside, all grassy—it was gradual, the slope—and at the bottom there was a glassy gray sea, perhaps a harbor. Out on this sea there were no ships, but craggy rough islands came up from the water, black and white thrusting to pinnacles, piercing upward like mineral icicles. The waves curled around their bases, no shores, white. I looked back at Jessica, her eyes nodded to left, then right. Mine looked to where hers had glanced and I was astonished to see that we were surrounded by babies in a ring, each naked and seated upright, happy children with beneficent expressions on their faces. A curious sensation of liquid warmth began in my ears and streamed from inside my head down into my neck, my heart, out through my arms to my hands and fingers and down through my torso to my hips into my genitals and on through thighs into calves and feet and toes until I was a complete fountain of heat. I looked to Jessica and she was laughing now and the babies were not laughing but smiling, boys and girls, and I too was smiling and laughing. It was life and it was funny.

This would have been the most miraculously auspicious dream but for what followed. Perspective changed. Now I was no longer inside the circle of children, but just outside. I was standing, hands at my sides, rather stiff, and I was looking at Jessica and she wore a smile still, maybe superior now, maybe more gracious and distant. I smiled back, worried, scared even. And I looked at myself—or a double of myself—across from her.

Kip.

It was Kip staring ahead at no one in particular, this is what I thought. He wasn't looking at Jessica, and though I called his name he wasn't willing to look at me either. He was in robes, and I had the distinct sense that his arms were missing. I wanted to ask him about his arms and opened my mouth to speak. But rather I woke up bathed in sweat, and was never able to get back to sleep the rest of the night. It crystallized into an omen, for me, and instead of seeing it as a stark private drama that played out once more my fears and guilt toward Kip—wondered what his armlessness could mean?—I took it as a warning. Of what I couldn't say.

In the morning, I began to tell Jessica about the dream. I described the hill, the ocean, the vertical isles, and the ring of babies. She said, —What a wonderful dream, before I'd gotten to the crucial shift to Kip at the center of the circle. —I wonder what brought it on? she smiled, and so I left it at that.

Despite all attempts to forget about it, the nightmare continued to come to mind, began to inhabit me. Maybe it made such entrée by the very nature of its simplicity. Maybe a more complex dream would have been easier to forget. But whatever the reason, I found it returning at unlikely moments, while accompanying Jessica on an errand, reading a brief in court, slicing bread for breakfast toast. It became a colleague, a confrère. I would shake my head and say to myself, You again.

It is impossible to know whether the dream inspired what was to happen next—my sightings of Kip—or whether it merely marked the beginning of these occurrences, served as prologue to the waking drama of my sudden seizures when I would glance across the street and see *him,* manifest, alive, the living Kip tramping along, an itinerant or homeless, once as a man in a suit—which took me aback since the only suit I'd ever seen on Kip was his military uniform—another time driving a cab. Altogether I must have seen him on half a dozen occasions. Only once did I decide to cross the street and approach him. It just seemed impossible that it wasn't Kip, and for me to continue ignoring him was ridiculous. What was I afraid of?—by this time we were both well past forty, Jess and I long married, Ariel now legally adopted. There was nothing to fear. And so I walked out into the traffic, kept one eye on him so as not to lose him in the crowd while I darted around cars. A bicyclist and I nearly collided, he shouted something over his shoulder at me but I didn't hear him. I was intent on Kip, who lengthened the distance between us before I could reach the walk opposite, and rounded the corner into a side street. The street traversed, I began to run. Turned the corner and there he was, his back to me, just a few paces ahead. I stopped to catch my breath, gather myself. What would

I say? The long slow arcing movement of his arms—surely this was Kip, I thought. And so I closed the space between us until, just at his side, I hesitated. At that very instant he turned to me with a look of apprehension clouding his face.

—What do you want? he asked.

—Nothing, I said, marveling at how much this man actually did look like Kip. —I'm sorry, I said, —I thought you were someone else. The man turned and went his way.

Somehow, something was learned, so I thought, as a result of that experience. I decided that were Kip alive, it would have to be he who reached out to me, that this would be the appropriate way in that it was he who left. I also settled on an interpretation of the dream that presumed the Kip-figure in the circle was an extension of the Brice-figure outside; both were me, within and without, and as such there was no reason to obsess about it anymore. Whenever it tried to resurface after that, I ignored it as if it were so much dross. Kip, I thought, should neither be so honored as to haunt me like a specter would an old abbey, nor so dishonored by me as to be seen as an embodiment of dread and doubt.

One thing I did allow myself to retain from the dreams and sightings was a profound belief that despite everything that spoke to the contrary, Kip was going to return one day, and when it came to pass, it would be wise of me not to turn away from him. I could fear the moment if I had to, but I could not resist it.

Kip, having heard this, says to me, "You know what's the most peculiar from where I sit?"

Having forgotten that he was here with me, listening to what I recounted, I utter "What?" before I'm fully aware of his presence.

"It's that there were times I thought I saw you, too. After I was invited to leave Laos, after the couple of years over there in the refugee camps, I decided to try to come back again and there were any number of places I lived. Here, Europe, Italy for a time, Spain, down in South America, then back toward Laos, Thailand, on and on. I was caught between one abandonment and another, I guess, and so I was condemned to being a permanent stranger. Talk about a man without a country, that was me. And I'd be lying if I told you there wasn't a freedom to it. The minute I felt myself settling down, that was the moment I would pull out. So on the one hand nowhere looked like home to me, and on the other, everywhere looked like home. One of the places I tried on, like you try on clothes, was the city. I didn't last, though. This day I swear I'd see Jessie, another day, at the edge of one of the fields in the park, walking along near Belvedere Castle or out on the Great Lawn, I was sure it was you. Maybe it even was."

I am stunned at the thought of Kip so nearby when I'd thought him dead. Also, that he'd become a helpless electron circling the atomic heart of the world, just as I once thought of myself. I say, "So you left."

"So I left."

"When was that? Was it three years ago?"

Kip shakes his head from side to side. "Does it matter?"

"It matters only because, I don't know, maybe it was you I saw one of those times."

He looks me in the eye and says, "No, it wasn't three years ago that I was there, it wasn't me you saw," and I can tell at once that he is lying and that it is one of those rare mistruths whose value transcends fact. Lay aside your speculations about what might have happened if this were different, or that. This is what Kip's small falsehood is about. Just as when we were children, I'd admired Kip for the wildness of his spirit, I find myself now in awe of such natural charity.

A cricket between the floorboards. Music of its spiky thighs rubbed together. The shutters were open and out the windows shouts rose, a few individuals, then a few more, until there were many.

—Wagner, he slurred. —Wagner, coming more and more awake from the sleep of his flu.

Wagner didn't say anything, because Wagner was not there.

There was such an uproar and he pulled the sheet away from him and swung his legs around, planted feet on the floor, and then he stopped to listen, though the tingling in his soles—an indication of his fever—captured as much of his attention as the cries from below the open window.

—What is it? he managed to shout back. The influenza could be heard in the thickness and weakness of what he'd tried to ask. His cheeks were so cold, his forehead wet. He mumbled, then cried out with as much clarity and volume as his fluey body would allow, —What is it? Wagner?

Even the cricket desisted after that. Kip struggled with sore muscles but got up and in short steps made it across the broad room to a window looking out over the main road. His eyes worked against the blackness. He heard no further sound. He whispered the name of his colleague once, twice, three times, more times than that over the course of the next hour.

The crowd had run along to homes in the night. Nothing more was heard. After a while, Kip returned to his bed. He sat down slowly, then lay back. Chills shook him, but nothing agitated him more than the possibility that Wagner had been caught. Please don't let him be seen, Kip prayed, shaking like a dead leaf in an autumn gust. Don't let him be captured.

In the morning, hot sun spilled into the room and made soft shapes on the floor.

—Wagner? Kip tried, as he walked down the stairs from the upper to the ground floor. —Wagner.

But Wagner was history, all over. They told him that day, and they repeated themselves, quite hysterical in their solace and support, the next day too, and the day after that. Wagner was gone, had been seized by the authorities while helping a family in their fatally desperate effort to leave this admirable country. He was gone and the several people who were trying to escape were gone with him. Nobody could say where they'd been taken, when they'd come back.

The fever left, Kip got well.

Does a person have to have a cause to explain what he's doing? I ask him.

"Wagner thought so," says Kip.

"And what do you think?"

"I didn't think so then."

"But what do you think now?"

"I think now that you have to have a reason for what you do. 'What's your cause, Calder?' I can still hear those words over all the rain splashing down in the mud."

Kip is looking down at his hands and I look at them with him, maybe as a way of avoiding what I must say next.

"So my cause, what was my cause, that's what Wagner wanted to know, and then I realized something back in the room, when I was reading this letter that was old by then, that it was too late for me to come running back—I mean, I did come back, but there was no real coming back for me."

This is it, I am thinking, now we're coming to it, and say nothing, but wait for him to continue, which he does. "I came back as much to leave as anything else. Leave for once and for all. If I'd suspected you and she were in love before I left, I knew it for a fact the first week I was there with you."

And I decide to leap ahead. "Jessica and I are married, Kip."

"I know," he says.

"You do? How?"

"Because she's written all over your face. It happens with people who live together. I see her in you and hear her, too."

"I see."

"Brice, I'm glad for you. All right? Since you've brought it up, may I ask how is Ariel?"

"Ariel's fine," I say, listening to how pinched my voice has gotten just now. "Ariel's wonderful, Kip. She's a wonderful young woman."

"Is she your only child?"

"We tried to have another. It didn't work," I said. "Ariel's had more energy than three children all on her own anyhow. She had a way of filling the house like a gang of kids. Reminds me of someone else I know."

That made him grin, and as he did a breeze shook the highest branches of the cottonwoods and the scads of colorful rosaries swayed where they were draped over either of Jesus's outstretched white arms, whose paint was peeling.

"Do you think it's possible for a person to change?"

"It's possible."

Kip asks, Brice answers.

I think, this is hard, what I'm doing here is hard. Do I need to do this? And the answer from my mind to my mind, as if they were separate entities, is: Of course I do. My knees are sore, my bones are damp from the ground, my back hurts. Far cry from the child who'd vaulted drunken down here and leapt onto the low tin roof and crawled through to the nave from the dormer window that is still there, with unglassed frame and crawl space that would lead you from outside to inside. Not dead yet but these bones draw in the chill unlike times buried in the dry, dry past. And I am thinking, Brice, your friend is dying, and you're worried about your brittle bones? I am thinking, Brice, will you never change?

"I never used to think so. I always figured a person grew up a certain way and that was the way they were, you know. Like they would learn more and know more things but the basic person stayed the same underneath. But I don't think that's right anymore. You had every reason not to come here, and you came. You know how I used to call you a traitor? I don't think that's fair anymore."

I move from inside to out. I say, "Maybe it was never fair, Kip. Did you stop to think that?"

"Don't hate me for saying this, Brice, but fair or not, that's what I used to think about you sometimes, and when I came back from Laos that first time and saw the way you were with Jessica and with Ariel, too, I thought, Man, there he is in his final flowering, the ultimate traitor incarnate, the fucking Judas of Judases. I still loved you, but I felt the knife at my back."

When I hear those words I know that Kip will never believe he hadn't been betrayed by me. Rather than protest, I remain silent. We look each other straight in the eye.

"But I was wrong. It was Wagner, when he got caught instead of me, and when they came and asked me about him, what did I do but obfuscate in order to save myself? I was the traitor, then, too, and saw how it looked from the inside looking out. Sometimes I told myself that Wagner'd have done the same thing if the tables were turned, but I don't believe that's so. If I'd told them the truth, at least they would have taken me away too, maybe to the same place they had him, and if we were both alive still, maybe we'd have found a way out together."

"Those are pretty substantial maybes, Kip."

"They're pretty empty maybes is what they are."

"From what you've told me about him, I think that Wagner would forgive you if he knew the circumstances."

"But he doesn't and he can't. And that was what I was left with. I packed up as quietly as I could and left Laos soon after that myself. Partly because I knew my days were numbered there, partly because everywhere were reminders of my failure. It was in Nam Yao that I began to think about how I'd treated you in the past, labeled you the traitor, even though you had never really sold me down the river any more than I had Wagner."

"That was why you ran away to Bandelier that time without me, isn't it," I say.

"Runners run and traitors are left behind. That's how I had it added up."

"Maybe all these labels and definitions don't mean much in the last analysis."

"Maybe not, I don't know. What I do know is I used to hate you for loving Jessica even more than I did. But no more." Kip looks at his hands again; that old habit of his, staring down hard at his fingers as if there were signs there that, if he could only read them, might give him the answer to any question he'd ever want to pose. "I'm sure you've raised Ariel better than I ever could have," he says.

"Who knows and who cares?" I hear myself say. The words are out of me before I have a moment to ponder them. Very unlawyerlike of me, although not out of character. In fact, I think Kip might well have been wrong.

"Brice. Will you believe me when I tell you I've come a long way to say these few simple things? Our lives turned out one hell of a lot unlike anything I'd ever have been able to guess. I have spent half my life knowing you were my best friend ever, and the second half knowing you were my worst enemy. And now I can at least be sure that I've been wrong for half my life. It was like I just woke up one morning and realized, Man, that's probably wrong, you're probably way off, and for all these years it's been doing a slow rasp against you and it's going to ruin whatever days or years you've got left if you don't face a few things. And that's why I'm here. I don't want to go down like my poor dad, unresolved and like a puzzle done in parts but with other parts scattered all over the floor. One last question?"

"Of course."

Kip's hesitance gives me just enough time to gather what is coming. When he says the words it is almost as if they were my own, which reminds me of the days when Kip and I were so close that we barely had to speak to know what the other was thinking. It brought to mind something I could remember thinking when I stood at the door all those years ago in New York, after he'd pulled me to my feet, shook my hand, heaved his duffel bag up over his shoulder and departed my life—left me there thinking how easy it once had been for us to walk in unbroken step, side by side, and how that had been made impossible after we'd come down off the Hill and entered into the ways of the world. But here it was again, in its curious way, that synchronicity we once took for granted, in the form of a question we seemed to utter at just the same moment, Kip aloud and I silent. "If I'm her father, or one of them, does Ariel know about it?"

"If you still are unsure of it yourself, why would you want her to know?" are the words that come out of my mouth. No sooner do they touch the air between us than I begin to feel some deep shame. Kip is quicker to seize on it than the lawyer in me might have anticipated.

"It's a simple question, you don't need to answer, really. But it's a question I thought you might want to ask yourself once you knew what did happen to me. I am Ariel's father, aren't I."

I want to change direction and say, "It's late in the season for us to be asking and answering these questions," but he had forestalled that by being so unguarded about why he asked that we meet. It was not too late, was his perspective. I could almost viscerally feel Jessica's fear rise inside me as we approached this subject. I say, finally, "I answered that question over twenty-five years ago, Kip. The answer is the same now as it was then. I wish you'd believed me. You might have spared yourself a lot of useless pain. Assuming you have suffered because of it."

"Assuming I have suffered . . ."

"You were wrong not to believe me."

"It's true," he says, which once more disarms me. "But does she know about me? is what I'm asking. Does she know who her father was—is, I mean."

"Insofar as it was I who raised Ariel with her mother, adopted her, and—"

"You never told her."

"I'm sorry, but as far as Ariel knows I am her father. And you are a mysterious stranger. That's what you are. You're a lost man we knew, a half-brother of some sort, an old friend who probably died in Vietnam, someone who it's been better not to talk about. You've been ambiguous to us and vague to her."

"Do you think she deserves to know the truth?"

"Look, there are times when I think Ariel does know the truth without her mother or me ever having told her a thing. I don't even know why I think this. There isn't any specific moment where she'd said something that I could repeat, that would prove what I'm saying."

"I see," he says, and is quiet. It is dawning on me so clearly that he is right to be bringing all this up, inspiring and intimidating both of us at the same time, just like my Kip of olden days. This is a harvest, an April harvest, marking the end of absence and winter. Ariel, I think, is a lucky woman. She has a father in Kip toward whom whatever love she might come to feel would be love wisely offered.

I have hesitated long enough, so I go ahead and say it: "Do you want me to tell her?"

"You would be willing to tell her?"

Question answered with question, my same old friend.

"Jessica and I had promised ourselves that on Ariel's twenty-first birthday we would tell her. But you know what happened? It came, and it went. We didn't do it, we can't even talk about it, it seems. It's been the greatest failing of our lives."

Nothing is spoken for minutes.

"I'm sorry," he says, finally.

"Maybe now that I have something I *can* tell her, something concrete—now maybe we'll be willing at least to think about it."

"Well, it looks like that's up to you. After all, you're her father, not me."

"Kip," I say. "Why don't you come back with me?"

"I can't do that."

"Well, at least give me your address, so that Ariel can find you if she wants to."

"I can't do that, either."

"How come?"

"I don't want her to see me like this."

"Like that? You look fine," I say.

The eyes with which Kip looks at me have in them suddenly

more diversity of meanings and emotions than I've ever seen in anyone's eyes. They call me a liar. They tell me that I am beloved. They ask me to be quiet. They let me know Kip is pleased by what he has heard. They well with dignity and sadness, mischief and disaster. For one instant I am in the presence of Kip as a being full of grace that has been acquired through a process so unenviable as to be sickening, and yet so complete as to be holy. "I have something for her, by the way," and he pulls from a leather satchel that has been lying on the ground at his side a bound notebook. "I still haven't had it in me to read the thing. It may be a big disappointment, it may bring shame on me, I just don't know. But it's something I'd like for Ariel to have, if you might see fit to give it to her."

It is his father's diary, the one Kip hid away for safekeeping after his parents had died in the accident.

"And there's this, too," as he hands me an envelope. I open it and there is an address and a key inside. "Your mother told me to put their possessions in storage and so I did. It's all still there and since I'm the end of the line so to speak I thought it ought to be passed along to you. After all these years, I don't know what's there or even if there's anything left of it that the mice haven't found. I set it up a long time ago that the rent would be paid every year from interest on the money my parents left."

"I'll take care of it, Kip," I say.

"If it's a burden—"

"No burden." I stand. I reach out my hand and he says, "Did you know that there are twelve cottonwood trees down there, one for each disciple?" as he takes it and is pulled to his feet.

"Ariel will know," I say. "I promise."

Kip looks out across the outdoor chapel at the cottonwoods,

then back at the willow where we stand. "Did you look at the one we've been leaning against?"

I had, I tell him.

"I like this tree," he says and I know what he is trying to tell me and I say, "So do I, Kip."

*T*he superstitious have always found Good Friday an ideal repository for their delusions and credos. Like a hat under which you place your head when you are in your most imaginative, hopeful, churlish mood, Good Friday has been there for the wildest oracles and most earnest fanatics. It is a day, according to the laws of antiquity, to take heed of what you accomplish, to pay attention with the same liberality a fishermen pays out line in hopes of catching his fish. A day to fear and embrace. A reflection day.

Bread baked on this particular Friday is said to preserve one's house from fire, for instance. An egg laid on this day will never become stale, the old wives have it. Good Friday is the best day of the whole year for a mother to begin to wean her child, and it is said anything sewn on this day will never come undone.

Likewise, there are things best not carried out on Good Friday, according to those who are keepers of the flame of superstition. We are warned that clothes washed and hung on the day Christ died are likely to become spotted with blood. There are few greater sins than doing laundry on Good Friday, they say. And woe to the baby born during the light of this day, because his or her life will be full of nothing but sadness and wretched bad luck.

One thing Kip and I never did share was a similar regard for superstitions. Kip deemed them ridiculous from the first, whereas I always thought it better not to press my luck.

And so a ladder leaning up against a building back on the Hill when we were kids would cause me to step out into the street rather than put a foot forward under its jinxed rungs and struts. But Kip? The opposite. Out of his way he would go to prove its impotence, and if a black cat were there to cross his path once he ducked beneath, so much the better.

—Come on, boy, he would say. —What're you so afraid of?

—Nothing, I'd reply.

—There's something. What is it?

—I don't know, I'd say. —Leave me alone.

If I spilled salt, salt would be tossed over my shoulder. If there were a mirror, well. There was never a mirror I didn't shy away from. And cracks in the sidewalk? I would leap to clear them while Kip's foot stamped on every last one a sidewalk had to offer him.

Sometimes I've thought this superstitious bent is the legacy of my mother. I wasn't weaned on Good Friday: could that have been the problem all along? No knowing.

One other thing they say about Good Friday is that if work is done on this day, it will have to be done all over again. While there was a time I might have given in to whatever it is in me that's willing to believe these silly old dicta, that time is not now. Kip's and my work today is permanent. For whatever it's worth that is what *I* say.

*M*aybe it shouldn't come as such a blow when someone you used to know but haven't seen for half your life brings you the news of his dying. In a way, he was already gone. For all you had known, it might have been just as well if he were. But then he appears before you, and you remember that your life, insofar as it has any design, is defined by those you love and hate.

"Yellow rain is what it's called," Kip says, and I am reminded of the black rain that fell after they dropped the bomb so long ago in Hiroshima. "It comes in other colors," as if reading my mind—"blue rain, red rain, white rain, black rain too, a colorful rainbow of venom, and it comes in washing over you and you begin to feel sick, nauseous, and you get the chills, vertigo, and a fogginess sets in on what you see, and then you begin to bleed, from your nose and mouth and ears. You cry blood. And I'm one of the lucky ones because I didn't get that big a dose of it. You get hit directly and you die vomiting your own lifeblood and excreting your blood while your lungs hemorrhage and your legs run with red, your own gore and heart's blood. There's no stopping it and what's more, the government denies it and just about everybody believes that it doesn't exist, isn't happening. And so I may be sick with that, and to be honest with you, Brice, I think I'm sick with the other war, too. You remember where we used to play? I wonder about some of those canyons, what they buried down there before they even knew about radiation. Maybe I'm just worn out and it has nothing to do with rain of any color, just the marathoner coming to his wire a little earlier than others. Strange race where you lose by coming in first. I don't know."

Am I trying to push Kip's illness away from him and me when I picture the scene from the film they made of that novel *Black Rain*, the devastating scene where the young Japanese woman sits by her mirror and stares at herself and then combs her hair? She cannot find a husband because she has radiation sickness from having walked across burning Hiroshima with her aging aunt and uncle in search of shelter. The families of potential suitors continually reject her, even though she is beautiful and very sweet, because they know one day her health will leave her and she will begin to hallucinate and finally go mad and die. I picture the scene where her malady manifests itself. Doing her toilette, she is seated before a mirror, and begins to comb her hair. Sensing that something is wrong, she looks up and sees that it readily comes out in shanks, beautiful black hair. Her hand touches her head and in knowing disbelief she runs her fingers from crown to ear. Her hair in bunches, clumps. And she stares into the mirror, and without a word having been spoken we know that she is seeing herself dead.

"Why do we do this to ourselves?"

Kip says, "What?"

"I'm sorry," I say. "I was thinking of something—I was just thinking aloud. How did you get sick? I mean, you don't have to tell me if you don't want to."

"Do you remember when we were growing up how people used to have the strangest ideas about the Hill and what was *really* going on up there? Well, it was the same overseas. I knew that Wagner was dead, or I thought I knew. But then I would keep hearing rumors about this guy who was way up north in Laos, an American, a former pilot who had married a princess and created a kingdom of sorts, a dominion separate from the rest of the world. He embraced all gods and he walked with a limp. So I decided, even though I sensed deep down that all this was rot, that he hadn't survived, decided anyway to try to get in there to find him. It was the only way I could make peace with myself, exorcise this guilt, push Wagner's ghost out of my shadow. It's gotten easier to get into the country these last years, if you know people and you know who to avoid and how to avoid them. I made the arrangements and crossed the Mekong, it would have been about two years ago, now. I was surprised how little things had changed physically. It's true that I wasn't able to travel the

routes I once traveled. The road from Vientiane to Luang Prabang, just for one, I knew better than to use. Trails, and friends
got me to where I'd heard he was. It was like a pilgrimage to find
Kurtz, a crazed Marlon Brando up the river and through the war
to Wagner's house we go. But the war was over, gone, at least
on the surfaces, and it wasn't a movie I was in, it was me hoping
that what I thought had happened hadn't happened at all, hoping
that though it was true I'd failed him, he might have survived
anyway, that though I'd run, been a traitor—"

How it surprises me to hear him use the word again. He must
have sensed what I was thinking because he interrupts himself
long enough to make acknowledgment.

"Traitor, yes. But Brice, this is half of why it was only you I
could come to now. Because you're the only person who possibly
could understand what this has meant to me, my act of traitoring,
and I guess the only one who could forgive me."

"Did you find him?"

"Wagner. He was like a figure out of some mystical religion
all of his own making. He seemed to be there, out there ahead
of me somewhere, but he wasn't. All threads without anything
tied to them once you reached the end, that was Wagner, or I
should say that was the many Wagners, all these manifestations
that I heard in echo but never could discover. It was like trying
to touch a sound, like trying to close your fist on a beautiful
passage of music. The music went on even while you held your
fist tight and it went on after you opened it up and saw there
wasn't anything there. Wagner defined the term *missing in
action*—he was still active and still missing, and that's what he'll
be for me for as long as I live, and it's the cruelest thing, Brice.
Anyway, when I was in-country deep, to get back to what I was
saying, I began to notice that there were many Wagners out there,
rumors of servicemen who'd established fiefdoms, or who were

living in caves with seven wives, or who were still held captive by Pathet Lao who were keeping them like human wampum, trading chips against the day when Laos would want to open up again to the world, and America in particular. All of it seemed, as the days went on—and believe me I knew that I couldn't stay in there very long before somebody would say something to someone else and the presence of this unwelcome drifter would come to the attention of people who didn't want me or anybody else wandering around the countryside untended—all of it seemed fantasy, with every new story I heard. My Lao was good, so it wasn't that I was getting the information wrong. It was that the information itself got bent and mangled as it went from mouth to ear. But one of the things I'd heard about was the yellow rain and how the Laotian government was waging a discreet war now against those who fought on the other side back a decade and a half ago. So before I left, I wanted to try to work my way down to Alternate, see what was there, find out if anything was left of Long Tieng, and even see if I couldn't find Kha Yang's family. I never made it that far and so I'll never know the answer to that one either. I was staying outside a village just south of the Plain. In the village there were Hmong with others, but the Hmong set up at the edges, up on the higher stretches of this mountainside. When the chopper came in, I was sleeping off a ways from the Hmong village. I knew that they'd been using chemical weapons in there as far back as seventy-nine, they'd been torturing these people ever since we abandoned them. Trichothecene mycotoxin, the poor man's atom bomb as it's been called, is what they use on them. Early in the morning. The dawn breeze carried it down with the help of polyethylene glycol, very gently blew it through the settlement. And then, like that, the chopper was gone and the cloud had slipped away into the land and the trees, and into our lungs and eyes. People crying, standing up in the first light and sobbing, and I knew that it was time for me to move quickly, as much for their sake as mine. I had friends of friends in this village and knew that if I was discovered here, there would be more for them to pay yet. No end to vengeance. So I left. How I made it back down to the river I couldn't tell you, it was like a dream, I just ran in the direction the compass needle told me to go. I ate roots, weeds. When I found the Mekong I did what I had seen others do so many times, I built a little makeshift raft of bamboo and once it got dark I paddled my way across as quietly as I could. Unlike those poor Hmong, once I was in Thailand I was more or less safe. I'd gone all that way and found nothing of what I wanted to find. But I began to find other things—and it was the beginning of my trip back here."

On a summer day back when Kip and I were ten years old, as part of the civil defense program, all our townspeople were evacuated from the Hill. A warm June afternoon, cloudy skies. The threat of atomic warfare was forever in our minds, and all across the nation exercises such as this were conducted. People gathered in underground shelters, streets were deserted as sirens pierced the air, radios broadcast a pairing of notes meant to hurt the ears and alert the populace that nuclear war was under way and that they should find sanctuary.

The evacuation that day was remarkable for its scope and, to those of us who were possessed of healthy imaginations, for its realism. Our fathers were frightful in their seriousness as they came home from the Techs to fetch us after what was called warning blue had sounded, at three-thirty in the afternoon. Eight thousand of us left our houses and schools and places of work and fled through the three main exits from town. Catastrophe

and heartache were mirrored in every face. Were the bombs coming, we truly would not have seemed to one another more grim.

Downtown, as we left, they simulated looting so that the police
could practice panic control. Other teams of men gathered at sites
to prepare for the identification and counting of the dead, and
town doctors grouped to ready themselves to treat the wounded.
Overhead, we saw jets twisting in the skies, having been scrambled from nearby Kirkland base. The local radio station issued
reports about the evacuation as we streamed down the canyonside
out toward the desert foothills where we were told to park our
cars along the shoulder and huddle ourselves beside their great
rounded bulks as a hawk's cry riffed against the screaming of the
jet planes above.

Kip and I swore that if this ever came to pass, we wouldn't
get separated. We had plans of our own. We told each other that
if the time came, and the war came, and that if we survived the
blast, what we would do was get ourselves somehow to safety in
one of the Indian ruins, wait for the cloud to blow away and the
radioactivity to thin out, and then we would walk across the desert together until we got to Chimayó, because we were convinced
that the Hill would be gone and the rest of the world might even
be gone, but that the church somehow would still be there.

—Water from the creek, he'd say.

—Good fresh water.

—Yeah.

—And if we have to, I bet we could live on the posito dirt
until the first crops'd grow, I would say.

—Yeah, 'cause we'd grow corn and beans ourselves.

—And we'd make bread.

—Or our wives would.

—And we'd build houses side by side.

—Sure would.

—And that's where we'd live.

—Sure would.

Thus, our plan, but we managed that afternoon to get separated along the road. Guards at the gates directing traffic in the confounding exodus must have signaled Kip's father to go one direction and mine to go another. In the newspaper, the civil defense director for our town called the operation successful and said that he was "extremely well satisfied with the results." The town had been almost completely evacuated in something less than an hour and "threatening planes," he said, "were destroyed fifty miles north of Los Alamos," whatever that was supposed to mean.

—Did they really shoot down planes? I asked Kip.

—I think so but I don't know, he answered.

We couldn't bring ourselves to admit the failure of our own scheme for a week or two, until one day walking along barefoot over at the border of one of the mesas, Kip said, —That whole thing they did where we had to leave the Hill and go down there to escape from being blown up by the bomb? That was stupid.

—I know, I said.

—No, I mean it was stupid, Brice, stupid just like we are stupid.

I didn't get it. —How come we're stupid? We're not stupid.

—Did we do what we said we were going to do if that happened?

—But it wasn't our fault.

—Doesn't matter. We weren't together and we would of died.

—No, I said. —We'd have made it down to Chimayó separate, and then we'd have gone ahead like we said.

—Once we got separated that'd be the end of it, boy. It would have been like this . . . and Kip traced the tip of his thumbnail across his neck. I was flattered by the thought that Kip would

consider it the end if he and I were separated during the course
of a war.

—You're right, I said. —If they do another one of those drills,
what we do is we stay behind. We'll hide and let them all run
down into the desert. We'll get through it somehow, boy.

—Shake, he said.

We reached our small hands out to one another and shook.
As it turned out, civil defense exercises after that one were more
modest. We were never evacuated again and so our resolve was
not tested until our days in New York, when again we failed to
live up to the standards and principles of our friendship. I still
have a copy of the newspaper clipping announcing the success of
the civil defense drill that June—the makers fleeing what they
had made, fleeing with such efficiency and dispatch—and in it
there are lines that never fail to rouse wry laughter from me. A
certain percentage of police were evacuated along with Hill residents, the paper reported. The police chief said this measure was
taken to insure that authorities would be available to help out
"after the disaster let up."

After the disaster let up? Since when was it the nature of
disasters ever to let up? I wondered. Disasters don't let up, they
only let us down. Always down.

*T*he New Mexico afternoon was dissolving toward evening. This
had always been my most cherished season here. In other parts
of the country, late winter into early spring seems desolate, the
buds ripening, yes, but still like promises not yet kept, and the
trees stand naked without so much as a shawl of snow to cloak
them. Elsewhere, back east, upstate where Jess and Ariel and I
often liked to go to get ourselves away from the city, it was im-

possible to walk this time of year. The frozen ground gave way to mud, a mucky mud that bore a petrified crust at midnight, then thawed at dawn and never dried out during the course of the sunniest day. The grass was pale, the hyacinth and crocuses —pathetically tiny and vulnerable to late snow—might have perforated the dark damp clay, but all the perennials remained dormant. Fallen limbs, broken branches, the roads white from salt and sand. And the sky, the sky interminably white, a blister upon the firmament, like a soreness from the ice and wind. That, to me, was early April elsewhere. Here it was different, always. The desert too can be muddy, but of a pregnant red. Here the sky never stopped with its constant performance, it did not matter which season. The densest, strongest, most muscular, meaty clouds anywhere on earth. Now clear, now rain. Now palest blue, now deep gray-blue. The sky here was an improvisational genius.

And I suddenly realized that Kip had stopped talking and my eyes had wandered away from him, up the ridge of Tsi Mayoh. What did the Tewa words mean? flaking rock?—they'd once mined obsidian from this valley. The sandstone cliffs, the fallen boulders, all of it the color of a fawn's coat. Nothing had changed an iota since the last time I glimpsed it. What solidity there was to the earth, despite the best efforts of we rascals who run about enacting our dreams on its back. And look at us, me and Kip, look at what the quarter century had done to us.

We'd walked a little, other stories came forth. One night he thought the mosquito netting had fallen on him and he woke up clawing at it in a fever to get it off his skin. He wrestled with it in the dark for some very long minutes before coming to the realization that it wasn't netting but just a thick pelt of his own sweat. He stood up in the dark and held his arms out at ninety-degree angles from his sides, partly to let the air dry him off, partly as a self-punishment for being maniacal. Held himself there for an hour, like a Christ without a cross but crucified anyway.

There was a story about a formal dance that was held in the royal capital at the ambassador's residence, and how several of the Ravens had flown in for the party, changed out of their flight-suits and into rented tuxedos. At the ball were the entire lot of warring factions, represented by embassy staffs and local ministers. The Chinese were there, smiling and enjoying themselves, the Russian ambassador's wife assented to Kip's offer to dance to the music of a small but adequate band. Champagne, crudités, caviar. It was as if the war were not going on. There were spooks and Pathet Lao who earlier the same day might well have been out in the field trying to kill each other, but tonight was a night off, a temporary truce held to the strains of swing music. And then, everyone left, having bid one another goodnight, having shaken hands, and the next day were right back into the business of fighting. "That's a true story," he remarks, as if even he can hardly believe it in retrospect.

He told me about how once, just for a lark, he and Wagner had taken their planes up on a clear Sunday morning, out from Luang Prabang, and headed north. Rules of engagement prevented them from flying above the twenty-first parallel, but they wanted to see what was going on along the China Road. China Road was known as no-man's-land and they wanted to find out why. They had, by then, so many hundreds of missions between them that their aircraft had become metal extensions of their bodies. Wagner loved nothing better than to show off—shine his ass, as they used to put it—so as they flew along he cruised with the plane's wings at vertical, one wing pointed down to the earth and the other straight up toward the sky. He could pull this off for a while, but then would arc over and fall toward the ground. He rolled his airplane and snapped it upside down and flew along inverted, hanging in his straps until Kip heard him say, —Get on my tail.

Kip pulled in twenty feet behind him intrail. Nose to tail, elephant walk, down low enough to stay out of the propwash.

The next thing Kip knew, they were going straight up. The sun was in his eyes. Up into a hammerhead climb, a steep ascent, until just before his wings began to complain, before they ran out of airspeed and went into a stall, Wagner rolled ninety degrees and let the nose sink into the horizon until they fell straight down. They gained velocity faster than a scalded ape—another pilot idiom—plunged into a nice roll and came to a perpendicular with one wing pointed to the earth again, and the other straight up to the clouds.

Kip didn't know why Wagner had to make these gestures, but he went along with them for a while, as ever, then finally said, —This isn't getting us to the Road.

—Calder, you don't know the value of zazen.

—What's zazen?

—*That* was zazen.

—What was that?

—That was something of value you're too blind to see.

China Road was hardly a road. It was more a muddied gorge, a furrow across the thicket of gnarly green. There was nothing going on here, it seemed. No smoke rising, no sign of encampment. Wagner radioed Kip that they return, and the two banked away from one another in order to reposition and head home. Halfway through Kip's turnabout, however, he glanced down fifteen hundred feet and his eye caught the front end of a bulldozer partly covered with tarpaulin.

—Got something here, Wagner.

Wagner asked what did he have.

—I'm going in to find out. Stay high.

Wagner stood away as Kip dropped down to see what was there. As he came in low over the sightment he had just enough time to note the covers coming off two of the three guns situated in a perfect triangle around the lure. He saw tracers coming at him from three directions. He was suddenly in the convergence zone. The tracers were flaming heavy, and he knew that for every tracer he saw, there were four invisible slugs. The sky was a stream of fire. He couldn't hear the sound because he'd shoved the throttle forward, pushed the stick hard down and headed toward the trees. Climbing up would be the end of him, so he dropped to the tops of the green. Two hundred feet. His one hope of escape was to dip below the line of fire. The only reason they missed was that they were as surprised to see him as he was to see them. The flight back to Luang Prabang was quiet. "That's true too," he says. "Maybe all wars are strange, but that was one strange war."

*I*s it in a poem by Horace that merchants in a town are standing in the doorways of their shops watching soldiers march off to war, and these merchants think to themselves, How fortunate the soldiers are to go off to battle where they'll either die in honor or come home heroes, while the soldiers look in envy at the merchants thinking, How lucky these shopkeepers are, getting to stay home while we have to march off to our deaths. I think of this as Kip is offering me the most unexpected judgment I'd ever heard about the war.

"What's strangest of all is that I've come around to your way of thinking. Maybe not exactly the same, but closer than I'd ever thought possible. Like we were both walkers in that meditation I described, it's like we've come to the same point on the path, just that one of us walked down while the other ascended."

"What do you mean?"

Kip says, "How can I put it. To me it's like this. If Nagasaki was our national orgasm, the fall of Saigon was a postcoital depression."

"What do you mean?" I say again.

"I started to get it, how those wars linked up—War Two and Vietnam. It took me long enough, but I finally started seeing the light just recently."

He has aged into this new individual, I am allowing myself to see, but it is less an overt physical change than a difference in articulation, in how he expresses himself, how he moves—little, in fact—and the modulation of voice, which is a kind of spirited monotone. The creek rattles in its muddied banks. Someone has set a grand bouquet of plastic flowers on the concrete altar down here, bright reds, blues, pinks. The services finished, the priest has left the outdoor sanctuary, and Kip and I are alone.

He is speaking. I can hear him. I'm listening to him and what I am beginning to hear is a part of me speaking. Listen, I think.

"I started to get it that 1945 only began to perish in 1975, it took that long. Just as you fight fire with fire, it took one kind of shame to begin to erase another, Brice. And in that way Vietnam was the best, most wonderful tragedy that could ever befall our country. One of the catchphrases you used to hear during the war was frontier sealing. We were doing some serious frontier sealing over there is what. But it was we who needed the damned frontier sealing, not them. We were in desperate need of a confidence reduction, and our failure in Vietnam was the leech Fate, like a wise physician, applied to our impudent body politic. Not that the Communists were heroic, don't get me wrong. Because they weren't. They were corrupt and savvy and deceitful and they were ruthless. Their comeuppance is already upon them and don't they deserve it, too, in their way. But we had to lose, the dominoes that Eisenhower was so worried about falling in Southeast Asia—and for all his blindness Eisenhower did have the foresight to see Laos as the first domino—they had to fall, or else they'd fall the other way and our sick narcissism would carry us across the face of the world to yankify and cartoonize everyone and everything, and turn—sooner rather than later—the whole planet into an American theme park, a grotesquerie. You get what I'm saying, Brice?"

I understand, I tell him.

Kip adds, "I'm proud that I was there to witness it, man. I am proud to have taken part in the loss. My only regrets, and don't think they're not colossal, have to do with what happened to the villagers in Laos to whom we made all our pretty promises. We'd help them help themselves. That's what the CIA told them. That's what the ambassador told them. Help them protect their homelands against the aggressors. We set them up sure as hell in Laos, we gave them just enough rope and now the ones who the Pathet Lao didn't exterminate or reeducate out there in the jungles where no roads run, no houses are, where there's nothing but the gulags that we here in the West to this day don't know about, the ones who didn't have *that* for their fate are still waiting, in dismal camps along the Mekong in Thailand, waiting for nothing, for deportation. The Thai want them out and before too long we'll send them back, repatriate them to the mountains where one by one their old enemies will quietly annihilate them with yellow rain or worse."

But it doesn't matter anymore to America, I wanted to tell him. Wars have come and gone between now and then. A generation has blossomed in the interim, a generation that might respond to the fashion of the period, but doesn't know more than what they're fed by the same blighted media that only half covered the war in the first place. Afghanistan, Lebanon, Iran, Nicaragua, Iraq, Croatia, Somalia, where hadn't war broken out to carry our limited attentions in the exhausted wake of Vietnam.

"Exterminate them, murder them, feed them to the dogs, and then slaughter the dogs and eat the dogs, too."

I told him I understood. And as I watched him talk I realized that we had somehow come full circle. Here I'd always considered myself to be the antiwar saint of sorts—not, to borrow one of Kip's terms, that I should cartoonize myself, or indulge in self-slander—but it seemed to have turned out that it was Kip who'd gone up against his superiors and denied war some victims it would otherwise surely have devoured. Reminded of that Goya painting of Saturn eating his young, I mixed mythologies and saw Kip as a David, sighting the old bastard cannibal between the eyes and releasing that stone to find its mark.

Kip, the fighter turned eccentric peacemaker. And I, who abandoned this place over half a lifetime ago, the runner.

"Will you help me to figure out a way to tell them about this? Everyone wants reconciliation and forgiveness now, everyone wants to see Vietnam as a chapter in our history come to an end. But it's like Hiroshima and Nagasaki. These things, if they're to come to an end, have got to be looked at square and clearly. Do you know that we have detonated eight-hundred-and-fifty-plus nuclear weapons, and that you can get a list from the government when and where each of these tests took place, whether it was an underground test or one out in the Pacific Ocean—and that Hiroshima and Nagasaki are right there with all the other detonations, right there listed as tests, no mention of casualties, though the list does acknowledge they were tested in combat, but fails to put in a little footnote at the bottom of the page that would explain what they mean when they call them *tests*?"

I still am not sure what it is Kip wants me to do about all this.

He is looking at his hands and they are palms up with fingers opened into a symmetrical basket, as if he were holding a globe of air in them, bobbing it gently up and down, shaking it like you do a birthday present in order to hear if it makes a noise so that you can guess what is inside.

"If they tell you that the yellow rain doesn't exist? if they tell you that these people are dying from the urine of giant bees— and don't laugh, because that's one of the stories I've heard— that swarms of bees deluge the skies over their villages and rain yellow on them and that's what's behind all this illness? If they tell you that? It's lies."

"What did I used to say back when we were in school?"

"I won't argue. You were right, in certain ways, wrong in others."

"Just like you."

"Just like me, like most everyone. But I *know* this, Brice, and with what I know and what you know maybe something good and decent could come of it for somebody else. For me it's neither here nor there, finally. It could just as easily have been something else. And it's not that I didn't deserve it, when you get down to it. But there are those that don't."

"What are you asking me to do?"

"I don't know," he says. "Nothing. You're a lawyer and I'll bet you turned out to be a good lawyer. When these things come up before Congress, which they have already and will, as the curtains get drawn aside on what really happened during Vietnam and afterward, then you can take my story there, maybe, and set it alongside all the others, and that way we'll have done something together, just like we once wanted to, way back when."

"Let me get you some medical care, Kip. Come back to New York with me and we'll have somebody really good have a look at you. If what you want is to be my friend, let me be your friend, let me help you."

Kip looks at me and says, "You know what we should do? We should go inside."

"Take Communion?"

Kip laughs, "Oh hell no," which I must admit makes me feel affectionate toward him—all this reconciliatory spirit is wonderful but also is weird, like the pleasure of pain, or eros and thanatos, it holds conundrums in it that I like and do not like. At least Kip has maintained his distance from certain things. What am I saying? At least his illness hasn't forced him into orthodoxy.

"You mean, the dirt?"

"What harm can come of it?"

He seems suddenly filled with vitality. He puts his hand on my shoulder, "Brice, you remember way long ago when you talked me into coming down here with you—"

"Of course."

"—well, I thought I owed you the favor in return."

The line has dwindled away to a hundred. There are many people still milling about in the plaza. We walk up the dusty common and take our place. Soon enough we cross a footbridge directly in front of the archway. Birds chirp in the pressed cedars just within the brown walls. Kip and I are nearly out of words. We watch the others, hear the children screaming gleefully as they skip about barefooted, and wade in the acequia. Pilgrims who might have walked a very long way to be here cool their feet in the rushing water of the irrigation ditch. A family just beyond has laid out supper on one of the wooden picnic tables, the mother being helped by her daughter, setting out paper plates covered with tinfoil. Dogs run up and down in the water, splashing everyone. When I hear the father of this family shout at the dogs to get away, his expression, *"Váyanse,"* has a shock of fa-

miliarity to it. *Váyanse, hijos del demonio!* and my eye finds him
—not the old custodian who'd cried out at us so long ago—but
Fernando Martinez, and I think to myself, You're seeing people
who are not there again, Brice, and turn to Kip and begin to say,
"Do you see that guy over there . . . ," but Kip doesn't hear me.

His focus is on the two steeples of El Santuario. "Did you ever
notice that only one of the towers has a bell in it?" he asks.

I'd noticed, but I didn't know why it was so. As he tells me
about how expensive bells used to be, my eye goes over to the
family once more and I see that they are sitting down now to
their meal, three, four, five children all dressed for the day's festivities and look once more at the man with such concentration
that he's somehow willed to glance up at me. Our eyes meet, and
when I see him nod and smile, without the faintest trace of recognition, I nod back and hear my Kip. He's telling me that everyone in the parish would give donations—not just from the little
money they had, as this was always a poor place, but spoons,
a broken axle, anything of metal—and the bell was especially
smelted for the church. In Chimayó they could afford only one
bell. The other tower to this day remains empty. And as for the
bell that does hang in its belfry, it is only rarely rung—when a
local parishioner dies—and then it must be chimed by hand, with
a hammer or a rock, as it has no clapper.

"I've heard it," Kip says. "It gives an indescribable sound. They
chime it in syncopation with the bell over at La Capilla del Santa
Niño de Atocha. They'll ring this one fifteen times, then the other
one fifteen times, then this one ten times, then the other ten
times. The ringing just seizes you in such a way that you *feel* the
soul of the dead person lifting away from the valley."

"You sound like a believer," I say.

Kip shakes his head with a calm smile. "I always thought

of you as the tower with the bell in it, and me the empty one."

"That's funny," I say. "Just the opposite is how I've always thought."

"I'm not sure that the towers aren't perfectly equal in their way. One has wind and birds in it, the other has a clapperless bell. They're both flawed."

We finally pass through the walled cemetery, around the wooden cross mounted on a small adobe base with its black millstone inset, and into the church.

Thousands of pilgrims have already passed through here this day, and the peace candles warmed the nave, their smoke giving it a smell of antiquity. Kip wants to sit for a while, and we do, together in a pew several rows back from the altar. Just to think, the two of us had stumbled down this very length of flagstone, having guessed with youthful wisdom the impact our community would have on every other community on earth. I stare at Kip, whose head is bowed and whose hands are folded in his lap, and feel a merging of passions to which words would never attach nor from which come forth.

*T*he sky, I swear, is even bigger than it once was. Its midnight blue is bluer than midnight, its moonstruck clouds more capricious, building and building up into massive plumes over against the grand stretches of distant mountains from Trampas Peak to Thompson Peak, then changing shape within the pocket of time it takes slowly to close your eyes and open them again. The daylit pinks seem browner, the pinks of the rock formations, the piñon grayer in its greens. There are more twinkling lights out on the desert, more houses with people in them.

The light, like ghost snow, hints of afterglow in the desert night. I have said goodbye to Kip and know that he accomplished what he'd wanted to do, that he had given me a gift which I could possess for the last third of my life, a quiet and glorious gift, whether it came from largesse or not. Not the diary, that was for Ariel. Nor his inheritance, which was for charity—or rather, for Ariel, too, if she wanted it. The gift was that my youth and my adulthood could now be of a piece, a whole entity with beginning, middle, and yes, an end. Without asking for it, he allowed me to forgive him, and by the same token had forgiven me without my having asked. Forgiveness was the touchstone of redemption, and I hope that Ariel will be able to forgive me for what I've failed all these years to tell her.

Whenever she would ask me about how Jess and I met, I answered tangentially, avoiding the whole truth, and thus denying her a birthright. I knew why, of course. Always knew what it was to hedge and shift and equivocate. —We met at Columbia. I've already told you that story a hundred times, I would say. And Ariel'd confound me with her Kiplike eyes, looking right through me but not knowing what if anything there was to see there. It has been, almost without my knowing it, my great dark secret—so secret that it's often invited its possessor to forget. But Kip has changed this. He had so many secrets to hang like clothing around the nakedness of his life and, as it turns out, so have I. But by telling me his, he's liberated me from holding on any longer to mine. It is as great a gift as anyone has ever given me.

You're her father, Kip. She will know it, know both her fathers now, and so know her mother, the woman that both of them have loved.

The amber lights on the Hill shine, up ahead. Within the hour, I will be at my mother's. Time cannot move fast enough for me now that I have the power to tell.

*W*hen I awaken, I hear her in the kitchen, humming a song to herself. She still has a fine singing voice, though the melody seems to stray—is she improvising? I recognize it, and remember it was one of her favorite tunes, "Someone to Watch Over Me." Whoever wrote it, I can't recall, the Gershwins maybe. In the days when I was growing up, she would sit at the piano and sing it; there was a double entendre she relished, at the expense of the military and the AEC and everyone else who watched over her, who even after the greatest secrecy of the forties carried on into the new decade with a vigilance that beheld a spy behind every rock. But hearing it this morning, it sounds like the wistful love song it was meant to be.

> There's a somebody I'm longing to see,
> I hope that he turns out to be—

I sit up and look at my hands—Kip's old tic—and see that they are still dirty with the soil from the sanctuary desert chapel.

> Someone who'll watch over me—

Look at my watch and see that I had better get a move on if I want to get the car back to Alyse, and make my flight in Albuquerque. I doubt there will be time to drink the coffee I smell that she's made. My father's jacket, buttons ineptly but tightly resewn in the middle of the night with needle and thread from her old tin sewing box, lies folded over a trunk at the foot of the bed, offers me the certain pleasure of fulfilling a promise.

Then she's there in the room before me, and she is smiling. "I'm happy you came to visit, Brice," she says.

"I'm sorry I've been such an absence—"

"Don't," she says.

She asks me do I have time to call Bonnie Jean to say goodbye. True to form, I say I'll call her from the airport, or else from the city later tonight. Not all things change, or at least not all at once, I think.

"All right," she says.

Then I think, Damn it all, call the woman, she's your sister. I ask my mother for Bonnie's number, pull the rotary around in tight incomplete circles, and when she answers begin to thank her for everything.

True to form, she says, "I didn't hardly do anything. Not that I wouldn't be happy to if you'd stick around for a change."

"I'll be back soon," I say.

"Right, Brice."

"No, honestly. I mean it."

"Say hello to Jessica for me," she says, finally.

We hang up and I begin to throw together my few things before I realize that probably, yes, I will come back soon. "You mind if I leave this bag here?" I ask my mother. "Just a few clothes. I don't need them for the trip home."

This is fine by her. I think, I ought to wash up before I go. But then I realize that my hands might guide me better with a little sacred earth on them. I kiss my mother goodbye, a solid filial kiss with her beautiful, fragile head held firmly in both my soiled palms.

Down from the Hill, down the broad switchbacks of the familiar road that would lead me back past San Ildefonso pueblo, to the crossroads near Pojoaque. I have for Alyse a token of blessed soil for which, being the friend she is, she will thank me ardently before calling Martha to come, see what Brice has brought, touch it because it has magical properties that will make you live forever. Then she will drive me from Santa Fe to Albuquerque for the flight home. I spoke with Jessica last night, and said there was so much to tell her. She asked me how Kip was, and I could only say he was finer than I'd ever seen him but finer, as always, after his own fashion. For her I have some holy clay too, and some as well for Ariel—a humble birthday present to accompany that, or should I say those, for there are so many, from her other father.

The party's a few weeks after the fact, but what difference does it make. Ariel, twenty-four. I've been her father for twenty-four years. I wish she could see what I am seeing here now. I begin to wish she took more of an interest in my history, but catch myself with the thought, Listen, man, you have hardly known your own history, how should you expect her to contemplate what's never been disclosed to her? That would change, of course. Our histories, set straight, might finally intertwine, ironic as it may seem.

I take in a deep breath of air, look east as I round a hairpin curve. The Sangre de Cristos have been rinsed by rain, and above them rise those inveterate clouds like a second range much grander in scale than the mountains themselves. Released my breath, breathed again. Thin, sweet air.

My thoughts go back to Ariel, Jess, Kip, myself. All parents wish their children took more interest in their histories, I guess.

It is unfathomable to me still that I am a father—and I *am* a father—and even more unbelievable to me that next year I will be celebrating my birthday of half a century, and seven months later there will be another birthday, as the successful construction of the bomb continues to chase me around the calendar of years. Los Alamos already has commemorative festivities under way, with many more activities planned for the months ahead. The nation will honor (or not) the half-centennial of its magnificent, dubious achievement. Now that we are told the cold war is over and the threat of nuclear war is diminished, the celebrations on the Hill can be mantled in a kind of dignity that pure history offers anniversaries of events mixed with equal parts glory and sadness. Pure history is history sealed from the present. Is safe history. The Trinity blast down at Alamogordo will be commemorated as pure history, if possible. But, of course, it is not. The arsenal Trinity fathered is vast and there are despots not born yet whose pleasure will be to make it vaster and threaten to give us another glimpse of its fearful magic. If only the posito in Chimayó could generate healing soil enough to bury the silos around the world forever, that would be a day truly to celebrate.

At the foot of the pass where the highway no longer holds to the steep beige and charcoal walls of the long mesas, and begins to open out into the straightaway across the flatland, the traveler crosses the Rio Grande. Known to some as Otowi, it is the sacred site the Indians call Po-Sah-Son-Gay, "the place where the river speaks." There is a love story associated with Po-Sah-Son-Gay.

So many different things connect here. The old Otowi bridge still spans the muddy river to the right of where the new concrete four-lane bridge crosses over. It is a restored but fragile sculpture of an honest, old design, its concrete verticals holding strong, its necklace of cables graceful, a narrow suspension bridge, the remnant of earlier times. All our families, back in the forties, crossed that bridge, and much of the equipment that went into building our homes and the myriad materials that were assembled into the bombs on the Hill were carried across that bridge. And back in earlier days it so happened that there was a woman who lived by the bridge. Her name was Edith Warner, and when she came here in autumn 1922 to exchange the air of Philadelphia for that of a small guest ranch in Frijoles Canyon her life underwent a revolution, such was the beauty of the landscape surrounding the stone house and cabins that stood near the Rito de los Frijoles —Bean Brook, as Kip used to call it—edged by alders and willows and grama grasses. The sun-warmed cliffs, the dry talus that lay like unmarked amulets at their feet, the smoke-blackened ceilings of the caves covered with line etchings of deer and birds and the cliff dwellers themselves, the Plumed Serpent at Tsirege mesa from whose height she could see mountains in every direction, the stars that at night lay overhead like a quilt—Edith knew she could never leave, that New Mexico was to be her home for the rest of her years. A man named John Boyd and his wife, Martha, who operated the ranch that winter, took Edith into their lives, and they moved on to an even more remote valley, higher in the Jemez where they built a log cabin and settled together for a time into a life of pioneers. If Edith harbored second thoughts about abandoning the East, a trip back to Pennsylvania in the mid-twenties laid them to rest. Ill health forced her return to the Southwest, and in 1928, unmarried, unemployed, thirty-five years old, Edith agreed to take the only work she could find, as care-taker of a rundown house that stood near the tracks of the Denver & Rio Grande narrow-gauge railroad. The train came through, spewing smoke and hot cinders in the fashion of old iron horses of the last century, and deposited in the boxcar station supplies and mail destined for Los Alamos Ranch School. Edith would sign for the shipment and with the help of a pueblo boy named

Adam ready things for the truck that came down from the mesa to pick it up each week. She was very poor, but considered it a good life to be paid twenty-five dollars a month plus what she could earn selling tobacco and canned goods, soda pop and gasoline to the Indians, the occasional sheepherder, boys from the ranch, tourists making their way from Santa Fe to the ruins of Frijoles. Gradually she fixed the house up, and gradually the Indians from the reservation began to accept her, this white woman who lived on their land at the place where the river speaks. They helped her plough her garden, they gathered firewood for her, they repaired her leaking roof. O-ne-a-po-vi, an elder woman of the pueblo, knew she had a special fondness for blue cornmeal paper-bread, and saw to it that Edith would have some for dinner. Likewise, the scientists from up on the Hill came down to have supper at her table. Edith developed a special fondness for Niels Bohr, his perpetual pipe and his straw hat, the way his sentences meandered, explored, often trailed off into silence, then picked up once more, always in pursuit, never at rest. Others from the Hill befriended her, too. Parsons, Fermi, Compton, Oppenheimer, the lot of them. Edith, like the trestle span by her house, bridged things. Then she met Atilano Montoya, known as Tilano, who came one day to build for her a fireplace of adobe brick, and her life changed again. Tilano told her of his travels through Europe—Paris and London, Rome and Berlin—as a member of a troupe of Indian dancers. His gypsy days behind, he was now one of the elders of San Ildefonso, with glorious braids that reached his waist, character charged with warmth and wit. He was a widower, and in time his visits to the house by the river became more frequent, until eventually his presence there was permanent. They never married, but were seldom apart. When the engineers came in 1947 to inform her that the Otowi bridge was outmoded and that they were going to have to build a new bridge, which would cast a shadow across her cornfield and into her kitchen window, she was saddened, of course, but it was said that she and Tilano accepted the inevitability of progress, and felt fortunate that they'd spent those decades down by the river. With the help of Indians from the pueblo and scientists from Los Alamos they built an adobe up in the canyon where, on quiet days, they could just make out the ruffle and shush of the talking river. She died a few years later, in the spring of 1951, and Tilano himself died two years after that.

I have read a book about this woman, which was written by the daughter of Ashley Pond, the gentleman who first founded the boy's school up at Los Alamos, and in this book the author appends the texts of Edith's Christmas letters, which she sent to all her friends, and which were famous for their humor and wisdom. The last of these laments the news of Korea. "Co-ha and Hagi, the boys who worked with Tilano in the garden from the time they could pull a weed, came home on leave before going overseas," she writes. "Five of the boys from the Pueblo have gone and again, after so short a span, the postman is always awaited anxiously." In the letter she speaks of cycles and of renewal, and of how the snowy peaks of Truchas are lit up by the sun. She delights in thinking of the long-ago people who walked just here in the world and thanks their gods for what generosities life can allow. Then, remembering the war once more, as if the war extinguished the glinting light above, she gives voice to her impatience with just that same world. "How to endure the man-made devastating period in which we live and which seems almost as hopeless to control as drought." It is as if I can see her leaning intent over the blank page before her. "I only know that the power recognized by those other sky-scanners still exists, that contact is possible. I know, too, what depths of kindness and selflessness exist in my fellow man. Of this I have had renewed assurance recently, when those about me have shared self and substance. When Tilano lights the Christmas Eve fire, perhaps against a white hillside, I shall watch from the house where some have felt peace and hope that in your sky there are some bright stars."

I climb back up the bank, duck between lengths of the barbed wire fence, having gone down to take a picture of the two bridges, so that I can show Ariel, and tell her this story about Edith Warner and Tilano. The Rio Grande is as silty as ever, rushing along with its yellow clay from Tierra Amarilla, with the red sand-stone remnants of Gallina dumped into the river back where the Chama merges, with all the earth washed down through the wild arroyos, all the basaltic sediment from its tributaries, reworking the desert as it makes its way down to the ocean. I found a perfect place to capture the image of the two bridges. It would have been a fine remembrance, bygone time bordered by time present, but I am overwhelmed with the thought that the day will come when those going back and forth over the new bridge would be so many that yet another bridge inevitably will be built, so there would be one bridge used by those ascending and another for those coming down. That's the way the world works, at least from the window through which I see it.

It is as if the image before me resists being photographed, as if the voice of the river disdains the impulse. One more object for reminiscence? it seems to ask. Another piece of evidence to prove the impermanence of that which endures? Bohr, author of the term *complementarity*, who understood that matter remains harmonious through the interplay of apparently conflicting forces, crossed this bridge many times. No need to photograph these two bridges, one not quite old, one not quite new—the image would be obsolete before the print so much as began to yellow.

Why? Because they love building things here. The river's not going to go away. It will continue to speak with its watery brown tongues. And people will continue to want to cross it to make their way up to the Hill, no matter what may happen in the world. It may change, but it will continue, and so another bridge will be built. I cannot get myself to snap the shutter, can't expose the film. Instead, I look at the bridges long and hard, do not want to forget a single detail, know so well how ruinous forgetfulness can be. A magpie settles in the poplar near where the narrow-gauge railway used to run, a jackrabbit disappears under sagebrush.

When I cross the highway, and get into the car, I think of that night all those years ago when we came careening across the desert toward Chimayó, and crossed the river just here. I smile and think, Kip, I'll always love you, too, my brother. The day is warming and I smell the earth and the dust on the dashboard and the metal of the body of the car. It smells good: earth, dust, metal. A breeze walks up the gradual rise from the river. The river splashes along in its ancient bed. I try to understand what it is saying to me, as this is the place the river traditionally speaks. There are many noises, scrapes and burbles. I cannot make out what they mean. I try harder, but the river only babbles, or so it seems. When I give up and reach to turn the key, I hear it. The words aren't in any language, really. The river doesn't bother with words, doesn't use the shapes and structures of human utterance. It says what it has to say. It is time to be moving on, it says. Like the water that had come down into the valley and ventured into the river, it was time for me to leave the Hill once more. Time to go back home.

ACKNOWLEDGMENTS

Above all I owe a debt of gratitude to my parents for introducing me to New Mexico during our many summer expeditions away from home in Littleton, Colorado. I first set eyes on Pojoaque Valley when I was ten years old, thanks to them, and revisited the little church in Chimayó with them on Easter 1992.

Without the help of retired air force pilot Lieutenant Colonel Roger Daisley of Fox Island, Washington, Kip might not have discovered the Steve Canyon program and Brice might never have noticed the convergences of Los Alamos and Long Tieng. I thank him for answering hundreds of questions about his experiences as head Raven during years of covert operations inside Laos, for sharing personal memories with me and opening to me the hermetic world of spookdom, not to mention the eccentricities of FAC pilotry. Thanks, too, to his wife, Alyse, and family, for putting me up in their home in August 1993. I am also grateful to another of the surviving Ravens, who prefers to remain anonymous, for helping me with details about Kip's experiences in Laos and refugee camps in Thailand during and after the Vietnam war; and to his Vietnamese-born Lao wife, who was so gracious in receiving me at their home.

Hedy Dunn, director of the Los Alamos Historical Museum, not only gave me access to very useful tape recordings and documents during my visits to the Hill, but spent many hours going over the manuscript with me. Also helpful during my research days at Fuller Lodge were archivist Theresa Strottman, curator Rebecca Collinsworth, and intern Eric Alexander.

Native Chimayóan Raymond Bal, who runs the Potrero Trading Post next to the Santuario, and Chimayó historian and artist Elizabeth Kay were most helpful with remembrances of Chimayó in the fifties and since. Sister Antonette Ahles, pastoral assistant to pilgrims, answered my sometimes very secular questions (such as how to go about breaking into the church in 1959) with patience and charm.

I am grateful to Robert Friedman, who edited the *Spectator* at Columbia University during the stormy late sixties, for walking me so vividly through his experiences of antiwar activism during that period.

Jennette Montalvo, faithful research assistant from the summer of 1992 to completion in October 1993, looked up arcana, ran down references, followed fragile threads, was hardworking on the novel's behalf throughout. Ariel Kaminer, namesake of both Wills' daughter, excavated considerable data for me in 1992. Beth Herstein helped me with legal research. This *Trinity* would not have come into being without *that* trinity.

Books of particular value to me were Jane Hamilton-Merritt's *Tragic Mountains*—hers is my source for the rodeo scene in Long Tieng; Christopher Robbins's *The Ravens*; Marta Weigle and Peter White's *The Lore of New Mexico*; Richard Rhodes's *The Making of the Atomic Bomb*; and Peggy Pond Church's *The House at Otowi Bridge*, in which the story of Edith Warner is told. The Los Alamos Historical Society has published valuable books and pamphlets about the history of the Pajarito Plateau and surrounding area too numerous to list.

Mei-mei Berssenbrugge and Richard Tuttle loaned me their house during my first research trip to New Mexico, April 1992, and kindly put me up again the following year. The idea of writing about Los Alamos hatched five months before that, during a sleepless night in Janet Rodney and Nathaniel Tarn's abode out on the desert, from whose windows I could see the lights of the Hill thirty miles toward the west. Anne and Patrick Lannan opened their home to me in Santa Fe last August—what eerie pleasure was to be had when I looked out the window of their balcony and could see both Mei-mei and Richard's old adobe at the foot of Cerro Gordo, across the river, where the book was begun, and Los Alamos once more far in the distance. I can't thank them enough for their hospitality.

Among others who were particularly supportive: Allen Peacock, Paul West, Dr. Bruce Fader, M. Mark, Jeanie Kim, Donald McKinney, Peter Straub, Nomi Eve, Deborah Eisenberg, Kate Norment, Anthony and Annabel McCall. But for Dr. John Daly and Dr. Mark Wallack I wouldn't have lived to tell the tale. Martine Bellen read the book as it was being written and I want to thank her for crucial encouragement.

Lynn Nesbit, my friend and agent, I thank for believing in this novel from the beginning. I am grateful to everyone at Janklow & Nesbit for their kindnesses and hard work, especially Lydia Wills and Cynthia Cannell.

Nan Graham, like an inspired *santa,* presided over the editing of this book with constant vitality, grace, and intelligence. Others at Viking—Paul Slovak, Courtney Hodell, and Barbara Grossman in particular—have worked persistently and astutely on behalf of this project, and I thank them. Elizabeth Ruge and Arnulf Conradi of Berlin Verlag contributed a number of important editorial suggestions, and my British editor, Jonathan Warner, whose tragic death prevented him from seeing this book into print, motivated me in my further investigations of Ariel and of Nambé pueblo.